GW01079961

VICTORIA WREN

The Last Hickory

VICTORIA WREN

The Last Hickory

WILD SPIRIT *The Last Hickory*

Printed in the United Kingdom

First Printing, 2021

Cover Designer Thea Magerand
Critique Partner Bethany Votaw
Interior Book formatting by Enchanted Ink Publishing
Family Tree by K.A Winters

ISBN: 978-1-8382146-8-5 (Hardback)

Readers please note this book was written and edited using American English Grammar.

This book was written for a teenage audience to enjoy and is suitable for young adult readers, but I would like to warn in advance of mild sexual content, some graphic descriptions and language that may make a younger reader uncomfortable.

WWW.VICTORIAWRENAUTHOR.COM

Mum and **Dad**, this one is for you.

Thank you for everything. x

Readers, please note that this book was written and edited using American English Grammar.

The characters in this book are entirely fictional of the author's invention. Any resemblance to actual persons living or dead is entirely coincidental.

This is a book written for young adults to enjoy, though it is my hope that older age groups will read the story and enjoy it. I would advise that for younger readers below the age of sixteen, there may be some action/fight scenes, and the occasional use of profanity that they could find uncomfortable.

Wild Spirit: The Last Hickory

Victoria Wren

WWW.VICTORIAWRENAUTHOR.COM

The Last Hickory

The Hickory Family

Vivienne
Hickory
1787-1805

Louis
Hicko
1788-1

Anna Jar
Warrick
-184

Cora
Ramsey

Thomas James
Hickory
1857-1935

Willard
Hickory
1903-

Winifred
Hickory
1905-1969

Gloria
Hunson
1952-2010

John James
Hickory
1927-2020

Alice
Hickory
1980-2007

Ben
Adler
1980-

Rowan Alice
Adler
1999-

Winifred Louisa
Adler
2004-

ah
Sewell
810
Joseph James
Hickory
1765-1811
Eliza
Hickory
1792-1907
Rupert
Black
Mary
Hickory
1794-1807
Franklin
Hickory
1818-1896
Carole Anne
Hickory
1822-1834
Annie Talbot
Hickory
1860-1924
Iyke
oodward
Iris Mary
Hickory
1929-
Robert
Fraser
1927-2020
Rose
Cullen
Jake
Fraser
1980-
Olivia
White
-2010
Luke
Fraser
2004-
Spencer James
Fraser
1999-

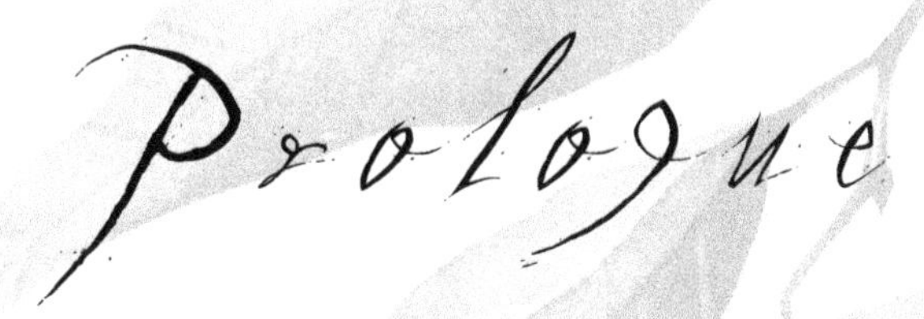

Prologue

Darkness swept through the forest like an inky blanket, swirling up dead leaves in its wake. Win walked under the stars. Barefoot, skin cool, her arms exposed to the chill of the night. Narrowing her eyes, she stepped lightly, her heels cracking over old, dry twigs. Rubbing her arms, she wandered into a clearing, gently bathed in soft moonlight. Above a half-moon, glowed down at her like a crazed half-smile, like it knew something she didn't. It was sinister, cold. Win ducked her head, not understanding why she was out of bed at this hour, why her dream had brought her to this place.

This had to be a dream. Win remembered falling asleep, her cheeks damp against the pillow. *Crying again*. Her heart ached, her insides were oddly hollow. Falling asleep night after night, with her mind whirling, images of that night constantly flooding back the moment she shut her eyes. She saw the fire, the cabin, groaning under the pressure of heat. Grayson's eyes in the light of the fire before he'd vanished inside. Win buried her face in her pillow, willing sleep to come so she could forget, for a while, anyway.

But she hadn't expected to be brought here.

She was light, her feet like paws padding through the thicket. Up ahead, there was a gentle, soft humming noise. When she stepped out of the clearing, she saw the stone. It loomed over her like a giant totem, pointing skyward toward the dense night sky. Why was she here? Her fingertips burned, vibrated at its nearness, an oppressive, sinking sense of doom crashing over her. Something was wrong here. Win was enveloped in sadness, a foreshadowing of death. The ground remembered what happened here, and like a ghost, she was swept up in its retelling. Leaves and trees rustled behind her in the undergrowth. Someone was headed in her direction.

Panic set in, and Win scrambled to the safety of the long grass, pressing herself between a small group of trees, densely packed together. Her lungs filled with cold air, ducking into the protective cover of the undergrowth as six figures emerged from the darkness.

Win chewed on her lip, watching intently as they strolled into the clearing, darkened figures all wearing long tunics and hoods pulled over their heads, covering their faces. One carried a long baton, a flaming torch, illuminating the darkness. They approached the stone, bowing before it then settling in a semi-circle with the stone at the epicenter.

Tickles of apprehension broke out across Win's neck. She badly wanted to run, to flee this scene. Something was going to happen here, and the rock in her stomach plummeted. One of the figures stepped forward and addressed the rest of them.

"Brothers and Sisters," she spoke in a grave voice. "We know why we have come here tonight. To put right a terrible wrong, to seek vengeance on the invaders, who raped and brutalized this land."

Win swallowed a knot in her throat. What the hell was this? Where was she? She'd phased into memory before, her memories, times she had suppressed and forgotten. This was another *time*, another place. Her thighs ached from crouching, so she carefully rolled onto her knees, keeping her head low.

The figures chanted in an unfamiliar tongue, but for some reason, it filled her with a sense of knowing, something deep, primal. It called to her blood. Warm, she fanned her face, her cheeks burning. Behind them, the stone hummed, a glowing blue light piercing through the black. Despite the sense of dread creeping up her spine, the whole thing was oddly serene.

"Bring us the *monster* Joseph Hickory," the woman spoke urgently. The peace was disrupted. Out of the treeline, two men appeared dressed in black tunics. Win's eyes widened as she watched them struggle with a man, a man with wild, red hair and a long, unkempt beard. His feet skidded over the mud, legs flailing under him, and his teeth gritted in agony as he continued to fight, wrestling in their grasp.

Win gasped, her hand covering her mouth. Her stomach rolled in anticipation. Yelling and kicking his bare feet, he fought as the two men forcibly dragged him to the stone. Despite his mature years, he wasn't giving them an easy time. The hooded figures murmured in confusion, watching as the men struggled, binding him to the stone, securing him with a thick, knotted cord. It bit angrily into his flesh, welts across his arms and back. He was wearing an old, faded shirt, torn and frayed. He looked like he'd been kept locked away, his clothes dusty and disheveled.

Win calmed her breathing. Her brow furrowed so hard it ached, her temples throbbing. She didn't want to watch this. One of the females stepped into the circle and pulled down her hood, revealing long, shiny black hair. Win's hairs stood to attention, something unearthly about the woman's face, something old gleamed in her onyx black eyes, moonlight shone off her fawn-colored skin. Win recalled the story of the curse, at least the story she'd read in books. Her stomach rolled, the clawing suspicion that something was wrong with that story.

*This isn't right....*Win narrowed her eyes, suppressing a shiver. She sensed a deathly cold. The black emptiness of the woman's eyes was frightening and void of feeling.

"Come, gather around," she spoke, her voice oddly serene. "We must take a part of him for the gods."

Oh...god, no. Win clenched her jaw. The man howled in fright, kicking his legs as four of the figures surrounded him, crawling on their knees, obscuring him completely from Win's view. She craned her neck in time to see the woman draw a long, thin dagger from her robes.

"Don't do this to me!" he begged. His sobs filled the night, and Win wished she could block it out, knowing she'd be hearing that sound in her dreams forever.

"Don't listen to him! He is the invader, the monster. The people of this land deserve to be avenged, and he must sacrifice a part of himself."

Win shivered, despite sweat gathering on her neck. Sacrifice part of himself? Her head swam, she was suddenly nauseous. She didn't dare speculate what it could mean.

Oh no, god, please, why am I looking at this? A gentle stirring in the bushes made her jerk in surprise. The falcon hopped out of the darkness, settling next to her, filling Win with relief. Her mother was here.

"I don't want to see this!" she pleaded with the falcon, her eyes wet. The falcon said nothing, its beady yellow eyes strangely focused. Win frowned. "Mom?"

We woke them up, Win. We woke them all up.

Win's eyes pulled back to the clearing, the terrible noise of sobbing filling her head.

"No, I'm begging you...what are you doing?" Joseph screamed as they crowded closer.

Win's head snapped to the falcon.

"Mom, don't make me watch this!" But the falcon was gone. Win blinked down at the space it only just occupied. Had she imagined seeing her? Brought out of her daze with the soft sound of chanting, her gaze followed the chorus of voices. Like tremors that began in their lungs, their voices bled together in union, the chant becoming hurried, frenzied. The cloaked woman lifted the knife; its blade gleamed in the moonlight.

Win choked on tears, covering her mouth. *No, no, please.*

"No, don't do this!" Joseph screamed. He gurgled, and Win covered her ears as the woman with the dark hair cut into him.

Win squeezed her eyes shut. Joseph howled in terror, his voice thick with fear.

"Please!" he begged faintly, as though he were losing consciousness. Win couldn't see a thing, but she thought perhaps it was a good thing. "Please don't do this."

"The gods thank you for your sacrifice, Joseph Hickory."

An awful noise made Win dare to look. Flesh slicing, blood, thick and wet, god she could smell it from here. Hickory blood. *My blood.* She drained of energy and gagged. The woman held something up to the glow of the firelight, a shiny wet *thing*, blood dripping through her hands. Win's fingernails whited from gripping her knees so tightly, and she could only guess at what it was.

The women in the semi-circle chanted feverishly as the stone glowed. Its harsh light filled the clearing, rolling off it in waves.

"Brother Nassuau!" the woman chanted, elated, her smile wide and wicked. "I give you his body. Curse his family and this land. He will know retribution for what he has done, the men he has murdered, the children he orphaned. They will all know. They will all pay."

They stepped away, out of the light from the stone, and Win could finally see the full spectacle of what they'd done to him. Slack against the stone, his head lolled, his upper body straining against the cord that bound him. Blood oozed down his shirt, blossoming out from the wound like an ugly flower.

Is he dead? Win waited to see what would happen, her mouth dry. A blinding light bled from the stone, a flash bright enough to send stars dancing across her vision. She shielded her eyes with her forearm, and when she managed to blink back to clarity, the organ in the woman's hand was gone.

Then one by one, they left, as quietly and stealthily as they arrived. With a ragged breath, and once they'd vanished into the trees, she rushed out of her hiding space.

She jogged across the clearing, stopping at the feet of the man whose demise she'd just witnessed. Kneeling at his feet, her fingertips tentatively stroked his wiry beard. He was still so young. He couldn't have been more than forty. She brushed his mop of red hair off his damp forehead, revealing thick brows, his lashes wet against his cheeks.

Grandpa, she nearly choked. *He's just like you.*

He wailed, and Win jumped back in fright. *He's still alive!*

Win inhaled a shaky breath, her mind whirring. How was this even possible? She wondered if she could somehow untie him. Standing on numb legs, her feet like wood, she stumbled back, looking for anything that might cut rope. The knife lay discarded in the grass, sticky with blood. She narrowed her eyes at the blade, the hilt carved from bone; she peered down at it. Then he moaned behind her.

"Joseph?" She fell to her knees on the grass. Taking his shoulders, she nudged him gently. "Joseph?"

He fluttered his eyes, slowly, painfully. His irises focussed on the face in front of him. Saliva coated his beard, thin strands between his lips as he tried to speak.

"Eliza, no," he babbled, raising a hefty arm, landing heavily on her shoulder. "You shouldn't be here."

"I'm not Eliza." Win's heart ached. She recognized the name, annoyed at herself for not paying better attention when Uncle Willard gave them the family tree. "I can't explain. I'm Winifred… you're alive. You'll be okay—I think. I need to get you back home."

She glanced up at the stone at his back; it was cold and spent, its magic used up for the night. For the first time, she noticed the faces carved into the granite, along with the carvings of animals, bears, wolves, and birds. With a deep shudder, she recalled the last time she'd seen this thing—it nearly killed her.

Joseph rotated his wrists, rubbing at the cord marks on his free hands. He gaped at her, bushy, red brows narrowing.

"Who are you? Another Witch?"

"No." Win shook her head. "I can't explain—you won't understand."

Torches of light flickered in the thicket of trees, voices calling out his name. It was a woman, terrified, screaming for him over and over. Win exhaled in relief. "They're coming for you!" she said, smiling, turning back to him. His breathing was shallow, raspy, eyes fluttering closed.

"Joseph, no!" She shook him hard. "Don't go to sleep, stay with me…I need to ask you something."

Eyes opened, watering at the creases. "What?"

"You'll be alright. Help is on the way," she attempted to reassure him, but the wound under his ribs was leaking, pooling around his thighs. Win looked around frantically. With shaking hands, she darted for the knife, slicing the hem off her nightgown. Bundling it into a ball, she pressed it to the wound, then placed his large hand over the top. "Hold it there!"

His lips quivered. "Who are you?"

Win shook her head. "I don't think you'd believe me if I told you."

His eyes opened, studying her for the first time. "You look like Eliza."

Win smiled shakily. "Yeah. I guess that's true. Look—who were they? Those women?"

"*Witches*," he breathed it out painfully. "Dark ones. They know what I did."

Win nodded grimly, not having forgotten his crimes. "I thought the Atoloa did this…they cast our curse in revenge for what you did? But that woman, she wasn't one of them, at least I don't think so—she was…."

…something else entirely…

"My orders…" he spluttered, and Win tried to settle him. "I killed…so many of them."

Her eyes darted away as the torches got closer; she got to her feet, waving her arms to try and catch their attention. But she was sober, slack, and her feet wouldn't move. When she turned to look back at Joseph, he was gone. Win cried out, an icy chill running the length of her body. The space he'd occupied was empty, black mist fading into nothing.

Win clutched her chest, a strange feeling of being enveloped in hot liquid spreading through her legs like she was being sucked back in time through a vacuum. It was over.

Win shrieked herself awake, drenched in cold sweat, her sheets tangled around her legs. She gasped and choked on her breath, blindly reaching for her lamp in the dark. Warm light cascaded around the room. She flew out of bed, tugging at the sash of her window, flinging it open, and cold air floated in. Still breathing hard, she stood numbly, staring at the strange, unfamiliar surroundings of her room. Her books, her old stuffed animals, photos of her friends pinned to her cork board—they all looked strangely out of place.

What the hell was that? She padded into the hall barefoot, still dressed in the nightgown she'd worn to bed. Breathless, dizzy, she stumbled in the dark, and around her, the walls moved. Win squeezed her eyes tight, trying to quell the dizziness. In the dark, her eyes refused to adjust, and she called out her sister's name. Panting, she put a hand on the wall to steady herself, but her hand left a print. It stuck to the wallpaper.

"What?" She felt vomit brewing in her gut. Rowan's door crashed open. The hazy shape of her dashed forward and held out her arms. Before Win blacked out, her eyes focussed, she stared down at her hands, coated in thick, sticky blood, and as she crashed to the floor, narrowly missing her sister's arms, she saw the grimy remains of a bloodied hand print on the wall.

One

Rowan touched down in a drooped cedar, her talons clutching the branch as it buckled under her weight. She lifted her elegant neck, yellow eyes flicking across the canopy. Below, a giant cat crept through the undergrowth, her purr rumbling in the distance.

The jaguar tilted her head, pupils like black pinpricks as it spotted the eagle, her brow drawing the densely packed rosettes together. A mass of black markings etched into her short, velvet fur, a long sleek tail whipped back and worth as she prowled the woods. She padded into a clearing, muzzle sniffing the air.

Anything?

Rowan landed deftly on the ground, stretching out her wings. She bowed her head in disappointment. *Nothing. I'm starting to think we need to go further afield. Lincoln or Mickleford?*

Win's shoulders sagged in disappointment. *I can't even get her scent. Where the hell is she, Rowan?*

The eagle fluffed out her wings, gold and white gleaming in

the moonlight. *We should head back, Win. It's after midnight. You have school. I've got a shift. We can look again tomorrow.*

Win stretched and yawned, revealing long, sharp fangs, the languid movement extending to her splayed claws. *Okay. But I'm getting anxious now. This isn't like her.*

Rowan shifted on the ground, pecking loose earth for bugs. *You need to let the dream go.*

Win sank to the ground, laying out her long paws. The dream still lived in her mind, on constant replay. It was hard to forget. Witnessing one of your ancestors get brutally mutilated was hard to shake off. Win told Rowan and Evan, seeking their advice. She couldn't shake the feeling she'd seen something important. It was the night the curse was cast, the start of, well, *everything*. Evan assured her she was still traumatized by the events of the summer, losing their grandpa and then Grayson. But Win couldn't forget it and the nagging suspicion that everything she thought she knew about the curse was a lie. The stone, the witch, and most of all, her mother and what she'd said.

We woke them all up…

Evan said she was overthinking things. She was still healing, learning to cope with her Therian body. But to Win, it had been real. She had felt the grass under her feet, and she'd laid hands over Joseph to attempt to staunch his bleeding. It was as if she had been there. Plus one other startling detail, Rowan insisted she had imagined. When she had woken and run into the hall, her hands had been covered in blood. Win clearly remembered the stain of a bloody handprint on the floral wallpaper. Dazed, and exhausted they'd forced her back to bed, and in the morning, the handprint was gone, leaving Win to feel that she'd imagined it. Evan and Rowan insisted she had been dreaming, but it left Win rattled and unsure.

Mom went missing around the time I had the dream, Rowan. Don't you think they could be connected?

No honey. You are still grieving, and the mind does some crazy things. And a Therian mind…anything could happen.

A low, guttery chug emitted from Win's chest. She wasn't about to argue, but she was sick of being treated like an invalid. Like, she was in some kind of recovery program. The truth was, Rowan or Evan had no grip on what had happened to their mother, and neither could explain her dream. She had been close enough to smell Joseph's blood. They treated her like a loose cannon; she could erupt at any second. Win supposed she could hardly blame them. Her hot temper, biting remarks flew out of her mouth uncontrollably. No wonder her father was working more in Boston. He'd been gone two weeks on this trip, and his phone calls few and far between.

Rowan said nothing, but Win swore she heard her sister exhale before she beat the air with her wings, lifting into the sky. Win was burdened with worry, a pang of anxiety surging through her as she decided to make one last sweep. Under the light of the waning moon, she took off, bounding across the ground, leaves kicking up in her wake. Keeping her eyes peeled, she swept through the trees, like a ghost, so fast you could swear you hadn't seen anything at all.

Alice was missing.

Saying it out loud had been hard for both sisters to admit. Two nights after the cabin fire, her absence had been felt, like a door opening, leaving a cold chill in its wake. Their mother was *always* there. Even if you didn't see her, which was often, her warm, reassuring presence surrounded the woods. And now she was gone, missing for six whole weeks.

With the arrival of September, school began, and Win had to learn to start from scratch. She was returning to her senior year as a Therian. A radically different person to the one who'd left in the summer. And what a fantastic summer it had been, for the most part. For the first time in years, she had friends, a social life, her mother, father, sister, and grandfather all in the same place.

The soft, bubbling noise of the brook rushed up to greet her as she dashed past. Somehow she always ended up here.

She'd also had a relationship—a boy she'd loved. Win couldn't bring herself to look at Grayson's camp, an area of the woods she knew only too well. She sniffed at the charred remains of the fire, now a sludgy mess after so much rain. Being here stirred up so many memories, feelings leaving her aching and tired. Grayson was gone too.

The summer had taken a dramatic turn. After uncovering some family secrets, learning of their relations to the Frasers, John Hickory died, leaving a gaping, hollow void in their happy but chaotic lives. Win tried to harden up after losing Grayson and accept her new life. When Alice vanished, it was enough to pull her into a dreary depression, not unlike the way she'd felt when she first arrived at Cedar Wood.

You have friends, she assured herself. *And you have family, what's left of them. And Luke and Ella.*

Win lifted her head and sprinted through the trees, running parallel to the road which ran back into town. Car headlights flashed through the trunks, and if anyone was to look close enough, they might get a fright. Her hind legs tingled, her back ached, the tale tells signs she must soon merge back into her human body. She was still young, a baby in her calling, and Rowan warned her to stay in her animal form for a couple of hours at best before she became too exhausted to make the change at all.

Since the calling in the summer, Win found she experienced signals, warning flares shot through her body. It was a call to return home from her sister.

Come back now, she said. Win could hear her voice as bright and clear as a sun flare. Rowan was the family alpha, which Win found came with some reasonably humiliating traits. She had to obey everything her sister said. In animal form, Rowan was the boss, the primal leader, and whatever she said, you did. It wasn't even an obligation; Win found herself pulled back through the woods, her muscles responding to her sister's cry. If Rowan said to come back, you went.

A smile threatened her lips. It wasn't like Rowan was some kind of dictator, but she sure as hell got a kick out of bossing her around, especially after their epic fight at their grandfather's funeral. Win dared to accuse her sister of being weak.

Yep, I definitely won't be doing that again. She rounded the old Mercy place, standing empty since the summer. She spied the large building looming against the night sky, cutting an imposing shape. She shuddered, wondering when the new owners would be taking ownership. It had been taken off the market a few weeks ago, and Luke remarked it would be the first time the building would have been owned by someone *other* than a Fraser. Win cowered as she passed; the ground always felt cooler here, and the old place never failed to spook her. The shadow of the building was large enough to blot out any shards of sun streaming through the trees walling the estate. Or maybe the ground surrounding the house really was haunted? She spotted lights on the top floor, flickering in the lead-lined windows.

So they've moved in already! She would tell Luke when she got in if he was still awake.

Win found herself at the base of an incline, the spot she'd used to morph and stash her clothes. She hunched over her paws, belly close to the ground as she waited for the pullback. Her spine arched and snapped. Jaw clenched as she breathed, her organs shifting and her bones cracking into the resemblance of the seventeen-year-old redhead she was. Panting, she felt around for her clothes, tugging her sweater over her head, slightly damp with spots of rain. She wriggled back into her jeans, her skin still crawling. It was the oddest, skin creeping sensation, and her vision had to adjust, merging back to clear. Existing inside an animal was weird and terrifying. Adrenaline pulsed through her veins for hours after. The pin-point beam of a LED torch made her squint, shielding her eyes with her hand.

"Who is that? Rowan?" she groaned. "I told you I was coming!"

"No, it's me." Luke's voice floated out of the dark. She smelled him as he stepped closer, leaning on his shoulder until the white beams faded from her eyes.

"You blinded me!" She pinched the bridge of her nose. "What are you doing out here? It's freezing!"

"You didn't come back with Rowan." He guided her along the incline and across a small clearing. She clutched his sweater, rubbing her eyes. He never said the words, *I was worried* out loud, but she knew it was his ulterior motive.

"I'm fine!" she snapped, annoyed he'd rushed out here in the dark. "I was taking one more sweep."

"Anything?"

"No." She couldn't hide her worry. "Nothing. But we'll keep looking."

"Maybe she flew south for winter?" Luke's remark tumbled out of his mouth before he could shut it, and Win shot him a filthy glare. He held up his palms in defeat. "I was joking!"

"You're hilarious," she said, wanting to change the subject. It hurt to think about Alice and where the small falcon might be. "Hey, guess what? We have new neighbors!"

Luke's expression soured. "Hope they managed to get the old place exercised."

"Isn't it weird a new family will be living in your house? A house your ancestor built?"

He smirked, pushing his thin-framed glasses up his nose, the light of the moon bouncing off his ebony hair, which had grown long, around his ears. "Nah. It could do with bulldozing if you ask me. Maybe another family will breathe new life into it? Make it a happy home."

Win linked her arm through his as the lights of Hickory house twinkled in the distance; despite her little growth spurt this summer, he was still a good foot taller than her. She loved how firm he was, safe, and he didn't shove her off anymore when she napped on him during a movie. Having him around was like having her very own big brother. Though, her father warned her repeatedly not to keep walking around the top floor in her underwear. She'd been appalled when he pulled her aside one day.

"I know he's your cousin…."

"Third cousin," Win reminded him curtly. Her father had exhaled, in the way dads do, exasperated and resigned at once.

"Whatever. He's a young man. And you might not *think* he's looking, but trust me—*he is*!"

Win waved him off but took care to wear her robe more. It was bad enough they shared a bathroom. Luke complained she left her underwear on the floor or her cosmetics around the sink. Luke got his revenge, trailing his sweaty sports socks on the landing, knowing full well she'd gag and have to tidy up after him. Theirs was a grudging closeness, forced together in odd circumstances, but since the summer, he'd been her rock, and she didn't like to imagine him not being around. The very thought of him leaving for college in another year with Ella made her insides crumble. Knowing they'd be leaving her behind, still too young in her calling to risk being that far from home.

"Rowan is getting testy. You really shouldn't have followed me out here. Now she'll be at your throat too," Win said as they rounded a corner, only a few yards from the start of the Hickory property. Luke was saying something, she was aware of his hand on her shoulder, but her attention was pulled back into the forest. She narrowed her eyes. "Oh god, can you smell that?"

Luke paused, craning his neck in the direction she had taken off in. He sighed and jogged after her. "Wait up! I can't smell… oh…Jesus!"

Win stood back, cupping her hand over her nose. "What the hell is it?" she said, her voice muffled. "Is it a dead animal?"

Luke heaved; his tan complexion turning grey. "That's disgusting…maybe a fox or something?"

Win stepped forward, but he grabbed her shoulder. "*What* are you doing?"

"Checking it out!"

"No, you're not!"

Win shook his hand off her shoulder and linked her fingers around his wrist. "Fine. Come with me then. But I'm fairly certain I can handle it myself."

Luke rolled his eyes skyward, relenting, then waved his arm. "After you."

Win pushed back branches, bending low as she followed a rancid stench wafting under her nose. She bristled, her spine tensing. Something had *died* around here. Luke's feet crunched on leaves behind her; when she stopped abruptly, he nearly toppled over her. He righted himself and puffed irritably. "Can you warn me if you're about to stop? I don't see as well as you."

"Sorry!" she muttered, squeezing his fingers. "I think we're close." Luke's flashlight hit the ground, the beam wobbling in his hand.

"Uh, you think?" Luke gagged, bunching his sleeve over his hand and covering his mouth.

The smell was foul, so pungent it had to be a large animal, perhaps a boar or a fox. Win scratched at the soil with the tip of her sneaker, prodding a massive pile of leaves. Something dense rolled out of the pile, landing at their feet. Luke yelled, the flashlight dancing in the air, and Win managed to cover her mouth before she let out a shrill scream. The narrow beam of light rolled around on the ground, illuminating the gruesome discovery.

Shit! Rowan! You need to come out here now!

Win scrambled back, her jaw sagging with fright as she stared down at the bloodied remains of a human hand.

Two

"The sheriff is sending an officer over," Rowan said. She placed a mug of chocolate on the table, and Win instinctively leaned back. Her skin was pale, and she felt bile rising up her gullet.

She nodded in thanks but pushed the chocolate away. "I don't think I can manage. I can still smell…."

"Dead hand," Luke choked out, covering his mouth with both hands and taking deep breaths through his nose. "I'm never going to forget it as long as I live."

The back porch door crashed open, and Evan bundled in, bringing with her a stiff breeze. She rubbed her arms, her teeth chattering. With a grim look on her face, she tossed the flashlight on the table. "It's freezing out there. I think—whoever it was, it was a guy. There isn't much left of him."

Rowan's complexion paled. She raked her hands through her mass of red curls cursing as she looked at the ceiling. Then abruptly, she banged the kitchen table with her fist. "Shit! A dead guy on our land? Great, just great."

Evan put a hand on her shoulder, but Rowan shrugged her off, and Evan drew back in surprise. "Rowan! The poor guy got mauled. Whatever did that to him—well—it was an unpleasant way to go."

"I know." Rowan exhaled, pacing the floor, her shoes squeaking on the polished wood. "But it draws attention to us—the house, the old rumors. We don't need this crap right now."

Rowan's fierce eyes snapped in Win's direction, and she slunk in her seat, feeling the heat of her sister's glare. "Whoa. Why are you looking at me?"

Rowan licked her lips, leaning her palms on the table top. "You haven't…done anything odd, have you? Had any weird killing dreams? Meat cravings?"

Win laughed out loud. "What? No! What on earth makes you think I would?"

"It's quite common in the first years after the calling. At night you can be plagued by dreams of hunting prey—especially a predator like you. And things get fuzzy. Sometimes the lines between dreams and reality get blurred."

"So, you think I went and hunted some poor guy and dragged him onto our land? No—no way!"

"That's absurd!" Luke leaped to her defense. "You can't really believe it? Besides, she always carbs up before going out. Check the cupboards if you don't believe me."

As much as Win appreciated his help, being reminded of her enormous appetite was humiliating. She hated he knew how much pasta, potatoes, and starchy food she'd been craving.

Rowan's face melted into a reluctant smile. "Of course. I'm sorry. But maybe—try some steak. You know, just in case."

Win chuckled darkly, but Evan cleared her throat, reminding them of the seriousness of the situation. "Well, we need to deal with the poor dead man outside in the woods. This is awful!"

Lights flooded the kitchen, casting gaping shadows across the ceiling, followed by the short wail of the siren. Rowan drew in a jagged breath. "The officer is here. Just…" She eyed Win. "Try not to act weird, okay? Like we had something to do with it."

Luke's hand slapped the table. "We didn't. You stop acting weird!"

"You're being twitchy!" Win warned her. "Calm down."

"Okay," Rowan breathed. There were heavy boot steps on the porch and a hard knock on the door. Rowan ran to the hall, and Win pinned back her ears, listening as her sister threw it open. Win's stomach was a mass of yarn, she felt breathless and edgy, and she couldn't forget the grisly discovery. But to Win's surprise, she heard Rowan let out a shaky, relieved laugh. She wandered back into the kitchen, followed by a young officer in his twenties, dressed in tan uniform with cropped dark hair and a deep olive complexion. He was wearing a black, heavy coat over his uniform. Rowan showed him into the room, her hand on his shoulder.

Win straightened in her chair as the officer glanced at her, and ducked her eyes bashfully.

"This is Noah Chase," Rowan introduced him to the room. "We went to high school together. I'm so pleased to see you! Though not like this. I heard you were back in town."

The young officer took off his hat, nodding politely at everyone in the room, his eyes lingering on Evan for longer than they should have. Evan usually had that effect on people. She was all long dark swathes of hair and deep tanned skin that gleamed, with striking features it was hard not to gape at her. "I took the position two weeks ago. I've been in Boston for two years as a beat cop, but my old man finally convinced me to come home."

"All the better for us!" Rowan flashed her best smile. "But you haven't been to see me at the bar?"

Noah laid his hat on his table, adjusting his belt under his jacket. "I had no idea anyone I went to high school with still lived here. But I'll sure come by now."

"This is Evan," Rowan said, waving her hand proudly in the pretty woman's direction.

"Her partner," Evan said in a clipped tone, which Win didn't miss. Neither did Luke. They both shared a grin across the table. Noah nodded, taken by surprise.

"And this is Luke and my sister Win."

Noah smiled at Win, nodding to each of them in turn, his gaze finally resting on Luke, recognition sparkling in his eyes.

"Luke Fraser, right?" Noah beamed, wagging a finger. "Spencer's little brother? Wow, man, you shot up. Think the last time I saw you—you were a little kid. God, you look like your old man. How's your brother doing these days?"

Luke grunted, and Win could tell he was holding back some acidic remark. He stared hard at Noah and unbelievably let it pass. He lifted his broad shoulders in a shrug. "I parted company with my family over the summer. I go by Blakely now."

"I'll have to catch up with him now that I'm home," Noah said, and Luke's shoulders stiffened.

"He's in Hawaii."

"Oh, that's too bad. Guess I'll catch up with him online." He cast Rowan a sly smile. "Didn't you two used to date?"

Rowan balked. "Uh, no. No, no. Just a rumor. Should we go out and look at this thing they found?"

Noah grabbed his hat and planted it back on his head. "Show me the way. I'm getting eased in gently to life in Cedar Wood—a dead body in the woods already!"

Rowan locked eyes with Win. "Aren't you coming? You're the one who found it."

Win drew her knees up to her chest, shaking her head. "I really don't want to go back out there, Rowan. It was too awful."

"No, of course!" Noah held up his hand. "I can go. You guys stay warm."

"I'll come with you." Rowan followed him out into the hall.

"You'll smell it before you see it, Rowan, trust me," Win called out, then instantly bit her tongue, her cheeks growing pink as she realized her blunder.

Noah made an odd face at her remark as he followed Rowan out into the cold. Her sister shot her a glare over her shoulder, and Win mouthed a humble sorry. When the porch door slammed, Luke flung a scathing look in her direction, which earned him a punch in the shoulder.

"Don't say anything!"

"Nicely done. You'll smell it before you see it." He chortled but wriggled his shoulders as if experiencing a visual recall of the bloodied, severed hand. Evan slumped in the chair across from them, leaning her chin on her hand.

"At least he *seems* nice," Win said, wringing her hands under the table. "Like a nice cop who won't automatically jump to conclusions about our strange family history."

"I hope we can get this sorted quickly," Evan said. "I hate to have to take off when something weird is going on."

Luke snorted. "Something weird is going on. It's a good family motto."

"Where are you going?" Win narrowed her eyes, ignoring Luke's sarcasm.

Evan leaned heavily on the table, dark hair tumbling across her shoulders. "I have to go into Boston for a week or so. One of my family members is sick, and they want me to come home."

"Oh no, is it serious?"

"It could be." Evan looked pale, tired, and heavy with worry. "I shouldn't be gone too long. But I do need to go. It's my mim."

When Win's brows drew in confusion, Evan smiled and filled in the gap. "My grandma—it's what I call her."

"Oh no." Win reached for her hand. "I hope she'll be okay. We'll miss you."

Evan smiled warmly. The two had bonded over the last few weeks, despite the rocky start to their relationship. Evan provided the comfort sometimes Rowan skirted around, especially when it came to Win's doomed love life. Win was grateful for a shoulder or an ear for listening when she broke down over Grayson. Win loved

Rowan, but when it came to Grayson, her sister drew up an invisible wall, her sympathy well run dry. She shut Win down and didn't want to talk about him, encouraging her sister to move on. Win guessed it was because Grayson slept with her and left her when Win needed him most. *And* he'd lied to her the entire summer. Funny how big sisters could hold grudges. Win hardly blamed her; she'd react the same way. Despite Win not trusting Evan at first, they were closer now, and Evan had a calming, balm effect on the entire family. Even Ben loved having her around.

"I'll miss you too, but I'm sure I'll be back in no time."

"I'm sure the good-looking officer will do plenty of bar visits now he knows where Rowan works," Luke joked. Evan scowled at him but brushed off his teasing with a wave of an elegant hand.

"Your smart mouth will get you in trouble one day," she remarked, to which he grunted a laugh. The porch door banged open, and after a moment, Rowan appeared, her face pale from the cold. She rubbed her arms briskly.

"He's calling it in. The place will be swarming with a team from Lincoln soon."

"Take it easy, please!" Evan took her shoulders, running her hands up and down her bare arms, "You're acting like we killed the guy."

"It makes me uneasy, is all." Rowan frowned, a deep line appearing on her forehead. She took a steady breath and pulled away as the door clanged again, the officer talking into his phone as he trudged into the kitchen. He shot a worried glance around the room, and Win stiffened in her chair, not liking his grim expression.

When he hung up, he stood with his hands on his hips. "They'll be a team here in twenty minutes, I'm afraid. But they already have some suspicions on who the victim might be."

Rowan gave a short laugh of surprise. "Already?"

"Well, this is Cedar Wood, and apart from our town's odd ancestry, nothing much goes on around here." His phone beeped, and he slid it open, his thick brows pulling into a frown. "Have you seen this man at all?"

He showed Rowan a picture on his phone. "He had a report filed on him over a week ago. Missing person."

Rowan bit her lip, shaking her head as he showed the photo to Evan. "No, I've never seen him."

"His name is Paul Ames. He's a Zoologist from New York. He was here visiting. You wouldn't have happened to have seen him in the bar in town?"

Luke hopped out of his seat. "I work there too, let me see." He peered through his glasses at the photo and then shook his head. "I dunno. Maybe. He looks familiar."

"He was staying at Sally's bed and breakfast."

Luke shrugged. "Like I said…maybe. Not helpful, is it? He was a Zoologist?"

"Yeah, he was. Apparently in town due to the strange sightings recently…but I'm sure you guys are sick to death of all those old rumors?"

A hush fell across the room. Rowan looked as if she were about to faint, her nails white as she gripped the edge of the chair. Finally, it was Evan who spoke up. "Sightings?"

Noah laughed as if he were a little embarrassed to be bringing it up. "Well, you know the town's history…wolves, big cats…giant birds? This guy was here tracking a supposed big cat spotted on the main roads around here of late. Up near the Boxford tunnel?"

Win's legs drained of energy, her fingers going numb. Had she been careless? So reckless to be spotted so near the main road? She knew she sometimes ran the road parallel, but she'd always stayed well hidden. You'd only really see her if you were looking hard enough. Her stomach sank, reality hitting in, and Rowan was glaring daggers at her across the room. But perhaps this man *had* been looking?

Rowan…I didn't mean to…

Just stay calm. He doesn't know anything.

"Has someone actually seen a big cat?" Evan asked, tilting her head, her face incredulous. "I mean, we live in a forest. We would have seen something."

"There's been some evidence of an animal in the vicinity larger than your average wolf. There has been the odd sighting, plus some carcasses of its kills." Noah laughed it off. "It's ludicrous, of course. I remember all the stories back in school about this old place. I never believed any of it."

Rowan's lips spread into an even smile. "It's all small-town stuff. We're used to it by now!"

"I'm sure! Animal sightings, ghost stories. Sure is good for bringing in the tourists, though."

"We haven't had any paranormal investigators for a while now, not since Luke's family sold the Mercy estate," Evan cut in, giving Rowan a reprieve, and Noah made a noise of surprise in the back of his throat. He cast a long glance in Luke's direction.

"It has new owners?"

Luke folded his arms. "I guess. I wouldn't know."

Noah shook it off, looking a little confused. "Funny…"

"Is there anything else we can do, Noah?" Rowan distracted him, and he snapped his attention back to her.

He flashed the photo in Win's direction, and she reluctantly craned her neck, not keen on seeing the face of the man who potentially owned the butchered limb laying only yards from their back door. It sickened her to think someone had been killed in this secluded patch of woods. Her mouth went dry as she glanced at the picture, a clean-shaven man with a hooked nose and a pair of thick-framed glasses. "Sorry, no," she answered, her voice cracking.

Noah straightened. "So you're the one who found him?"

"Both of us," Luke corrected him.

"And do you mind me asking what you two were doing in the woods this time of night? I mean, don't you have school in the morning? It's late." He checked his watch and whistled. "Or early, you might say."

Win's cheeks colored pink, her startled gaze finding Luke's across the table. He awkwardly cleared his throat. "Uh," he laughed, a sheepish smile crossing his face. "You don't need details, do you officer? I mean—you surely have an imagination?"

Win stared at him, open-mouthed in disbelief. "Uh…*Luke!*"

"Honestly, you two are a nightmare!" Rowan cackled, punching Luke's shoulder. She threw Noah an exasperated stare. "They can't keep their hands off one another! Teenagers!"

Rowan! This is humiliating! Win wanted to dissolve into the floor, heat spreading over her chest and neck.

Shut up, will you? He just saved your ass.

Win closed her lips around her protestations, and Noah clicked his tongue awkwardly. "Well, maybe you two should try practicing restraint? If you got caught, you'd be up for a public indecency fine."

"Sure thing!" Luke nodded, clapping his hands. "Restraint at all times. Well, if I'm not needed here…."

"Me too!" Win leaped out of her chair, not stopping till she had squeezed past Rowan and Officer Chase and was safely in the hallway. Luke disappeared into his den bedroom, formerly her grandpa's old office, hastily shutting the door. Annoyed with him, Win chased in after and slammed his door.

"What are you doing? I need to sleep. It's one in the morning!"

She crawled up his bed and dragged a pillow behind her back, drawing her knees to her chest in a hug. "What were you thinking? Telling him, we were…*doing it*…in the woods?"

Luke sniggered, clearly enjoying her humiliation. "What did you want me to say? You were back from a hunt? It seemed like a perfectly reasonable explanation at the time and was pretty much all I could think of."

"That figures!"

"What? C'mon. He bought it, didn't he? And I didn't notice you offering up any decent explanation."

Win exhaled and waved her hand, admitting a short laugh. "It's fine. I guess. Just keep it to yourself. It's embarrassing!"

Luke sagged onto the bed, his eyes going wide as if the thought had only just occurred to him. "Don't say anything to Ella!"

Win laughed, thinking if her best friend had been there, she would have come up with a far better excuse than a steamy encounter in the woods. She rubbed her eyes, weary and bone tired. Soon their yard was going to be filled with cops crawling all over the place. They had a field trip in the afternoon tomorrow and a chemistry test first thing. "I can't stop…seeing the hand. It was awful. That poor man!"

"I know," Luke agreed, a quiver erupting over his shoulders. "It's odd he was even here in town, studying wildlife. Maybe you should be more careful? Stay on the property?"

Win frowned, stretched out her long legs. It was easier said than done. The jaguar tended to go where it wanted. She could cover miles of terrain in one night, and keeping to the yard would be like being trapped within a zoo. The urge to move, to roam was undeniable, built-in muscle memory. "Maybe I haven't been careful," she admitted. "But I don't go far, and I have been trying to find my mother. At some point, we will have to go further out. And besides, I don't kill other animals." She cast her eyes down. "That I know of."

"That's the point, isn't it? It's what has Rowan so worried. You can't be sure of your actions in animal form." He saw her pained expression and altered his tone. "But for what it's worth. I don't think you've killed anything—judging by your carb cravings!"

Win threw a pillow at him, which he dodged. "Thanks. I should go."

"Good plan. I need to change for bed Win, you might be able to walk that test tomorrow in your sleep, but I won't!"

He started to undress, and Win made a hasty retreat, jogging up the stairs to her room two at a time.

"Win, can you come here for a moment?"

It was Evan's soft, feminine voice catching her as she passed the bedroom she shared with Rowan. Win yawned, eager to try and forget the night's grim events, but stepped into their room. Evan perched on the end of the bed; she was in her robe, her lovely dark hair pulled up on her head. The lamps were on, it was warm and cozy, and Win noted the new pink and white bedsheet Evan replaced Rowan's old sheets with. If anyone could force Rowan into girlishness, it was Evan.

Win crept in, noticing Evan appeared anxious. "Is everything okay?"

Evan's expression was gentle, but there was something concerning in her smile. "Come sit down for a minute. I need to talk to you."

"Where's Rowan?"

"With the cop," she replied, making room for Win to sit. "I think she'll be a while, they've cordoned off an area, and they are looking for the rest of the poor guy."

Win shuddered. "That's awful." She eyed her with suspicion and then noticed Evan had something bundled up in her lap, hiding it under her hands. "What's going on?"

Evan took a shaky breath, pushing back a strand of hair. "Rowan and I haven't been entirely truthful with you. And to be honest, the fact I'm doing this will really piss her off."

Win's eyes rounded, and then admitted a small sigh. "She isn't exactly hard to piss off at the moment..."

"She worries about you," Evan pressed on, despite Win's remark. "The responsibility of being alpha has been an adjustment, and—well—we made the decision not to tell you together. But I don't think we can hide it anymore. Not after tonight."

A cold chill ran across her neck, her insides whirring. She didn't like the direction this was headed in. "Tell me. You're scaring me, Evan."

Evan sucked in her breath, pulling out the garment, and Win recognized it instantly. She thought she had lost it, but it was her long, white nightgown, the one she had worn the night of her dream. But the worst thing was it was saturated in dry blood, dark, inky, and splattered everywhere. Win gasped. She didn't need to sniff it to know it was human blood, rich and coppery. It sang under her nose. She gagged and pushed it away.

The bloody hand print on the wall...

"We cleaned the blood off the walls. And in the morning you were so tired, you thought it was a dream," Evan answered her thought aloud.

"It was real," Win hissed sharply. "Why...why did you hide this?"

"We were terrified," Evan answered. "We found you in the hall, covered in blood, delirious, and you were muttering about Joseph Hickory...and if you look, the bottom of your nightgown is torn."

Win grabbed it, looked closely, her heart beat starting to whip out of control. She remembered holding the knife in her hand, ripping off the hem to staunch Joseph's bleeding. "I did that!" she insisted. "I remember tearing the hem. I told you, and you wouldn't believe me. I *was* there!"

"Win, it isn't possible." Evan shook her head. "I believe, you *believe,* you were there, and it was a vivid dream...but astral phasing through *time*? It's a stretch, even for someone like me to consider. You'd have to be..." her voice trailed off, distant, her mouth not willing to form the words.

"You'd have to be what? What Evan?" Win choked, her eyes filling up. "Please?"

"Someone connected with the stone. Someone extremely powerful."

Win deflated, her mind whirring. She recalled Uncle Willard, all tucked away in a tiny house in Lincoln, and she remembered what he said the day she had seen him.

You could be the one to set us free. The words sprang to her lips, but she pushed them away, her secret for now. After all, they'd hid this from her. She would find out herself. "We don't even know what the stone does."

"I believe," Evan continued, and Win could sense she was carefully choosing her words. "The stone is some sort of conduit for old, dark magic. It was responsible for casting the curse on your family. And I think it hides and shows itself when magic is present or has been used. The night in the clearing, the night your grandpa died, the four of you, *miraculously*, called it out of hiding."

"That was Ella," Win gave her friend credit. "She was the one who figured out how to contact Iris."

"Well, maybe she has a hidden talent. But, it is not something to be messed with. It's dangerous and rooted in evil. Your Uncle Willard told you that."

"In my dream, I saw what those…I think they must have been witches. I saw what they did. They woke it up…I'm telling you what I saw was real!" Win felt like she was talking to a wall. Evan's expression was unreadable. She closed a hand over hers.

"I don't doubt you think it's real. I think your subconscious conjured up something. Like with all nightmares, usually, there is a logical explanation for them."

"But why did you let me believe it was a dream?" Win was exasperated. "Like it didn't happen?"

"We didn't want to scare you. After losing your grandpa and Grayson…you were heartbroken. We wanted to wait until we found the right time."

Win's fragile temper frayed at the edges. She drew back. "That isn't good enough, Evan!"

Evan jerked at Win's loss of temper. "I know…"

"No, you don't. We aren't supposed to keep secrets from one another. Not after this summer." Her thoughts spiraled, arguing the reasons they would have kept this from her, and only one pushed to the forefront. They were scared she was a killer, and she was unstable, not to be trusted.

"So you both think, *that night*, I was covered in blood because I *somehow* slept-walked out of the house and killed someone? And you think I might have killed the poor guy out there?"

Evan looked alarmed. "No—we don't know anything. Only it's all a weird coincidence."

"But Evan, if I'm right about this…and what I saw was real…

then everything we believe about the curse is a lie…" she trailed off, noticing Evan's downcast expression and refusal to meet her eyes. The Atoloa shouldered the blame for years, but doubt nagged at Win's insides. Something darker lurked in the shadows.

A figure stepped in the door, and both women looked up sharply at the intrusion. But it was only Rowan, her cheeks red and cold, her hair around her shoulders. Win didn't have the energy to fight her sister on this. She understood Rowan's misguided attempt to protect her, even though she wished Rowan would occasionally let her guard slip.

"I think we may have waited too long to tell her," she said, wringing her hands, anxiety etched into the creases of her eyes. Evan shifted on the bed.

"What is it?"

Rowan paled in the yellow lamps of the room, casting a sickly glow across her face. "They've found more of him. A torso—and his head."

Win recoiled, sucking in her lungs; she started to babble, shaking her head. "Rowan, you know…I wouldn't…It can't have been me!"

"Win, I don't know what to say." She looked crestfallen, defeated, and very worried. "But the police are speculating, and they think it's an animal attack."

"No, *Rowan*," Win burst. "*No!*"

"Win…" She shook her head in dismay as if trying to shake away the awful thing she had seen. "The guy…he was ripped apart."

Three

Win thumbed a message into her phone. The truck juddered in the drive, the engine warming up. She nestled into the driver's side while she waited for Luke to haul his backside out of the front door.

Dad, I need to talk to you. When are you coming home?

She hit send before she could talk herself out of it. The ache to hear her father's voice was too hard to bear. After the cops cleared out, about three in the morning, Win managed to catch about four hours sleep, hot, exhausted, and restless under the covers. The coppery tang of blood lingered in her memory, causing bile to rise up her throat, leaving a caustic burn in its wake. She'd watched them carry out the body bag, the remains of the mangled victim jangling around inside. Win fought off images of his face, the picture Noah had shown her.

I didn't kill that man, she told herself over and over. Part of her was reeling, in shock, wondering if there was a chance she could have blocked out doing such a thing. She remembered the urges she experienced back in the summer, chasing after a poor woodland squirrel and squeezing it till its eyes bugged. She'd wanted to kill it, to feel it die under her hands.

But you didn't, a voice said. *You stopped yourself.*

Win threw her eyes, laughing at her own self-denial. *Grayson was the one who stopped me. If he hadn't…*

Guilt coursed through her, wondering at how many times Grayson had come to her aide, her defender, her white knight, and on that fateful night, she wouldn't forgive him. She'd been in the room, knowing he'd been locked in there, abused, starved, and yet she didn't give him the chance to explain. And now he was gone along with two others, who she'd loved and depended on, her mother and grandpa. Win empathized with her sister, how alone Rowan must have been in the early days, now more than ever. Perhaps this was why Rowan was hard on her now?

Time to tough it out, she thought—time to be brave. *And find Mom! She wouldn't have left us. Something must have happened.*

Luke bombed out of the porch, jumping the last two steps with his backpack strewn across his shoulders, drawing her out of her downward spiral. When he spotted her in the driver's seat, he groaned.

"Are we going to make it to school alive?" he joked, sliding into the passenger's side. Win scowled, struggling with the stick shift in her hand, the truck groaning as she thrust it into gear.

"I have to practice, and dad isn't here." She ignored him, staring open-mouthed as she roared the engine, feeling a blush creeping up her neck as she missed the choke point on several occasions.

"Why are you in a mood? You've had about as much sleep as me." Luke ground his teeth as the engine chugged down the driveway. Win's white fingers gripped the wheel. Anxiety boiled up inside her, his eyes on her face, waiting for her to choke and stall. Her exhaustion got the better of her. The truck jerked violently over a wide pothole, bumping them left, and right and Win stalled the engine before they'd even left the front-drive. She put her hands over her eyes and pressed back embarrassed tears. Luke scoffed.

"You aren't crying over a pothole, are you? Your dad really needs to fix this track."

"I'm not crying…." She sniffed, shaking her head. "I'm just tired!"

"What's *wrong*?"

"Nothing. Rowan said something last night, and— never mind."

Luke unstrapped his belt and then unhooked hers, waiting as it slithered back over her chest. "C'mon, swap!" Impatiently, her irritability rising, she slammed the door and swapped seats with him, then after a few seconds, they were on the road into town.

"Look, clearly something has you rattled," he said over the chug of the engine. "Can you manage to keep your shit together to get through the Chem test this morning? And then me, you, and Ella can talk on the way to Mickleford this afternoon?"

Win groaned. She had forgotten they had the field trip to the old Varga Museum in Mickelford, the small, historic town lay half an hour away, between Salem and West Point. "Yeah. I can shelve it. Why are you so worried about me taking this test?"

Luke threw her a mischievous grin. "Because I was hoping I could sneakily peek over your shoulder? My grades suck, and I'm supposed to be proving myself to the court, so I can actually be rid of my dad."

Win sniggered, then shut her mouth, recalling Luke's very serious predicament. He had to prove he could support himself, and had grades passable enough to get him into a college. Only then, he'd be granted the emancipation he dearly wanted. "Then you'll have to make sure you sit with me."

"Oh, I will. I should have studied, but I've been busy, work, practice…."

"Ella?"

"Yes, she's distracting too." He winked. "She was supposed to help me study."

"Well, that only works if you let her and don't distract her with…other things."

Luke laughed out loud. "Point taken. But I thought we should try the mind-melding thing you and your sister do…" his voice trailed away, and Win was about to come back with a witty retort, about as good as one she could come up with when she noticed him slow the truck to a crawl. He stared past her, through the passenger window toward the road or what lay beyond, through the trees. Win followed his gaze. He was staring at Mercy.

She punched his shoulder. "Luke?"

His lips parted, and he drew in a shaky breath, but his blue gaze firmly fixed on the large set of iron gates jutting out from the treeline, the old house lying beyond. Win shivered, a chill erupting out of nowhere, the blower on full in the cab. She prodded him again, and he jumped.

"Sorry," he laughed breathily. "Sorry."

"What's wrong?"

He pulled the truck away, and Win noticed his firm grip on the wheel. "It's nothing. I just…it's weird not driving straight in there."

Win narrowed her gaze, knowing full well he was unnerved, she could tell. Something just happened. "Luke, if you want to tell me anything…."

"No, it's fine. I just got a feeling. What do they call it? When someone walks over your grave?"

"That's creepy."

"Yeah. Ignore me. I'm sleep deprived."

He refused to be questioned anymore, and within a few minutes, they were parking in the school lot.

"So, like I was saying, we should try the mind-reading thing you and Rowan do?" He slammed the cab door, falling into step with her as they walked across campus. "It would be so handy for tests, and I might actually stand a chance of going to a decent college."

Win ignored the stab of envy in her gut, the pain of denial creeping up on her. The college word again, like a distant dream. Luke and Ella were destined for things she would never have, and Ella was pumped about New York. She had announced it excitedly, her heart set for a college place in the city once the time came to apply. Win expected Luke would follow. Being Therian, Win's options were limited. She was bound to Hickory land by the curse, never able to travel too far away. Life at a city college would pull strings too tight, and she could end up like her mother, permanently trapped in her animal form. She pushed down the terror of being alone like they had already left her behind. But she smiled at him, hiding her fear.

"I think you would have to be a pureblood Hickory for that to work." She nudged him. He waved her off, jogging slightly ahead, so he looked back at her over his shoulder.

"It works when you're a cat," he said, taking her shoulders. She stood on the stone steps leading up to the main building, and he took the step below, hands both firmly near her neck. "Close your eyes!"

"Nope." She did her best not to laugh.

"Ah, come on—look, I'll do it!" Squeezing his eyes shut, he made a loud humming noise through pursed lips. Win exploded into giggles, shoving his hands off. He opened one eye. "Knew I could make you laugh."

She playfully ruffled his hair. "It's a good thing you're pretty because you are *so* dumb!"

He laughed, but then his face melted into a more somber expression. "Look, whatever's bothering you, we'll deal with it. We'll talk later."

Win pressed her lips together, so he wouldn't be able to tell she was ready to cry. He wandered off to his homeroom, throwing her a boyish smile over his shoulder, and she wished he wasn't so adorable. She'd do just about anything for him, but the feeling was mutual. He walked backward like an idiot and shouted back at her, cupping his hands to his mouth.

"Clear your mind so I can probe you later!" He burst out laughing as a couple of heads turned in their direction, and Win flushed hot in humiliation.

"I'll tell Ella you said that," she teased, her smile vanishing when his back turned, her buoyant mood sinking the moment she was alone.

Win waited, having grabbed a seat near the rear of the large, orange and white striped bus, chugging loudly in the school lot. Outside the sky was a dense, monstrous grey, the wind batting the vehicle. Win pressed her forehead to the glass, cooling a dull ache forming between her brows. She gazed at her reflection, glassy green eyes looking back at her, her nose and cheekbones tapered since the summer, her mouth fuller. The Therian calling had caused a subtle disruption to her appearance. Fuelled by an inner heat, her skin lit with a permanent glow, which she supposed was better than the sallow appearance she'd sported when she first arrived in town. Her hair was thicker, heavier and most of the time, she wore it off her neck to keep from sweating.

The doors opened at the front, and a cold blast of air filled the bus. Win huddled into Grayson's coat, leaning her face into the lapels, the scent of bonfire remained even after all this time. She wriggled her toes in her boots, they pinched uncomfortably, and Win wondered if, like the rest of her body, her feet had grown. After the calling, she had struggled to adjust, her spine oddly loose, her joints extra flexible. When she'd dragged her winter sweaters and jeans out of hibernation, she'd noticed a sizable gap between her socks and the hem. Her arms stood proud from the sleeve of her sweaters, and suddenly her thicker waist caused the top buttons to dig into her stomach. Win's figure was lean, long, and shapely, with soft curves hinting to the animal she was hiding under her clothes. Every part of her body erupted, and she'd had to do a mad dash to the shops before the weather turned to kit herself out for school.

The doors opened again, and Win spotted a couple of students she knew from social studies pile on. One was Rosene Trent, who managed to throw her an icy glare of disdain before she slid into her seat. Luke and Ella finally appeared laughing about something as they wandered to the back. Win waved, and Ella grabbed a seat across the aisle. Their balding teacher Mr. Rainer climbed on, followed by a boy she knew was on Luke's basketball team, a moody kid with a shaved head and an attitude, who was ushered near the front, probably so he could be watched with a keen eye. It was Cole Ward, and he was a flight risk.

"Hey!" Ella beamed as Luke huffed and climbed over her, hustling the window seat. She held out a paper bag of pink and white striped donuts. "Bus snack?"

Win grinned, her mouth-watering as she dived for a donut. "I can always count on you for sugar."

"Well, you ate barely anything at lunch." Ella lowered her voice, leaning across the aisle. "Luke kind of explained what happened last night."

When the bus finally pulled out of the lot, Win settled back, and Ella crossed the aisle to slink into the spare seat next to her. Luke popped in his earbuds and, within thirty seconds, dozed off, his forehead touching the window. "He's exhausted. But then again, I don't think I'd sleep if I found a dead person in my yard."

Win inhaled deeply and explained what happened after the police left, and Evan called her into their room, watching as Ella's expression changed with grim fascination. It didn't matter if Luke was asleep; she knew Ella would relay it all to him at some point.

"So Rowan thinks you mauled this poor guy?" Ella sounded incredulous, which gave Win a moment of relief.

"She hasn't outright *said* it, but I guess you can't blame her? She found me in the hall covered in blood after a nightmare. Human blood too."

"And there isn't any way of telling whose blood it is? Or was?"

"No. But it was weeks ago, just after school went back…the guy in the yard was…." She swallowed sickly. "Fresh."

Ella went green. "Uh. That's awful. But…. I don't believe it.

Neither does Luke. Rowan is probably terrified. Have there been any other missing people reported around that time?"

Win hadn't thought. "The cop didn't say anything. But…" she exhaled, preparing to be gaped at like a crazy person. "It was Joseph's blood. I'm telling you. I was there, and I saw what they did to him."

Ella pressed her lips thinly, sticking her head into the aisle, making sure no one could hear them. "Win…I don't know. How could you time travel in a dream?"

Win sagged, defeated. She wanted to talk about what Uncle Willard told her. She was the one who could break their curse. But she knew she was hanging by a thread, and there was only so much Ella could take in. Would she look at her the same way Rowan did? Like, she was unhinged, still reeling after Grayson and her grandfather. So instead, she nodded. "It's crazy," she agreed.

"Well, the blood belonged to someone," Ella said. "I mean, could it even be yours? Could you have hurt yourself sleepwalking? You heal pretty quickly. It would explain why you had no cuts or marks."

"It does, I guess." Win mulled it over. "I never thought of that."

Mr. Rainer courted their attention from the front of the bus by waving his hand, and the chatter died away. "Guys, I need you to group into pairs, find your study buddy for the afternoon. Now, Mickleford isn't a huge place, and I've no doubt you'll all be fine wandering around but if you do have any problems, head back to the old courthouse on Essex street. It's on your maps!" He was walking the length of the bus, handing out paper maps to each student. "And can we please remember, although this is a historic town, tourist season is officially over for these folks, so show some respect and no wandering into anyone's yards!"

Rainer reached Win's aisle and stuffed two maps into Ella's eager palm. He cast a disappointed glance at Luke, who'd curled himself into a fetal position against the wall. Rainer rolled his eyes. "Does he have a partner?"

"Uh yes, me," Ella answered. Win huffed, feeling like a prize gooseberry, not loving the idea of trailing behind them all afternoon.

"No need to look so dour, Winifred. You can partner with Cole. I actually think you'll be good for him."

Win's jaw dropped, and Rainer smirked. "But Sir! Didn't he beat up the last guy he was partnered with?"

"*No*, he didn't," Rainer corrected her. "He's just…misunderstood. I'm sure you can handle him."

He handed out the last of the maps to the students who were lounging at the back of the bus. The rain beat gently against the glass, and Win drew deeper into her coat. Ella snickered, folding her map away. "I think you can handle Cole Ward, Win. You'd probably put him through a wall if he tried anything."

She laughed. It was true. It was the awkwardness of having to exchange pleasantries with anyone outside of her small but cozy circle that made her worry.

When they go off to college, Cole Ward might be one of the only ones left behind. You'd be stuck with him anyway.

Win recalled what Noah said last night, and he was surprised anyone was still left in their backward town.

Nope, the Hickorys will always be here, Win thought dismally. *We literally can't go anywhere else.* Win floated the idea of going to college in Boston, and her father was delighted and enthusiastic, but Rowan hastily shut the idea down. Win was still young in her calling, probably too young to have gone through it at all. How could she manage in a city when the pull to morph into her animal form became too hard to ignore? Rowan wanted her to go to college but not leave the area. Ever.

The bus bumped and wound through narrow country back roads, fine mist curling across the ground like a veil. Win stared dismally out of the passenger window, gazing at rustic, open farmland, lonely trees stripped of leaves dotted the landscape.

"So, where exactly are we going?" Win peered out the window just as the bus drove down a steep incline between a grassy valley.

"Mickleford. It's kind of famous around here." Ella practically burst with excitement, and history was her thing. She had been talking about this trip for weeks. "It's the *other* Salem."

"Oh?"

"Well, kind of," Ella corrected herself. "I've only ever been here once on a field trip. It's an odd place like it's caught in time or something."

Strangely as Ella uttered the words 'caught in time,' the bus drove through a vast patch of fog. They went down another steep incline and then a sharp gradient back up. The mist parted and revealed the start of a small town, so quaint Win made a cooing noise. They drove past a battered-looking sign for 'Mickleford' stating it was first established in 1693.

"It's cute!" she marveled, pressing her nose near the glass, peeking out at the streets lined with cobbled sidewalks and black-clad buildings. Ella made a face.

"It looks cute, but its history isn't," she replied.

The town appeared to be getting Halloween ready. Straw wreaths and paper garlands hung in doorways. Huge, overripe pumpkins crowded porch steps. Passing a play park with a huge sprawling green, Win admired the houses lit from inside with flickering lamps while smoke curled from chimney pots.

Win was taken by how antiquated the town seemed. It was like being on vacation with its hilly streets, multi-colored homes, and little coffee shops. Ella leaned across the aisle and prodded Luke's shoulder, and he blinked at her. "We're here? I swear I shut my eyes thirty seconds ago."

"Come on, wake up." Ella hauled out of the seat, stretching her back. The bus pulled up outside a tall, red-brick Georgian building with white wooden window frames. Once the old courthouse, now converted to a visitor center and gift shop, Win could smell coffee, even inside the bus.

"Why are there so many black houses?" Win asked, her fascination growing.

"It's an old town. It was a style back then, I guess," Ella offered, buttoning up the new red coat she had bought on their last shopping trip. One by one, they disembarked, and Win allowed herself a long stretch as her feet hit the sidewalk. It was chilly, and Win wished she had something warm around her neck. She detected a whiff of salt in the air, sniffing it in.

"Are we near the ocean?" she asked.

"West Point is about five miles east from here." Ella nodded. "Good nose."

"Can everyone gather into their pairs?" Rainer headed up the steps of the courthouse, where the group of thirty students had gathered in a semi-circle. Win groaned, spotting Cole's shaved head hustling his way toward her. Luke threw an arm around Ella's neck, kissing her nose as she glanced up at him. Win allowed herself a small smile at their mutual affection, but a pang of envy exploded in her gut. She missed Grayson—she missed his arms and pushed the dark thoughts away, content to be happy for her friends instead.

It hurts, she told herself. Missing him made her ache to her bones.

"Guess we can let you tag along with us?" Luke teased Win, having dozed during the part where she'd been assigned Cole as a partner. His facial features tensed as Cole approached, his lips set in a thin, disappointed line. "You want something, Ward?"

Cole ignored Luke. He was easily as tall and built heavily, more for football than basketball. Cole had a reputation for being difficult. He wasn't native Cedar Wood, having moved from another town two years ago. He was wearing a hoodie, pulled up around his neck, and a wool-lined denim jacket thrown over the top, his backpack trailing over his shoulder.

"Hey, Win," he greeted her, eyes downcast. He had a deep, rumbly accent. "You get stuck with me for the afternoon."

"That's okay." Win shifted from one foot to the other, giving him a reluctant nod. It was cold, the air nipped at her fingers, and she shoved her hands into Grayson's coat pockets. As Rainer talked over their heads, Luke whispered something in Win's ear, brushing her hair off her neck.

"Just watch him."

Win ignored him. "I think I'll manage."

"So unless you've all forgotten your Cedar Wood history, we have a very close link with this little town. One word, *witchcraft*." A couple of kids mocked Rainer's enthusiasm with 'oohing' noises, while others laughed jovially, and Rainer ignored them and carried on.

"Now, in the true spirit of fall and with Halloween being three weeks away, I'd like you to explore the town in your pairs and take as many notes and photos as you can for your history assignments. Plenty of notable places are marked on the maps, including the Varga house and the All Souls cemetery, where the Varga victims are buried."

Win shuddered inwardly; Cole noticed her sour expression and laughed. Win glanced back at Ella across her shoulder. "Victims?"

"I told you, it's not as pretty on the inside!" Ella chirped. She'd already pulled out her backpack and marker, her arm linked through Luke's. It was clear Ella was about to drag him off on a quest. Win didn't like the idea of trailing around a graveyard alone with Cole, not one bit.

"Can we follow you?" Win asked, and Ella laughed as many of the students broke off in their pairs.

"Come on," Ella ordered, stalking off down the cobbled street.

"Meet at the park for a break in an hour," Rainer called, handing out extra maps to some students who were still milling around the visitor center. Breath fogging on the afternoon air, the four of them took off. Win fell in line with Ella and Luke while Cole dragged behind, lighting up a cigarette when they rounded a corner and were out of sight. Win struggled not to laugh at Cole's blatant, willful disobedience, even as Luke threw her a knowing look.

"So, where too, Adler?" Cole asked, smoke billowing in the air.

"I plan to follow you around for the afternoon." Win held out her map, narrowing her eyes.

"Well, Ella is the expert, but perhaps the Varga house? It's just off Burial Hill."

Cole shuffled his large shoulders, blowing warm air through his hands. "Whatever you want."

"You know you do have to write this thing, don't you? So you should probably take some notes," Win chided him, which earned a not so unpleasant smile from his hard mouth.

"We could be study buddies? I'd buy you dinner if you wrote the damn thing for me." He finished up, sucking on the last drags from the butt of the cigarette, and then he flicked it. It landed nearby a flowerpot. Win glared at him, and he quickly apologized and stamped it into the ground.

"I won't write it for you. But I can help you if you need it?" she found herself offering. They'd fallen behind Luke and Ella, and Luke occasionally glanced over his shoulder to check they were still following.

"Is History your thing?"

"No," she replied, hauling her pack across her shoulders. "But English is. So you moved here from…where?"

"Uh, Wilder in South Carolina," Cole uttered after a while. She detected an accent, a slight drawl compared to the Bostonian accent she was used to. He dared a sideways glance at her profile. "And you?"

"Oh, Boston," she replied. "But my family are….born and bred here."

"Still, this place sucks, doesn't it?" He scratched his chin, agitated. "It's cold, its rains all the damn time. And the leaves! So many leaves!"

Win laughed, shooting him a coy smile. "Aren't there many forests in South Carolina?"

"There are, but there's also water—it kind of balances it out. You're a city girl. Don't you miss Boston?"

"Yeah, but my family is here." She couldn't help the resignation of her voice. They walked by a small children's park, an old leafy maple sat off to the right, drooping over their heads. Win bounced, picking off one of the leaves, a bright, burnt orange. "It's pretty here. You'll get used to it."

"You blend in with the trees," he said, smirking. "Everything's red like your hair."

"Good, that means no one takes much notice of me," she said, referring to her wallflower nature, but when she glanced back at him, he was frowning.

"I wouldn't say that was technically true, and *he* certainly keeps making sure you haven't wandered off the path!" Cole nodded in Luke's direction, who, at that precise moment, looked back and scowled. Win laughed and stuck out her tongue.

"Take no notice of him. He thinks it's his job to look out for me, a family obligation kind of thing."

Cole seemed relieved and smiled at her. Win ducked her eyes, feeling heat creeping up her chest. Within ten seconds, he'd gone from sullen and frosty to misty-eyed. She could sense the pulse of his heart speed up under his shirt.

She called after Ella and Luke, who'd walked ahead, and they strayed back to wait for them to catch up.

"Up this hill and to the left, we'll find the Varga house." Ella ran her painted nail along the map. The cobbled lane swept up a steep hill, lined with pretty colored houses, with slatted shutter windows. Some of them were storefronts, quaint little gift shops, or coffee houses.

"So, who were the Vargas?" Win trudged along behind as the hill steepened, her achilles pulling. "Or dare I ask?"

"Two sisters." Ella puffed as they reached the brow of the hill. Luke had broken out into a sweat, despite the cold. "Vecula and Eunice. Vecula was hung for murder in 1805, but Eunice disappeared before they could bring her in." She deepened her voice to add drama. "Never to be seen again!"

"And was Vecula guilty?"

Ella stopped to catch her breath while Luke dropped right back. "She was tried and found guilty of the murder of eight men, all buried here in the cemetery. But Eunice claimed she was only ever a healer, you know, poultices, herbs, and stuff, but Vecula… liked to keep parts. Which they found in jars, so it was a pretty foregone conclusion."

Win screwed up her face in disgust. "Parts—as in organs? Or…"

Behind her, Cole said, "Uh, gross. Don't even finish that sentence."

Ella laughed despite the grisly subject. "No, I meant organs, not boy parts!"

"Not any less disturbing," Cole quipped.

They met the peak, and Cole let out a shallow breath. A chill, resulting in a cold sweat, crept up her back. Maybe it was all the talk of bloody anatomy. Win's mouth filled with saliva, tasting acidic bile as she blinked back a memory.

A woman holding up something small, round…sticky. She swayed on her feet, her vision swimming. Staggering sideways, she bumped Cole's shoulder, and to her surprise, he put a hand out to steady her. He narrowed his eyes, staring into her face. "Adler, you okay?"

"Um, yes," she said shakily. "Out of breath, that's all."

They carried on, passing several pretty boarded houses until they arrived at a small blackboarded cottage with an iron fence around it. Ella exhaled. "This is it."

It was a small, black-clad two-story building with a pitched roof and, from the outside, looked as quaint as the others, but Win could feel dread building in her chest. She wasn't sure she wanted to go in at all. A few other students had made their way there, and they hung around the gate chatting and laughing. Win noticed an attendant wearing a uniform waiting by the weathered oak door, only letting a few people in at a time, and Win wasn't surprised. The place looked tiny.

"The floorboards are old and rickety, so watch your step." The blonde attendant turned her gaze to the four of them as they rocked up. "You'll have to wait a few minutes. It's a full house in there."

Ella nodded, grabbing a guidebook, and struck up an animated conversation with the attendant on the door. Win hung back, a little unnerved but happy to let Ella carry this one. Something about this place felt icky, unwholesome, and the walls ingrained with memory.

"Fraser, you okay?" Cole's voice made her head snap behind, where Luke slumped to his backside on the sidewalk. His head hung in his hands. Win crouched next to him, placing her hand on his shoulder. He jerked away from her, but Win had already felt the heat from his skin under her fingertips.

"Luke…you're burning!" She touched his forehead, and he pushed her away.

"I'm fine," he lied, his lips pale. "I've got a headache."

Win dug in her bag, finding an old pack of Advil rattling around at the bottom, among her wallet and spare makeup. She hadn't needed to medicate for a long time, and there were a few left in a blister pack. She shoved them in his hand. "Take them with water. You look sick."

He rubbed his eyes, taking off his glasses and wiping them on the edge of his sweater. "It's probably my eyesight. I haven't been tested in a while. Came out of nowhere."

"Or, you're getting sick." She took his glasses, wiping off the sweaty fingerprints he'd managed to make. She held them up to her face, peering through the prescriptive glass, and then gasped. "Oh god! How bad are your eyes?"

"Can't be sick. I have a shift tomorrow."

"Well, you can miss it." She went to touch his forehead again, and he snarled, his eyes flashing. Win drew back in alarm. "Luke?"

"Leave it, okay!" He stood fluidly. "I'll be fine. Look—Ella's calling us in."

The moment he stood, his color returned, his cheeks flushed, and Win handed him back his glasses, which he pushed over his ears. Win couldn't believe she'd never realized quite how bad his eyesight was, never once having tried on his glasses for fun. She squeezed her eyes to ease away her fuzzy vision.

Ella waved, and she didn't have time to question Luke further. He pushed past her with a nudge, and Win could tell how riled he was. He hated being fussed over, but Win rolled her shoulders, letting his agitation slip off her.

The old place had been set up like a town museum, with place cards and facts dotted all around the room for children on field trips. A vast brick fireplace was set with old pots and pans, a huge black pot for cooking, the old floorboards worn and rickety. The dark, heavily beamed interior smelled stale from lack of fresh air. A long oak table was arranged with a pestle, mortar, and a neat line of ancient, small glass bottles holding various herbs.

Not sure what to do, she looked to Ella, who was furiously scribbling notes. Win suddenly lacked the energy for writing; instead, she took lots of photos on her phone, her flash accidentally beaming in Luke's face. He looked pale in the hazy white light and scowled at her. She nodded at a set of branding irons nailed to the wall, complete with a poster about marking potential witches with crucifixes to cast out the devil. "Nice," she said through gritted teeth. Luke scoffed.

"Got to keep the women in line!" he joked.

Ella was lost to them, reading all the information cards placed around the room, ducking her head into the fireplace to get a closer inspection of the 19th-century cookware. Win's lungs squeezed, feeling immensely claustrophobic, and darted for the door. She breathed in the cold air outside, waiting by the gate. Within moments Cole had joined her.

"Too creepy for you?"

Win thought of the severed hand she'd found in her yard twenty-four hours ago. "Not really."

Awkwardly, Cole scratched the back of his neck; he was building up to something, a blush crossing his cheeks. Win tensed. "Thanks for not treating me like a criminal," he said. "Most people get annoyed at being stuck with me." Her smile mirrored his, his admission making her sad. He sounded about as lonely as she felt. "You three…seem okay."

"We're really nice!" She laughed. "And you…you're not as bad as you pretend to be…though the smoking, not attractive."

"I don't even like it much. Just something to do with my hands."

Win figured as much. He swayed slightly nearer, his hand brushing hers. Her palms itched with tickles of anxiety. A blush streaked his cheekbones, his blood pressure rising, and his scent wafted toward her. Win forced herself not to react. Boy smell, hormones running unchecked. Cole wasn't a bad-looking guy in a shy, quiet way. *Not happening*, she thought. Instinctively she stepped away, but this only seemed to tease him. He crowded her, and words came bubbling out of her mouth before she had time to take them back.

"So, if you need help with this thing, I can be your study partner?"

His eyes lit up. *Damn!*

"Really? I mean sure…I won't be much of a partner."

"Oh, that doesn't matter." She wished she could turn back time. Now his pupils were dilating, and he looked misty-eyed and hopeful and not about his history paper. "I like helping the needy."

He laughed, his face warming up. "Ha, thanks!" He scratched at his short hair. "I'm not exactly a high achiever. You have your work cut out. What about this weekend? I could come to your place?"

In her peripheral, Win spotted Luke hovering by the sidewalk, pinching the bridge between his nose. He was pretending not to listen in, even though it was clearly his motive. Cole spotted him and pulled a face. "That's if your guard *dog* over there doesn't mind?"

Win waved off his sarcasm. "He's not like that…he's..."

Win's eyes were drawn back toward the brow of the hill, where the winding road spiraled down into the town. The dry, woody smell of sawdust lingered in the back of her nose, her gaze following to a lumber yard sat at the base of the hill. Its main double doors were wide open, the sound of men chattering inside floated out on the breeze, and Win inhaled sharply. A man, tall with hunched shoulders, dressed in a bulky sweater, passed through those doors. A flash of white hair caught her attention. And in the moment, she froze. As if Cole had vanished, and she was standing alone on those cobbles.

Her breath juddered in her chest, and Cole moved nearer, he shook her by the shoulder. But she couldn't look away. She watched as the man hauled a massive yard of timber across his shoulder, flexing his arms to accommodate its weight. Win couldn't move, the strength wilting from her legs.

Before he disappeared inside the yard, he turned, and she saw his profile, his chin, and lower lip. Win started to jog, but her legs were jello weak, like wading through thick tar.

Cole was talking to her, but she'd fazed him out. "Win…Win what's wrong with you?"

Sound wouldn't come to her lips as much as she forced it. Instead, she padded down the hill, her eyes blurring as at once her voice finally emerged, and she screamed after him.

One word. One word to bring Ella hurtling out of the house and make Luke jump to his feet. Win sped down the hill.

"Grayson!" she screamed. "*Grayson!*"

Four

Her knees buckled as she hit the bottom of the hill. Behind her, Win could hear footsteps pounding on the cobbles. Someone was calling her. It was Luke, wired and frantic.

"Win, wait!" He caught up with her, sprinting past Cole with a speed she hadn't expected. Cole sagged, out of breath, hands on his knees. Luke hauled her back. "Will you stop?"

"No, I saw him!" Win shook his hand away. "I saw him!"

"Where?"

Win pointed wildly at the lumber yard, the screech of the buzzsaw drowning out her voice. "He went in there. Luke, it was him!" She bent double, her hands shaking. He caught her by the shoulders and forced her to stand, and she could barely breathe. "He's alive…."

"Wait, okay?" He held her, and she crashed into his chest, finding his shirt with her hands. "We'll go in together."

"What's going on? Is it him?" Ella braved the steep hill, followed by Cole. A group of students at the top of the hill gaped at them, confused, wondering what the chaos was about.

"You both took off like lightning!" Cole finally got his breath back. "You ever think about doing track?"

Win stood back on her heels, hands-on-hips. "I swear it was him, Ella."

Ella folded an arm around Win's slim waist, half holding her up if she dipped again. "I believe you."

"Who is this person?" Cole butted in, and Win could feel her agitation rising. As if reading her mind, Luke lifted his palm, waving Cole back.

"Maybe you better leave." His lip curled, his temper wearing thin. "This isn't any of your business."

"It's hard to explain." Ella softened the blow, touching Cole's shoulder. "We'll be up soon. Why don't we meet you at the coffee shop near the town hall in half an hour?"

Cole didn't seem to hear, only concerned with Win, staring past Luke's shoulder. "Is she okay?"

Luke's temper snapped. "She's fine. Take a hike!"

Win could barely look at him, an unbearable look of disappointment flashing across his face. She wanted to say she was sorry, but her heart seized in her chest. Cole trailed back up the hill, and as soon as he was out of earshot, she leaped toward the lumber yard door.

"Whoa, wait!"

"No!" She shoved Luke back by the chest. "I'm going in."

Luke caught her wrist in a keen grip. "I said wait!"

"Luke, back off for a minute!" Ella came between them. "Win, calm down. We can go with you. You!" She wagged her finger at Luke. "Calm *down*. What's up with you today? You owe Cole an apology."

Luke laughed shortly. "Like hell I do."

Ella puffed, exasperated, one hand bolted to Win's shoulder and one on Luke's chest. "Calm down!"

Win nodded. Her spine tingling, her nape hot, and she shifted her shoulders to expel heat inside her. Like she was going to combust.

It was a familiar ache in her bones; the call to transform was undeniable, like spiders crawling under her skin. She fought not to get worked up, to slow her heart. The three of them strolled to the yard doors, two heavy-set oak frames with the words 'Hank's Timber' printed in bold across a white sign hanging from the frosted glass window. The searing screech of the saws filled her head, the door sliding open easily. Dust clogged her nose, and she scratched at it. To the far right was a massive, metal stacking system, piled up with various lengths of timber, while at the back were some offices, a white door with staff only printed on it. A metal staircase ran up to a mezzanine level cordoned off by a thin partition wall. A big guy stood at the buzz saw working on a length, a cigarette dangling between his teeth, a cap on backward. He lifted his chin as he caught sight of them, waving them to stay back.

"That's far enough," he called, wiping his damp brow. Lifting off the cap, he revealed sweat-drenched red hair and a high, receding hairline. "It's dangerous in here. Can I help you, kids?"

Win's mouth turned as dry as the sawdust on the floor. What if he was here? Would he be happy to see her? Why hadn't he come back to find her? Finally, she managed a few words. "I think you have a guy working here. His name is Grayson? Grayson Riley?"

The man stepped forward, scratching his belly and shaking his head. "No one here but me, honey."

Win blinked in confusion. "But I saw a man walk in here? Minutes ago."

"Nope." He smiled, revealing a sizable gap between his teeth. "It's only me."

"But…" she stuttered, eyeing him. Was he lying? "I saw him. He's big, blonde hair, really blonde…."

"Sweetheart…"

"He has a scar down this side of his face." Win pointed to

her left side, hope dwindling. He was looking at her like she was insane. "Please…you can't miss him!"

"Are you deaf?" His tone stung. "I'm on my own here. There's no big, blonde guy with a scar working here."

Win eyes misted. "But…"

"Win, come on." Ella's hand was soft on her arm. "Let's get out of here."

"No!" Win covered her eyes. She wasn't going to cry! Not here. "I saw him."

Luke didn't say a word as they walked back out into the chilly afternoon, the sun already dipping behind clouds. She turned and met Ella's shoulder, arms crowding around her as she sobbed into her friend's hair. Luke's hand found the back of her neck.

"Why don't we find Cole?" he suggested, letting Win rest her head under his arm. "I'll buy you cake."

Win jerked away, her cheeks hot and flushed. "You don't believe me, do you?"

Luke rolled his eyes skyward. "*Come on,* Win. You heard the guy. He hasn't seen him."

"What if he was lying?"

"Why would he lie? You said it yourself. Grayson is quite hard to miss. I think the man would know if a huge, blonde dude worked for him or hung around his yard?"

Win stalked away, hating, of course, he was right. But she couldn't shake away the feeling. She'd seen him, so close, close enough to grab hold of, and now hope had been snatched away. Cole was waiting in the coffee shop; his legs kicked up on one of the chairs, holding the seat for them as they piled in the door, the air thick with coffee and sugar. Win knew she must look a mess, her face blotchy and red from crying. Luke slid into the seat opposite Cole, grunting out some kind of half-assed apology. Ella ordered them all drinks at the counter, casting Win a worried glance over her shoulder.

"You okay, Adler?" Cole studied her, his expression concerned, and she knew he wasn't looking at her like she was crazy.

"She's fine," Luke said stiffly. Her cheeks throbbed from being outside in the cold, crying, to settling in the stuffy interior of the shop.

"She can talk for herself," Cole bit back, and for a second, something dangerous flashed in Luke's blue eyes. Territorial, protective and annoyed.

Win kicked him under the table. They drank in silence; Win dipped her finger in the froth of her chocolate, sucking it off her fingertip, her mind elsewhere.

She wanted to go back; her feet itched to leave. Finally, she spoke. "But...What if...?"

"Win, for god sake, will you stop?" Luke slapped his palms on the table. "It wasn't him. You must have made a mistake."

"Who are you talking about?" Cole repeated the question, and all three passed a conspiratorial look between them. How to explain Grayson? A man who'd lied to her all summer, who she'd fallen for hard, slept with and then discovered he was harboring her dead relations, under the instruction of his crazy mother. It was intense.

But she would give anything to see him, to take back all the nasty things she'd said, to try to forgive him. He wasn't her boyfriend; he'd never taken her on a date or bought her flowers. But he'd been in her life. And she'd loved him.

"Win's ex-boyfriend," Luke finally admitted it out loud. "But that depends on your definition of the word boyfriend."

Cole's face dropped in disappointment, and Win made sure to throw an objectionable look in Luke's direction, his sarcasm and bad mood starting to irritate her nerves.

"Oh," Cole said, biting his lip. "Oh, I see."

"I need some air." Ella dragged her hands through her shiny ponytail, flipping it from side to side. "And I wanted to go to the town hall before we get back on the bus. Do you want to walk, Win? It might make you feel better?"

Win shook her head. "You guys go. I want to stay here."

Luke's chair scraped across the floor as he stood. He swiped up his coffee, landing a warm hand on her shoulder. "We'll see you on the bus."

The bell tinkled above the door as they left, but Cole remained. Win wrung her hands in her lap, nervously picking at the skin around her nails. He gazed at her across the table, sipping his coffee, appearing to be deep in thought, drumming his fingers on the tabletop. The coffee machine screamed in her ear behind the counter. Her nerves were raw and shot.

Why would the guy in the yard lie?

Because he doesn't want to see you. Horrible thoughts dwindled, clawing from the back of her mind to the forefront.

Win's stomach dropped, lifting her eyes to Cole's. "I'm sorry. You must think I'm crazy."

He shrugged, nonchalant. "Crazy is okay."

She curled her hands around her mug. "You have no idea. How weird it gets."

"So…you want to break into the office at the back of the yard?" His voice made her jerk in surprise.

"What did you say?"

Cole grinned, pleased he'd gotten her attention. "I *said*. Do you want to break into the office? I'm a pro at breaking and entering. It's kind of the reason I got kicked out of my old school."

A rush of warmth spread up her neck. She could have hugged him right then.

The air temperature dropped by the time they paid the cashier and got outside, Cole wrestling his arms back into his jacket. His shoulder bumped hers as they walked briskly back to the foot of Burial Hill. He was consumed with a cloud of tobacco; the smell burned the inside of her nose.

He'd lit up and sucked it back, holding it carefully between his thumb and forefinger. "So that ratty thing, you have on? I'm guessing it was his? It looks like a guy's coat. A guy with very little fashion sense."

Win huddled deeper into Grayson's coat, his remark stung. "I like it."

He walked ahead, finishing off the cigarette and tossing the butt end into a nearby front yard. She groaned aloud. "Why are you helping me anyways?"

"I believe you." His expression was sullen, exhaling the last of his smoke into the air above her head. "The speed you took off… you saw something. I don't think I've ever seen anyone move so fast!"

"Well, thanks. I don't know what I'm going to do exactly—break into the back door?"

"Nah, you leave it to me," Cole told her, his pale eyes full of mischief. "You're a top, high achieving student. I can say I dragged you along, your clean reputation undamaged. They *expect* this shit from me."

Win ground to a halt. "Cole, no." She shook her head. "I don't want you to get in trouble. Not for me."

He grabbed her hand, tugging her along, grinning. "How about we try *not* to get caught? And if we do, you can make it up to me." He winked, and she blushed involuntarily, not liking what he was implying.

They reached the foot of the hill, the lumber yard ahead, one of the doors was open, and they ducked behind a dumpster as the man who'd shooed her away earlier appeared carrying several yards over his shoulders. Cole gripped her wrist, dragging her down an alley, a cobblestoned, narrow space leading to the back of the yard. Out the back, the yard opened out onto a narrow river, running all the way through the town. A metal staircase ran up the wall, leading to a second floor. Win craned her neck, her foot setting on the bottom rung. "Is that the guy's apartment?"

"Could be." Cole dropped to his knees, eyeing the lock in the thick wooden door. "Don't you want to break into the office?"

She knelt beside him, panic exploding in her chest. "Can you do it?"

"Can I do it?" he mocked her, devilishly. Out of his jacket, he produced a small Exacto knife, and Win hid her disapproval, guessing all the rumors about him weren't exactly a lie. He jammed the sharp end into the lock, twisting it, till he felt the lock wield and click. The door sprang open as if the puny lock was all that held it shut. Cole puffed. "That was easy."

Win slipped in past him, her heart pounding. She'd never done anything like this before. The room was small, square, and untidy. A filthy coffee machine sat on a run of filing cabinets. A desk overflowing with paperwork and dirty mugs crowded the middle of the room. A porcelain sink sat in a lonely corner, filled with old rags. It smelt awful. Her nose wrinkled from the distance of the door. Like burgers and old fat.

"What are we looking for?"

Win didn't know how to answer. Evidence—anything she could link to Grayson. She didn't want to say out loud that she should be able to smell him. She lifted up piles of paperwork, looking at the fine print, scanning for his name, hope draining every second nothing sprang out at her.

"What's the guy's name?" Cole asked, breathing down her neck. Her eyes pricked, wet at the corners. What the hell were they doing? This was wrong.

"Grayson."

"And he was your boyfriend or something?"

Her mouth dried up, heart sinking; she let a stack of papers fall through her fingers. This was insane. There was nothing here.

"Did he break up with you?"

Her shoulders stiffened, ducking to her knees and opening cupboard doors. She ignored him, not even knowing what she was looking for. Footsteps thudded lightly on the other side of the door, heading purposefully toward it. Win grabbed Cole's wrist, and they padded carefully back outside, shutting the door quietly behind them. Win sagged against it, shaking, and Cole fixed the lock back in place.

She exhaled. "Oh my god, we shouldn't have done that!"

He gave her a cocky grin. "You wanted to. Did you see anything?"

Win peered up, her fingers finding the metal wrung of the ladder. Before Cole said another word, she started up and reached the platform, it was seconds before Cole called her back with a hiss. She spotted a dingy window, spying a neatly made bed in the room, an open door leading to a bathroom. "Win, get down!" Cole cried.

Annoyed, she groaned and dropped to the ground, landing squarely on her feet, ignoring Cole's expression. Cole had a strange, expectant look on his face, as he edged closer.

Win got distracted by footsteps, wide feet slapping through puddles, but she knew instantly who it was, knowing his tread anywhere. Before she could speak, Cole's hands circled her waist and she stumbled back against the wall of the shop. He bowed his head, her back pressed against the cold brick, time slowed, and she quickly realized in horror he was going in for a kiss. Cigarette smoke overwhelmed her.

"What are you doing?" she squawked, taking his coat and shoving him off. Cole smiled cockily.

"Uh…kissing you?"

"The hell you are!" Luke's voice exploded in her right ear, and Win groaned inwardly. He yanked Cole away and threw him to the ground, where he landed on his back with a thud. Cole scrambled back in surprise. Luke lunged, grabbing him by his shirt, his biceps straining as he lifted him clean off the ground.

"What the hell, Fraser!" Cole wriggled in his grip.

Win wiped her lips, even though he hadn't gotten close to kissing her. "Luke, stop! He didn't do anything." Her eyes snapped to Cole. "What were you thinking?"

Cole grinned sheepishly. "I thought you wanted me to. I thought..."

Luke shook him. "You thought wrong!"

"I didn't want you to kiss me!" Win was affronted, hideously hot around the neck. Her heart pounded in humiliation.

Cole kicked his flailing legs, weaseling out of his grip. Then he got up, brushed off his pants. "My mistake...I'm sorry! I thought....I misread things! Sorry!"

Win's stomach dropped. It had been his intention all along, hadn't it? To get her alone? She felt such an idiot. "Cole, leave us alone," she said wearily. "We'll talk on the bus."

Rubbing his backside, Cole stalked off down the alley, looking confused and rattled. Luke whirled in her direction, nostrils flaring, his chest rising and falling rapidly. She would have to look at him eventually, and his eyes drilled holes into her skull. "Luke..."

"What the hell, Winifred?" he fired. "What are you playing at?"

"He offered to help me look..." her voice flattened. She couldn't say it. Overwhelmed by her foolishness, she stared past him. "I wanted to check out the office. He offered to help. I didn't know he was going to jump me!"

"Of *course* he was. He's been drooling over you all afternoon."

"I didn't know that."

He placed his hands on slim hipbones, chuckling.

"Then you're a moron. I thought you were supposed to be, you know, *sentient*? Learn to read guys better!"

"I'm sorry!" she burst, hating being scolded by him of all people. "I just wanted….to find Grayson."

Luke huffed, raking his hand through his hair, so roughly he made it stand off his head before smoothing it back down. "I know what you were doing. I wish you had asked me, is all."

"I ask you for everything, all the time." Win exhaled, hating he'd witnessed it, knowing she leaned too heavily on Luke at times. If she had asked, he would have been there. She sagged against the wall. He leaned on the wall with one hand next to her ear, towering over her; she wondered when he'd grown, her eyes running the length of his arm all the way up to his shoulder. She was fairly certain his arms had gotten bigger.

"Have you been working out or something?"

He grunted. "Don't change the subject. I hate he tricked you into doing that. Makes me want to…."

"Hulk smash?" she teased, wanting to disperse this male display of testosterone.

"Do not make fun of me," he accused, cocking a brow, but she could see his facade slipping. He balled his fist, and Win threw back her head and allowed herself to laugh, which was a relief.

"Well, don't. He didn't come close. I'll be prepared for him next time."

"Next time?"

"Seriously, have you been weight lifting?" She smirked up at him, and he laughed, his smile creasing his eyes. She knew he couldn't stay mad at her forever.

"It's just kegs at the bar," he said, shrugging. "They make me lift them. But thanks for noticing."

"Lucky Ella, huh? Where is she?"

He pushed away from the wall. "On the bus, waiting. That's why I came to find you guys. We have to leave. A road got flooded on the way back to Cedar Wood, so we need to divert through Lincoln."

He threw his arm loosely around her shoulder as they walked back down the alley. Win cast one more dismal glance back at the yard. She questioned herself. Maybe she was going crazy? Her phone buzzed in her coat pocket; she grabbed it out and slid the screen, revealing a text from her father. She sighed in relief.

I'm home and cooking dinner. Evan has moved everything. I can't find the pans. See you soon.

A wash of relief burned through her, hardly able to wait to get home to hug him. The normalcy of his message filled her with warmth. She would be able to go home and talk things through with him. He'd tell her Rowan was just worrying, she wasn't crazy or a killer, and the dream, was only ever a stupid, meaningless dream. Luke fell into step behind her, their day at Mickleford coming to an end.

As they climbed onto the bus, she avoided Cole's gaze, heading to the back. He caught her hand as she passed.

"Look, I'm sorry, Win. I really thought...it doesn't matter what I thought. I don't know what I was thinking. I really screwed this up, and you've been so nice to me." A guilty flush crossed his cheeks, but perhaps it was just an act too? She pulled her hand out of his grip.

"If you still want help with the paper, I'll do it. But don't even think about trying that again!"

He set his mouth in a firm line, nodding grimly. Wandering to the back aisles, Luke threw himself in with Ella, throwing his arm around her and pulling her against his chest. He looked content to close his eyes again, jaw propped on curled fingers, and Win wondered if his headache was finally gone. Slipping into her own seat, alone, she huddled against the glass, wishing she had someone to cuddle into, how wonderful it would be to feel warm again. Right now, all she felt was anxious, irritable and she badly needed to get home and explode out of her skin.

Swallowing a lump in her throat, she cast them a quick glance, and Ella met her eyes, smiling briefly, before turning away to stare at her reflection in the glass.

"Luke didn't take long finding you." Ella stretched and yawned, her cheeks rosy.

"No, he didn't," she agreed, sleepy and warm herself. It hadn't occurred to her to ask him how he'd managed to find her so quickly.

Five

The afternoon passed in a blur. Clouds threatening rain finally exploded and washed out the roads, leaving giant, ankle-deep puddles in the potholes in the Hickory yard. Win tried to forget the man she'd seen in Mickleford, telling herself she must have imagined it, the part of her mind so lost to him she was conjuring up his image from thin air. When they'd arrived home after the trip, Luke avoided her, sleeping off his headache and perpetual bad mood, and Win had been content to see her father, who'd been gone for two weeks. Before dinner, she excused herself, taking off to the forest, stripping off and kneeling in the dirt, shrouded by trees as she morphed, her feline companion springing free of its confines. She ran off her energy, keeping to the perimeter of the land, her muscles languid and free, even if only for a short time. She cut it short before hunger could strike, before she lost herself and strayed from the borders, the memory of a severed, bloodied hand still fresh in her mind.

She lifted her eyes to the treeline, scanning the shadows, convincing herself she'd seen movement. *Mom? Mom, are you there?*

Win's hope dwindled, feeling plops of dew land between her eyes. She flung them away, shaking her thick neck. Where was she? Even though the falcon lived apart from them, there hadn't been a time since Win had arrived in Cedar Wood where she hadn't felt her mother. Even in the early days, she'd been present, hovering, watching with a protective eye. But Win didn't want to admit it. The thought churned her guts. She couldn't *feel* her here.

By the time she sprinted back through the puddles, her breath chugging against her chest wall, her father was serving up something charred and burned to the base of a wok.

After dinner, Ben claimed exhaustion, yawning and stretching at the dinner table before excusing himself for the night. Win tried to relax, watch television, and distract her mind. Her phone beeped, and she spotted a message from Cole, apologizing for his unwanted attempt at a kiss. Win smirked, thinking of Ella, the *betrayer* who'd no doubt been cornered into giving him her number.

She thumbed back a half-hearted reply, not really mad at him; she was too wrapped up with thoughts of Grayson to care. When night drew in, she attempted to sleep after scribbling some notes for her paper on Mickleford and finally collapsed back against the pillow. She was hot and irritated, her run having done nothing to work off her jangled nerves. Evan had already left by the time she'd arrived home, leaving a space in Rowan's bed. So there was only one thing for it.

Win snuck in around midnight when she couldn't sleep, and Rowan rolled in her direction, her fire-red hair splayed across the pillow.

"I saw him, Rowan." Win made quick work of her strange afternoon. Rowan sighed softly, taking her sister's hand and squeezing it.

"You know." She bit her lip. "I think I see Grandpa, sometimes."

"You do?"

Rowan shivered under the covers, her eyes misty. "Sometimes. Around the yard, in my peripheral. But it's always my imagination. I want to see him so badly. I miss him."

"Me, too."

"I wonder what he'd think of the job I'm doing here," Rowan mused. "If he'd be proud of me."

"Of course he would!" Win was alarmed she would even have those thoughts. "He loved you so much. You were his girl!"

Rowan chuckled fondly, but then any lightness in her expression melted away. "This is so hard. Being alpha. Second-guessing everything I do, every decision I make. I want to be more for this family."

Win nestled closer, snuggling under Rowan's arm. "You are everything. You're strong, powerful…."

"Come on, Win!" Rowan scrubbed at her face with her hands in the dark. "My pay at the bar isn't going to cut it. Dad is supporting us financially, and I never went to college. I just—drifted."

Win shifted to her side, letting her head sink into the pillow. "You are way too hard on yourself. Grandpa died only months ago. We haven't had any time to grieve. You're doing great… maybe I should get a job, like Luke?"

"No!" Rowan shook her head. "I want you to study. I want you to have the options I didn't have. You have to be the one who gets out of here."

"Rowan, you're twenty-two years old. You're not dead!" Win wondered where exactly Rowan thought she was heading, certainly not to the lofty heights of a New York college or even Boston. She'd practically run out to the yard the moment she got home from the school trip, her body aching and ready to change. How would that go down in a big city? She was fairly certain the central park rangers would have something to say about a big cat running free night after night. She'd end up like the white wolf in Lincoln, stuffed and put on display. Win shuddered at the thought.

Rowan's breathing was shallow in the dark. "I've been thinking I could get a better job. Maybe even something at the school?"

Win propped herself on her elbows. "Rowan, that would be amazing. I could see you as a counselor, you know? You'd be wonderful."

"You sound like Evan."

"Well, she's smart, and she loves you too." Win flopped back down, thinking she could smell Evan's shampoo brand on the pillow.

Win could tell her sister was smiling. She felt her warm hand reach out and shove her shoulder. "Come on. I need to sleep. Settle down or go back to your own room."

Win laughed. "I'm not five years old. Fine, I'll leave. I can't sleep, I'm too wired after today and what I didn't see…" her voice trailed away, sadly. Anxiety bubbled up in her chest. "Rowan?"

"Hmm?"

"You don't think I killed that guy, do you? Not really?"

A long pause stretched between them. "No," finally her answer came, and Win let out her breath. "But someone did… or we have real-life furies around here to deal with. I'm sorry if I made you worry. It's my natural state of mind to be guarded."

"I wish Mom were around," Win said.

"Me, too. Something else I feel like I've failed at. Where the hell is she?"

"It's not your fault…." Win rose out of bed, not wanting to voice her true fears. Perhaps something awful had happened. "She's a falcon! She can take off whenever she wants."

"But, the dead guy in the yard…Mom going missing…it's all weird…."

Win felt like she had missed out on a massive chunk of the puzzle. "My dream?"

Rowan whistled through her teeth. "Don't even get started. Then I'll never sleep."

"I was covered in blood!"

"I remember. It wasn't your blood either…but it was strange…."

Win sank back. "How?"

"Blood has a scent. It's unique, like a code, and we as a family share the same DNA, so the scents are familiar but still distinctly your own. But this blood on your gown….it smelled..."

"Like us?"

"That's what worries me."

Win wanted to shout the words lingering between them. It was Joseph's blood. But then, how was it possible? The fact was, it wasn't. She couldn't time travel. In the dark, Rowan's hand closed around her wrist, and it startled her.

"Evan and I will get into it when she gets back, and we'll double our efforts looking for Mom. But please, go to sleep now?"

Win nodded, knowing she wouldn't settle in Rowan's bed. She was too jittery. She was half tempted to crawl in behind her dad, but he'd looked so exhausted after his drive she was likely to give him a heart attack. Plus, he snored. Instead, she crept downstairs, her toes curling on the wooden staircase, as an icy blast of air snaked around her bare legs. Fall had really kicked in. She tiptoed into the kitchen, quietly padding around, heating some milk in the microwave and stirring in some cocoa, keeping the lights off in case it cast any rays under Luke's door in the den.

She wandered back into the hall, clutching her hot mug, and a jet of cold air attacked her legs again, causing a shiver to ripple up her spine. Where was it coming from? Frowning, she craned her neck around the stairs, noticing the back porch was wide open, letting in the frosty air.

What the hell? A splinter of fear nestled at her nape; she set her mug down at the foot of the staircase and ran out onto the porch, looking left and right. There was no one there, just an eerie lingering silence, and the empty yard had been turned into a bog with all the rain. It reminded her of a dystopian disaster movie, old machinery sinking into muddy pits of water. She longed for the sunshine again. She stared out to the woods, trees rustling, her keen eyes narrowing. A flick of movement among the trees, a shadow moving, Win choked.

"Who's there?" she called, her voice lonely, her breath fogging. "Mom?" Tears pricked her eyes. Maybe she wasn't going crazy; maybe she *had* seen him in Mickleford. "Grayson?"

Something crashed inside the house. Win jerked, hurtling back inside, taking one more glance at the treeline.

Your mind is playing tricks…shadows…

Whatever it was, had gone. She ran back into the hallway and skidded to a stop, nearly falling over a hard body in the dark.

"Luke, what the *hell!*" she shrieked, her legs wobbling. He was standing motionless, his eyes wide open but empty. She touched his arm, and his skin burned under her fingertips. Alarmed, Win peered up into his face, his glasses off, his mouth slack. She waved her hand in front of his face. "Luke? Can you hear me?"

When he didn't register her, she guessed he was sleepwalking. She had no idea he slept walked. He'd never mentioned it before. Ella hadn't ever mentioned it, and he'd stayed over her house on many occasions. Win didn't know how to deal with a sleepwalker, and she'd only ever read they could get angry when disrupted. Gently she took his arm. "Luke? It's time to get to bed…" She tugged him, and like a boat on still water, he moved.

Phew, okay…. She led him back to his den, flinging open the door, his room smelled sweaty, and she was reminded of his temperature. She placed a hand on his chest. He was radiating heat. "Jesus, you must be getting sick."

"Not sick," he mumbled, and his voice sent shock waves through her. It was guttural, deep. She dropped his hand, swaying in the doorway of the den; his eyes were open and had locked on her. Oddly, something in his expression terrified her. He was emitting a scent, not his usual laundry smell, more like…

An animal… Alarmed Win met his gaze. He wasn't seeing her. He was just looking straight through her, his eyes were alarmingly blue, cerulean, his lip curled.

"Luke…come on, bed!" She took his hand again, giving him a pull, and to her surprise, he went. She placed a hand on each of his shoulders, heat rising off him in a haze. Nervously, she pushed his shoulders, and he fell on the bed. He was so hot she had half a mind to pull off his shirt but decided against it. She knelt on the edge of the bed, biting her lip hard as she shoved him down; he jerked, fell back on the pillow, and then snapped awake.

He seized both her wrists. "Win? What the hell?"

She had managed not to scream, sagged in relief. "Oh, thank god you're awake!"

He let her go, scrambling up the bed. "What are you *doing*?"

"Easy! You were sleepwalking."

"No…I wasn't!" He patted around on his bedside cabinet, feeling for his glasses. "There was someone knocking on the back porch."

Win exhaled in relief. "You opened the porch door?"

He shook his head, confused, and dazed. "I swear…I heard knocking. I don't remember opening it, but I guess I must have. I've never done anything like this before." He sat up, patting down his body as though he'd lost something.

Win crawled on the bed, leaning across him to feel his forehead when he batted her hand away. "What are you doing?" His heartbeat rocketed up ten notches, his pulse exploding under his skin. She could hear it throbbing in her ears.

"You were burning up. I'm checking your temperature," she explained, crawling closer, and he pulled the covers around his neck. "What's your problem?"

"Win, the nightshirt you have on covers nothing! *Nothing!*"

Her face flamed in the dark. "Oh, sorry!"

"Sorry, won't cut it if your dad comes down here!" He pulled his knees up to his chest, and Win slipped off the bed, wondering why he was suddenly so bashful. It wasn't like he hadn't seen her completely naked! Only in the summer, he'd practically carried her home in nothing but a thin shirt.

"Are you sick?" she questioned him. "Do you remember anything?"

"No. Only knocking in my dream. And then you were straddling me."

Win scoffed. "I wasn't straddling you! You were acting…really strange!"

"Well, I'm fine now!" Abruptly he turned over in bed, hugging his pillow. "I should sleep."

"Do you need anything?"

"Nope. Just you out of my room!"

She bristled. That was gratitude for you! He'd scared the crap out of her. "Fine…goodnight!"

He whisked over, shooting her a fiery glance across the room. "By the way, it is not okay to come in here half-dressed. Try putting some clothes on!"

Her fists balled, but she bit her tongue. She hadn't thought twice about how she looked, but now he mentioned it, a draft blew up her shirt, and she remembered the porch door was still swinging open. Shaking her head at his attitude, she pulled the door closed tightly, snapping the lock in place, and peered out into the dark. She didn't dare look out to the yard, to the trees swaying on the breeze, in case she did see something out there, watching her. For a brief moment earlier, she could have sworn she hadn't been alone.

Six

Rowan's cross trainers sloshed through a deep puddle as she skirted through the outer edges of town. Her lungs full to bursting, breathing out good, clean air, she jogged until her calves ached, stopping to stretch against a fallen fence. Holding her arms above her head, pulling her upper torso into a good twist, she surveyed the skyline, the fluffy clouds still blocking the morning sun. It was just before seven am, before the morning traffic whittled through town, folks heading out to the larger areas for work. Rowan loved the quiet and the stillness before the hum of the cars hurtled by. The road was hers, as open as the sky. Looking to the trees, she searched for a familiar shape, hoping to spot the falcon, who, up until a few weeks ago, was always hovering nearby, knowing she was needed.

I need you now. Where are you?

Ducking through trees, she jogged back through the forest, on the old muddy path which ran past Mercy and then into the deeper woods before Hickory House. Up ahead, she spotted yellow and black police tape wound around the trees to cordon off the area under investigation.

Rowan shuddered, staring at the tape flapping in the breeze, beating against the bark of an old white pine. Something was wrong here; she felt it, along with her despair, creeping up on her like an old friend.

An animal had done this. Ripped apart that poor stranger. And Win was the only animal she knew was capable of such carnage. Standing with her hands on her hips, she ducked her head and crawled under the tape. She skirted around the perimeter, sniffing the air, staring hard at the ground, searching for any evidence her sister could have done this. But it just smelled like pines and mud—like home.

"Rowan? You're not supposed to be in there!" a familiar voice barked behind her, and she whirled about, clutching her chest.

"Noah…God!" she said. "You scared me."

Her old classmate stared at her as though she'd stepped in the middle of a field of landmines. Noah was on duty, staring at her with his mouth gaping open. He shook his head in disbelief, motioning her to come back. "What the hell? Come over here!"

When she skirted back across the tape, he took her hand and tugged her away. "This is a crime scene. It's not for you to go poking around in. You need to go!"

"I'm sorry!"

"What are you even doing out here?"

Rowan's mind went horribly blank. She smiled sheepishly. "I was out running. I thought I'd take a look…." She knew how lame it sounded. But to her relief, Noah scratched at his hair under his hat and whistled through his teeth.

"I'll give you a pass. But you *cannot* be here. This is serious, Rowan. I should book you for this!"

Rowan gave him her best smile. "You won't, though, right?"

He huffed and waved his hand. "Flirting with me doesn't work, Rowan."

Rowan grinned, hopefully. "It used to!"

His walkie buzzed relentlessly at his hip, someone intent on getting hold of him. Still annoyed, he waved her away. "There's a cop car parked through the trees a few yards away on watch, and a team will be arriving here in ten minutes. Go on. I'll pretend I didn't see you."

Feeling foolish, she marched away, as she dipped her back and went through the trees. Her eyes were drawn up, an old knobby elm ahead of her, but it was what was sticking out of the elm that grabbed her attention. It made her stomach drop. Warily she cast an eye over her shoulder, but Noah had already vanished back through the trees. He'd looked stressed and edgy. She hated to imagine why. When she was sure he'd gone, she glanced back at the elm.

Oh, shit. Not this again. She marched up to the elm, breathing rapidly, and yanked the rusty arrow out of the bark, sagging on the trunk as she turned it over in her hands. How long has this been here? Months? Days? It had been deeply embedded in the tree, and through the tip of the arrow, there was a tiny piece of paper. Rowan didn't have to unfold it to know what it said. It was another note, damp and ruined, his writing barely legible. She scrunched it in her pocket.

"I saw him, Rowan…."

Rowan bent the shaft in two with ease and tossed it in the bushes. She jogged back to the house, wet leaves sticking to the bottom of her trainers. How many times had this happened now? How many of these little signs had she found planted around their land? It was a wonder Win hadn't seen any herself. It was a stark reminder that he slipped in and out like a ghost, even with their attuned senses. She'd lost count of the number of arrows she'd found, all the notes she'd folded away and kept in a box in the back of the closet. Rowan breathed through her nose, the sincerity in the messages almost pathetic.

Please forgive me.

Win, please come back to me.

I love you. I'm sorry. Can we talk, please?

Her treachery overwhelmed her, and when she reached the drive, she bent double, heaving and squeezing her eyes tight. Win *wouldn't* forgive her for this. She'd never understand. Rowan was thankful Grayson had never confronted Win. He'd not had the balls to walk up to her front door.

But Win said many times, the man was socially awkward, painfully shy, and private. God, he'd lived in the woods all his life! And after what he'd allowed to go down this summer, was it any wonder he was a little nervous? He was trying to draw Win out in the only way he knew how, and Rowan, so far, managed to block every attempt.

Rowan looked up at the house, *her* house, looking over every loose tile, every broken shutter. Her home, and she wasn't protecting it. She wasn't as strong as John. How could Win ever understand what she was trying to protect her from? She was seventeen and besotted with a dangerous man. And didn't Rowan know something about dangerous men?

She stretched and mounted the steps, wishing Evan was here. Evan didn't know about the arrows or the notes, and nausea swelled in her gut as she imagined the horrified look on her girlfriend's face if she told her. She missed Evan's warmth in her bed, ached for her to come home. Dismally she thought of her mother, notable by her gaping absence. What would she think? Rowan wished she was here to talk to. Evan was a pure soul, forgiving and prepared to look past Grayson's misdemeanors. She'd been able to comfort Win when Rowan couldn't— when it made her sick to the stomach to see her wasting away over him.

I understand more than you think. Rowan wandered into the hall, kicking off her shoes and wriggling her toes. She understood the pull, the need for him, like a craving you can't satisfy. It had been that way with Spencer. The more John ordered her to stay clear of him, the more she wanted him.

Rowan wandered into the kitchen, preparing her even smile. Spencer might have shot her through the wing, but there were worse ways to kill someone. He'd swallowed her up, betrayed her, and she didn't want the same for Win. Grayson would never be good for her.

"Hey." Ben looked up from the newspaper. "Good run?"

"Hmm." Rowan skirted past him, grabbing a bowl from the cupboard. He reached out and patted her hip, and she dodged his touch, but she told herself, at least he was trying. Win folded herself into his lap sometimes, like a six-year-old, and although the scene tugged fondly on the corners of Rowan's mouth, it made her hurt. Rowan emptied some cornflakes into the bowl, sloshed in the milk, and then sat opposite him, one leg folded under her.

He stuffed his mouthful of toast, eyeing her across the paper. "This police matter is a little worrying, isn't it?" he said after he'd washed it down with coffee. "Do we need to put up some high fences or something?"

Rowan paused, thinking about admitting she'd just potentially contaminated a crime scene, but she was still bristling from being told off by Noah, so she said nothing.

"Sure." Rowan watched her cereal dissolving into the milk, along with her sanity. "I'll just dive into my massive amount of savings, shall I? I wonder how many more shifts I can fit into my week."

Ben exhaled at the giant wall his daughter had thrown up. "Don't be like that. You know I can help."

Rowan scratched her head, rubbing her eyes, a headache forming. "I'm being shitty. Sorry."

Ben folded his paper away, peering at her across the new glasses he'd just had to buy, his dark hair long and untidy. It struck Rowan how grey he looked lately and tired. And when he thought no one was watching, he talked to himself, muttering and mulling over words in his head.

"We'll draw up a list. Everything needs doing in this old place," he suggested. "All the jobs John never got to. I think he lost interest after Gloria died. He only ever seemed interested in engines. You know I think we could convert the old barn out back?"

Rowan barked a laugh. "So you can have an escape room from the crazy house?"

His worried expression melted, replaced by a charming smile. "I was actually thinking of you and Evan. A place of your own?"

Rowan's heart lifted, she smiled. "Really? You do like her?"

Ben laughed. "Like her? I love her. She made sense of this kitchen for a start!"

Rowan laughed, a blush creeping up her neck. "I love her too."

"Look." He leaned a little closer. "Stop shutting me out. We're a team, and Grandpa never meant for you to take this place all by yourself. We can handle this together…or as much as you want me involved."

I want you involved. Rowan bit back the words longing to erupt; instead, she nervously tapped her fingers on the tabletop. "I was thinking of getting a job. In town. I can't stay at Hardy's all my life."

Ben's smile lifted. "That's great! Have you thought about what you'd like to do?" When she didn't reply, he jumped back in. "What about a teacher? Or something at the school?"

Rowan rolled her eyes. "That's what Win said!"

"Well, she's smart like me."

Rowan's shoulders slumped. "I think a teacher might be a bit of a stretch. I don't have the grades to go to college…not to mention the time!"

"Come on, why not? You could do it!"

Rowan sighed, her headache suddenly getting worse. "Dad…"

Their conversation was broken by an almighty crash of a door slamming upstairs, followed by Win's distinctive voice yelling something obscene through the bathroom door. Ben and Rowan exchanged a pained glance. Rowan sniggered as she stared down at her wilted cereal. Luke ran downstairs, skidding on the wooden floor as he threw a huge bundle of colored socks in through the door of his den and then locked it.

A mischievous grin splitting his face, he took a place at the table, scraping back the chair before pouring milk into a bowl, followed by his cereal. He ate ravenously, chuckling to himself when Ben puffed out a sigh, finally giving in.

"What have you done?"

Luke threw back his head, utterly thrilled with himself. "She brought it on herself."

"Oh, Luke." Rowan kicked back in the chair. "I have a headache, and you two make it worse."

"Then maybe you should teach your sister how to share? She uses all the hot water *every morning*…or she deliberately turns on the faucets when I'm trying to shower. The plumbing in this house sucks."

Ben laughed. "That's because no one has fixed it since the fifties. Something else to add to our list?"

"Maybe you want that escape room after all?" Rowan joked, busy watching Luke and trying not to find him funny. His teasing was adorable; he riled Win into a frenzy, leaving her a raving mess sometimes. "So, you've exacted revenge, how?"

Luke grinned. "I stole all her socks."

Rowan burst into giggles. "I hope you're prepared for her wrath. She hates having cold feet."

"Yeah, I know. She should think herself lucky I didn't steal her underwear."

Ben cleared his throat. "Don't do that. Ever."

Rowan studied Luke's face, his eyes bright but his skin slightly paler than normal. Then she remembered he'd gone to bed feeling unwell, but clearly, he'd slept it off, judging by his buoyant mood. Win trudged downstairs, her lips pursed. "Dad, I've borrowed your socks. This jerk thinks it's hilarious to hide all mine."

"Why mine? Can't you borrow Rowan's?"

Rowan lifted a skinny ankle, wiggling her barefoot, her toe rings glinting in the sunlight. "I'm a barefoot girl. Even in this weather."

Ben sighed. "Fine. I have to work online today, if the internet doesn't die on me. I'll see you guys later." He gave Win a kiss on the head as he passed. "Have a good day at school."

He hadn't even reached the foot of the stairs when his voice brought Rowan out of the happy little family scene, jarring her back to reality. "Rowan, there's a cop car pulling in the drive."

Rowan watched as both Luke and Win's expression fell— the pained shared glance and the way she instinctively moved just an inch closer to him. Rowan wrung her hands, wiping them on her pant legs. Darting to the window, she spotted Noah slamming the car door shut. "Damn," she muttered. "Why is he back so soon?"

Was he here to question why she had felt the need to go wandering into a cordoned-off area? She thought of her best excuses, hoping he might be dumb enough to buy whatever she came up with.

Noah lifted his hat, taking the steps and meeting Ben at the door. He walked in, followed by a blast of frosty air. Rowan attempted to smile as he walked into the kitchen, but her tongue went sandpaper dry. He scanned the room, smiling half-heartedly.

Wipe the guilty look off your face, for god sake. She wished Evan was here, to feel her warmth, her strength. She noticed Win's stance, how she was standing behind Luke. He'd risen from his chair, half blocking Noah's view of her with his body, and her fingers had wound around the bottom of his shirt. Rowan wished Win would stop *fiddling* with him. She did it all the time, completely unconsciously, fixing his hair, straightening his shirts. Was it any wonder the poor guy couldn't take his eyes off her?

"Hey, Rowan." Noah bestowed a kind smile. "Sorry to have to bother you guys so early."

"It's fine," she managed to blurt out. "Do you want breakfast?"

"Uh no." Noah glanced at the array of leftovers on the table. "I had to come by—to give you guys a heads up. A forensics team needs to come by today and take some more samples in the area where the body was found."

Ben was leaning in the door. "Why? I mean…of course, you can have all the access you need. But is there something more?"

There was. Rowan's legs drained of strength. Her fingers found the edge of the table, taking all her effort to remain upright. Noah fished in his pocket, pulling out a piece of paper with a black and white photo on it. He showed it around the group, and eventually, Luke piped up.

"I've seen her." He paled, raking a hand through his hair. "She's been in the bar a few times."

"Her name is Lucy Weaver, and she disappeared from a nightclub in Lincoln two weeks ago. Her parents live near here, so maybe it explains why you've seen her around. No one reported her missing because she was due to go on a vacation, traveling south, so everyone assumed she'd left."

"What's going on?" Ben asked, his eyes wide, alarmed.

"Well." Noah coughed into his hand. "I shouldn't really be saying this at all."

"Say it!" Luke snapped, and Win punched his shoulder.

"There was more than one body out there. They found stripped bones among those of the zoologist."

Stripped? Rowan swallowed sickly. *He means eaten.* She swayed on her feet. What the hell was happening?

"They have identified Lucy's remains." Noah looked sick, exhausted, and weighted. "They need to come back and comb the area, and I'm hoping to god they don't find anyone else."

"Are we under some sort of investigation?" Ben asked.

Noah whirled in his direction. "Ah no…I mean, it's all really weird." He wiped his mouth. "And nasty. With the family history and all the strange animal sightings over the years. I hate you guys are at the center of all this. They want to set up some surveillance cameras in the woods."

Ben swayed, and across the room, Win dropped into her chair. Rowan met her eyes.

Shit Rowan…what's going to happen? I won't be able to go out!

We can handle this! Stay calm!

Unaware of the silent dialogue going on across the room, Noah plowed on. "They are setting up the cameras and night sensors. A team will come and set up, but we might need to commandeer some of your space. They want to try and catch whatever…or whoever did this. ”

"Whoever?" Rowan maintained her composure. "They think this could be…a murder?"

The cop chewed the inside of his mouth, clearly uncomfortable, and Rowan wondered how much gristly stuff he'd seen in his time. He was so young and baby-faced. "The girl's remains," he stumbled on his words. "There was nothing left."

"That's awful." Luke heaved, covering his mouth. Win's expression caught Rowan's eye. Her sister was staring up at him from her chair, studying the planes of his face. She looked anxious, worried.

Noah seemed nervous as he turned his eyes toward Ben. "It's going to be intrusive, I'm afraid, and we'd have to ask you to refrain from going anywhere alone or leaving the house, other than work or school, or in a vehicle with someone else." He glanced at Rowan, a smirk curling at the corners of his mouth. "No running in the woods."

Rowan flushed, staring hard at the floor. Ben had appeared at her side, the warmth of his arm pressing against hers. "Of course, you're welcome to use the place, and we'll help you however we can. Have you found anything else?"

Noah's expression soured. He looked warily around the room. "The zoologist," he continued. "The forensic team found more of his remains."

Ben made a noise like he was going to be sick; his tanned skin had paled to a sickly white.

"And," Noah breathed through his nose, about to deal the final blow. "It's odd. There's no evidence of him being dragged or attacked or any kind of tussle or fight. It's like he went in willingly. And he had no idea what was about to hit him."

Seven

"Willingly?" Ella's usual creamy olive complexion had turned a sickly green. "You mean like he was lured in there?"

Win rubbed her eyes, a dull ache piercing her temples. She necked from her water bottle, staving off any dehydration. The school cafeteria was bustling, noisy, trays clattering, drink cans popping open. Win was used to filtering out background noise by now, but today her focus waned, and she was exhausted after the morning's reveal.

Across the table, Luke devoured his second burger. Win admired his appetite right now and wondering where he was storing all the fat he consumed. His figure appeared leaner than ever. "It's awful, and I have no idea what it could mean." Win groaned, playing with the remains of the sandwich she'd bought. "The poor girl, too. Can you imagine? She must have been terrified."

"Don't think about that," Ella told her. "You guys are innocent. This is some awful coincidence!"

"I wish we knew more." Win sat back against the plastic seat. "I'm hoping Noah will be back as soon as he has more news."

This seemed to draw Luke's attention away from his lunch. "You mean the Officer with his head up his ass?"

Win threw him a scowl. "Don't be a dick. He's nice. At least he gave us a warning."

Ella checked her watch. "We have to get to class. Uh, basketball again."

Win hauled from her seat, the thought of having to dribble a ball up and down the court filling her with dread. Luke shoved the last of his fries into his mouth, grabbing his pack and falling behind them as they trotted through the halls, teaming with students hurtling along to their next class. They stopped by Ella's locker, and Win retrieved her own sports kit from her locker across the hall. Luke banged open his locker door, pulling out his own kit before slamming it with such force it echoed down the narrow hall and rocketed through Win's skull.

"Can you *please*, turn down your testosterone level for the afternoon?" she shot at him. "What is with you, Mister Mcsnappy?"

Luke burst out laughing, tossing the bag over his shoulder. "I thought you were supposed to be smarter than me. Is that the best you can come up with? Mister McSnappy? I expect better from you, Winifred."

Win's mouth curled into a reluctant smile, despite his annoying prank on her earlier. "It's the best I can think of right now. What I'd like to call you is too obscene to say out loud."

Ella puffed loudly, putting herself between the two of them. "Will you two *stop* bickering? You are driving me *insane*!"

Luke threw an arm around her shoulder, and they sauntered off to the gym changing rooms, leaving Win to dawdle, watching as they retreated down the steps, her loneliness creeping in. She gave herself a shake, telling herself she was being insular, depressive, and what with everything going on, she needed to snap out of it.

Having parted ways in the corridor, Win joined Ella in the changing room and pulled off her hoodie, quickly changing into jogging bottoms and a tee-shirt. As Ella pulled her ponytail free of her tee-shirt, she sat to fasten her shoes. Win folded her arms, looming over her, unsure if she should say what she had on her mind.

Without lifting her head, Ella said. "What is it?"

"Nothing," Win lied. Ella tutted, fastening up her sneakers, and then stood up. Her full height only reached Win's collarbone.

"Out with it."

Win huffed, waving her hands. "It's odd— I don't know. Does Luke ever sleepwalk? When he stays over?"

Ella looked puzzled, then she bit her lip shyly. "My mom makes him stay in a separate room, but usually I tend to sneak..."

"I don't need the details!" Win cut her off, holding up her hand. Funny how in the summer, she had loved learning about their relationship, even if they'd kept it quiet at first. Now she could hardly stomach it. The thought of them being intimate made her spine shudder, like imagining your brother having sex.

"Then no, he doesn't. That I know of," Ella finished, slamming her locker door shut. "Why?"

"Last night, he did. And it was strange. He looked kind of… wild. Not like himself at all."

"Was he okay?"

Win nodded. A group of female students wafted past, their cloying sweet perfume filling her nose. When they'd passed, Win said, "He was fine. He didn't remember what he'd done."

Ella seemed deep in thought, a blotchy stain blushing up her neck. She pressed her lips together, opened her mouth to speak but then sealed her mouth again, having changed her mind. Win narrowed her eyes, smirking. "What?"

Ella grinned sheepishly. "Nothing…it's nothing. *Wild*?"

"Hmm." Win sensed something was brewing. "Say what you're thinking."

Ella blushed furiously. "I don't know if this is related, but..." She cleared her throat, looking around, checking they weren't about to be overheard. "But he's been acting differently lately… more amorous?"

Win leaned in closer, though she could hear just fine, and burst into a laugh. "You mean horny?"

"Yes."

"Then *say* that!"

Ella giggled. "You said you didn't want details. But yes—I've noticed. Apart from the stroppy mood swings, he's been fairly… energetic in other areas."

"Hmm, lucky you," Win teased, though it made her spine shudder again. "We should go. I won't be able to look Luke in the eyes."

"Oh, for god's sake, don't say anything!" Ella laughed, grabbing her arm as they walked out onto the indoor court. Coach Reyes had already started splitting them into teams. Luke was practicing shooting hoops by the time Win, and Ella arrived. Ella was split into a different team, and Win groaned. She'd been forced to the other end of the court. She sidled near Luke, who had broken into a sweat, his glasses replaced with contacts.

"Hey, Romeo," she teased, swiping the ball out of his hand. He cocked a brow, smirking.

"Am I supposed to know what that means?"

Win jostled the ball back and forth between her hands, daring him to take it off her. She thought about teasing him some more, but then she noticed how grey he looked under the eyes, and she thought better of it, passing the ball back to him. Coach Reyes paired Win into a group, along with Luke, and they were forced to the benches while the first group warmed up.

Rosene was in their group, along with six others, she passed Luke, flicking her long blonde ponytail, so it practically swiped him in the face. Making a big deal of stretching in front of him, she bent low, ensuring he had a great view of her backside. Win snorted, disgusted, and looked away, glad Ella wasn't here. Luke politely tried to avert his gaze.

"Ella looks so great since the summer, Luke." Rosene straightened, curving her spine to the right, bringing her long arms over her head. "How much weight did your girlfriend lose?"

Luke hovered over her as she flipped forward to stretch her spine. "She's the same size as last semester. She looks amazing, doesn't she?" he retorted, and Win was proud of him, though what was about to come out of his mouth made her cringe. "I hear you're dating another football player, Rose? Wow, going through them like a bad rash, huh?"

Rosene shot him a spiteful look. "Adam is smart and will probably get a scholarship to college. Unlike you, Luke. How is it pulling all-nighters at Hardy's?"

Luke's jaw hardened, his fists balling. "It's work, Rosene. You ever try it?"

Rosene's smile was brief and acidic. "I prefer to concentrate on what's important, my studies and ensuring I get the grades to leave this town behind."

Luke squared up to her, his eyes flashing a bright shade of blue. "Well, you sure need to concentrate. We all know there's more going on between your legs than your ears."

"Luke!" Win shot out of her seat. She jerked him back by his shoulder. "Apologize to her!"

Rosene stepped back, flinging her ponytail over her shoulder. "There's no need. I know it's hard for him, falling from grace." She flicked her eyes over to Ella, oblivious at the other end of the court. "And having to make do with the dregs."

Win's temper flared. "Okay, back off." Her eyes flashed, and Rosene withdrew, her chin high and her mouth curled into a cruel smile. Win stared dumbfounded at Luke, who was rolling the ball between his fingers, balancing it deftly on his middle finger and letting it spin. He cackled.

"You see that, Adler? You see what I did there? That was a *comeback*. None of this Mister Mcsnappy pants bullshit. You could actually learn something from me!"

Win waved her hands in exasperation. "You shouldn't talk to her like that. I know she's a jerk, but you used to date her."

"So?"

"*So*, you should be a gentleman. I would hate it if you ever spoke to Ella that way!"

His face dropped, letting the ball bounce to his feet. "I would never do that."

Win was called away, and along with several other students, was tasked with practicing hoops for twenty minutes. She was irked by Rosene's horrible behavior but also by Luke and his attitude. He'd been put into his own team and was practicing down one end of the court, dribbling the ball back and forth, swiping it from other players without blinking. She watched him, noticing how quickly he'd changed; everything about him seemed bigger, which included his personality. After some time, Ella and Win were reunited, and Win wrapped her friend a huge hug.

"You missed me?" Ella laughed, hugging her back. Win hated her friend was the sole focus of Rosene's wrath; she couldn't stand it if she ever overheard what had been said in her absence. The court emptied as everyone jogged back to the locker rooms to change. Luke barrelled up behind them, his face white and sweaty. To Win's surprise, he sagged against the wall, rubbing his eyes. She touched his shoulder, and he jerked away.

"Are you okay?"

"I'm fine," he growled. "Just dizzy. I didn't eat much this morning."

"You ate two burgers for lunch."

He straightened, his lips an odd tinge of green, then without warning, he hurtled toward a trash can, overflowing with cartons and juice boxes, and threw up violently. Some of his teammates cajoled him, made disgusted noises, or clapped him on the back. Ella ran across, rubbing him between the shoulder blades. He batted her hand away, wiping his mouth, humiliated as he jogged into the locker room.

Wordlessly, both girls changed in a hurry, and Ella made a dash for it, intent on catching up with him before their next class. Win made her way to social studies alone, worried. She thumbed him a text, which he'd seen but didn't reply to. She took a seat at the back, eyeing the door, waiting for them both to appear. As the minutes ticked by, she grew more anxious, and something was battling to take hold of her subconscious. A thought, a feeling nudged her, guilt creeping through as much as she tried to ignore it. It plagued her right after Ella revealed the titbit about his increased sex drive, a spark of memory, something her grandpa said to her before he'd died.

"I was after any woman I could get my hands on…or let me get my hands on them!"

Nausea swelled in her gut. How could she have not seen this?

What if you did this to him?

"Can I sit here?" a voice came from above, striking her out of her daze. She peered up, registering Cole Ward, standing awkwardly next to her, with his backpack slung over his shoulder. Win reluctantly pulled out a chair, wondering what happened to Luke and Ella. She eyed her phone, saw a message from Ella, and breathed a sigh of relief.

Took Luke back to yours. I'll see you in Math!

Then seconds later, another message popped up. *He says he'll come get you from school. I'm at book club tonight.*

Win quickly replied as Mr. Rainer closed the door, signaling for other students lurking in the door to settle down. *I'll make my own way! Tell him to stay put.*

"Can everyone get their notes out from our trip earlier this week? Or your photos?" He ushered a few stragglers to their desks. "We are going to write up some first drafts of our papers this afternoon."

Win slipped her phone on the table, remembering she had taken lots of pictures inside the Varga house. Cole shrugged out of his jacket, he smelled like a spicy men's cologne, and Win edged a little further away as he threw his jacket on the back of the chair. He smiled at her sheepishly.

"Told you I was going to need some help."

Win puffed, a churlish tone in her voice. "You should have taken your own notes. I'm not writing this for you!"

"How about I come by this weekend?" he pressed, folding his arms on the desk, peering up at her.

"Fine. You can buy me lunch as payment." She couldn't believe what she'd just suggested. Cole's face brightened like a pup that hadn't seen his owner all day. She remembered his attempt at a kiss and wagged her finger at him. "But you keep your hands to yourself. Got it? I'm not interested!"

"Sure! And no problem," he replied eagerly. "And I'm sorry for what I did. I just...I'm an idiot. I misread the moment."

"There wasn't a *moment*."

Cole raised his brows. "I get it and I'm sorry. Can we start over? Hands firmly in pockets I swear!"

Win recalled Rainer's words. He was misunderstood. If Grayson were here, she'd give him a second chance. Maybe Cole deserved one too? "Sure," she relented. "It's fine. I want to help you."

"Why?"

Win threw him a smile. "I'm nice." *And probably very dumb.*

Cole cocked a brow, slinking back in his chair. "Well, guess there's always a first time for everything."

"We can work on your paper," she added, her cheeks rising in color. God, Luke would kill her, especially as they had a bunch of cops crawling all over the property. Win took out her phone and thumbed back through the photos she'd taken in the old Varga house.

There were a few shots, bad ones with other students getting half their heads in the frame—one of half of Luke's face illuminated in flash. Win giggled at one of Ella's round backside as she was bending to look at the cookware in the fireplace. Most of these were next to useless. She pinched her fingers on the screen, seeing if she could close in on the *fascinating* 18th-century pots and pans when a panel at the back of the brick laid fireplace caught her attention. Win froze, zooming in as close as she could, her eyes struggling to adjust. There was something painted into the back of the fireplace. It looked like a black, swirled mosaic, with a mix of faces, bears, wolves, all knotted in an intricate pattern. Win shuddered, and the phone slipped out of her hand.

"You okay?" Cole asked, and she snatched up her phone and tossed it in her bag.

"Fine," she lied. The painting was a replica of the pattern she'd seen somewhere before. On the face of the stone in the woods, the night Joseph had been butchered. Shivering, she rubbed her arms, listening to Cole as he chatted, but her mind was distant, elsewhere.

There was only one person she could ask about this, someone who didn't much like unexpected guests. But she had a feeling her uncle was the only one who could explain this to her.

Eight

Win found herself walking off-campus the moment History ended. She ran to the school office, made a weak attempt at an excuse, and managed to avoid Ella as she returned for their last class. Win pulled on Grayson's coat, huddling inside as she stepped out into the bleak, rainy afternoon. Sprinting along Main Street, she picked up speed as she neared the woods, her eyes keen to find a place she could use to change. She ran into a thicket, stripping off her coat and shoes, shivering as she slipped out of her clothes. She wasn't catching a bus to Lincoln. There weren't any, not till tomorrow afternoon, and she needed answers now. Her fears over Luke forced her forward, convinced she was doing the right thing.

Naked, trembling, she skipped around looking for a place to stash her clothes, stuffing them under a bush and kicking leaves to cover them. *I hate this part.* Nude and alone in the woods, her skin on display, vulnerable and raw, she had prayed on many occasions not to run into a hiker.

Squatting to the ground, she clenched her teeth and closed her eyes. A deep rumble emitted from her chest, and what would have been a human cry became a lulling ripple of a purr. Her arms lengthened, her spine stretching to the point where her eyes bugged, the pain never any easier. Within moments the cat emerged, and Win sprang out from her hiding spot, her belly low to the ground as she sniffed the air.

Then she ran. Muscles working like a well-oiled machine, she pelted through the woods, jumping vines and scattered debris, keeping hidden in patchy undergrowth all the way to the Lincoln Bridge. Win assessed the steep rocky incline down to the water, hopping deftly from stone to stone, her paws sliding as she got nearer to the rushing river. With a leap, she crossed the gap, her back legs landing in the shallows. Win ducked as a car hurtled across the bridge. She snaked up the incline on the other side, peering over the top, knowing the road was her next hurdle. She sprang across the asphalt, her claws clapping over the shiny black road before she ducked in the bushes on the other side. Following the road into Lincoln, she was out of breath but exuberant by the time she reached the dismal row of cottages. She'd never traveled this far before, especially not alone, and so far, she hadn't been seen.

Smoke billowed from a broken chimney pot as Win leaped the short fence into her uncle's front yard. A magnolia, asleep for the winter, provided a good place for her to catch her breath and hopefully to change. She picked up a rock between her teeth, and with a sideways lunge, managed to throw it toward the window where a lamp flickered. It clattered and fell into a gangly rose bed. Win waited and groaned inwardly when he didn't make an appearance at the door. This time she tried again, throwing a rock squarely at his front door.

Rain pelted her fur, drizzling from a heavy grey cloud. She hid in the magnolia, her purr rumbling through her chest. A loud click of a shotgun inches from her head made her freeze.

She whirled about, her old uncle standing right behind her, his shotgun aimed straight and high, the barrel pointed right between Win's eyes. Win squealed inwardly, her ears flattening, submissive. She ducked her head between her paws.

Uncle Willard! It's me, Win!

He cocked his head, wiping rainwater off his bald, shiny scalp. "Winifred? What the devil are you doing? You've trampled my azaleas!"

I'm sorry! Please…I need to talk to you!

He dropped the gun, using his sleeve to wipe his mouth. In the daylight, he was quite a sight to behold, tiny in stature, thin, and his skin like paper. And his eyes were more animal-like than any other part of him, small, round and beady, unused to the glaring light of day. Win ran her gaze along his arms, where his small, clawed hands held the gun, tiny, sharp talons emerging from the beds of his nails.

He opened the front door. "You'd better come in…once you've shifted. I don't trust you in that form."

I don't have any clothes! Win panicked, and he grinned, revealing sharp, yellowed teeth. Inside she grimaced. He looked like he'd got stuck during a transition.

"I'll get you a blanket." He kicked the door open, giving her one last long look. "You smell like death to me—a predator. And I've not gotten to this age to end it by being chewed on by a juvenile jaguar. So if you don't mind, I'll keep my gun by my feet."

Flames from the crackling fire warmed Win's skin. Wrapped in a woolen blanket that smelled like it hadn't been aired for a century, she huddled on the couch, drawing her knees up to her chest. She glanced around the room, as ramshackle as when she'd last been here. But there was a whiff of something in the air, staleness hadn't been present before, and she half wondered if Willard was getting out these days. With every drape pulled tight, dust motes were visible through narrow cracks seeping in light. Every wall was lined floor to ceiling with boxes, paperwork, books stacked precariously. An old television was buried under crates of books, the coffee table, on which her uncle had placed a tray of coffee and some cookies, coated with dust, so thick Win could taste it.

"Please help yourself!" he urged, pushing the floral plate of chocolate chip cookies toward her. Win took one and sniffed it when he wasn't looking, spotting tell-tale flecks of mold around the edges. She hummed in mock appreciation and then tucked it under the blanket.

Willard sloped into a rocking chair on the right of the fireplace, hidden partially in shadow, and she wondered if he preferred it that way. Across the way, his eyes glimmered, there was a sharp tapping sound from the floor, a clicking, and when she glanced down, she saw he wore no shoes, the relentless tapping coming from the clawed toes poking out of his socks. Win drew back in alarm, hoping he hadn't noticed her staring. Was this what happened when Therian got older? Her uncle was as old as the invention of the lightbulb.

"I'm sorry to just drop by like this," she said, trying to distract herself from his cloven feet and the clawed fingers holding the cup he was sipping from. "But I've got no one else to ask."

"It's wonderful to see you," he replied. "Though you must be curious about my appearance. I seem to be getting stuck— between phasing. I'm old and tired, I guess."

Win drew her brows together. "Sounds grim!"

"I look a fright! You, however, are only at the beginning of a long life. I yearn for the day where I can sleep and not wake up."

Win was unhappy that he wanted his life to be over. "Can you help me?" she asked.

He rocked in his seat, and his little feet tapped on the wooden floor. The sound made her neck tingle. "If I can, I will." He nodded. "Tell me everything."

Win took a large gasp of breath and didn't leave out a thing. She recounted her nightmare, waking to find herself covered in blood. She told him about the bodies in the yard, the strange pattern in the Varga house fireplace, and then finally, the subject she was most dreading. Luke.

When she finished, not only did her shoulders feel marginally lighter, but she had the sense he'd listened. He wasn't about to palm her off, tell her she was crazy, or fearing the worst. He clicked his tongue, rocking back and forth in the shadows. "Well, where to start!"

"I know!" She let out a raspy breath. "I know how it all sounds. I'm sorry to burden you, but Rowan is worried all the time. She looks at me like I'm about to implode. You are the only one I know who can possibly help me!"

He rocked forward, close enough to touch her hand resting on the arm of the couch. He tapped it with a palm soft like the pad of a cat's paw, and she shuddered. "This is why I'm here. First of all, we need to talk about Luke."

Win braced herself, swallowing as heat rose up her chest. "Okay."

"I feel like you already know what's happening."

Win dipped her head, the realization hitting her. Her heart ached. "I did this to him, didn't I? If he hadn't come with me…if I hadn't made him. Oh god!"

She was referring to the night that everything changed. The night Win Adler died in the woods, and a very different teenager emerged. The night Grayson vanished into the flames of his cabin, the very same night she and Luke set her ancestors free. But Luke hadn't come away entirely unscathed.

Willard shushed her with a wave of his hand. "What you did for us was a marvel, Winifred. You had barely come through your calling. Then you went back to set our trapped ancestors free. Don't regret that for a moment!"

Win hissed through her teeth, the memory of the horror outside Grayson's cabin unfolding before her eyes. She saw Luke, in terrible pain, suspended as blue light washed through him, her ancestors running at him, escaping through him and into the night. "Luke nearly died!"

"But he didn't!"

"I've done this to him. He's in pain right now because of me. He's going to suffer…."

"Win, he lived through it because of the blood running in his veins and in yours. Blood is the purest, strongest link we have."

"What are you saying? Luke is a Hickory?"

"He's not a Hickory, not by a long shot. He's an offshoot, Jake's son. His blood, no matter how diluted, remains linked to our curse. But he's lived apart from us, locked between a feuding family for decades. The connection to the Earth is weak, but there is still a connection. Surely you must sense that? You two, are… bonded?"

Win flinched, never having thought of it that way. She recalled the moment she first met him on that fateful afternoon in Hardys. Admitting to feeling an attraction, a spark, she'd pushed it away the moment she'd laid eyes on Grayson. Luke was like her brother. But perhaps this was the spark? She loved him so much. The image of him not being there crushed her, made her struggle to focus. He belonged with them, with her.

Win gasped inwardly, an idle thought striking her. *Rowan and Spencer!* Like pulling back a heavy drape and light flooding in through a window, the truth dawned clearly. *Of course!* Their attraction, the obsessive nature of their relationship. It was programmed into them, like a primal, old pack mentality. Rowan couldn't have helped falling for him. Win thought at least she could give Rowan that knowledge; it might make her easier about the whole situation. She had been doomed from the get-go.

Like they were made for one another. Win rolled her shoulders, not understanding why that made her skin stand on end, and she was thankful the guy was no longer in her life.

"So, whatever blood is inside him, it's dormant?"

"Of sorts."

"And," she concluded. "The blue light woke it up?"

"You'll have to forgive me, but this hasn't ever happened before. It's the only conclusion I can come to. The light—the magic you encountered is powerful!"

Win struggled to keep her thoughts on track. Her mind was spiraling. "What's going to happen to him? Right now, he looks sick… and he's snappy, moody, and ...."

Willard chuckled wistfully. "You don't need to say another word. I've been there, remember? Oh, the joys of being a teenager—and a Therian one too. But on a more serious note…." Willard clicked his palms together, his voice lowering. "This is what worries me, Win. If what you describe is happening to him now, the calling is ripping through him at an alarming rate. Therian begin their calling around fourteen, and sometimes it presents even earlier, mild symptoms, changes in taste and smell. It ends, usually at eighteen, sometimes early twenties. There have been late callings before. How old is Luke?"

"He'll be eighteen in November," Win answered, uncertain where this was headed. She didn't like her uncle's grave change in tone. It made her insides tighten. Willard looked upset.

"Then he missed four years of gradual, slow mutation. His body is going to try and hurtle him through, catch up for what he's missed…but—I fear it might be too much."

Win drew back, her bottom lip dropping. "Too much? You mean…?"

"It's violent, unearthly. Surely you remember what happened to you that night? The pain, your body collapsing in on itself… deconstructing..."

"Stop!" she cried, drawing in a jagged breath. She shook away the image, the memory. Yes, she remembered. God, she could still feel it, the slow decline of her heart. The moment she had closed her eyes and given in. And her remains left behind in an ugly, sticky pile. She heaved. "You mean….he could die?"

"Win, whether you were aware of it or not, your body spent many years preparing for that night. And when it came, you were ready for it. He's had nothing!"

"It's going to kill him." Her hands weakened, and the cup slipped to the floor out of her grasp, cold coffee spilling out onto the rug. She started to shake. "I'm sorry..."

"Leave it, leave it!" He waved both his paws when she lifted out of her seat. "Win, I'm surmising all this. I don't know *anything* for sure. But I know what the calling does, how it rips the body apart. There is a chance you could get him through this. But it's slim."

"How?" she spluttered. "I'll do anything!"

"I know you would," he whispered. "I wish I had better news. But I believe one thing. If anyone can find a way, it'll be you. You know what I think about you. Do you remember what I told you in the summer?"

Win, defeated and tired, looked skyward. "Oh, don't start all that again. Not after what you just told me. I'm not special. I can't lift the curse!"

Willard rocked back and forth, a tiny growl emitting from his chest. "Do you think it's a coincidence you had that dream? You saw what *really* happened in the clearing that night! You are the last Hickory, the last pureblood in this line. Your blood runs thicker, richer, filled with memory…and power!"

Win wiped her face, hardly aware she had been crying. Rocked to her center, she sat, arms tightly folded around her knees. "I don't understand."

Abruptly he stood, his nails clicking as he scampered out of the small room. "Wait here!"

She nearly laughed. As if she could go anywhere wrapped in a blanket. Right now, she could barely lift her head. Guilt weighed heavily on her chest, forcing her to breathe slowly, harshly. No matter what her uncle said, Luke's death was all she could focus on. And she had unwittingly brought this on him! So what if she was the youngest Hickory? It didn't make her special. She couldn't fix Luke.

She tried to distract herself, gazing around the room. Something long, like poker in the fire, caught her eye. She got to her feet, padding across the rug to look closer. It was a fire poker, long, densely black, but the end was shaped like a crucifix. Win shuddered; it reminded her of the branding irons on display in the Varga house, a horrific way of marking a witch back in those days. She ducked back to the couch the moment Willard shuffled back into the room.

He was weighed by a heavy wooden box and heaved it on his lap when he sat back down. Intrigued, Win leaned closer, wrapping the blanket around her chest.

"This belonged to my mother," he said. "It was in your attic for many years, and before she died, she wanted me to take care of it. Your grandpa was a little wilder in those days, and she worried he wouldn't be able to keep the house in the family—that it would be sold. But this is something you really need to see."

He handed Win the box, and carefully she lifted the lid, coughing as old dust filled her nose. Inside were several leather-bound journals, the paper crinkly and thin. "What is this?"

"They are from a time long forgotten. Journals, memoirs, letters. They all belonged to the women who lived in your house. Eliza, Vivienne, Louisa, and Mary Hickory. Some of it makes for some disturbing, if not illuminating reading!"

Win was confused. "But what..?"

"Look under them."

One by one, Win carefully lifted out the journals, laying them next to her on the couch as though they were written in precious gold. Something caught her eye, an old, stained rag, crumpled into a ball, partially flattened by the weight of the journals piled on top of it. Gingerly, she picked it up between her thumb and forefinger, her nose wrinkling, and like an old, moldy bandage, it unraveled, revealing it to be a long, blood-soaked length of moth-eaten cloth.

Win's eyes widened, her hand froze. "No…what is this?"

She didn't need an answer to her question. She smelled him on the cloth. His blood dried into the fabric, long forgotten, hidden away for years. It was the hem of her nightgown, the piece she had ripped off with the knife, the cloth she had used to soak up his blood.

"No, this isn't possible," she spluttered, fear coursing through her. "This isn't real!"

Willard had eased forward in his seat, fully visible in the lamp-light, his frail face paper white and his teeth sharp were bared in a grimace. "Yes, it is Win. You were there. You…were there!"

Nine

Rain fell in sheets, but Win hurtled back through the undergrowth, as fast as she could manage. Cold, wet and tired, she crossed the fast road atop Lincoln Bridge, her paws slipping as she jumped down the rocks below it. She couldn't think, she could hardly breathe. As she fled, keen to get back home the last part of the conversation with her uncle replayed in her head. Win sprinted across the freezing river, her feet splashing over the rocks.

"Evan told me she believes the stone is some kind of conduit, for dark power?" Win had countered, after he had shown her the bloodied fabric of her ruined gown. How was it possible she had passed through time, allowing her to be there, at the exact moment her ancestor was mutilated? "How can this be related to the house in Mickleford?"

"There are so many things we still don't know," Uncle Willard said. "But I know, somehow, you were there that night. You harnessed the stone's power."

"Through a dream?" Win cocked a brow.

"You've done it before. Didn't you say you accidently phased once to a time you'd supressed?"

"Yes," Win agreed, remembering her awful memory of the pit. The day Spencer tried to kill her. "But I phased into my *own* timeline, this is different. I never existed back then!"

"What if I told you, this wasn't the first time this has happened? That you weren't the first Hickory this has happened to?"

Win drew back, unsure as he handed her a green and gold, leather bound diary, one that had been placed on the couch when she'd opened the box. "This." He placed it in her hands. "Is Mary's journal. It's an unsettling read, but I think if you read between her adolescent ramblings, she makes reference to the stone, on more than one occasion, and what it can do."

Win held the book on her lap, uncertain whether to lift the cover. "Didn't she die young?"

"She was thirteen," Willard replied. "But this goes on before, long before—it's disturbing. But, you need to read it."

Win huffed, impatient and growing tired. Outside it was growing dark, gloomy and rain was hitting the roof in torrents. "I don't understand how this will help Luke."

"Silly girl," Willard scolded her, tutting. "You have to learn where you come from. What you are! Haven't you listened? She was powerful, and she somehow harnessed the power of the stone. Something none of her sisters did. And she died because of it."

Win bit her lip, thoughtful. "She was the youngest of them. Like me."

He nodded, relieved she was finally catching on. "She was the last of them until she died, and then Eliza had children and carried on the line."

"But it makes no sense!" Win argued, finding a flaw in his logic. "Iris was younger than Grandpa. Why didn't she survive? If she was the youngest in line, she should have lived…had more power? And…how is this anything to do with the Mickleford house?"

Willard held up his palms. "The house, I'm afraid, is a mystery, and as for Iris…how can you be sure she didn't have power? I'd also like to point out, we aren't invincible Win, and we die, *eventually*. We don't know a thing about Iris after she entered Mercy, only she had a son. And there have been more Hickory's, after Mary and long before you. They may have had no idea of the power they held in their blood."

Win tried to hand back the book. "I don't know if I can take this right now. I just want to help Luke."

"Then read it!" he urged. "I'm going to have it couriered to you. You can't take it home in this weather in your mouth. But promise me, you'll try. I believe the key to understanding your power lies in this book, and unfortunately, a rather unpleasant family member."

Win rose to leave, needing to be free of his watchful gaze, confused, upset, but before she left, another thought sprang into her head. She could hardly believe she hadn't thought to ask it immediately. "Uncle Willard...our mother is missing. She has been for weeks. Do you know anything?"

He clicked his tongue, his expression wearied. "She always was a headstrong little thing, Alice. A flight risk, if you will excuse the pun. But I haven't seen her."

"Could this be connected? She vanished not long after we burnt the cabin."

He shoved his hands in his pockets. She could tell he was edging to say something. "The magic which pulses from the stone is old and powerful, and the night when you set them free, dark magic was given back into the night. There may well be a connection—or she's off on one of her adventures. Alice did love to fly."

Win made it back to the spot she'd left her clothes. Shivering, her teeth chattering, she found a secluded patch of brambles and eased back into her own body, diving to retrieve her underwear. She groaned, slipping on damp socks and her mud-splattered jeans, before pulling on Grayson's coat and fumbling in the pocket for her phone. She slid it open, the screen spotted with rain, checking her messages as she jogged back through the woods. Missed calls and messages, one from Luke, several from Rowan. Win hurried, now officially late, they would have been expecting her home hours ago, and the sky grew darker.

Win found a muddy path back through the woods, one running around the back of Mercy. The old house appeared out of the gloom, its chimney stacks spitting out puffs of grey smoke, clouding the place in a foreboding aura. Win studied the building, trekking around back, the little rusty gate she and Ella had snuck through on the night of the bonfire, still swinging in the wind. It was too tempting. Someone was in there, and Win was propelled to push through the gate.

She folded her arms around her waist, as she peered across the building, the lead-lined windows staring down at her like dead eyes. She'd been here many times, the last time it had been left to ruin, all the topiary hedges overgrown, weeds escaping the flower beds. In a way, it warmed her to know someone was taking care of the place. They were trimming back the topiaries at last.

Win froze. Up ahead, she saw the topiary Hare. Iris's Hare. Win's mouth went bone dry, a chill running up her back. The last time she was here….it had been overgrown.

Oh, god…

Daring to get closer, she crept up to one of the lower windows on the ground floor. Standing on tiptoe and using her fingertips to pull her up on the ledge, she pressed her nose against the glass. It was the family room; she narrowed her gaze, spotting a large cream leather couch, ornate candles on each end of the enormous stone fireplace. A moment too late, Win spied the steaming mug of coffee on the tabletop.

A shadow moved inside.

Shit! Win dropped to the ground, landing awkwardly on her ankle. Breathing hard, she didn't dare look again. Keeping her back to the wall, she crept close to the building, jumping over muddy flower beds until she reached the gate to the meadow.

Panting, she sprinted back into the safe canopy of the trees. So *someone* was living in there. Adrenaline coursed through her. Wiping her brow, she jogged back through the bushes, picking up the muddied path back through to the Hickory woods. The bushes rustled behind her, but when she turned, she noticed a pair of squirrels catapulting from branch to branch.

It was eerily quiet, shadowy; the clouds were heavy above her head. Cold nipped at her fingers, her solitude becoming more oppressive every step she took.

A crawling sensation exploded down her spine. Win lifted her chin, determined not to give in to fear. She walked faster. Eyes were hot on her back. She paused, her feet in the mud, closing her eyes, picking up the soft rise and fall of breathing nearby.

Goosebumps broke out across her arms, delicate mist coiled around her legs like a spider's snare. She whirled about, hearing something rustle behind her. The rain fell, soaking her through, so her hair stuck to her head. The lights of Mercy flickered in the distance, and something moved. Win choked, a shape, large, lithe, and muscular, moved through the trees at speed.

Her feet wouldn't budge. Utterly rooted to the ground, she gaped as the animal moved closer. It was too big to be a wolf. Rain glinted off its short fur. And the smell…even in the wet weather, she could smell its predatory scent. A flash of silver flickered through the trees, a long, solid tail appearing before it vanished into a thicket, keeping low. It was hunting her.

"Who…are you? Who's there?" she called, her voice cracking.

We woke them up….we woke them all up…

"Who are you?" she cried, her heart hammering. "Come out. *Now*!"

Keen, yellow eyes edged closer, and she was paralyzed with fright. With a wooden step, she crept backward, every muscle in her body preparing to flee, adrenaline flooding her blood. Win attempted to call to the earth, her focus too splintered and her body exhausted, and fleetingly cursed herself for not being able to phase back, gritting her teeth and trying to force the change. What was the point of this gift if when she really needed it, her body betrayed her?

You have to run. You have to move.

The creature hissed, long sharp fangs glinted with saliva, its eyes following her, and she knew she was looking into the eyes of a killer. It snarled, still hidden in darkness, and darted away into the undergrowth. Something had scared it off.

Win squinted through the misty dew, trying to track it, as a different smell suddenly filled her nose. Her heart caught as she tumbled backward. Hitting a body, a pair of hands landed on her shoulders, startling her out of her daze. Thick raindrops dripped down her chin as she recognized the familiar smell. "Luke, what are you doing here?" she cried, whirling around throwing her arms around his waist in total relief and shock.

Thank god! The warmth of relief quickly washed away the moment he laughed, a deep rumble right above her head. In alarm, she drew back. "You're not…!"

"*No.*" The man smiled, boyish, handsome, and about twenty years Luke's senior. "No, I'm not Luke. But after that greeting, I'm starting to wish I was!"

He held a black umbrella, dripping trails of rainwater, dressed in a large woolen overcoat, sweater, and jeans, and wearing a smile and a mischievous glint in his eye, said he remembered exactly who she was. Win's stomach dropped. It was Jake Fraser.

"You're not meant to be here." She fumbled for her words, blushing hideously. He was supposed to be in Hawaii, thousands of miles away. Reality came crashing around her like a tidal wave.

The animal! Where had it gone?

Win whirled about, her eyes scanning the trees. It was long gone. Reluctantly, she turned back to Jake, who was eyeing her, amused at her bedraggled state, gleefully enjoying the upper hand he'd somehow won from her.

"Hey, redhead girl." He winked as he tugged her under the umbrella. "How about we go inside? And you can tell me exactly why you're trespassing on my land?"

Ten

Evan unlocked the door to her apartment, a small building with a room above a pharmacy in Lincoln. She put her bags down quietly in the hall, rubbing the back of her long neck. A dull ache spread out from the nerves behind her eyeballs, making her queasy. The hallway was dark, all the doors closed off, but the air was ripe with the smell of unwashed bodies. Evan wrinkled her nose, kicking off her shoes.

"Are you here?" she called down the dark corridor. Silence wafted back, lingering eerie. Evan wondered what she expected.

Her phone went off in her bag; she jerked in fright then scolded herself for being so jumpy. She grabbed it hurriedly.

"Is everything okay?" came the worried male voice at the other end. Evan breathed a heavy sigh.

"I've just walked in. I've been to buy groceries…and shampoo. See if I can convince her this time?"

"I didn't have much luck either," Ben said. Evan leaned against the wall. Even the sound of his concern was draining. But then, hadn't she brought this all on herself?

"Let me try again," she whispered, spying movement in the corridor, a wisp of a shadow darting across the hall. Evan shivered. "I've got to go. I think she's awake."

"I'm scared, Evan," Ben said aloud. She wondered how long she had waited for him to say it. "I'm scared this isn't going to work."

Evan bit her lip. "I know."

"We need her. The girls need her…but we need her—better. Better than this!"

"I know, Ben. Let me try again. We are making progress!"

"I can't keep slipping away. The last time was two weeks. I'm lying to my company. I'm lying to the girls. Rowan needs me home…God." She could envision him on the other end of the line, clawing at his greying hair. "Maybe, she should never have come back."

"Ben…no!"

"I don't want to say it. I don't. I love her, and I want her home. But this is hell."

"Give her time, Ben. We can't send her home in this state."

"Things were okay, Evan, you know? They were okay. And now…this is so messed up."

"Ben, I have to go." Evan spotted a figure trail into the hall, lank hair, long-limbed. The creature, resembling a woman, glanced at her through yellow eyes before drifting back into the bedroom. Evan suppressed a shudder. With all she'd witnessed over the years, this was as creepy as hell. "I'll call you. Just concentrate on the girls."

She hung up, her headache finally splitting across her skull—time to face the music.

Poor Ben hadn't known what to do when she told him about Alice. He hadn't believed her at first, not until he'd stepped through the door and seen for himself the wretched creature cowering in the corner, her stringy hair covering her face. Ben hadn't been able to speak. He'd sat at Alice's feet and wept, unable to believe his eyes. Alice didn't react; she glared at him blankly, her eyes empty vessels. She didn't even know who he was.

But it hadn't stopped Ben from coming back. Five weeks he'd spent his days and nights here, talking to her, pleading with her. She had refused to move, to budge from her hiding place; her only response was to growl if he came an inch too close. Evan watched pitifully, her heart-wrenching. She wondered if she had done the right thing.

Alice didn't want to be here. And yet, Ben never complained when she hissed at him or lashed out with her fingernails. He was so happy. And very determined. But she questioned how far he was prepared to go now, after his phone call. He was losing the will to carry on.

Evan wandered into the living room. Alice rocked in the corner. It stank in here; Alice refused to wash, no matter how hard Ben tried to persuade her. Her long, strawberry blonde hair fell in string vines across her shoulders.

Evan crept carefully around the couch. Alice lifted her chin, peering at her across her knees. She could move if she wanted to; god, they had learned that lesson. In an effort to get some fresh air in the room, Ben opened the window. It had been enough for her to squeeze through.

Evan had nearly passed out from panic. Alice had fallen fifteen feet, and landed miraculously unharmed. She was quick when she chose to be, they found Alice on a bus at the south end of Medford, and no one dared speak to her. She was a terrifying sight to behold, a long, thin woman with spindly arms, wearing a tatty, stained nightdress.

Evan and Ben wouldn't make the same mistake again. Evan perched on the end of the couch, one foot solidly behind her in case Alice should make any sudden moves.

"Hey Alice," Evan said. "How are you doing? Are you feeling any better?"

Evan was met with the crawling silence, only her steady, rhythmic breathing filling the gap. Evan shifted, lifting to her feet. "I'll get you some dinner."

She walked briskly to the kitchen, her neck prickling as the woman watched her leave. She bustled about in the kitchen, switching on lights and rattling pots and pans, anything to make her feel less alone. She boiled up some water, planning on cooking some pasta for Alice, something plain. Alice hadn't been able to tolerate many foods, often throwing them back up in the corner.

Evan felt a pang of guilt, watching as the water frothed and simmered, thinking of Rowan back home and how, for the past six weeks, she'd lied to her face. Even now, Rowan messaged her, wishing her grandma well, wanting to hear the news. Lying next to her in bed, watching her sleep, so many times she'd wanted to wake her and reveal what she'd done.

How could she ever explain this? Where would she even start? Her power, her lies, right from the start, the moment they'd met. Win was the reason Evan dared come back to Cedar Wood, a place haunting her for so many reasons. Win was the light, the ray of hope Evan had longed for, her redemption in the form of a suspicious, red-haired teenager.

She never expected to fall in love. Rowan had been her undoing, and it killed her that she'd lied her way into her life, driving the smallest wedge between the two sisters. And what made it all the more horrible was that right from the outset, Win had seen straight through her. But Evan gained her trust, rendering her invincible. God, she loved them all. She loved Rowan, and Win, even Ben. She even loved Luke, the way they'd embraced him. Could she come back from this lie? Would Rowan trust her again?

Lying to her had been agonizing. She had been on the brink of spilling everything so many times. Evan longed to see the look in her eyes when she told Rowan she'd brought back her mother. She longed to see elation, her reaction when she learned she'd been given the ultimate gift, to have her mother back in her life. But this creature wasn't the woman Rowan or Win would remember.

Alice needed to be fixed. There was no other choice. Rowan *had* to forgive her. There was no choice in that either.

Evan stepped into the hall, swallowing, ensuring Alice was still crouched in the corner. Stepping back into the kitchen, she stood on tiptoe and reached for a box of fusilli, pouring a handful into the boiling water.

She tried to keep her face neutral when she walked back to the living room, the smell of cooking spilling out into the hall. "Shall we watch television?"

Alice glowered at her, a snarl erupting from her throat. Evan slunk back. "Or we could talk? I could tell you about what the girls are doing? Win did really well on her English paper…."

At the sound of her daughter's name, Alice's blank eyes flicked up. Evan smiled, hoping she was onto something. "She's doing so well, Alice, the way she's coped with everything, she astounds me. You'd be so proud of her."

Alice sniffed and lowered her arms, folding them around her ankles like a small child. She was listening. Evan edged onto the couch cushion. "Rowan is working nonstop at the bar. But guess what, she wants to quit and get a better job? Isn't that great!"

When Alice didn't answer, she only continued to stare at a moth crawling across the rug; Evan retreated back to the kitchen. She paused to give her one last look before darting inside, her skin crawling. Evan reached for the pan. The tiniest creak on the floorboard behind her made her shoulders stiffen.

She whirled about to find Alice standing in the doorway of the kitchen.

Evan shrieked, knocking the boiling water off the stove. It rained down on the tiles, pasta and scalding water, trickling over Alice's bare feet as she closed the gap between them. Frozen in terror, Evan choked as Alice moved like a cat, her hand closing around the younger woman's neck.

Alice hurled Evan backward, and she cried out in agony as her lower back collided with the worktop. Alice pressed her face close enough so Evan could smell her sour breath.

"Why did you do this to me?" her voice, strangled, choked, and unused for so many years. Frightened tears filled Evan's eyes as Alice's thin, nimble fingers tightened around her windpipe.

"I wanted…I wanted to help you…to bring you back…."

Alice's glassy eyes flickered. "Help me? Why? I was complete. Don't you know? I was everything I was ever *meant* to be."

Evan spluttered, "But I wanted to reunite you with your daughters….they need you."

Alice's eyes filled with tears. They spilled over white lashes. "But I was finished here. I had my time. You don't even know what you've done."

Evan's hand closed around Alice's wrist, but it was useless. She squirmed against her. "I wanted to help."

Alice cocked her head, sneering. "Why? Do you have a guilty conscience?"

Evan choked under the pressure of Alice's hand, her feet slipped on the watery tiles, but the older woman held her there firm like she weighed nothing. "I don't understand."

"I *know* you." Alice grinned, revealing yellowed teeth. "I know who you are. And what you did."

Evan slipped, choking. "No."

"Yes. Oh, I know all about you. But you don't know what you've done. Nothing good can come from that stone. Do you understand? *Nothing*."

Evan gripped the counter behind her, taking the weight off the pressure Alice was putting on her throat. She gritted her teeth, feeling the sharpness of her nails against her flesh. "I don't believe that, not anymore."

"You should believe it. It's all true and now…." Alice let her go, and Evan sagged, gasping as fresh air burned her lungs. The older woman spun away, clutching at her stringy, lank hair. She looked at her hands— hands she hadn't used in a long time. "You don't know what you've done."

"What?" Evan spat, gingerly feeling her neck, sucking in lost air, her oxygen levels wilting. "What have I done?"

Alice leaned against the doorframe, weak from exertion. "You woke them up."

Alice fled back to her ratty, disgusting corner of the apartment, tearing at her hair and wailing. Evan followed her on wobbly legs; the strength knocked right out of her. Alice sobbed into her hands and then stopped abruptly. She stood, quicker than expected, her movements light, fluid. Like a bird.

"I want to wash. A bath…please!"

Evan was elated, trying to brush off what had happened. "Yes…of course!" She ran to the small, pink and white tiled bathroom off the hallway. She ran a bubbly hot bath, and steam filled the room. She turned to grab some clean towels, and once again, Alice's ghostly figure filled the door.

"Shit!" Evan gasped, clutching her chest. "Alice…you need to stop doing that."

Evan's fingers trembled, reaching for the bath cream and making sure the suds filled up the tub. Alice was beyond filthy. "Is the water too hot?" She glanced over her shoulder, and Alice moved toward the tub, dipping her fingers into the water. She clenched her jaw.

"Hotter."

"I don't think..."

"Hotter, please," Alice begged, crossing her thin arms.

Evan ran the hot tap, watching as steam rose off the surface. Alice was struggling out of her nightdress, it was stained yellow under the arms, and she had refused to wear anything else after she had come home from the woods. Evan helped ease it over her head. She winced at the deep, red scratches on Alice's thighs and upper arms, raw and weeping. "Did you do this to yourself?"

"My skin." Alice's voice was weak. "It's not my skin."

What have you done to this woman? Evan's stomach dropped. Alice had been wrenched back into her human form after more than ten years of living as the falcon.

"I'm sorry," Alice moaned, her pale eyes drawn to the bruises blossoming across Evan's throat. Evan rolled her eyes, it wasn't the first time she'd been hurt. Evan shivered, gripped the edge of the tub, and pushed away old memories. Her scar ached, but she straightened and projected the peaceful aura of calm she'd practiced over the years.

"It's alright," she assured her. "Let's take this first step together. I'll wash your hair."

"I want it cut off," Alice said, pulling at the ratty lengths around her face. "It's heavy."

"Of course."

Alice shook as she lowered herself into the tub, the water rippling over her skin. If she was in any kind of pain, she fought not to show it. Evan used the shower attachment to wash Alice's hair, lathering up with both hands, filthy dark water filling the tub. Rinse and repeat, after a couple of washes, Evan was satisfied the woman's hair was clean. It even looked brighter. She grabbed some scissors from the kitchen and got to work.

"How short?" Evan peered around Alice's shoulders.

"Up to my ears."

"But—your lovely hair!"

"I can't stand it. It itches!"

Evan snipped at the soft, blonde wet lengths. They fell in the tub like angel hair on a breeze. Alice let out a long sigh as if she were free, her tangled mane of hair chopped in a blunt bob around her ears. Evan made the mistake of leaving the scissors on the edge of the tub. Alice was too fast.

She moved like lightning, grabbing the silver implement and ramming the pointed, sharp blade into the back of her hand. Alice cried out as blood pooled out of the wound, leaking between her fingers and into the murky water.

"What have you done?" Evan snatched a towel and made an attempt to bandage her hand. She slipped an arm under Alice's and hauled her out of the tub, water cascading to the tiles. Shivering, bleeding, Alice allowed Evan to wrap her up and yank her back to the living room.

"Am I real?" Alice studied her hand, the blood trickling between her fingers. "Is this real?"

"Of course, it's real. You just stabbed yourself!" Evan snapped, avoiding the spilled water and pasta in the kitchen as she went for the first aid kit. Kneeling before Alice, she bandaged up the hand tightly. "Why did you do that?"

Alice's eyes went wide, haunted. "I heard him on the phone. He doesn't want me to come back."

Evan sagged to her knees. "Oh, Alice…he didn't mean it. He's scared."

It hadn't occurred to Evan that Alice even heard her phone call to Ben. But Alice was still Therian, her hearing as sharp as a blade. The poor woman was in turmoil, learning to deal with being back in a human body, her senses heightened, nerve endings raw and frayed. It must be like endless torture. "Give him time. He'll come back. He loves you."

"Can you call him back now? I want him now."

"No, he has to stay with the girls. Rowan and Win, need him too. He'll be back, though, I promise. He's so happy you're here."

"Ben looks after me. He always takes care of me."

Evan sat next to her on the couch, her body cold, skin like paper. She was so frail, compared to Rowan, even Win, they would tower over her, and yet she was the one who brought them into the world. It was a good step; she was talking about Ben. She finally registered him.

Evan wrapped an arm around her, transferring some of her warmth. "I'll get you something to wear."

Alice nodded weakly, and Evan was relieved. This was a breakthrough—the first glimmer of hope in weeks. Evan was gone seconds, ripping through her draws and finding a pair of loose pants and one of Rowan's oversized sweaters. She wondered if the smell might help her, might calm her. Or, Evan debated, would it set her off again?

Evan had to try. She helped Alice into the clothes, winding the pants up her legs, easing the sweater over her head. Alice tucked her nose into the fabric, a ghost of a smile playing on her lips. It was a good idea. Evan knelt at Alice's feet, placing her hands on her knees.

"We can do this, Alice. *Together.*" Evan was positive, the smile she wore, her well-practiced exuberance. "We'll get you strong and get you home, to the girls. They need you."

Alice's bottom lip dropped. "I won't ever fly again, will I?"

Evan's smile froze. She shook her head. "I don't know."

"That's the price—the price for being here. I won't fly again. I won't ever….be weightless."

Evan fought back tears. She'd ripped this poor creature out of a life she'd been happy in. Being the falcon was Alice's destiny, her end game. It was all she was ever meant to be, her purpose fulfilled. Like being snatched out of heaven and forced back to earth, walking the ground like a ghost. But Win needed her mother. What was coming…Alice *had* to be here.

"You know you'll never be absolved," Alice muttered, drawing her knees up to her chest. "If that's what you're looking for."

"I'm not." Evan hid her eyes. "I don't want redemption or forgiveness. I just want to help."

Evan broke the eerie tension by going to fetch a blanket; she switched on the television, which lit up the dark room. Alice's pupils contracted at the sudden attack, squinting, but she huddled into the blanket and watched an old episode of a nineties comedy show, tilting her head, occasionally her mouth twitched into a smile. "Ben liked this show," she called, and Evan lifted her head. She had been trying to clear up the mess of the bathroom, scrubbing at the grimy ring Alice had left around the tub.

"He still does!" she called back. "Win watches it too, with Luke."

Evan wandered back into the room, the television still casting a bright glow across Alice's pale features. Armed with dirty, blood-stained towels, she switched on a lamp, and Alice flinched. She was shaking.

Evan dropped the towels and ran. "Are you alright? Is it your hand?"

"No...no," she cried, scrubbing furiously at her face the second a tear escaped. "It's only...this is all such a mess. I don't know if I can go home...."

Evan hugged Alice's knees. "You can!"

"No, you don't understand. You woke them up!"

Evan's calm faltered. "Do you mean Luke?"

Evan had been watching him for weeks. He'd altered, right from the night of the cabin fire, and she'd quelled her horrible suspicions, set them aside, and tried to focus on Rowan and Alice. The night Win set her ancestors free, *something* touched Luke, woken a part of him that had been lying dormant. The changes were minuscule at first, so subtle you could barely tell. But Evan noticed and tried to laugh it off as teenage hormones, his mood swings, his appetite, his *size*. And she noticed the way he looked at Win when he knew she was distracted. How he studied her, watched her every move, the longing in his gaze was painful. Win was oblivious. In fact, she *actively* made it worse. She was so open, tactile, craving physical contact with him. The poor guy was in agony.

"I didn't wake Luke up...it happened when Win set your ancestors free," Evan said in protest. She was happy to accept the consequences for Alice, but she hadn't had anything to do with Luke.

"I mean all of them," Alice's voice snapped her out of her train of thought.

"All of them?"

"Our blood is *linked*. We are bound together," Alice spluttered. "Surely you must have known that?"

"I didn't think...!"

"Now...I'll have to face him. If I go back, eventually, he'll come to find me. He always does."

"Who are you talking about?"

Alice cried, her shoulders shaking, her face growing blotchy. "It's always been him. It's always about Jake."

Evan blinked. "Jake? Jake Fraser? Luke's father?" Evan swallowed and her palms broke out into a sweat. If she meant Jake… then she also meant…

Oh, god! Oh, no!

"You can't possibly understand," Alice sobbed. "Ben and I didn't just decide to move our lives to Boston. We wanted to stay here, to raise our family here. We left because of Jake….we ran away!"

Eleven

Win's feet barely touched the stones as Jake ushered her through the ornamental courtyard, and wished she'd never set foot back in the place. She could have been home by now! The key cranked as Jake unlocked it, placing a hand on her lower back, showing her through the glass-paneled door. He tossed her a look, daring her to run. The smirk on his mouth said he expected her to bolt, but Win held firm, trying to prove she wasn't afraid of him. *Don't panic. You can get through this!*

The Virgin Mary could prey all she wanted. She was such an idiot. Water pooled around her feet as Jake shook out the umbrella, dropping it in a stand by the door with a clunk that echoed through the hall. She crossed her arms over her chest, not daring to meet his sardonic gaze as he showed her down stone steps and into a back kitchen. Win paused in the door.

"I saw something out there!" she burst. "It was a huge animal…didn't you see anything?"

He slipped out of his coat, hanging it on a hook, throwing her a smile over his shoulder. "Perhaps it was a wolf? I've heard this area is quite renowned for them."

She cocked a brow, pursing her lips. "That's not funny."

"I wasn't trying to be." He leaned against a long, chrome kitchen counter. "I haven't got much of a sense of humor when it comes to young women snooping around my home."

"I wasn't snooping!" Except she absolutely was, her cheeks flamed. A deep shiver tore through her, her lower teeth chattering. She glanced around the massive kitchen, five times bigger than the one at Hickory. It was wall-to-ceiling chrome, with huge cooking stations, triple ovens. Everything was neat, clean, but something sad hung in the air. It was lonely, unused, and long since served its purpose. In its day, Mercy was a fine home built after the American Revolution. It echoed history.

"Are you on your own here?" Win asked. Jake filled up a kettle, letting it boil on the hob, and was pulling mugs out of the cabinets, which surprised her. He didn't look like the type of man who knew his way around a kitchen. "Your wife?"

"She's in Hawaii."

Win gulped. "And, Spencer?"

"Oh, he'll be along at some point." Jake didn't look up. "He always turns up, eventually."

"But he's not in Hawaii?" Win tried to disguise the anguish in her voice. *Please don't let him be here.*

"I haven't seen him for some time." Jake clattered the mugs onto the steel surface. "Tea? Coffee?"

"No, thank you." She edged back, still lurking in the doorway. Jake snapped his eyes in her direction, clicking his tongue and running his eyes up and down her body, his steel gaze landing at the sodden mass of leaves and water leaking out of her sneakers.

"You are making quite a puddle on the floor."

He walked by briskly, pressing the red button on an intercom. It beeped, and then a female voice answered at the other end. "Judy, can you come down, please?"

Judy? Win groaned, recalling Luke's old housemaid. That lady did *not* like Win. The last time they met, it had ended with Win nearly giving old Robert Fraser heart failure. Within a couple of minutes, a portly, tanned woman with bushy blonde hair bustled down the corridor behind her, forcing Win to take a step into the kitchen. Judy startled, not having expected to see the bedraggled teenager lurking in the door. "Winifred?"

"Judy, can you fetch me some towels, please?" he asked, throwing Win a wicked grin. "I'm going to pick you out something nice to wear!"

Win spluttered, "I'm not changing!"

Jake rolled his eyes. "Win, I'm going to get you some warm clothes because you'll catch something if you don't get dry. Can you manage to stay put for five minutes while I'm gone?"

"You won't have anything that fits me," she protested as he sauntered down the hall, hands in pockets.

"I have three ex-wives. I'm fairly certain I've got something that'll fit you," he threw back casually. "Oh, I can see you— eyeing the exits. I'm not blind. If I come back and find you've bolted, I'll call the cops. And what with your family being at the center of a murder investigation right now, that'd go badly for you."

Win did all but stamp her feet. Jake laughed as he disappeared down the hall, whistling to himself. She knew he was right; she was trapped in a snare. *So stupid!* Why hadn't she just gone straight home?

What was *he* even doing here? She shuddered, reminded of the creature she'd spotted right before he'd turned up. Her heart beat faster, having an awful premonition, thoughts wildly exploding in her head. Where the hell was Spencer?

"Here!" a female voice startled her, and Judy thrust two large fluffy towels into her arms. They were warm and fresh from the dryer. "You'd better strip off!"

"In the kitchen? Uh, no thanks," Win bit. "I'd rather freeze."

"Then come upstairs!"

Win followed the older woman through the hall and into a large, marbled hallway, an epic staircase wound up to the first floor. Win had been here before, and she recalled Luke warning her last summer about this being Jake's side of the house. She passed his office, remembering the day she'd confronted him about the box of sentimental items he'd left discarded in the attic. Judy stomped upstairs, and Win had no choice but to follow, running her hand up the polished banister, aware of her feet sinking into the plush, cream carpet.

"There's only one room up here." Judy showed her into a bedroom. "So keep your hands to yourself!"

Win ignored her remark, flitting past and closing the door firmly behind her. Within seconds she'd stripped, not sure what to do with her coat, drenched and ruined. She folded the towel over her chest, securing it, and then wrung out her hair, wrapping it up in a towel. Curiosity getting the better of her, she wandered around the room. A massive, comfy-looking four-poster bed sat proudly in the center of the room. On the bedside cabinet sat a pair of reading glasses, a pile of books, and expensive-looking watch, and silver cufflinks. Win gasped. This was *his* room!

Win spotted a bathroom, pushing open the door and peering in, admiring the Jacuzzi tub, the lights flickered on, and she wandered in, stepping into her dream bathroom. She could spend an eternity here! Everything was cream, gorgeous and expensive, built for a woman to get ready in, pretty led lights dotted around a huge mirror. But he'd just said he had three exes who'd made use of this room. There was an empty wine glass left by the side of the tub, and when Win narrowed her eyes, she spotted a red lipstick stain curled around the edge. She sniffed a floral, delicate scent lingering near the tub, a woman's fragrance.

Win screwed up her face in disgust. A woman had been in here, *very* recently.

Win blushed, heat creeping up her neck. He was a complete *womanizer*. His wife was in Hawaii, wasn't she? She darted to the mirror, shaking her towel free and drying off her hair till it hung limply down her back. Her gaze drawn to the bathroom cabinet, wild curiosity taking over as she flung it open, poking her head in to inspect the contents.

"Oh god, you really are a cliché!"

Win jumped in fright, clutching her towel, and narrowly missed whacking her head on the cabinet door. Jake stood in the door, arms folded, watching her with avid interest. His mouth was pressed into a thin line, but his eyes shone. "Are you really going through my bathroom cabinet? What did you expect to find in there? Sleeping pills? Chloroform?"

Win lifted her chin, feeling how incredibly vulnerable she was. She was wet and naked in a strange man's bathroom. But instead of stuttering out a response, she crossed her arms, mirroring his pose. "I don't know… maybe Viagra?"

He chortled, putting a hand on his heart. "Now, that hurt."

"You're cheating on your wife," she accused. His mouth curled into a smile, and Win's cheeks burned. She really needed to learn those snappy insults from Luke. She threw a gaze at the stained wine glass. "Does she know?"

His smile dropped, which was more terrifying than being teased. "My soon-to-be ex-wife is perfectly aware of what I do in private. She's in Hawaii now, no doubt screwing the pool boy. Not that it's any of your business. Now, when you can drag yourself away from my bathroom cabinet, I've left some clothes on the bed. I would like to see you downstairs in ten minutes."

When she opened her mouth to speak, he shut her down with a wave of his hand. "I don't want to catch you poking around anywhere else, Winifred. Come *straight* down."

Satisfied he'd left, she hopped out of the bathroom, grabbing the neat pile he'd left on the bed. There was a pair of grey sweatpants and a hoodie with a faded logo on the front. Pulling it over her head, she smelled Luke. This was his and something he'd probably left behind when he'd moved out. It was comforting. Shoving her arms in, she hugged her waist. She had to see him soon. He needed to know what was happening to him if he didn't already. Tears pricked her eyes, brushing them away; she spied a pair of fluffy socks.

Okay, maybe he isn't a complete monster, she thought, stuffing her feet into them.

He'd left her socks after all, and he'd kept Luke's clothes and items from their past. Maybe he wasn't going to be too harsh on her? Maybe he'd just yell at her and then let her leave?

Her body ached. Cold had crept in and taken hold. Exhausted and emotional, she trotted back down the sweeping staircase, finding him leaning against one of the kitchen counters, a mug of coffee by his side. Dark hair fell into his eyes; he looked up from his phone, the glare of the screen flashing across his face.

"I want to go home," she said, hopelessness filling her voice. "Please."

He exhaled, raking his eyes upward. "Of course. I'm not kidnapping you, Win. I'll take you right home after you've told me what you were doing."

She trembled, all her bravado gone. "I wasn't doing anything."

"Clearly, you were."

Don't be nice. Yell, please. She thought she might start crying. "I wasn't going to break in or anything. I was curious. I saw the lights and wanted to see who was living here."

"You've heard the old adage about curious cats, haven't you? You don't just walk onto other people's property on a whim. Now, what were you really doing?"

Her stomach plummeting, she fought for her excuse, but there was none. It was exactly what she had done, walked into his yard without blinking, without stopping to think if she should. With her head lowered, Jake's gaze bored into her skull. "You're right," she finally admitted, though it irked her to do it. "I shouldn't have. I wanted to see who was living here...and…." She thought of something else that might make her look less guilty. "…I know about Iris, your mother."

The smile on his face vanished, and he scratched at the scruff on his jaw. "I see."

"I know who you are…we're kind of…."

"Related," he filled the gap, his tone curt. "Yes. I've known for years. I'm well aware of our unfortunate relations."

And I've gotten your son killed. He's going to suffer because of me.

He narrowed his eyes, spotting her bottom lip quivering, and with a sigh, he tore his hands through his hair. "Oh…you're not… urh!" He pushed away from the counter, closing the gap between them and catching her by the shoulders. "Don't think you can turn on the waterworks and wheedle your way out of this!"

Win sniffed, tears bubbling up out of nowhere. "I'm not!"

"Do *not* cry!" he begged, eyes thrown to the ceiling. "Pretty girls and tears do not mix, *please*!"

He relented, grabbing a tissue from a box nearby and pressing it into her hand. "If you cry, then I'll have to hug you, and that would be inappropriate, so quit it right now!"

Win gave an almighty sniff and recoiled. She wiped her nose. "Fine." When she had gotten her head clear, she looked up; he was still towering over her. Lazily, he grinned.

"You've never been in real trouble before, have you?"

Are you kidding me? If only he knew the last six months of her life.

"I mean, with this kind of thing, trespassing, sneaking around, breaking and entering. I bet you get away with all sorts. You've never been caught. This scares you…or…." He grinned. "It's more the look on your dad's face when he finds out what his baby has been up to. That's what terrifies you."

Win firmed up her chin, her eyes fiery. "That's not true!" But Jake smirked like he could see straight through her, into her soul.

"You have a sister, right? Yeah, I met her once, years ago. I bet *you* are his favorite—his little princess."

"You are way out of line!"

"Am I? I don't think so. We have favorites, we don't like to admit it, but we do. It's natural, to love one just a bit more. And I can tell. You're his!"

Win recoiled, but his grip on her arms tightened. Something nestled in his gaze, something dark, hateful, and jealous. He reeked of envy. "You'd know something about favorites, wouldn't you? Judging by the way you've treated Luke all these years!"

His hands dropped away, and she sagged. For some reason, being gripped in his attention was like being caught in a tractor beam; she could neither pull nor look away.

"You don't know what you're talking about," he said darkly.

"Are you home because of Luke?"

"No, as you recall, he's trying to ditch me. Rather publically."

"Then why are you here? Back in Cedar Wood?"

The Frasers were broke, or so she thought. According to Luke, his father had run their family company, once a profitable law firm, into the ground, accepting bankruptcy and liquidation. But nothing about his appearance suggested this, his expensive aftershave, clothes leaning toward significant designers. He was a walking men's catalog. She stepped out of the space they shared, feeling like he was surrounding her, crowding closer.

"Well?" she snapped when he didn't answer.

"I hardly think it should be you demanding answers, *but*," he said, non-comitial. "I'll tell you one of my secrets if you tell me yours?"

Win laughed shortly. "I don't have any."

"Oh, you are a little *liar*, red. We both know that's not true."

It took all Win's effort not to smack him. He was so annoying. Now, who did she know who managed to irritate her like this? "Can we please stop with the games?"

"Fine. I'm home because I'm in the middle of a nasty divorce. My father died last summer, and he left me enough to clear the company debts. I was delighted to hear that my family home was still available, sitting here unsold. So I bought it back—excuse the lack of furniture, it's still rather empty. In short, I mulled over my options and thought, why not start again, in the place I grew up?"

Win wasn't buying it. *There's nothing here for you—nothing you want.*

Jake wasn't being truthful, and his expression now demanded her secret and wasn't about to allow her to wheedle out of it. Her mind raced, trying to drum up any excuse. But a half-truth seemed like the best option. He took a step nearer.

"Your turn."

"Okay…" she began. "I know you think I'm crazy. But I *did* see something out there. Something big, and you already seem to know about the dead bodies in our yard. I guess that must be all over town by now. Something killed a man and dragged him onto our land. I was walking home, thought I saw something, and I followed it here."

He cocked a brow. "You? On your own?"

"I'm tougher than I look."

"Hmm, maybe. I still think you're hiding something. Nice of you to look out for your new neighbors? Maybe you wouldn't have bothered if you knew it was only me."

"I don't care about your stupid feud. No matter what happened back then, you are a part of our family. Luke is too." Her little statement seemed to have piqued his interest.

"Well, isn't that sweet," he cooed. "I'm sure your grandfather will feel differently when he finds out we've been getting to know one another? Trust me, he *hates* me."

Win opened her mouth, lips parted, she gasped. "My grandpa is dead. Didn't you know?"

Jake's sardonic smile vanished. Ducking his eyes, he scratched at his hair. "I didn't. I'm sorry."

Win rubbed her arms, a chill crossing them. "Don't you even want to know?"

"Know what?"

Win moaned, exasperated. "About *Luke*? Don't you even want to know how he is?"

"Oh," Jake sighed. "You can tell me if you like."

Win shook her head in dismay; his refusal to meet her gaze was infuriating. "There's that favoritism thing again."

"It's more a question of loyalty over favoritism."

Win gave up. He was about as impenetrable as a brick wall. "Can I go home now?"

He looked thoughtful, sweeping back his hair, finally relenting. "Yes, of course. I apologize for keeping you here this long. Your family must be worried, judging by the amount your phone has beeped."

He sauntered away, returning seconds later with her dry clothes. They were hot and fluffy against her skin. She pulled on Grayson's coat; it was still damp with rainwater, smelled claggy, and hung heavily on her shoulders. "What is that thing?" Jake made a face.

Win drew back, a little insulted. "It belonged to someone I knew. Why?"

"It stinks."

"Thanks." She averted her gaze, her eyes growing wet again. She was a mess today. Jake leaned closer, mildly fascinated, having caught her reaction.

"Oh, interesting!" he mused. "Did it belong to a boyfriend your dad has no idea about?"

Win clutched the coat tighter around her chest. "He doesn't have a problem."

"Liar!" Jake wagged his finger, pleased with himself. "I'm betting he doesn't know the half of it, which is probably a good thing. Because if you were *my* daughter…."

"I'm not. So you can drop the chivalry act. Good thing we are only distantly related."

Jake grumbled and grabbed his coat, and she followed him into the hall after having slipped her feet into slimy, wet shoes. Ignoring Judy's glare as she walked behind him outside, Win broke out into a chill, jumping into the front seat of the black Mercedes. He held the door for her and gave a mock bow as she slipped past him.

He jumped in the front seat, started the engine, and turned on the heater, aiming it at her midsection, warm air billowing around her cold legs. Her skin broke out into goosebumps, her eyes drawn to his hands on the wheel. He slipped an arm around the back of her seat, reversing out of the drive at speed. She couldn't help notice the way he stared at her, his eyes locked on her profile.

"I could have walked this," she said, anything to break the tension.

"Win, you just told me a crazed animal is wandering around in the woods. Do you honestly think I'd let you walk home?"

She fanned herself, growing uncomfortably hot, what with the blower on her chest, plus he kept looking at her, his eyes searching the planes of her face.

"I'm sorry…if I'm making you uncomfortable?"

Was he some kind of mind reader? When she said nothing, he continued. "It's only…you look so much like Alice. In profile. It's…weird."

"Hardly. She's my mother." *Was, should have said was! Idiot!* "You knew her?"

"Of course I did. We went to high school together."

Win didn't pursue the subject, even though he'd let the words trail in the air between them. He wanted her to ask, to beg to know more. And he hated she wasn't biting. The car rolled to a stop in the driveway of Hickory House, the long dirt track running into the woods. He pulled on the handbrake, twisting his body to face her. "If you don't mind, this is where I leave you. I don't think your dad will appreciate seeing me right now."

Win's forehead creased in a frown. "What do you mean?"

"Try asking him about me sometime."

A dull ache formed in the base of her skull. She was bone tired and her nerves raw, and she didn't think she could take one more second of his presence, his cryptic messages. Especially as it was clear, he was having great fun at her expense. Jake whipped around to the front passenger side and opened the door for her. Win attempted a half-hearted smile as she squeezed out. "Thanks," she muttered. Another question weighed on her mind. "What shall I tell Luke?"

"Whatever you want, I don't care. Neither does he."

"He will. He'll want to know you're home."

"I'll leave that one in your capable hands, Win. You know him best."

"He's your son!" she barked. Jake got back in the car and slammed the door. The window whirred as it rolled down; he left her with a charming, almost wistful smile.

"Not anymore."

Win knew there would be consequences the moment she stepped in the door. Her father rose from the dinner table, his eyes raking over her appearance, checking she was all in one piece, before deciding it was acceptable to let rip.

"Where *the hell* have you been?" he roared. Rowan appeared behind him, arms crossed, her face as grey as stone.

"Win, this is not okay. Not after Noah's visit this morning. We've been worried sick!" she barked, shaking her head.

I'm sorry…

Rowan's face clouded. She pulled back as Ben continued to yell at her, oblivious to their private communication. His face contorted, his dark eyes narrowed. He looked wrung out, aged another five years since she'd seen him this morning.

"*Where have you been?*"

"I stayed at school. It was book club tonight!" she said, thinking quickly. Ben threw his hands in the air.

"Since when do you go to book club? You read all the time here!"

"I was trying it out, okay?"

"A call or a text would have been nice, Winifred. Especially after this morning!"

Her eyes blurred with tears, humiliated and feeling very small. It occurred to her, maybe Jake was right. She hadn't been told off before, reprimanded. Not by him. Maybe she was his little princess? "I'm sorry…I was caught up, having fun…and there's a guy I've been seeing…Cole. We were hanging out."

You're lying. Rowan narrowed her fiery green eyes. Win shot her an imploring glance.

Please, not now…just not now! I saw something in the woods…something big…

Rowan nodded, giving her father a sideways glance. She clenched her jaw. *We'll talk later.*

"So you were with a boy?" Ben probed, hands-on-hips. "I'm going to find out, Win, if you are lying to me! It's not like you!"

Win had a vision of standing semi-naked in Jake's bathroom, drying her hair, in a room where he'd taken other women to do things she didn't like to imagine. Though no longer a virgin, the thought of it made her squirm. It left her feeling dirty as if the word liar had been stamped onto her forehead, like a brand. She burst into tears, and Ben's face melted. "Oh…*Win!*"

"No, I'm sorry. I should've called." She held up her hands. "Please…can I just go shower?"

Not waiting for an answer, she stomped upstairs and threw open the bathroom door. She flung her clothes to the floor, climbed under the spray, and cried into her hands. When her skin was red raw, she stepped out weakly, sniveling like a toddler, and put on pajamas. Her bed was warm, soft, and it was hers, her home—a place she was loved and wanted. Luke belonged here with *them*, not in a house with a man who didn't even care to ask about him.

As if on cue, the door creaked open, and Luke popped his dark head around the door. He winced on her behalf. "Hey. I heard you getting yelled at."

Win scrubbed at her face, her eyes sore and swollen. "It's nothing."

Luke slipped in. He was fresh from the shower, his hair curled at his nape and damp, dressed in his black Hardy's shirt, ready for work. "Well, dating Cole Ward isn't nothing."

Win fell back on the pillow. "I'm not dating Cole…" she fought for an excuse. "I'm helping him with his paper."

Luke heaved in relief, clutching his chest. "Thank god. There was a rumor he gave two girls at his old school something nasty, so for god sake, don't go there."

Win chuckled weakly. "I won't."

"Then where were you?" he asked, his voice low. "We tried calling you."

Win could feel it kicking off again. Close to tears, she couldn't stand to look at him, his face, how he was smiling at her, in curiosity. What had she done to him? She was bursting, aching to confide in him. He was always her first port of call. But she couldn't stand to see his expression, the resigned disappointment when he learned his father was home, and he didn't care enough to let him know. She would find the words the right way, but not tonight.

"Do you think there's any chance we can talk about this tomorrow? I've had a really, *really* crappy day."

Luke nodded thoughtfully, hands in his jean pockets. "Sure, though I'm more worried you *don't* want to talk to me. You're usually bending my ear about something."

"I know," she laughed, her voice thick with tears. "Are you feeling better?"

He scratched at his head, tugging on his hair. "Yeah, it must be stomach flu. I feel fine. I'll be home around midnight if you're still awake. Though, you look beat."

"Have a good shift," she said. He shrugged, accepting he was being dismissed when she charged out of her bed and flew across the room. Win practically winded him; he lost his breath as she flung her arms around his neck, burying her face in his hair, till her own breath grew hot against her skin.

"I love you." She hugged him tighter. "I just want you to know."

Gingerly he wrapped his arms around her back, patting her. "Uh…What's going on?"

"Nothing. I'm hormonal," she lied, pulling out of his arms, wiping her face.

"You've cried all over my shirt."

She brushed at the damp spot on his shirt, feeling the beat of his heart underneath, it pulsed faster, and when she glanced up, a red blush had sprawled up his neck. His throat bobbed. "I've… got to go to work!" He pointed at her and then waved at the bed. "Sleep this weirdness off!"

She smiled, waiting for him to leave before she started up again. But she had a horrible feeling he could hear her bawling from the other end of the corridor.

Twelve

Rowan circled the canopy, drawing up her talons and descending in a sharp dive. Eyes narrowing to pinpoints, she splayed her claws, the air rushing through the rivets of her golden feathers as she swooped onto unsuspecting prey. A small, brown bunny made a frantic dash from its burrow. Rowan snatched it in her claws. The small creature struggled, its chest heaving as she took it higher, rendering it unconscious from shock.

Poor little thing. Rowan dropped it to the ground, giving its belly a sharp slash with her talons before picking it apart with her beak. She made quick work of it, necking the remains of its entrails, leaving the carcass for the foxes.

I saw that. Gross Rowan! A voice came from below, and Rowan went into a dive, meeting Win in a small clearing. The sun was rising above the dank, miserable clouds, another day of heavy fall rain predicted, but the sun gleamed off Win's sleek back.

Rowan landed. *Just doing what I do, Win. You should try it sometime.*

I'd rather starve.

The jaguar let her jaw sag, panting lightly, and lower fangs gleamed with saliva. She made a deep, chugging purr, emitting from the center of her chest. *Anything?*

Rowan had a sense of déjà vu. They'd been out here before, but now not only were they searching for their mother, there was another, very large and very dangerous predator on the loose. Rowan and Win talked late into the night, long after Ben had gone to sleep, looking up possibilities on Win's laptop.

"Was it a lynx? Or some kind of leopard?" Rowan had grown tired, irritated. How could a cat that large be circling their land and she not know?

"It was silver? At least, I think so."

Win had been entirely rattled after her meeting with Jake Fraser, which she had filled her in on. Rowan promised at first light, they would both go out together. Except Win didn't seem to have any firm details, other than she'd been spooked. After being dragged into Mercy, she was massively unsettled.

Win found the log they had stashed their clothes under. *I'm not helping much.*

Rowan landed next to her. *You're here.*

Win vanished into a thicket, appearing five minutes later, nude and dashing to the log for her clothes. Rowan was already dressed when she got there. The more you phased, the quicker you got, and Rowan was a pro these days. She'd even managed to phase mid-flight on the odd occasion if she concentrated hard enough. This often resulted in falling several feet from the sky, stark naked, and a bumpy landing, rolling through broken twigs. Still, it was fun to push herself. Before Win appeared, she scanned the tree line, her heart sinking. Taking a deep, lungful of air through her nose, she tried to detect any signs of the falcon. But the air was light and fresh, and her stomach sank.

I'm going to fly out tonight, Rowan promised. *Scan the outer areas and see if she's nearby.*

What if the animal I saw is connected…?

Don't go there yet! She's out here somewhere…

Rowan sat on the damp grass, her back to the log, and took out a water bottle she'd hidden in among their things. She threw back her head and drank greedily, washing away the taste of vermin; it had left a tang on her tongue. Win plopped down beside her, and Rowan pulled out another bottle. Silence wafted between them, neither wanting to admit their darkest fears. That something unspeakable had happened to the falcon.

"Thank you," Win unscrewed the cap. "I don't like this, Rowan. How could we not know this thing was out here?"

Rowan waved her hands. "Because, whatever this thing is, it's damn good at hiding its tracks. I've seen nothing out here, and trust me, I'm looking. I've been out looking for Mom."

"I know what I saw." Win necked her water, wiping her chin. "At least I think I do."

"Well, we've run out of time," Rowan said. "The police are going to be here today. They'll set up the equipment and tents. Maybe they'll have better luck than we have?"

Win threw back her head, resting her neck on the log. "I'm going to have to be careful."

"They'll shoot you, Win," Rowan warned her. "You can't go anywhere near these woods after today. In fact, we'll have to take you out for you to phase, find somewhere else safe, out of town."

"Makes me sound like a dog that needs walking." Win rolled her eyes.

Rowan noticed the way Win bit relentlessly at the skin around her nails, her edgy tone. She leaned nearer, placing a warm hand on her shoulder.

"Have you said anything yet? To Luke?"

Win shook her head, chewing on her lower lip. "About his father? No."

"You're going to have to, soon. A guy like Jake will want to make his presence known eventually. And you don't want Luke finding out by his father walking into the bar or something. It'll be gentler coming from you."

Win listened but stared into the distance. "He was so cold, Rowan. I can't believe he's just given up on his son. He didn't seem to care at all, and he's not going to fight this emancipation."

Rowan half-smiled. "Nah, I don't buy it. I think he cares. He's here, isn't he?"

"Then why is he acting like this?"

Rowan sipped from her bottle. "Because fathers can be weird. Trust me."

Win threw her a look of disdain. "Dad's not weird. He loves you."

Rowan heaved a sigh and decided now wasn't the time to get into this conversation. Win had a cloudy view of what had occurred in the early years. She didn't want Win to remember how she was drugged, how she used to lose hours, sometimes days of memory, thanks to her meds mixing with her Therian blood. Before Cedar Wood, so much of Rowan's early life was a hazy mess. Ben did his best, but his refusal to accept the truth set her back years.

"And," Rowan paused for effect. "You should talk to Luke about what's happening to him. We have to figure out a way to get him through this."

"I'm working up to it. It's hard to know how to break the news that he's about to change into…" her words dried up, tears filling her eyes. "If he makes it…."

Rowan squeezed her hand. "He will. Uncle Willard doesn't know everything. We'll get him through it—somehow—but you can't keep this from him. And…" she paused. "Keep this animal thing to yourself for now. Let's not terrify everyone. Everyone is being careful, and we are literally about to be surrounded by police. No walking off alone, no phasing on the property without me—especially at night!"

Win's features pulled together, and she nodded like she was mulling something over, something she couldn't put into words. Rowan could only imagine the guilt she must feel. When a minute passed, and her sister said nothing, Rowan touched her hand gently. "Evan will know what to do. We can figure this out."

"Rowan?" Win's voice pulled her out of her daze. The sun was beaming through a cloud now; it was nearly six in the morning. "Did you ever meet Luke's dad? When you were with Spencer?"

Rowan drew her brow together, thinking hard, searching her jagged memory banks. "No, I don't think so."

"He said he met you once."

"I don't remember," Rowan said. "Sounds like you two had a long chat."

Win ducked her eyes, a red streak dashing across her freckled nose. Rowan's mouth dropped open in mock horror, and then she threw back her head and cackled with laughter. "Oh, *Win*."

"*What?*"

"You think he's hot!"

"I do *not*!"

Rowan rolled to her side, cackling. "Interesting."

"Shut up!" Win covered her face and then burst into giggles. "He's as old as Dad. That's gross!"

"I'm teasing you. Take it easy."

"He isn't a good guy. I'm fairly certain there had been a woman in that bathroom, like hours before I was in there. It was so strange…he gave off this vibe!"

"You mean like, a confident vibe?"

"Hmm, I guess."

"So, like an *attractive* vibe?" Rowan grinned, noticing her sister's neck breaking out in a rash.

Win punched Rowan's arm. "That's disgusting!"

"It's okay. I'm only messing with you." Rowan smoothed out Win's tumbled curls with the flat of her hand. Win puffed. "If it makes you feel better, Spencer was kind of the same."

Win's chin lifted. "He was?"

"Of course! He was confident, driven, and I couldn't stay away from him. But I was fairly clueless. And there was this pull, energy between us. Now, if what you've told me is true, and it's a weird Therian connection, it seems I would have fallen for him no matter what."

Win twisted her body in Rowan's direction. "Does it make it easier? Now you know you couldn't help it. That we are all... linked."

Rowan exhaled, staring up at the sky. "Look, Win. This might come as a shock to you, but my relationship with Spencer wasn't all bad. Do I wish he wasn't a distant relative? Yes, absolutely. Do I wish he hadn't spent five years gaslighting me? Hell, yes! But...I can't change what happened, and I'm a stronger person for it. There were parts of our relationship that were...okay."

Win made a disgusted face, her jaw sagging. "You mean the sex part!"

"That's not what I said!" Rowan argued. "I mean, there were moments when, genuinely, he got me through some tough times. But the guy *did* shoot me, so he loses any points he may have won."

"I guess that's how I feel about Grayson," Win added thoughtfully, drawing Rowan back to the present. "I can't hate him for what he did."

No, but I can. Rowan thought but then knew she had no right to judge. Grayson used Win, and then left her in the woods, breaking her heart. Rowan pressed her lips together and said nothing. They would only end up fighting. Win rested her elbow on the gnarled log, propping her chin on her hand.

"It's weird Luke isn't like them. He isn't like Jake or Spencer. He doesn't have the same vibe!" Win thought aloud.

For the second time that morning, Rowan burst out laughing. Win's brow drew to a frown, incredulous and defiant. "What? He *doesn't*!"

Rowan wiped her eyes. It struck her how utterly clueless her sister was, especially when it came to Luke. Rowan couldn't work out if her sister was blind, oblivious, or even if she secretly suspected something and was having a fun game of her own. But Win wasn't cruel, not in the slightest, so she came to the conclusion she was just naive. "If you say so!"

Win hopped to her feet, her skin red. "I've had enough of you teasing me. I've got school, and I need a shower!"

As she stalked away, trudging through the long, dewy grass, Rowan couldn't resist one last dig. "Make it a cold one!"

"*Shut up!*"

Rowan allowed herself a brief moment of respite, drawing up one knee to her chest and gazing across the clearing, Win's footsteps retreating into the distance. The birds tweeted as they hopped across the branches, the leaves rustled, and the air was crisp and clean—a perfect fall morning. Rowan breathed deeply and rose to her feet. It was perfect, so tranquil out here. It was too bad she was being watched.

Rowan squared her shoulders stiffly, lifted her chin, and jogged into the woods. Her senses were on high alert, though she couldn't be absolutely sure how long the stranger had been watching. While Win had been dying with embarrassment, Rowan sensed an odd stillness in the air, her eyes drawn to a flock of birds rocketing out of the bushes, lifting into the sky, like gulls sensing a shark circling beneath them. Her gaze flicked back and forth, watching for movement.

Rowan balled her fists, her neck tingling as the bushes rustled behind her. She held her breath, closed her eyes, and waited. When she heard the whisper of his breath, she catapulted around on one leg, her foot sailing behind her, kicking her intruder squarely in the chest. Air whooshed through the hunter's teeth; he grunted and landed on his back. Before he even managed to hoist himself up, Rowan was on him. She jumped, landing on his chest, straddling his hips.

His pale eyes went wide as she balled up her fist and smacked him in the jaw, his whole head flying right, and Rowan was able to grab a fist of his hood and yank it away, including the mask he'd been wearing. Out of the hood spilled a shock of white-blonde hair cut short around his ears. From Win's wistful, dreamy description of him, Rowan expected a character from Lord of the Rings. She grinned viscously. "I knew it was you!"

She went to punch him again, but he cried out and held up both his hands. "I wasn't going to hurt you!"

She'd left a nasty welt across his lower lip, her eyes drawn to the scars. Win had described them, but in the light of day, they were a sight to behold. Three long, clean claw marks ran from under his ear, under his cheekbone, and under his lower lip. Grayson panted, his eyes wild and hurt. "Get off me, *now*!"

"No way…not until you…!"

He grabbed her by the shoulders, throwing her over his head, but to his surprise, she tucked and rolled, landing deftly on her feet. When she uncurled and rose to her full height, he mirrored her stance, all six foot four of him towering over her. "I'm not here to hurt you, I swear!"

"Do you honestly think stalking is romantic?" she flung at him, holding up her balled fists. He wiped his lip, blood welling from the graze she'd inflicted.

"I'm not stalking…at least I'm not stalking you or Win. I'm…"

He didn't finish. Rowan picked up a rock and flung it at him, it hit him in the shoulder, and he growled as it bounced off his heavy jacket. He ducked the next one, which she aimed at his head. "Will you *stop*?" he barked, holding up both palms.

"Not until I hit you in that stupid, thick head of yours!" As he leaped out of her way, she managed to take him all in. Mostly everything Win described was true— the scars, the hunter camouflage, and the crossbow strapped to his wide back. He was broad, bigger than most men she knew. Slim hips, a narrow waist, and long powerful legs, with feet, shoved into heavy leather boots, covered with mud. His face was strangely wholesome, handsome, with straight features and those big, pale eyes. For a moment, Rowan could see why Win was so infatuated. *Almost.*

"Why...can't you..leave her alone?" she gasped between throws, her rock supply dwindling. She yanked a heavy branch from a tree, her upper biceps flexing as she lifted it with ease, even he looked marginally impressed.

"Are you going to beat me with that?"

"I will if you don't get the hell off our land."

"I'm here to help you!"

Rowan laughed. "Does it look like we need your help?"

Grayson shook his head. "I don't know. You don't seem to have much of a handle on this situation."

Anger bubbling up to the surface, she flew at him in temper, lunging with the branch, but he caught her waist, flipping her round so hard it slipped out of her hands. He seized both her wrists, crossing them over her chest, yanking her back against him as she struggled. Blind panic tore into her; she could feel his chest pressing into her back. "Let me go!" She wriggled and fought, her legs slipping from under her in the mud.

"Then *you* calm down!" he snarled. He was struggling, not expecting her strength. She could feel him waning, becoming tired. With a jerk, she threw her head back, head-butting his chin. Black spots exploded in her vision, a crack of splintering pain rocketing through her head, but it was worth it. He dropped her like she was on fire.

"Shit!" He rubbed his mouth. "*Time out!*"

Rowan whirled about, grabbing her branch and going in for another hit. He kicked her legs out from under her, and she landed, smack on her ribs, knocking the air right out of her.

"I said *time out!*"

Rowan rolled onto her back, cradling her ribs. "Ow."

Drawing a raspy breath, Grayson got to his feet and stood over her. "Are you alright?"

"Hmm," Rowan hummed, though her eyes watered. He held out a hand, encased in fingerless gloves, his nails short and bitten down to the beds.

"Come on. Truce." He grabbed her forearm and tugged her to her feet. Rowan whistled, rubbing her torso. She lifted the edge of her tank top to reveal a purple bruise blossoming over her pale skin.

"I think I cracked a rib." The pain knifed through her.

"I'm sorry…I never meant to hurt you."

"I'll be fine." She bent double as she wandered to a trunk and leaned her weight on it. "Give me a day to recover, and I'll be back for round two."

Grayson rubbed his jaw. "I wish I could say the same." He flexed his jaw back and forth, the welt on his lip swelling, he dabbed at it with his tongue. "I'm not here to hurt you. And I know Win isn't interested in seeing me."

For a split second, she let guilt creep up her neck, something about the way he'd said that sounded so lost, pathetic. "How do you know?"

"I've left signs and notes…I know it's crazy. I was hoping she'd want to see me…but I guess she's done. I can't say I blame her after what I did."

Rowan tensed her jaw, letting the guilt wash over her. Instead, she nodded. "She's dating some boy in school. She's moved on, Grayson. You should let her move on!"

His face crumbled, he chewed on his ruined lower lip, and Rowan's conscience was close to caving. He looked so crushed, and those eyes of his. Rowan looked away, knowing he was getting to her.

"News travels around here, and I heard rumors about the big cat sightings—and the killings. I had to see for myself," he said, changing the subject.

Rowan hardly believed what she said next. "The cops are going to set up surveillance around here today. You can't be here, Grayson. You'll get caught."

You could have let him walk straight into a trap! Rowan didn't think she could sink that low. He causally peeled off his gloves, his eyes flicking around their woodland surroundings.

"I've lived in these woods all my life Rowan. I'm used to staying hidden."

"Yeah, I know!" She rolled her eyes. "Win thought she saw you in Mickleford a few days ago."

He nodded. "It's where I've been living. I have a job there too, at the lumber yard."

"She came looking for you."

He ducked his head. "I know. I hid."

"Like a coward!" Rowan flung at him. He snapped his head up sharply, eyes narrowed and dangerous like a predator.

"Thanks!" He scrubbed at his face, raking his fingers through his short, blonde hair. "I wasn't ready…I didn't want her to see me like that!"

Rowan chortled, laced with pain as she slid to her feet, using the trunk of the tree to push her up. "Like what? Working at your job? I hate to break it to you, Grayson, but women look for certain qualities in a guy. A home and a job come pretty high on the list! Running around the woods in camo gear is a bit worrying and not the kind of quality I'd hope for in a guy dating my sister."

"I'm not dating her, am I?" he growled, wounded. "I'm not here for her."

"Bullshit."

"Well, maybe…but I'm here because something is very wrong. I heard about the girl who went missing from Lincoln. There is something dangerous in this forest. Other than you."

"We know. I have it under control."

"Do you?"

"Yes! You don't need to be here."

"There was another body, Rowan."

Rowan froze, her lip dropping. Grayson took a heavy step toward her, leaning against a tree. He smirked, glad to have rendered her speechless. "What?"

"It's true." He waved his hand in the air. "I wish it wasn't."

"Who is it? The cops haven't said anything…."

"Cops don't know. I found him in the woods near my old cabin, half washed away in the brook about four weeks ago. I went home to check on the old place and see what the cops left after the fire. I found the guy—half-eaten." He shuddered, wiped his mouth. "I buried him."

"Do you know who he was?"

"He didn't have anything on him. But he looked like a homeless guy. Perhaps he was a wanderer and using the cabin for shelter? I found a camp bed in the old place. But then the girl went missing, and then the zoologist. This thing has a two-week feeding pattern."

Wow, he was useful. Someone who, if not entirely unredeemable in her eyes, could be a powerful ally. Rowan allowed herself a moment to feel some gratitude toward him. She lifted her chin in defiance. "Thank you for telling me. You don't have to keep a lookout, though. We have it handled."

"This means, if the cops don't catch the thing, it'll feed again!"

"I get it!" she snipped.

"And I'm terrified it'll be one of you next."

Rowan puffed. He had a point. "We've lived in these woods for years, Grayson. It's our home. We can take care of ourselves."

"Can you, though? You're here right now, unprotected, unarmed. You brought her out in the woods, defenseless. And you all flit around like there's no danger. It may not be you or Win, but it might be the kid you live with, or your girlfriend—or your father. What this thing did…."

"Grayson, stop!" Rowan cried. He was horribly right, but she wasn't about to let him see. "This is my home. I'm the alpha now, and you need to let me handle it."

He smiled, wickedly which was disarming. "You're not *my* alpha, and I'm not leaving."

"Yes, you *are!"*

"You can't make me!"

"I can call the cops!" she spat back, angry at his defiance.

"You'll hurt Win if you do."

And I'll have to admit what I've been hiding. Rowan chewed the inside of her mouth, rubbing the back of her aching neck. She thought of all his 'signs,' the notes she'd been collecting in a box. Nausea welled in her gut. If Win found out…. Rowan wasn't sure why she'd kept them, only it felt a step too far to trash them. And something in his writing tugged her insides.

"Do what you want," she said at last. "But I don't want you near my sister. She's been through enough. She just about makes it through one day at a time."

Rowan wished she hadn't said anything because he crumpled again, exhaling and puffing like he was in some inner agony. It occurred to her how insane it was. Win had two very different but interesting guys fawning all over her. Luke, who was still young, cute, and about to explode out of his skin into god, only knows what. And Grayson built like a Norseman, who could flatten Luke with one hit.

And I ended up with a guy who tried to kill me! She nearly laughed. Thank god for Evan, beautiful, sweet, and hers. Rowan had missed her. Not having her in bed was hard enough, but she was her best friend, and she ached for her to come home. Grayson took a great stride toward her, took her hand, placed a folded piece of paper in her palm, then wrapped her fingers around it. "My number…I have a phone too!"

Rowan sniggered, willing down the heat creeping up her neck. She snatched her hand away. "Wow, you're really in the modern world now. You'll be tweeting next."

Grayson frowned. "I don't know what that means. But please, take it. And if you are worried, call me. I'm not Therian, but I know this wood, backward. And I don't want anyone getting killed."

Reluctantly, she nodded, folding the paper into her pocket, knowing she would have to trash it. If Win found out they'd spoken—she didn't even want to imagine how she'd react. Win was already torn up and broken, in bits over Luke and grieving over a man who stood less than a mile from their home.

Without saying goodbye, she walked out of the woods, wading through the wet grass until she reached the boggy backyard. Feeling eyes at her back, she turned and spotted him lingering in the treeline, a part of her touched he'd seen her home.

Inside the house, she walked in on Luke and Win arguing over breakfast, tossing insults to one another across the table. It amazed Rowan that Win still found the energy to annoy him. Win had raided his underwear drawer and stolen all his boxer shorts. Luke seethed and threatened swift vengeance.

Rowan slipped into the chair next to her father. He lowered his paper and smiled at her across the top. He threw her a long gaze, thoughtful, and part of Rowan wished he *would* notice she was in some measure of pain. It hurt to breathe, like a knife slipping between her ribs.

Luke threw a piece of toast across the table, hitting Win in the forehead. She squealed, rising from her chair, and dashed out of the room. Luke sprang out of his chair and chased her. Thankfully, upstairs Win's bedroom door slammed shut, with Luke safely on the other side and Win cackling in her room. The crash rocketed through the house, shaking the floor, and Ben whistled through his teeth.

"I want one pair Win! One pair—you can't let me go to school with nothing!" He banged on the door, and on the other side, she howled with laughter.

"He's not borrowing mine," Ben said. After a few seconds, Luke appeared at the foot of the stairs, wearing a beseeching look and a bashful gaze.

"Ben…"

"Oh, for god's sake, they're in the top draw!" Ben huffed impatiently, his voice following Luke back upstairs.

Rowan smirked. "He should've never touched her socks."

"It's like having puppies!" Ben exclaimed in exasperation. "You okay, honey?"

Rowan flinched but plastered on her best, false smile. The paper burned a hole in her pocket, and without thinking any more about it, she got up and tossed it in the trash.

Thirteen

The day rolled by, and in the afternoon, Win arrived home to find her home was now a major crime scene. Slamming the door of the truck, she passed several uniformed officers armed with shotguns, casually strolling the length of their yard. When one of them tipped their hat to her, she fell into despair, wondering how she was ever going to sneak past them. A small team headed into the woods, ready to set up surveillance cameras and bait, and a few tents had been erected close to the drive.

Already her skin itched and burned. This time of day was usually the hardest to endure, and eventually, she would have to phase into the animal before it burst out of her at the wrong time. But how was she going to keep a jaguar in her bedroom? Her options were severely limited right now.

On the kitchen table sat a rectangular cardboard box. Win peered at the label, seeing her name scrawled in neat handwriting in marker pen, and her stomach sank. It was the diary. Willard had made good on his promise to send it to her.

She clutched it to her chest, jogging up the stairs, passing Rowan's bedroom, surprised to see her father sitting on the edge of her bed. She was about to wave and make her presence known when she heard her father groan.

"I'll only be gone a week this time."

"Dad, it was two weeks last time, and you only just got back!"

His eyes flicked up when he saw Win lingering in the door. "Hey, baby."

Win's shoulders sagged. "You're leaving again."

"Look, I'm sorry." Ben threw up his hands in despair. "I have to take this job, the plans are being pushed through, and time is tight. I want to be here, but I also have to pay the bills."

Rowan perched on the window ledge, arms crossed, and she visibly recoiled at the mention of paying bills. "Fine, go," she said after a while. "We'll manage."

"What are you going to do about Win?"

Win made a noise in her throat, annoyed they talked over her like a three-year-old.

"Let us worry about that. We'll figure something out, even if I have to drive her out to a field somewhere."

Exhaustion pulled at her, and she retreated out of the room, closing the door and flopping onto the bed. The box lay at her side. She felt like a pet needing to be let out, the weight of burden settling on her shoulders. She yanked the box open, the smell of old, musty cardboard wafting up at her, revealing the green and gold, leather-bound diary inside. Tugging it out, she fingered the spine, a tingle of dread creeping up out of nowhere. Swallowing, tightly, she knew she must talk to Luke, who right now was getting ready for his shift.

Win had dallied with the idea all day, the knowledge of Jake back in town, eating her insides. But Rowan was right. What if Jake casually bumped into him? What if he told him she'd been with him, in his house? Luke would kill her. Still, it had to come from her. Staring at the diary, she sighed and slipped it under her pillow, thinking it would make some unsettling bedtime reading. She needed to talk to him about what would happen to him, his fate lingering on her conscience.

Start with Jake! She sucked in her breath. *And then, deal with the rest.*

Quickly, she stripped out of the jeans and sweater she'd been wearing all day. Ella was heading over, and as it was Friday night, they had planned to go to Hardy's for dinner to keep Luke company at the bar. Win supposed she could unload on Ella at the same time.

She grabbed a short, black floral dress from the closet. It was Evan's, one she'd loaned Win. Win complained she had nothing pretty that fit, and they were virtually the same size now. A prickle of fear nudged her conscience. She hadn't even thought about Ella. Her best friend finally had the boy she'd yearned after since they were five, and now, something awful was going to happen to him.

Something isn't going to happen. You'll get him through his… you have to.

It dawned on her that he might not be able to leave Cedar Wood. He wouldn't be able to travel, go to New York to college. Her breathing quickened. Nerves erupting in her chest, she jogged back downstairs and tapped on his door. *It's now or never.* When it swung open, he was buttoning up his shirt, peering closely at his reflection in the mirror. "Come on in, why don't you," he drawled, side-eyeing her.

"I knocked."

"I didn't say to come in, did I? I could have been naked in here."

She rolled her eyes. "Lucky me, you aren't. What are you doing?"

He tore his eyes away from the dirty mirror, it was dusty, and the whole room smelled like a boy's pit. "I need a shave, but I don't have time," he said, and Win chuckled despite the nagging feeling this was yet another side effect. *Start with Jake…see how he reacts.*

"It's fine. It works on you."

He laughed and turned to the mirror again, poking and prodding at his face. "It wouldn't be so bad if it grew evenly—look!" He jumped at her, holding out his forearms and pointing to the dark patches of hair running down to his wrist. "Where's this coming from? It's everywhere. I thought only old guys had this problem!"

Win attempted to conceal a smirk, but she giggled. "Guess you're having a surge of hormones?"

"I hate it! I might have to wax! What are *you* wearing?"

Win paused, her eyes dropping to her dress. "It's Evan's."

"It's too short!"

"It fits me." She fingered the hem. "I don't have anything pretty."

"Sure you do. What about –uh—the yellow sweater. The bulky thing you wear?"

Win narrowed her eyes in dismay. "I'm having a night out, not going for a hike!" This wasn't why she was in here. "I need to talk to you. *Now.* Before, you go anywhere else!"

Luke threw on his glasses, blinked rapidly, pulling them off again and cleaning them on the edge of his shirt. He fell on the bed and patted the space beside him. "Sounds ominous."

Butterflies exploded in her tummy. She plopped down on the mattress beside him, hardly able to look him in the eye as she recounted how she discovered Mercy was reoccupied and its owner. When she finished, she glanced up at him, and his jaw was tight enough to crack a nut. This wasn't the day for part two of this talk, she quickly decided.

"So that's where you were?" he asked stiffly. "And why you were so weird when I came up to see you?"

"Before you tear into me, I didn't know how to break it to you." Her words flew out in a stumbled rush. "I'm so sorry. I feel terrible I didn't tell you earlier. I was so freaked out by it all. And… he's such a *dick!*"

Luke sucked in air through his nose. "So…you went in the house?"

Her cheeks reddened. "Yeah. I got soaked from the rain, and Judy gave me one of your old sweaters to wear." There was a territorial gleam in his eye, protective and primal, but her nerves got the better of her, and she spilled out things before she had a chance to think straight. "I think he's dating again. Do you know he and Carla are divorcing? When I was up in his bathroom…?"

"*What?*" Luke exploded off the bed like a grenade had gone off under his backside. "You went into his *bathroom?*"

"I had to get changed somewhere!"

"What…you…*no*, Win *no*!" Luke collapsed down on the bed, his head lolling in his hands.

"What's wrong?"

Luke sat up, his face cracking in a sarcastic smile. "Wow, just *wow*. You must have made an impression. Do you know how many times I was allowed to go into my father's side of the house when I was a kid? Hardly ever. Do you know *why*?"

Win withdrew, feeling like she was about to hate the answer. "No."

"Because there was always some…*woman* he'd tucked away down there. I've lost count of the times I walked in on some hooker getting dressed or him making out with his secretary. While my *mother was* busy running his home!"

Win's face burned, she buttoned her lip, deciding rapidly she didn't need to say a thing more. Luke steamed, his eyes flashing, and if he could have growled, he would. Her eyes filled up.

"Please don't yell at me! I didn't know."

"I can't stand the thought of it!" He stood, paced, and loomed over her, hands-on-hips. "He didn't say anything *else*, did he?"

Win's heart sped up a notch, and she ducked her eyes. "No."

"Hmm, I find that hard to believe."

"Is that all you care about? I was sick with nerves about telling you."

He shoved his hands through his hair, then took off his glasses and pinched the bridge of his nose, leaving Win to wonder if he was in pain. "I don't give a crap he's here as long as he never speaks to me. Wait…Spencer wasn't..?"

"No," Win assured him. "Although he said something odd— he would be along eventually. Whatever that means."

"Nothing good. Sounds like you two had a cozy chit chat." He settled next to her again, having hopped up and down several times. He placed a hand on her shoulder. "Look, thank you for telling me. I know you were only looking out for me. But please, *please*, do not go on his land again. He's my dad, and I know what he's like. You were lucky he didn't call the cops."

"I won't— I swear!"

"Just be *good* for once." He rubbed at his eyes as if to nurse a dull ache. Win let her fingertips trail to his temple, pushing back a swathe of his hair, tucking it behind his ear. He jerked reflexively.

"Are you in pain?" she asked, but he was already on his feet, out of her reach when she went to touch his shoulder.

He jumped up, pulling her up with him by the wrists. "I'm good. Now let me get ready."

She wandered to the door, letting it creak open. "I'll see you at the bar."

He collapsed on the bed again, resting his elbows on his knees, rubbing his eyes, pushing his glasses up to his forehead. "See you there. And Win…?"

"Yeah."

"Put something on that covers your ass. Please!"

She huffed, shaking her head. "I'll borrow your jacket, then."

Luke, feigning exhaustion, fell back on the bed, covering his eyes. "Whatever. Only for tonight, and start buying your own clothes. You got makeup on it last time."

Win tried to smile, closed the door, wishing she could tell him everything. Only she didn't think he'd have the strength to hear it.

Ben paused before unlocking Evan's apartment door, taking in a shaky breath. He puffed, and then pushed it open. He never knew what awaited him on the other side. Often it was nothing good. Usually, it was a mess, clothes strewn across the floor, food smeared anywhere Alice could throw it. But as the door swung back and revealed the short corridor to the living room, it was dark and quiet, apart from the glow of the television spilling across the room, illuminating the features of his eldest's pretty girlfriend. She sat cross legged, barefoot on the rug. Her hair tumbled off her bare shoulder as he crept into the living room.

"How are you?" he asked before Evan waved her hand and signaled for him to shush. Alice was curled up on the sofa, a pillow tucked under her chest, hugging it tight. Evan jumped to her feet and guided him to the kitchen. When he turned the corner, his heart broke.

"She's been asleep for the last hour." He noticed the dark smudges under her eyes. "She's been frantic, asking for you."

Ben's heart lifted. "She asked for me?"

Evan nodded, rubbing her eyes. "How long did you say you'd be gone?" Ben recognized the guilt on her face. She hated every minute of lying to Rowan—he hated it too.

"I didn't give specifics," he answered. "But this can't go on much longer. We are needed at home."

"We should have been honest from the start," Evan agreed, and Ben recalled it had been her directive to keep Alice's whereabouts from Rowan and Win. He'd argued the point. Being home would help her recover, but Evan was urgent she remained undiscovered. Part of Ben wondered if Evan knew what she was doing. She seemed unprepared for this version of Alice.

Evan rubbed her arms, she looked so tired and small, and he thought if she were one of his girls, he would have hugged her.

The toll the lie was taking was becoming more evident, the creases around her eyes deepened. In the early days, they'd been so optimistic. Their objective was to get Alice well and bring her home. But as the weeks dwindled on, and Alice made no signs of wanting to communicate with them, his hope withered. And the lying became harder. Looking at Rowan in the eyes killed him, knowing how much she worried. It was cutting her in half, knowing her mother was missing.

"Alice said something odd," Evan said, glancing up. "About Luke's father?"

Ben did his best to remain steely neutral, his standard expression when it came to Jake Fraser. The name stuck in his throat. *Jake*. It churned his guts. "Oh?"

Evan groaned. "Ben. What the hell is going on? What did Alice have to do with Jake?"

Ben leaned against the kitchen counter, folding his arms, non-committal, avoiding her stare. "It doesn't matter. He isn't in Cedar Wood."

"I think it matters. It matters to her— she's terrified of him."

"She doesn't need to be. I'm here."

Evan made a face, narrowing her eyes, clearly not liking the answer he gave. "Do you think he could help her?"

Ben's eyes flew wide as though he'd been slapped. "No! He doesn't help anyone—certainly not her. I can deal with this, Evan, I always have."

Evan was prying now, and he was becoming irritated, feeling trapped against the counter with her leaning closer. "She said you both ran away? That isn't dealing with it, Ben."

The look he threw her was enough to make her back off. She didn't understand. She couldn't. "You ought to get back to the girls," he said with finality. Evan sighed, defeated, grabbing her suitcase propped in the hall. Ben didn't like disagreeing with her, he felt naturally at ease with Evan, and she'd given him the ultimate gift, his wife. But Jake...he couldn't talk about him.

"Fine. Move her to the bedroom—the lights from the cars

outside flash sometimes and scare her," Evan said, with the authority of a parent discussing the wayward behavior of a child.

Ben didn't reply as Evan shoved her arms in her coat. Before she left, she crossed the kitchen and put a warm palm on his clenched, folded arms. "I didn't mean to upset you. I'll do anything to help her. Anything that means we can move forward, and we can stop this awful charade."

Grimly, he nodded, patting her hand where it sat. "I know. I'll see what the next few days bring."

She smiled and closed the door softly after her as she left. Quietly, Ben padded into the living room, where Alice had rolled onto her back, her breathing even—spirited away in a peaceful dream. He lifted her, she weighed practically nothing, and instinctively she wrapped her arms around his neck. For a moment, he was twenty again, and he imagined carrying her into their first apartment in town, where Rowan was born. His thoughts darkened as he kicked open the bedroom door. The place they'd run from—the life they abandoned.

Ben shook the fear away, knowing Jake couldn't hurt them here. He carried his wife to bed.

Win and Ella had to linger in the door of Hardy's when they arrived. The building was rammed. Standing on tiptoe, peering over the sea of heads already crowded at the bar, Win spotted several students from school. Outside, the rain pelted the sidewalks, the red neon sign reflecting on the shiny, wet surface. Win hadn't bothered to change, only threw on a pair of boots and Luke's jacket, but now she had damp legs. She shivered and huddled closer to Ella, who waved down a waitress. "I think she just cleared the table!" Ella said in relief, turning her gaze to Win. She fingered the seam of the faded denim jacket Win was wearing, an odd smile playing on her lips. "You look great. That dress is cute!"

"It's Evan's. It's not too short?"

Ella beamed and winked. "You have good legs!"

Finally, they stuffed themselves into the bulk of the restaurant, and Hazel, one of Rowan's friends, showed them to a booth near the pool table. The air was thick, the rain driving everyone inside.

The bar was six people deep, and the restaurant was bustling with activity. Win craned her neck and spotted Luke tearing around, a pencil behind his ear, his apron stained with oil. He carried trays of fries, one perched precariously on his shoulder.

Ella pulled out the menu. "You want anything?"

Win's stomach was too acidic, the bubbles whirling around making her queasy. She was still uneasy after her conversation with Luke. Win hadn't had a moment to let the jaguar out of the cage. Her bones ached to stretch, her skin hot and itchy. She told herself she could make it one night without phasing, and hopefully, she'd sleep it off when she got home.

As Luke strolled away to the kitchens, she shook her head. "You order what you want."

Ella made a face. "But then you end up eating mine!" she complained but then shouted over to Luke for some fries. After a short while, her large brown eyes flicked to the door, and she ground her teeth. "Great, guess who just arrived."

Win stretched her neck, squinting through the dim light. Rosene walked in with a guy she knew from school on her arm. Then they were followed in by Cole Ward. Win groaned.

"Cole is here too."

Ella shrugged out of her jacket, fanning out the long dark hair curled around her shoulders. "You said you wanted to talk to me?"

Win's attention snapped back to her friend in anticipation. She drummed her hands on the tabletop, hardly able to find the words. The bar was busy, a thrum filling the air, she was confident no one could listen in. "Luke is sick."

"He looks fine." Ella's eyes widened. Her head snapped in his direction, he was oblivious, serving a customer and had ducked to his knees to take a small child's order.

"No," Win stammered. "I mean…he's changing. You know what we talked about? His moods? The sleepwalking?"

Ella's round, dark eyes pulled into a deep frown, she licked her lips then sagged back in her seat. When she didn't say anything for a long time, Win leaned forward. "Ella?"

"I should have guessed." Dismayed, she shook her head and Win guessed her friend would automatically blame herself for not noticing sooner.

"I didn't either!"

"It makes sense." She smoothed out her hair, her fingers trembling, and her eyes wet and shiny. "When will it happen?"

"I have no idea."

"*How* did this happen?"

Win ducked her eyes, hardly able to stand the heat of Ella's gaze. "It has something to do with the cabin fire when we released my ancestors. The blue light passed through him, and…my uncle seemed to think it woke up something inside him. In his blood."

Ella nodded, her gaze drawn away, staring into the distance. "But, he'll be okay, right? He'll just come through it like you did?"

Don't say die, don't say die….

"It's a little different for him."

Ella pursed her lips, her expression pensive. There was a fire smoldering under the surface. She was becoming hot, irritable and Win could sense the thud of her heart even in the dense atmosphere of the bar. It was precisely what Win had dreaded, Ella's wrath.

I've screwed everything up for her. I deserve it.

"Different, how?"

I killed her boyfriend.

Win's mouth was so dry she took a swig of her coke. "He isn't fully Therian. His body hasn't had time to prepare for what's happening to him. It'll be difficult."

Ella's eyes shone with wetness. "Difficult like he'll be in lots of pain?"

"Yes." She drummed the table. "But I think we have a way of helping him. I just need to figure this out."

"No, we figure it out together!" Ella snapped. "Tell me!"

Win lifted her gaze skyward and plowed through what her uncle told her, watching as Ella's face rapidly changed in expression. She didn't know if Ella could possibly take it all in. The diary, Luke changing, and most of all, how it was all linked to a long-deceased relative.

Ella drooped like a deflated balloon. Win could tell she was mentally going over everything.

"So, your uncle likes giving you cryptic clues, huh?" She laughed shakily.

"I don't know what to say." Win relaxed, her neck tightened with tension.

Ella stared over at Luke, exhaling loudly. "The only thing I care about is him."

"Me, too!"

"We have to find a way to get him through this, intact!" Ella was determined, her terror evaporating into decision. "We were going to spend the weekend together. I was coming over, but we could spend some time looking through the old diary?"

Win nodded. "I think Cole is coming by. I was meant to be helping him with his paper."

"You can still help him!" Ella seemed off, her gaze wandering and then falling on the jacket Win was wearing. "Have you told Luke about this yet?"

"No," Win admitted, ashamed of herself. "I was hoping you'd be there."

"You should be the one to tell him. You two are close."

Ella's tone worried Win. "What do you mean?"

Ella smiled, waving her hand breezily. "I mean…you're close… you're family. Why, what did you think I meant?"

Win drew back, her throat tightening. Then she smiled. "Nothing. You're right."

"Don't you think it's odd? How your mom went missing right after the cabin fire?" Ella thought aloud, bringing Win out of her melancholy. "The dream you had—your mom and now Luke. Do you think it could be connected?"

Win smiled, a rush of gratitude swelling inside her. She clasped Ella's hand across the table. "I'm so glad you're here. I feel like you actually hear me when I speak."

Ella managed a half-smile, squeezing Win's hand affectionately. "We'll get through this together."

Hazel approached the table with their fries, slamming them and the sauce caddy on the table before dashing off to her next customer. Win ate slowly, nibbling on the fries, but her stomach was in knots, and it didn't help that Ella seemed off, lost in thought. She washed her food down with coke, feeling like it might stick in her gullet. Rosene sauntered past their table, pausing to linger, throwing them both an acidic smile. She was wearing a black v neck dress, her long blonde hair billowing around her shoulders.

"You two look like someone died." Rosene paused by their booth, drink in hand. "Whatever could you be gossiping about?"

Ella visibly tensed, her shoulders drawing up to her ears. "Nothing you'd find interesting."

Rosene placed one manicured hand on their table, looming down over them, her gaze entirely focussed on Ella. "So I hear you're choosing to apply to a NY college."

Win ignored Rosene's fake sincerity as Ella's shoulders rose defense. "That's the plan—if I get in."

"Of course you'll get in, you'll walk it. A bookish type like you will have no trouble. Makes me wonder how you put up with Luke at all." At the venomous gibe Win's blood boiled, she went to open her mouth but Ella warned her with a look, and a sharp kick under the table.

"I wanted to speak to you, Ella. No hard feelings about what happened this summer with Luke, okay? I'm in a much better place now."

Win huffed, sitting on her hands, the blonde's fake sincerity irking her. "You know we never wanted you to get hurt, Rosene."

Rosene's pink lips pulled back in a sneer, veiled as a smile. "Of course. I completely understand how these things happen when you work together and hang out all the time. And you've lost so much weight, Ella…."

"I haven't, actually."

Rosene ignored her. "…it's no wonder he started to notice you."

Win bristled, leaning back in her seat to try and catch Luke's eye, but he was taking an order at another table. He'd broken out into a sweat. Ella straightened her shoulders and managed a bright smile. "But it worked out great. I mean…you're seeing Adam now, right?"

Rosene tossed the guy she'd arrived with a cool smile, her long icy hair whipping down her back. She lifted her fingers and waved at him. Adam was about six feet and had curly dark hair with deep ochre skin and dark eyes to match. He nabbed the pool table and was sharpening a cue. He smiled bashfully when he caught them all staring. Win met his eyes for a brief second and smiled back—poor guy, she almost felt sorry for him. Cole joined Adam at the table and pulled out a long cue. He gave Win a wink across the room.

"How about a game?" Rosene changed the subject.

Win's heart sank. She readied herself to say no, but to her horror, Ella slipped out of the booth. She lifted her chin in defiance. "I'd love to," she said, following Rosene across the crowded bar. Ella grabbed a cue and shot Win a look over her shoulder.

"Come *on*, Win!"

Oh, for god sake. Win reluctantly got to her feet, meeting Cole's appreciative gaze as she strolled across. Ella yanked Win down to hiss in her ear. "I know you don't play—but try! *Please.* I want to wipe the smug look off Rosene's face."

Smirking, Win nodded, loving Ella's secret competitive streak. Cole tossed her a cue, which she caught fluidly in one hand.

Cole grinned. "Whoa! Reflexes!" He laughed, and a mild look of panic crept across Rosene's pretty features. Win was usually content to watch from the sidelines when Luke and Ella played pool, protesting that she wasn't in the least bit competitive. But she sidled up to the table, hesitantly chalking her cue and dusting the flaky blue remnants on her dress. She leaned her hip against the table. "So, singles or teams?" she asked, trying to muster up some enthusiasm as Rosene threw her arm around Adam's broad shoulder.

"Teams, of course." She smiled sweetly.

"I'll rack them up." Ella wore a fierce look of determination on her face. Win hopped onto a bar stool, crossing her legs. Luke wandered past the table, giving her a death glare.

He mouthed to her, "what the hell are you doing?" to which Win could only shrug helplessly. Keen to break the tension, Win sloped away to buy a round of drinks. Adam decided to sit this game out, watching Rosene prance around the table in her black dress, which hugged her curves.

The game was already underway when she carried the drinks tray to the pool table, and Cole potted several stripes. He lined up the cue and aimed but missed the hole. Ella grinned in triumph and took her turn. She potted a red, flung Cole a grin, and lined up another. Win crossed her arms and leaned against a bar stool, trying to pretend she couldn't feel Cole's eyes hot on her face. "So, shall I walk to your place tomorrow?"

Win regarded him, dazed, and then realized he meant to study. "Sure, sure." She tried to sound keen. Cole leaned on the cue, his gaze intent.

"And then, we can go somewhere after? For lunch?"

"Um, sure. Do you drive?"

Cole's smile dropped, replacing it with a bashful look. "No, I was hoping you would."

"Fine," she relented after a pause, suddenly remembering her yard was currently full of cop cars. And they had been warned not to go wandering around alone. "Uh, call me when you get nearby, and I can pick you up in my truck. Home isn't good right now."

Cole made a face, and Win waved her hand, sighing in exasperation. "It's a long story. Just call me, okay?"

Luke passed by, a tray of drinks in both hands. Rosene pressed past Cole, blocking Luke's return as he made to dash back to the kitchen with empty hands. Rosene brazenly tugged on his shirt, pulled him into a dark corner of the bar, and whispered something in his ear. Luke's jaw tightened, his expression sour. Win sensed his train of thought. Only a year ago, this had been him, out on a Friday night with his friends, not even contemplating one day he would be working here, having to pay his way and proving he could support himself.

Rosene inched her hand around his back toward his pocket. Finally, he peeled away from her, removing her hand from his hip. Rose preened, clearly pleased with herself, as she returned to the game.

Ella's mouth dropped open, and Rose laughed. "Don't look so shocked, Ella. I was reminding him of all the fun we used to have together."

Don't react, Win told herself, even though her fists were balling at her sides. Win licked her lips as an image of stamping Rosene into the ground with her paws flashed into her mind. God, she wished she had phased before coming out tonight. She stretched out her arms to flex out the tension.

Ella lifted her chin, tried to aim, and then missed the ball. Rosene laughed sweetly.

"Rose, you do remember you came here with *me*, right?" Adam mocked before throwing her the cue. Rosene simpered and snaked her fingers up his back, ruffling his hair.

"Don't be sore. I was just catching up. Ella doesn't mind, do you?"

Ella's expression read otherwise, her jaw tight enough to shatter glass. Win met her eyes briefly. Win sidled up next to her and leaned into Ella's neck. "You want me to bite her? I don't mind. I would—for you."

Ella's face cracked into a wide grin, shaking her head. "I'll let you know."

"What's one more dead body in my yard, huh?"

"Win!" Ella burst out laughing, the sound distracting the other players. Cole cocked a brow, interested.

"What's so funny?"

"Nothing. Win just has a dark sense of humor." Ella squeezed her friend's shoulder. "I love that about her."

Who said I was joking? Win smirked, darting her eyes, and caught Luke looking at her from the bar where he was grabbing beers for a table of soaked truckers who'd walked in from the rain. He snickered, and Win frowned, puzzled. Her heart leaped. Had he *heard* that?

Rosene lined up her shots and pocketed one straight away. Cole grinned and high-fived her in appreciation. Win could feel the intensity growing around the table, hidden glances, and pulsing heartbeats. Everyone was edgy, irritated, and the two boys were fired up, their minds not on pool. Win grimaced inwardly.

The only one who didn't seem to be reacting was Rosene. Win guessed her emotions were as icy as her hair color. Cole flicked his eyes in her direction, his heartbeat quickening. Win tugged on the back of her dress, wishing she had covered her backside, as Luke tactfully suggested. Rosene noticed Cole's wandering eyes, became distracted, and hit her ball with such ferocity it pinged across the table and landed on the floor and the blonde huffed.

Cole groaned in annoyance. "Too bad, Rose."

The blonde stepped aside and let Win take her go. The music throbbed through Win's skull as she willed herself to concentrate. Her skin tingled like it didn't belong to her.

You need to hit one of the stripes. That's your best bet.

Win jerked, lifting her chin in the direction of Luke's voice. Trembling, she whirled about, he was serving a customer drinks, but he flicked his eyes over to her.

Don't look at me—just sink the orange stripe. You've got a clear shot.

What?? How are you doing that?

Luke smiled at his customers, swishing a cloth over his shoulder, giving her a sly wink as he jogged back to the kitchen. *I told you I'd get in your head eventually.*

Win covered up her laugh with the back of her hand, hoping no one had noticed.

Stop staring over here and kick Rosene's ass!

Win chewed her lower lip, her fingers unfamiliar on the cue, feeling awkward as she lined it up, leaning across the table, her heels lifting off the floor. She gave herself a stern shake, trying to focus yet still reeling from hearing Luke's voice in her head.

"Haven't you played before, Winifred?" Rosene pouted, and Win lifted her chin defiantly.

"Well, I'm sure if you figured it out, it can't be too difficult."

Okay, lean across, put your right foot behind a little. Otherwise, you'll topple. She gazed up briefly, and he was taking someone's money, stuffing it in his apron pocket. *Lean over, not too far! Jesus, why are you wearing that thing? I can see your underwear!*

Win bit back a laugh. *Then don't look!*

Come on, Adler, focus.

Win took a deep breath, brought her arm back, and hit the ball straight into the pocket.

"Yes! I actually hit it!" she yelled in triumph and was relieved she hadn't humiliated herself.

Ella laughed. "Want me to take over?"

"Yes, please!" She gratefully handed over her cue. "It's not my game!"

She wiped her clammy hands, hurrying across the bar to find Luke. No one noticed her slip by the kitchen. The air was cooler outback, where they stacked the drinks and cutlery. Luke leaned against the wall, his chin lifted, rubbing his eyes. He darted away through the rear door to the alley, leaving the door wide open behind him.

Luke bent double behind a huge dumpster, retching. Win ran after him. The smell of garbage from the trash cans wafted up to greet her.

"Luke." She paused by the dumpster, knowing he wouldn't want her to see him throwing up. "Luke, are you okay?"

He sank to his knees, and Win crouched next to him. He was trembling and sweating through his shirt. "Don't look at me." He covered his face. "I'm going to puke again."

"What's going on?" she asked, but before she got an answer, he collapsed and vomited behind the dumpster. He waved her away. Eventually, he got shakily to his feet, wiping his mouth on his shirt sleeve.

Win took his arm, his skin feverishly hot. "We need to get you home," she said, but he shook his head. His skin was grey, perspiration dotting his forehead. "You look terrible."

"It's nothing. I'll be fine in a minute," he insisted, but when he stepped forward, he swayed, and she grabbed his waist.

Panicked, she led him to the wall, allowing him to sag against it. He closed his eyes as water leaked out of the corners. Her heart dropped, she touched his face, but he caught her hand instead.

"Alright," he breathed. "Take me home."

Fifteen

Hickory house was dark, its windows like eyes reflecting in the moonlight. Ella's car sped up the drive and squeaked to a halt. Win jumped out of the car and ran to the back door. Luke flinched as she reached across the seat for his shoulder.

"I can manage," he growled sickly, and Win drew back, leaving space for him to crawl out of the car. Clutching his stomach, he shook Ella off as she tried to help him up the steps. Win ran ahead and unlocked the door.

She threw on the hallway lights, but Luke cried out behind her.

"Turn them off," he begged, turning his face into his shoulder. Shaking, Win flicked them all off, and the hall plunged back into darkness. Luke shuffled across the hall and flung open his bedroom door, slamming it shut behind him. Ella stood motionless in the doorway, her lower lip trembling.

Ella went to open it, but he'd locked it from the inside. Her eyes filled with tears. "Luke, please let me in!"

"Go home," Luke growled from the other side. "I don't want you here."

Win felt his words like a stab to the heart, her brow knitted, and she reached for Ella's shoulder. "Please…should we call you a doctor?" Ella did her best to convince him, she pushed gently on the door, and it squeaked against its locked bolt.

"Go home, El!" he moaned. "I'll see you tomorrow. I need to sleep this off!"

Ella and Win exchanged a helpless look. Her chin wobbling, Ella grabbed her keys and headed to the door. She didn't look back as Win called out. "I'll call you later!"

As soon as Ella's car crunched out of the drive, Luke's door opened, and he bounded to the kitchen. Win ran after him. He gripped the kitchen sink, breathing heavily, his nails white.

She went to his side, her hand finding the nape of his neck. "You're sweating," she hissed.

"I feel so cold," he managed to say through chattering teeth. The muscles in his biceps tensed as he gripped the basin. She ran her hand up his neck, pressing her chin against his shoulder.

"What can I do?" She blinked away tears. She hated seeing him like this, weak, helpless. He twisted his chin in her direction.

"You're warm," he muttered. "I'm freezing. Keep your hand where it is."

She flattened her palm against the back of his neck, and he closed his eyes as if it brought him some sort of temporary relief. "I'm so sorry."

"Don't be sorry."

"But it's my fault," Win's voice broke. "I've done this to you."

"No, you didn't." Even arguing seemed to cause him discomfort. He gagged and leaned over the bowl, retching up pale liquid. "It's just the pain—in my head."

Win remembered. She'd lived it. "You're going to be alright," she promised. "You'll get through this."

He wiped his mouth, swaying on his feet. "What's happening to me?"

"Let's just get you to bed, huh?" She took his shoulders, guiding him back into the den. The springs of the mattress groaned as he sank onto it. Win climbed on and peeled off his shoes. He lifted his head off the bed as she sprang to her feet.

"Don't go…where..?"

"I'm getting a thermometer," she said before rushing upstairs to the bathroom cabinet. In moments she was back, gently pushing his hair off his brow. The machine beeped, and Win stared down at the numbers flashing in red. "Oh, boy," she said through clenched teeth.

"I'm hot stuff, huh?" he drawled, a sleepy smile crossing his lips. His internal body temperature was dangerously high, unnaturally off the charts. Win didn't know if she should call the doctor or attempt to drive him to the hospital, but if this was real— if somehow Luke was going through his calling, what good would it do? Win's stomach turned. He was a ghastly shade of white.

With trembling fingers, she unbuttoned his shirt, pushing it off his shoulders. She turned him onto his side and eventually pulled it free. She pulled off his socks and then looked at the buckle of his jeans, chewing the inside of her mouth. Making her decision, her hands shook as she carefully undid his belt and pulled his jeans down over his hips, averting her eyes as she tugged it down over his knees. Taking a thin sheet off the bed, she laid it across him. The heat rose in waves off his skin, yet under the sheet, he squirmed.

"I'm cold, Win," he complained. "Get me a duvet."

"No, you're burning. You have to cool down. I'm going to call Rowan."

"No, don't go. Come here, please," he begged, and she climbed up the bed next to him. "I'm sure I'll sleep this off."

"Luke, this isn't something you can just sleep off," she worried, laying beside him. He opened his eyes, glassy blue and watery. He looked so lost, like he was in so much pain.

"I need sleep, that's all. Don't go."

"This is my fault."

He managed a weak smile. "It's mine. I shouldn't have talked to you—in my head. Learn to play pool."

"You know what I mean. You must have guessed what this is?"

Win ran her thumb over his brow bone, and the light touch caused him to shiver. A horrible grey tinge lined his mouth. Every breath he drew seemed raspy, painful. "I know, Win. I know what's happening. I knew the moment I got caught in the light."

"And you didn't tell me?"

"You were dealing with other stuff. I didn't want to worry anyone, especially after your mom went missing. I *knew*. I felt it the moment it happened, like being charged up by an electric current."

Bubbles of guilt welled in her chest. What did she want? Forgiveness? To tell her it was okay, even if he was dying because of what she'd done?

"I'm not going anywhere," he said as if he'd read her thoughts. "I'll live."

Win stroked his hair. "I'm not letting you go anywhere. Nowhere I can't follow."

"And bug the shit out of me."

"Absolutely!"

He groaned. "What if I turn into a ferret? Or, something tiny?"

Win's mouth curled into a smile, despite the situation. "Then I'll buy you a cool cage. With a hamster wheel!"

He breathed out a laugh, low and deep, closing his eyes. "I didn't mean to yell at Ella. I hate being like this and for her to see me puking my guts up. I hate you seeing me like it."

"I don't think Ella minds in the slightest. You know she adores you. Sick or not."

His eyes fluttered open, lips parted as though he was going to speak, but instead, he swallowed down whatever might have been chasing up his throat.

"Stay here, okay?" he said, after a long pause.

Win's throat clogged. "I'm right here." She ran her fingers through his hair, waiting until she was sure he was asleep before she peeled off the bed. Light flooded under the crack in the door, the latch rattled, and Rowan's voice floated in the air. Win hurried to the door, creeping into the hallway as Evan and Rowan slipped out of their jackets.

They looked at her in mild surprise, which turned when they noticed how pale she was. "You're home!" Win flew at Evan, burying her face in her hair. "Where's Dad?"

"He left tonight for Boston. He wanted to get on the road," Rowan explained. "Then Evan called and needed a lift from the bus station. What's wrong? You look like a ghost!"

Everything rushed at once, all the fear she'd been bottling for twenty-four hours spilling out of her like a geyser. They all ended up in the kitchen, where Win draped over the table, head in her hands.

"Luke's sick," she admitted, terror creeping out into her voice. She raked her hands through her loose curls. "Evan, can you please help him?"

Evan's face was grave. "I was afraid of this."

"You were?" Rowan was ashen; she pulled out a seat and flopped into it.

"The light on the night of the fire…." Evan said, wringing her hands. "When you first told me what happened, I thought maybe somehow he'd had a lucky escape…but…."

"But what?" Win cried. "Evan…he looks awful. Will you look at him? Do something for him, please?"

"Alright!" Evan panicked. She left and gently opened Luke's door, vanishing inside. Win got up, paced, and gripped the edge of the sink, her knuckles white. Rowan's warm hand was on her shoulder, and then she was in her arms. She burst, unable to hold it in any longer.

"I did this to him." She wept into Rowan's hair. "It's my fault."

"No, it isn't!" Rowan held her tighter.

"Yes, it is. I made him come with me that night. If we hadn't fought, it would have been you, I asked. And then I went off and found Grayson. It's all because of me!"

Rowan made a soothing, shushing noise, but Win pulled out of her arms. "Win, if you and I hadn't fought, you would've never found that cabin. All this was meant to be."

"Was Grayson dying meant to be? And now if Luke…if anything happens to him…."

"He would have never let you go alone," Rowan assured her. "He's your best friend."

Pain flashed across Win's eyes. "I can't lose him too."

There wasn't a life she could imagine without him in it. The thought of him gone, his empty bed and precious life snuffed out made her choke.

In the corridor, Luke's door opened and shut again quietly. With a pale, clammy complexion, Evan crept into the kitchen and collapsed into a chair. Rowan fled to her side anxiously, massaging her shoulders. She planted a kiss on Evan's head.

"Are you okay?"

"I took some off him," she said, sighing wearily. "A little healing incantation I know of to draw out the sickness."

"Evan, what can we do?" Win babbled. "My uncle told me this could kill him."

"Whoa!" Rowan fired urgently. "He isn't going anywhere!"

Evan shot her a look. The kind parents shared when they were trying to keep something quiet. "Rowan, this is dangerous. He's sick. *Gravely* sick. I'm not sure what I can do to get him through it."

Win covered her face with her hands, sobbing into them. "We have to do something."

"Let me think," Evan breathed, clearly exhausted after channeling whatever energy she took off of Luke. Win told them about the diary, but Rowan and Evan just seemed confused. To them, it sounded like the ramblings of a very old man.

"We'll look at it tomorrow," Evan brushed her off. "But right now, we need to focus on him. And how to get him through this."

Rowan made hot drinks, and all three escaped into the family room. Rowan dropped to her knees and built a fire in the hearth. She rolled up scraps of old newspaper, tossing them into the grate, before striking several matches and letting the paper char and crisp up. Win drew her knees up to her chest and hugged them. Inside she was raw. The fire crackled and sprung to life.

"Think back to when you went through this," Evan said, stretching out her long legs as Rowan stepped over her and came to sit between her knees on the floor.

"It wasn't too long ago. What triggered you? What helped you?"

Win cast her memory back, recalling the day a pair of fangs had erupted from her mouth. It had been the day she had learned of Luke and Ella hooking up, embarking on a steamy summer romance that had blindsided her. The stress had caused an involuntary shift in her body, and she'd fled shamefaced to the woods, in the direction of one person she trusted.

"Grayson," she answered. "He helped me. He distracted me."

Rowan made a face. "I'd hate to know how."

"Well, he *did*. He also didn't make things easier." She recalled how worked up she used to get. Even at a fleeting touch. "At least Luke has Ella."

"I'm not sure we should be encouraging that," Evan pondered, and Win frowned.

"Luke isn't dangerous."

"He could be," Rowan added, sipping her chocolate. "To someone like her. Things could get out of hand."

Win got the point, rolling her shoulders, as a shudder passed over. The subject made her uncomfortable, imagining them together and the danger if something went wrong.

"I'm not saying we should ban her or anything," Evan, said eyeing her carefully. "Maybe just keep an eye on them? Maybe give her a warning?"

Win bit her lip, recalling her frank conversation with Ella on this very subject. "I think she knows."

"Then we try to keep him calm, try to make him avoid things that piss him off, rile him up," Rowan offered, and Win laughed.

"This is Luke we are talking about." The guy could barely

tolerate waiting in line for his lunch or got mad when she took too long in the shower.

"I can take him out with me? Meditation could work?" Rowan suggested.

"I guess that could help if he can stand up for long enough." Win stretched and faked a yawn, anything to get away. Her upper canines throbbed; she probed them gently with her tongue, feeling two sharp points. Blood drained from her face, but she kept her expression neutral, hoping neither noticed. Rowan looked beat, and Evan was ghostly white. They didn't need to be dealing with her right now as well.

"I don't know what else to suggest." Rowan cast a glance at the clock at the mantle. It was nearly one in the morning. "I've never dealt with a young *male* Therian. I only know what Grandpa used to tell me. He was a little asshole!"

Win edged out of her seat. "I'm going to turn in!"

Evan smiled and reached for the younger red head's hand, giving it an affectionate squeeze. "Get to bed and try and sleep. I'll keep an eye on him tonight. He might bounce back in the morning."

Evan and Rowan were deep in conversation when she left the room. Before charging upstairs, she peeked in Luke's room and saw him sprawled out on his back, arms and legs flopping over either side of the bed.

Win ached with anguish. Closing his door, she got ready for bed. She changed and locked the bathroom door, brushing out her tangled mane and vigorously scrubbing her teeth. She checked for fangs and lurched in horror.

Her fingers clutched the bathroom sink, ten sharp claws protruding from her fingertips. She sucked in her ribs, squeezing her eyes tightly, and focussed on her breathing.

Keep calm. You're not going to change. You're not going to change.

Even as she thought it, the claws elongated, stretching the skin around her nail beds, she cried out.

Go away, go away.

She trained her thoughts and focussed on pulling her mind out of this state. She thought of trees, the ocean, birds, but her mind soon strayed to prey, imagining hunting something down and sinking her fangs into it. Her gums throbbed, teeth erupting from her lower gums. Her mouth filled with salvia.

Come on!

Then she thought of Grayson, her mind drifting back. The day he'd pulled her in the brook, ankle-deep, and kissed her. She imagined kissing him, pressing against him, his breath on her neck. Then her mind wandered to the day in the clearing, her pulse rocketing as she remembered what they'd done. Win's eyes snapped open, hot and uncomfortable, but for a different reason. When she looked in the mirror, her teeth were gone. She exhaled in relief.

Splashing her face with water, she slipped out into the corridor, hearing voices in the kitchen below. Rowan and Evan were tidying, and there was a whiff of bleach in the air, which meant Evan was cleaning.

"I don't know whether to bolt his door or set up some sort of tripwire outside her room!"

Rowan's joke echoed upstairs, and Win froze. Her hand paused mid-way as she reached for her door. She melted into the shadows and closed her eyes to focus on their conversation below. Evan laughed off the comment.

"Rowan, I think you're over worrying. Win doesn't have feelings for him, *not* like that."

"I don't think it matters. Ella is a sweetheart, but she isn't the one who triggers him. I'm pretty certain."

Her jaw sagging, Win dropped to her knees in the dark. What were they *talking* about? A tingling sensation broke out across her back, and like a curtain lifting, light-flooded in and blinded her. Dazed, Win sagged, pressing her face between the banister railings.

"Win is too wrapped up in Grayson to even notice. That's what worries me. We have a young, handsome guy in the house who is besotted with her, and she can't even see it!"

Oh. My. God.

"Rowan, right now, the poor guy isn't interested in anything other than not dying."

Win heard her sister laugh shortly. "He will trust me! I don't think I'd trust him around her *at all.* You were saying we should focus on keeping him calm when the very person who riles him up wanders around the house, stealing his underwear! She has no idea, but I see it. The way he looks at her…he's like a lost pup. It breaks my heart."

Unable to hear another word, Win scrambled back to her room, every fiber of her body on fire. Flushed, she stared at her reflection over her vanity, reality drawing on her.

You are a moron!

She fell back on her bed and raked her hands through her hair. How could she have not noticed? He didn't…he *couldn't.* They were best friends. He had Ella! He wasn't interested in her, was he?

With hands pressed to her neck, she attempted to stem the frantic knocking in her chest, but every time she closed her eyes, she saw every moment they'd shared, replayed every comment he'd ever made, any joke at her expense. Not once, even for a second, had she seen him as anything other than a brother. She drove him nuts, teased him, and in return, he batted it straight back. They fought. There had been times where they'd nearly throttled each other. Win was a pain. Luke was an immature idiot. One, she couldn't do without.

Win flushed, a strange heat scorching up her center, right to the base of her neck. Ella said something tonight which bugged her.

"You two are close…."

Win's insides plummeted, an ice-cold wash of fear enveloping her skin. Did Ella know? Did she suspect? *Oh god…*She could tear out her hair. *So stupid!!*

Diving under the duvet, she found the diary, and after several attempts at reading, she gave up. Her eyes wouldn't focus, she read the same line over and over, unable to concentrate, and with a sigh, she let it slip to the floor. She pulled the sheets up her chest but fell into a sweaty sleep, her mind in tatters. Half of her vowed she would get Luke through this no matter what. And the other half, the scared, miserable, and selfish part, loathed herself because if what Rowan implied *was* true, there was no way he could stay here if he came through this.

What if he admitted it, confronted her? What if he tried something? And then she'd have to push him away, and it would hurt them both. Humiliated, he would leave. And it would be like she'd lost him after all.

Okay, so maybe once you thought he was cute. She sat up in the dark, rubbing her eyes, admitting in those early days he could earn a flush with his smile. And the ease they shared, the comfortable air, it was a friendship born out of a shared experience in the tunnels and nothing more, especially after she met Grayson.

"Surely you've realized that you two are…bonded?" Uncle Willard's words haunted her.

Was this Spencer and Rowan all over again? The pull of energy flowing between them, the spark she denied. How had she been so blind?

No, it's different. It's different for us…

Her argument stalled. She wouldn't admit to anything, not even to herself, any lingering doubts she forced away. If she hurt Ella after everything they had been through, Win would never forgive herself.

As she drifted in and out of sleep, through all her turbulence, one thing kept pulsing in her mind. A strange, peaceful feeling hovered over her, stark clarity, that no matter how right it might feel she would deny again and again.

It wasn't love, not in that way. It was different, primal. It was completion, like finding the missing half of your soul.

He belonged *with* her.

Sixteen

The truck jostled up the flat planes of the beach, the tide out for miles, leaving nothing but wet, golden sand in its wake. The small, colonial town of West Point became a blur in the distance, as did the grassy, steep dunes. Win rested her elbow on the open window of the truck, the tips of her hair damp. She breathed in the salty air as the sun rose into puffy white clouds.

"Feel better?" Rowan asked. She took the truck off-road, back onto the crumbly dirt path leading back into town. Win drew up her knees and rested them on the dashboard.

"Better," she agreed. "But this is going to be a nuisance coming here every day."

Rowan had shaken her awake at four am, planted a mug of coffee in her hand, even though Win didn't drink it. Win dived under her pillows, and Rowan grabbed her sister's ankles, tugging her off the mattress. Her bottom landed on the rug with a thud. They'd crept out of the house, Win blurry-eyed, and as Rowan drove out to West Point, she'd wound down the window, letting in chilly air to wake her up.

Rowan explained it was necessary. Win needed to change. Her body would betray her eventually, and as if by some sixth sense, Rowan could read the signs and knew she needed to get her as far away from the camera surveillance as possible. Before the sun was even up, Rowan drove out to the dunes in total darkness and forced Win out of the truck. With the waves lapping the shore and plain open freedom in sight, Win hadn't argued.

"It's something we'll have to deal with," Rowan mused, throwing back her hair in the wind blowing through the window.

Win sighed. "I feel like such a burden."

"Oh, come on. I'm going to need to change soon. At least I have the option to go upward!" Rowan threw her a wink. "You aren't a burden. We'll all take turns coming out here. Evan won't mind, and Dad will do it when he's home. I'm sure even Luke would drive you."

"No!" Win snapped a little too quickly. "He's got enough going on right now."

"Okay, we'll manage." Rowan squinted against the rising sun. She darted a curious glance in her direction. "Are you…alright? You've been quiet."

Win smiled awkwardly, staring hard out the window. Words formed on her lips. She wanted to ask Rowan about last night about her suspicions, but she didn't dare start a conversation. Her stomach was unsettled, and she decided she wanted to push it away and focus on what was important, keeping him alive. Rowan cocked a brow. "Win?"

"I'm just worried about him," she admitted, which wasn't a lie. She struggled to keep a neutral expression while trapped in her sister's radar. Rowan had a talent for sensing everything she was thinking, and it didn't help they could resort to private telepathic conversations when they needed to. Between them weaved an open channel, allowing each other a permanent flow line. And now it was evident Luke possessed this trait, too, after last night at the bar. And she wasn't sure how much access she wanted to give him. Up until last night, she would have given him anything, but now, she wondered at the cost.

It was a sunny Saturday morning, and Cedar Wood was waking up as they drove back into town. A few runners were out on the wet roads, and some houses were getting ready for Halloween, stringing up paper ghosts and skeletons from their gateposts. Pumpkins crowded outside porch doors, and Win made a note to buy one for the house. Not that she expected any trick or treaters! Ben used to take her in Boston, going out for a couple of hours while they wandered their little town, the simplicity of the memory causing an ache to take root in her chest.

Ella's car was parked in the drive when they pulled in. "She's early! It's only just seven am!" Win said in surprise, not expecting Ella back so soon.

They both got out of the truck as Evan appeared on the porch and waved them away. Rowan stopped mid-step, leaning on the car. "What's going on?"

"Why don't we all go for a drive?" Evan suggested brightly. Win frowned, puzzled. She wrapped her arm around Win's shoulders and ushered her away from the porch.

"I'm exhausted," she complained, her stomach rumbled. "And I'm starving!"

"I'll buy you breakfast. Come on!"

Rowan's face broke into a sly grin. "Are we trying to give Ella and Luke some privacy?"

Win's head whipped back and forth between the two of them. Then she caught the expression on Rowan's face. "Oh…uh…." She rolled her shoulders in a shudder. "Okay…breakfast sounds good."

"They were having a heated discussion, so perhaps it best we give them some space," Evan said as they headed to the truck.

Win hopped in the truck. The thought of what was going on in the house made her nauseous. She wasn't an idiot, she was pretty sure there had been times where *things* had gone on downstairs, but she'd been oblivious then. Luke had still been fast asleep when she peeked through his door this morning and was relieved to see his color had returned, but she doubted he was back to full strength. But then again, he was a Therian male. What did she know? Now all she could think about was Luke's feelings for her. And after last night, after caring for him, she felt a strange sense of protectiveness.

Twirling her spoon in her chocolate, she was silent at the table in Evan's diner, a shabby little off-road place outside Lincoln. Rowan ordered pancakes, and Win had done the same, but now she just gazed at the murky syrup, too tense to force it down.

"One of the surveillance guys came to check the footage while you were out," Evan told them.

"Did they catch anything?" Rowan asked, stuffing the last of her syrup-covered blueberries in her mouth.

"Some birds, a rat or two, but nothing man-eater size," Evan sighed with disappointment.

"No falcons either?" Win muttered, utterly miserable. God, she felt depressed. She allowed herself a moment to feel annoyed, angry at their mother for *literally* taking off and leaving them. She was needed now! Half of her knew it was time to admit maybe something awful had happened to her. Perhaps it was something to do with the creature Win had seen near the Mercy land? She rested her chin on her arms.

"Oh, Win, for god sake, snap out of it!" Rowan nudged her arm. "We'll get through this. Luke seems…. better." She cleared her throat, smirking. "And I'm sure we can figure this thing out together."

"I'd love to know how," Win snapped, raising her chin. "You didn't see him last night. He looked like he was dying…and Uncle Willard said…."

"I know what your uncle told you!" Evan reached across the table for her arm. "But this generation of Hickorys are pretty tough. You got through it, and you weren't ready. Luke can too!"

Win's chin trembled. "Where is our mother, Rowan? Don't you think it's time we faced the truth? That she could be…!"

"No, I'm not giving up!" Rowan shook her head. She exhaled, rubbing her eyes, sore from sea salt spray and their incredibly early start. "We'll double our efforts. Keep looking! Grandpa always said she was a free spirit—a wanderer. She'll come home." Win's phone vibrated on the table, and all three of them saw Cole's name flash up on the screen. Win groaned, sliding the screen open.

"Ah, is the new guy?" Evan smiled, her dark eyes gleaming with mischief.

I'm walking to town, where shall I meet you? Win read the message, thumbing back a weak, half-hearted *Sure! Text me when you're nearby, and I'll meet you.*

"He's not a new guy! I forgot he was coming over to study," she groaned.

"On a Saturday? He's keen."

Win half-smiled. "He's not my type."

"Give him a chance. He could be sweet!" Rowan said, and Win shook her head in refusal.

"I'm not sure I want another guy in my life right now. It makes things complicated." For Win, there was only one guy—snatched away too soon. But Rowan grinned wickedly.

"Oh, pretty soon, I'm not sure you'll be able to help that."

Win's brow cocked, noticing the devious smile spreading across her sister's face. "Huh?"

Evan shook her head in dismay. "Take no notice, Win."

"No, tell me!"

Rowan sniggered into her palms, and Win was glad her sister found her predicament so amusing. Rowan kicked back in her seat, chuckling. "All I'm saying is, wait till you hit twenty...maybe twenty-one? Then you'll know."

Evan sighed, and by her expression, Win could see she felt obliged to fill in the gaping holes. "Rowan means the heat."

"The *what?*"

"The heat," Evan said, then blushed. "It's not my place to tell you."

Win had gone the color of the diner door, a cherry red flush breaking out across her skin. "If that implies...what I think it does... oh, god!" She stared furiously at Rowan. "Is this one of those I'll tell you when you're ready conversations? Except you end up forgetting like you did with my calling? Failing to mention I'd turn into a pile of guts on the floor?"

Rowan sobered, crossing her arms. "You're a smart cookie. I'm sure you'll figure it out."

"Shall I ask *Dad*?" Win threatened.

Evan and Rowan both shot forward in their seats. "Do *not* do that! Unless you want to live in your bedroom forever," her sister urged. Win slumped in her seat, and Rowan rolled her eyes.

"All I'm saying is, pretty soon, you won't be able to help it if you get more attention from the opposite sex!"

"Or the same sex!" Evan said, chuckling and Rowan grinned, reaching to squeeze her hand.

"True! It's something we go through when our bodies decide it's time for us to—*you know*—breed? Our biological clocks kick in. You'll be as frisky as hell, but don't worry—its fine!" Rowan laughed into her palm, with the look of a person who found her situation hilarious. Win's mouth dropped open.

"*Breed?*"

Rowan waved her hand and then burst out laughing again, while Evan huffed and looked skyward. "It's *fine!*"

Win's eyes went saucer wide. "I don't *want* to breed!"

Rowan laughed. "Yes, I know. But it's kind of involuntary. Trust me, you'll get through it like I did." Then she winked and lowered her voice. "It isn't *all* bad."

Evan pulled a face. "That's because you had a boyfriend as a giant shield."

"Spencer was many things, but he did come in handy. I didn't need to have any awkward conversations with guys at the bar. He scared them all away."

Win stared miserably at her hands, sighing loudly. Just when she thought she'd gotten a handle on things, Rowan dropped a bomb. Thank god it wasn't happening now. An ache lurched in her gut, missing her mother. She would have been the one to talk to about this stuff, the icky things. Instead, she had Rowan, who she loved, but tended to edge around anything too intimate like it was a basket of snakes.

Win waved her hands, batting away the heat under her skin and hoping it would signal an end to the strange conversation. "Let's go home now," she begged.

Once they reached home, Win shot up the stairs to her room, holding her hands over her ears as she raced by Luke's locked door. But Ella sat on the bed, waiting for her, the leather-bound diary open on her lap.

Ella looked up, bright eyes and flushed. "Hey, you're back!"

Win slipped onto the bed next to her, resisting the urge to heave. She wrinkled her nose; Luke's scent was all over her, like a cat marking his territory. It only made her queasiness worse. She smiled anyway, swallowing her revulsion, telling herself this wasn't the first time this had happened. But now, it left her unsettled. A part of her wanted to reveal what she had learned, another strange and gross Hickory family secret, but she clamped her lips shut for now. It was too weird to say aloud.

"You're here early!" She scrambled up against the pillows.

Ella threw her a sad smile. "I was worried sick last night. I couldn't sleep. And after he told me to get lost…!"

"No! I don't think he wanted you to see him like that." Win remembered she hadn't even texted Ella; she must have been going insane with worry. "I'm so sorry. I should have messaged, but things got so crazy!"

"It's fine! I totally don't blame you. He called me this morning and apologized, so I came over…."

"And made up! *Great!*" Win diverted her attention to the diary on Ella's lap. "Where is he now?"

Ella smiled. "He's asleep. He looks a lot better!"

Yeah, I bet he does! Win didn't understand why she felt so uncomfortable, but she was keen to distract herself.

This is all a bad dream. Rowan is reading this wrong, and Luke is crazy about her. Ella was crazy about him, and Win was not going to wedge herself between them. It was Ella's place to care for him, too, not just hers.

"You found the diary?"

Ella's expression softened into one of wonder. "This is insane, Win. It's *so* old. You don't mind me reading it, do you?"

"Of course not!"

"Because if there is anything in here, that can help Luke…!"

"Read it!" Win urged her. She was so grateful for her friend, knowing she wasn't alone. They both loved him, but differently. Win wrapped her in a hug, which caught her off guard. Ella smiled into Win's hair and held her tight.

"What's the matter?"

"Nothing!" Win sniffed. "I'm glad you're here. I don't know where to start with this thing. And Cole said he was walking here..." Win glanced at her watch. "Huh, ten minutes ago. He's late. Good start!"

She checked her phone and saw there were no messages from him.

"Do you like him? He is quite cute," Ella asked, glancing up from the weathered, thin pages.

"Only as a friend." *And nothing more!!*

Ella nodded solemnly, her eyes downcast. "Maybe it's time to move on? From Grayson?"

Win didn't say anything. It still hurt too much to admit he was gone. She'd fantasized about his return so many times, waking from bad dreams with her pillow damp and her chest hollow. Ella's gaze turned back to the book, and she beamed like a child on Christmas morning. "Do you mind if I read this while he naps? I'm so excited!"

Win rolled her eyes. "Knock yourself out!" She grinned, running for the shower, keen to wash the remains of salt spray out of her hair. Her curls turned to a mass of frizz, barely able to brush her fingers through it. Leaving Ella tucked in among the pillows, Win showered and changed, rechecking her watch, then her phone and frowning as she stepped into the hall. Cole was taking his time!

Luke was in the kitchen making a sandwich. He leaned away from the counter when she wandered in, checking her phone once more. Glancing up from her screen, she caught sight of him and went liquid hot. Luke walking around in nothing but his sweatpants had gone from no big deal to downright alarming. There was no question he'd filled out, his arms toned and defined. It was worrying, as was her reaction. Apart from a lack of color, he looked bright-eyed and nowhere as sick as the previous night. It was a quick bounce back. She turned on her heels, about to flee when he dropped his sandwich and bounded over to her.

"Hey, where are you going?" He laughed, catching her arm as she stalked into the hall.

"What…I'm fine…you?" she spluttered, her skin burning. He looked confused, a slow grin spreading across his face.

"Uh…I didn't ask, but that's good to know. I wanted to talk about last night…."

Win's legs drained of blood; she breathed through her nose and reached for the doorframe. Before she could ferret away, he grabbed her and pulled her against him for a hug. She was pressed against his warm chest, her hands hanging limply by her thighs. She could smell him, Ella, and a mix of sweat and hormones. She squeezed her eyes shut and prayed for it to be over.

Oh…god…

He dropped her, pulling back, a frown on his face. "You… okay?"

"Fine!"

"You look weird!"

"No, you look weird!" What a snappy comeback. Win died inside. She flapped her hands nervously. "I'm waiting for Cole."

"Oh." Luke didn't look impressed. "He's coming to study, right?"

"Uh-huh."

"Look." He took her hand, pressing his palm flat against hers. "I'm so sorry about last night. I don't think anyone, but my mom has ever taken my temperature, so thank you. And for getting me undressed and into bed!"

Win slapped his arm. "Ella's upstairs!"

"Uh, yeah, *I know*. I think she's more than happy you were here. You were looking out for me."

Win felt a tingle of relief, thinking Rowan had gotten this backward. He didn't have feelings for her. It was all just a silly, horrible misunderstanding. Luke shoved his hands in his sweatpant pockets, a wry smile playing at the corners of his mouth.

"I didn't say anything…*weird*, did I? In my delirium?"

Win's heart thumped. "Um, no. No, you were just your usual sarcastic self. Only paler and sweatier."

"Ha, thanks." He scratched the back of his head. "Well, thank you, anyway. Honestly, you…"

Win held up her hands, clutching her phone that was ringing. "I've got to go!"

Luke eyed her suspiciously as she marched out the front door. Outside, the sky turned a foreboding shade of grey. She rubbed her arms and answered her phone, only to hear a heavy panting at the other end.

"Cole? Are you lost?"

"Cole, are you there?" When there was no reply, only wheezy, soft breaths, Win gaped at the screen in alarm. She narrowed her eyes, a chill exploding up her back.

The line went dead, and the silence, the sudden click off, was more frightening than the raspy breaths on the other end of the phone. Shaking, she dashed back inside, where Luke wandered barefoot into the hall, pulling on a white tee shirt. He caught her expression and froze.

"Win?"

"Somethings wrong," her hands went clammy. "I think something happened to Cole!"

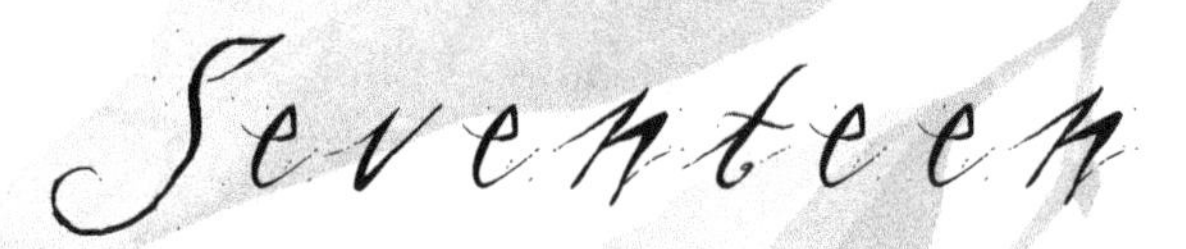

Seventeen

Across in Lincoln, Ben awoke to the guttural noise of his wife whimpering in the dark of the living room. He lifted his torso off the camp bed, the muscles of his upper back tight from sleeping on springs poking through the mattress. He rubbed the back of his neck. "Alice?"

His bare feet hit the floor, groaning as he stretched and padded to the spare room. Inside it was dark, tangy, and through the myriad of shadows, he could make out her shape, pacing the floor. "Alice, stop!"

He caught her shoulders, and she recoiled, her nails digging into his arms, shoving him away. Ben staggered back against the wall, a sharp reminder of the strength she still possessed. Even in this frail, tattered state, she could knock him sideways. "I'm going to open the curtains, okay?" he called, crossing to the window. "I can't even see you."

Alice crept to the corner, pulling her knees up to her chest and folding her arms around them, head bowed. She wailed as pale light flooded the room. She'd obliterated this bedroom. What once was a pretty, pastel decorated guest bedroom, was now a wasteland, wallpaper ripped by fingernails, blood stains on the rug and the bed clothes pulled off and ripped to shreds in fits of temper. Ben puffed out air, still bleary-eyed, exhausted, having spent most of the night trying to convince her to eat. He'd taken over from Evan, Alice duty, they called it. When one finished, the other took over, telling lies to cover their tracks. Though some progress had been made, she was nowhere near the women he'd lost all those years ago.

This Alice had eyes like the devil, pale, glassy, and able to stare into a void for hours on end. And this Alice wasn't settled in her skin. She scratched at her bare arms and legs, leaving ugly welts. The strawberry-blonde mane of hair he'd loved was chopped into a blunt bob around her ears.

Ben wondered how something that should have been so wonderful had gotten so royally screwed up. He squatted and crawled carefully toward her. "Alice, talk to me. Did you have a dream?"

She trembled, her voice thick with tears. Her hair fell over her face when she finally lifted her chin. Then to his surprise, she held out her arms. Ben choked, taking a moment to breathe before he reached for her, and like a child, she crawled into his lap, cradling her head under his chin. This was progress. He lifted her, carried her out of the room into the living room. He landed on his bottom on the couch, with her crowded on his lap.

Minutes drifted by, and neither spoke. He wrapped his arms around her, horrified at her bones protruding from her back. "You need to start eating, baby." He kissed her forehead. "A stiff breeze would blow you away."

"Food tastes like…ash," she admitted. "Everything here is so bright. And hard."

"You can't go back, Alice. I know you'd run away if I gave you half a chance."

She lifted her chin, her face inches from his, her pale eyes watery. "I do want to go home."

"Then you have to try," he insisted. "You have to try and live in this world now."

A tear clung to her bottom lashes. "I've lost everything."

He ran his knuckles down the back of her calf, up and down, ankle to behind her knee. She grew quiet, resting her head on his shoulder. "Not true. You have me, the girls. You have to come home to us."

"I was happy, Ben."

He sucked in his breath—the very words he'd dreaded. Though he'd never asked for this, never dreamed of having her back, the possibility of having his wife alive and human had been overwhelming. His family together, at last. Over the years she'd been gone, he'd dated, met women online, but knowing she was still out in the world kept him from becoming serious with anyone. When Evan told him what she'd done, this was what he'd been afraid of.

His Alice had so loved to fly.

"I'm sorry," he whispered. "I'm sorry you were torn away. But I need you. We should have had a life together. And the girls."

Her breathing deepened against his shoulder, and he wondered if she had drifted off. Instead, she ran her hands down his arm, linking her spindly fingers with his. "We shouldn't have left. We should have stayed and faced…him," she whispered.

She shook. A deep shudder passed through her, and he felt it. All these years, and she was still terrified of him. Ben shook his head. "I wanted to stay. I think you'll recall it was you who didn't want to face him anymore. I can hardly blame you."

"She woke them all up," Alice breathed, closing her eyes. Ben pulled a face.

"What does that mean?"

She clutched him tighter. "There's a fox in our henhouse."

Ben smirked. "You sound like your dad. I have no idea what you are talking about."

He held her closer. When she looked up, he smiled and did something brave—kissed her on the lips. When she didn't react, he did it again, and she smiled and stroked his hair. He grinned. "That's more like it."

"I'm old Ben. I got so old."

He chuckled. "Me too. We have two very independent, wayward girls who have given me a fair few grey hairs. Not to mention the guys they choose to date."

Alice gazed skyward, thoughtful. "I remember some of it. I know Win was desperately in love with the man from the woods, but I don't remember what happened to him."

Ben made a face, raking his hand through his hair. "Hmm, that's a story best left for another time."

"And Rowan…." Alice's eyes darkened. "And Spencer Fraser."

"Yet another one for when you're feeling strong again."

"But…isn't it incredible?" Alice marveled, her eyes clear, wide like she was finally having a moment of clarity. "After all we did, leaving Cedar Wood…and yet…one of our girls still ended up with a Fraser."

Ben clicked his tongue, keen to change the subject, the ghosts of the past sure to upset her. She rested her arm on the back of the couch, her knee drawn up, and one hand on his thigh, the way they used to sit when they were kids. Like no time passed at all, and she never left. It made him ache to think of the years he'd lost. And yet, given a choice, she still wouldn't be here.

"It was all for nothing, wasn't it?" she mused. "Our leaving was pointless, futile. It ended up the same. We should have stayed."

"Rowan is free of him now," Ben assured her. "She's stronger."

"But she suffered." Alice was becoming shaky, and Ben knew what she was thinking, even if she didn't voice it out loud. Once bitten, you were never truly free.

Across the room on his camp bed, his cell phone buzzed into the mattress. He ignored it and pushed back her hair, peering into her face. "I'm going to make you something you like." He kissed the tip of her nose and let her slip out of his arms. He even dared to let a smile cross his mouth as he jogged to the kitchen. Crashing about in Evan's small but immaculately tidy kitchen, he found pans and raided the fridge.

Milk, flour, eggs, he slopped it all on the counter, making a mess, heating oil in the pan. What a breakthrough. He would get her back, even if it took him a year or more. Alice's mind was fragile, delicate right now, and she seemed so afraid, but even if it was selfish, and he pushed, he knew he could win her back to him. He'd done it before, a long time ago.

The boards creaked behind him, and he turned, finding her standing in the door, holding out his phone. "It won't stop ringing." Her lips were pale. Ben looked away.

"Ignore it. I'm making you pancakes."

She held it out in her palm; it buzzed so hard it nearly slipped out of her hand. "Answer it."

Ben threw a dishcloth over his shoulder, huffing as he caught it before it fell to the floor. He peered at the caller ID. "It's Evan," he dismissed it. "I'll call her back."

"I'm sure it's fine," he said as Alice stared at him, imploring, wide eyed. He didn't want intruders here, not when he'd had this breakthrough, this moment of normality with her.

"Somethings wrong, Ben," Alice said, her shoulders trembled. "Pick up the phone!"

Annoyed, he slid the screen open, wiping his hands on his pant leg. "What's up, Evan?"

"Ben, you have to come home!" Evan's panicked voice bled through the receiver. The tone in her voice iced his blood.

He turned away from his wife, facing the window, hoping Alice couldn't hear. "What's wrong?"

"It's happened again…someone got hurt…you have to come home!"

"I can't leave her here alone!"

"You'll have to. We need you here. This isn't good, Ben. *Please!*"

"Is it one of the girls?"

"No, no, just get in the damn car…please!"

Behind him, a door crashed, a stream of cold air rushed through the apartment. Ben gagged, running into the hall, finding it empty and the apartment door wide open. "Shit!" he hissed. "*Shit!*"

"What? What is it?" Evan begged on the other end. Ben padded outside into the yawning stretch of hallway, empty and dark and no signs of his wife. He ran into the hall and grabbed his shoes, diving for his keys on the couch.

"I can't come!" he yelled. "She's gone!"

"What? No, come home! She might be heading here now!"

"I'll be there as soon as I can!" He hung up the phone, grabbing his coat and flinging himself down the concrete steps. Outside it was cold and damp, and Alice had escaped wearing nothing but a nightdress and one of Rowan's sweaters. He looked up and down the road outside, but there was no sign of her.

Alice did love to fly.

Eighteen

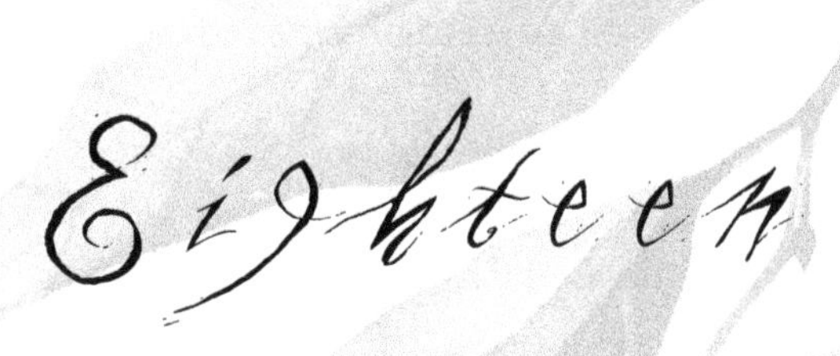

Win stuffed the phone in her back pocket and bounded outside onto the gravel. The sky was clouding up, once again threatening rain, which was a problem. She might not be able to track Cole. The air stung the back of her throat as she ran, and she suddenly got yanked back by the shoulder. Luke caught up, amazingly fast, his mouth pinched.

"Where are you going?" he fired.

"Something happened to Cole!" she spat, pacing back and forth. "I heard him breathing on the other end of the line!"

"So, perhaps he pocket dialed you?"

"No, I'm telling you something's wrong." Out in the woods, it was eerie, silent. "Can't you feel it?"

The question hung in the air between them, a heavy silence. Luke looked to the forest, raking both hands through his hair. The cops on surveillance earlier had been called away to an emergency across town. They were alone out here. Still, Win stalked into the woods, exhaling as he dragged behind. The air was oppressive.

She knew Luke could feel it, too, the sense of danger, shadows lurking in plain sight. Like a heavy veil hanging in the air. A coppery tang wafted under both their noses, Luke recoiled and gagged. "What is that smell?"

"Blood," she answered dismally. This wasn't good.

He sucked in his ribs, covering his mouth. "I think…I'm going to be sick!"

"You'll get used to it." She rubbed him between the shoulder blades as he heaved, bent double, and vomited up his sandwich. He straightened a little shaky and wiped his chin.

"I've never smelled blood before." He turned a sickly shade of green, made a face, and vomited up again. "Not like this." Win groaned loudly. She left him and started to track into the woods, listening for any signs of Cole.

"Wait!"

"Go home. You won't handle this!"

"I'm not letting you go in alone! I can't help it if it makes me sick!"

"Wait till your next basketball game with a bunch of sweaty guys. Then you'll know how it really feels." She pushed aside branches with her arms, ducking and sniffing the ground. A tangy scent of coppery fear lingered in the air. She darted toward it, following the trail. "He's nearby!"

"Shouldn't you get undressed?"

She whirled in his direction, letting a sapling branch slap him in the face. "*What?*"

"You know, get undressed? *Change?*" He was puffing air through his nose, and it was evident he wasn't fully recovered. "So you can protect me?"

He made a good point. But Cole was close, she could smell him, and nausea swelled in her gut, wondering what she would find if there were anything left. Why had she let him walk here? She should have guessed he might cut through the woods. Why hadn't she insisted on picking him up in the truck? If she changed now, if Cole was even still breathing, there was a risk he might die of fright if he spotted a giant Jaguar coming toward him.

She slapped a hand on Luke's shoulder. "Go home!"

"No!" he insisted.

Win waved her hands in the air, knowing he was too stubborn. "Then hold down your stomach!"

Win ran through the undergrowth, barely breaking a sweat, while behind Luke waned, holding a tree for support. She sniffed the air, the stench of wet, claggy blood filled the back of her nose, and she gagged into her palm. She waved Luke toward her, clutched his forearm, noting how heavily he leaned on her. This had been a horrible plan. He was sweating, his hair curling at his nape.

A scream tore them apart. It shrilled through the trees, echoed through Win's skull, so loud it banged around in her chest. Or was it just her heart? It was Cole. She ran toward it, dragging Luke along with her. The scream was desperate, lost, and terrified.

"Cole!" she screamed into the air, trying to will the desperate tone out of her voice. "Cole, where are you?"

She ran up an incline, grabbing vines to haul her over the top. She looked back, and to her surprise, Luke made it, though he'd gone a ghostly white. She dashed into a small clearing and froze.

An animal lifted its jaw, its white muzzle matted with dried blood. Luke barrelled into her back, seeing what she saw. "Oh, my god…" he whispered. "It's a panther!"

But it didn't look like any panther they'd seen in books or at the zoo. Muscular and lithe, this creature was massive, its eyes a haunting shade of yellow, and its fur a light silver. Its jaw sagged, revealing two long, sharp canines, stained berry red. It towered over a figure on the ground, its round ears pinned back. Win spotted the remains of rumpled clothes, blood-stained, and juddering fingers.

Cole was still breathing. Win squared off her shoulders, balling her fists, a low growl rumbling in her chest. Anger replaced her fear.

I'm going to rip you apart for this. She made to lunge after it, and the thing backed off. It snaked into the bushes and then ran. Both Luke and Win dropped to their knees next to Cole.

"How is he alive?" Luke asked in awe.

He was only just alive, cold to the touch and shaking.

Cole clung to Win's hand as she pulled off her shirt, bundling it into a ball and holding it over the gaping, raw wound under his ribcage.

"I don't think you can refuse me a date after this," he joked, voice trembling. She steadied him, laying a hand on his forehead.

"Cole, stay still. Don't talk!"

Win stared pitifully down the length of his body. Splattered in dirt and marred in deep scratches, blood pooled through his ripped jeans. A giant gash zigzagged over his calf, and on his right hand, his fingers were chewed to mush. Win hissed, and next to her, Luke swore.

"Cole, look at me. You'll be okay!" Win tossed Luke her cell phone. "Call Ella and Rowan. They're at the house. I'm going after the thing and ending this!"

Swiftly she rose, but Luke blocked her. "You can't go alone!"

"Yes, I can!" She shoved him away. "You stay here and take care of him! Get him to the hospital."

Luke staggered toward her, hardly able to stand on his own legs. He clutched the back of her neck, and for a horrifying moment, she thought he actually might kiss her. Instead, he said. "Don't die, okay? I can't do this thing without you."

She clutched his forearm and then pushed him away. "I'll be back, I promise. Take care of him!"

Win vanished through the trees, her heart hammering, as her feet flew across the dirt. There was no time to worry about shredding clothing or ruining jeans. She took a long breath into the hollow of her chest, finding the connection to her ground and drawing the strength running through the land under her feet. She was going to attempt something she'd seen Rowan do but never dared try herself. Without pausing, she ran full pelt, a long, moss-eaten log blocking her path. She leapt, air rushing through her hair, and jumped. On the other side, she landed, all four paws smacking the dirt. She growled, shredded fragments of her clothing floating down as though they'd evaporated mid-air.

That hurt, like being ripped in half, sliced with a knife. Her eyes watered, but she didn't stop. The panther was close, she could hear him breathing. Fear leaked out of him, and it stank, filling her nostrils. She growled, high pitch, viscous and primal, as she stalked into a thicket of densely packed cedar pines, their leaves wide, flat, perfect for hiding.

Her breath chugged, adrenaline coursed through her blood, thick and hot, and for the first time since her calling, she felt powerful. Win wanted to kill this thing. She hadn't been given this gift for nothing. A jaguar's bite was lethal, the most deadly jaws of all the big cats.

Leaves exploded mid-air, and Win sprang sideways. Her claws splayed as the panther lunged from the left. She batted it away with her paw, catching its flank, and leaving a deep scratch in her wake. Win regained composure as it pranced away, bowing low to the ground before springing, both paws up. They tousled and wrestled on the ground, leaves flying, rolling in the dirt as one toppled the other, over and over.

Pain blinded her momentarily, its fangs sinking into her shoulder, tearing surface flesh. She flung it off before it could deepen the bite. They prowled around one another, both snarling, saliva dripping.

It's too fast, she thought wildly. And it kept dancing away, every swat of her claws. *It's trying to tire me.*

Win panicked. It might be working, her muscles ached, and she'd never been in a fight before, especially not one like this. Win's body, strong and lethal, was built for this purpose, but she had no style, no flare, striking out blindly anyway she could. But this thing was a pro. Like it was born to dance this way. It lunged, rolled sideways to its back, and swiped at her underbelly before darting out of her reach. Win narrowly dodged the attack, its eyes yellow and mad. It was angry, but then so was she.

She focused, pulled back, and when it dove again, she leaped over him, flattening its torso to the ground with her back paws, tearing into its belly with her teeth. She felt it yell in pain, its ferocity only increasing. This time it rolled, but it caught her left leg, sinking its entire jaw into her upper flank, right by her hip bone. Her vision whited. She staggered out of its grip, clawing the dirt, dull pain slicing through her.

Panting, she crouched, fear rolling off her in waves. Low to the ground, she crawled away, not able to support her weight, as the panther crept around her, its jaw open, blood trickling from its gums.

It's killed me, she thought. Her mind was lost, exhaustion pulling at every muscle. She tried to stand but lost balance and toppled into the dirt. The panther crept closer. It bowed low, powering up, preparing its death blow and Win sensed an odd rush of calm. This was her end. Staring into its eyes, she saw her life, finished, nothing.

She closed her eyes. The air split. An arrow pierced straight through the panther's paw, the one it was about to use to strike. Blood spurted, there was a roar of agony, and it retreated. Win opened her eyes. A body stood between her and death, and she swayed as her world dropped away.

Grayson lifted his crossbow, aiming it straight between the panther's eyes.

Grayson! Win's mouth opened, but no sound came. *Grayson!*

Grayson stood with his legs at hip-width, one leg behind the other, ready to fire.

"Get the hell away from her," he snarled. The panther regarded him curiously. "I know you can understand me, you son-of-bitch. Back off, or this next one goes between your eyes!"

Kill it! Win willed. *End it now.*

Grayson fired, but the arrow missed, searing the creature's fur as it shot past. The animal backed away, hobbling into the bushes, whimpering as it attempted to run, taking one more look at her before it fled. And then she heard it speak, and what she heard iced her heart.

Tell your sister I said hello!

Grayson rapidly reloaded his bow, fired again, and then chased the thing into the bush.

No, come back!

Fractures of pain tore through her back leg. She hobbled through the dirt, too weak to stand. When Grayson appeared, he threw back his hood, tore off his mask, and dropped to his knees. He held up both palms. "Win…it's me. Take it easy!"

I know it's you! This was impossible. He was *here*. Every time she opened her mouth, an involuntary snarl came out. Her mind was shattered, broken. She'd been so blind. The thing was Spencer. How was this even possible?

We woke them all up…

Win witnessed the blue light touch Luke, tear through him like an unstoppable wave. And Willard's words echoed back to her. Blood was the link between them. Could it be that strong? It woke up Spencer too. And if it woke him up...

Grayson crawled closer, she snarled, and he winced, backing off. He was bigger since she saw him, not so wiry. And his hair was short, cut neatly around his ears. She sniffed the air. It was still him, only he smelled like woodchips.

I knew I was right. Spencer had been here in Cedar Wood the whole time, and apparently hadn't changed one bit. Jake's words came back to her. It gave her strength she could be right about something after her abysmal failings.

"Oh, I'm sure he'll turn up eventually…" He'd known the whole time.

"Win, you're hurt. Can you try to change back? I can't help you like this."

Win cowered, ducking her head, and Grayson stood, and did the gentlemanly thing, and turned his back, both his hands in the air. "I won't look. Even though turning my back on you is probably the craziest thing I've ever done."

Grateful tears snaked out from the corners of her eyes as she willed herself back into her own body. She noticed his shoulders stiffen as she cracked and contorted until she was folded into a human-shaped ball, drawing her knees up to cover her nakedness. It dawned on her he'd ran away from this before, from what she was. Her vulnerability struck her hard.

"I'm here," she said weakly. He turned and smiled, laughing breathily.

"Thank god."

She was hurt. Her hip was torn, flesh sliced loose from the bone. She dared to look but saw cartilage and bile charged up in her throat. Grayson pulled off his hood. "Easy, easy," he assured her as he wound it around her upper thigh, knotting it so hard she hissed. "Sorry! We have to get you home."

This was going to sting like hell. And to make matters worse, it was Therian. Spencer did this to her. Grayson shrugged out of his jacket, wrapping it around her, helping ease her arms through the holes. It was warm and smelled like him. He linked his arms under her legs, lifting her off her bottom and into the air. He staggered and then grinned. "You weigh more than I remember."

She gasped, mildly insulted. "Thanks. I filled out a little. Being a wild animal kind of has that effect."

He threw her a shy smile, one she remembered. "I like it."

She wrapped her arms around his neck, unable to do anything but allow herself to be carried through the woods, staring at his profile. She linked her hands, touching the back of his blonde hair, his hair short and fuzzy near his nape. "You cut it all off," she said, unable to keep the disappointed tone out of her voice.

"Yeah, well, long hair doesn't work in a lumber yard," he panted. "Work hazard. You don't like it?"

Win pursed her lips. "I liked it long."

"I'll grow it."

Dizziness swept over her, her thighs were sticky, and she was bleeding heavily despite Grayson's makeshift tourniquet. She rested her head on his shoulder, her chin bumping on his collarbone.

"Look, I know you don't want to see me," he said, pausing to heave her into a higher position. She kept slipping down his body, and he was trying not to hold her backside. "I know how badly I've screwed this up. But…"

"Why would you think that?" she asked, her voice fading. "I'm so happy…I thought you were dead!"

For a moment, he looked confused, his brow knitting. She touched his chin with her fingertips, her breath soft, lulling into a pain-induced sleep. "I missed you."

"Well…I thought…" He paused. "It doesn't matter. Don't sleep, okay? Stay with me!"

"Okay," she murmured, closing her eyes. They were nearing the house; she could sense the shift in the ground, familiar earth underfoot.

"Hey, Win." He jolted her, and she opened her eyes. "Will your dad be home?"

Dad? "I…uh…don't know. Maybe…why?"

"Because if I'm doing this, then I'm doing it right this time."

She blinked, opening her eyes. "Doing what?"

"If I walk into your house, I'm in this for real, okay?" He nudged her with his chin, making sure she heard. "I want to meet him, introduce myself…as….if you still want me?"

Even though he'd stumbled gruffly through that sentence, Win understood. "You think I don't want you? I've been going crazy without you."

He still looked confused, but he shifted her weight, taking the plunge and walking across the yard, avoiding the deep puddles of mud. "Win, wake up!" he barked, and she jerked in his arms. "We are together, okay? No more hiding, no more secrets!"

Weakly she nodded, passing out in his arms, hearing his voice call out across the yard. He was calling Rowan for help.

Nineteen

Rowan flew down the drive as the ambulance arrived, waving her arms frantically in the air. Her nerves in tatters, she wondered how the morning had gone from relative calm to chaos in less than an hour. The blue and white neon sign whirred to a halt as doors were thrown open and two paramedics jogged to greet her, darting through the police tents erected across the yard.

"He's inside," her voice cracked. "Please…there's so much blood!"

They nodded, sharing a grim expression before chasing her to the house, trundling the stretcher along after them. "Was he attacked?"

"Yes, I think so…it was an animal attack!"

Rowan showed them into the hall, where a shaven-haired kid she'd never met was laid out on towels, bleeding all over the wooden floor. Next to him, Ella pressed her hands on the wound under his ribs, and Evan cradled his head in her lap, trying to keep him calm. The kid was out cold, his dark lashes settled against his deathly grey skin. One hand was a bloodied, chewed mess, and leaked blood through the patch job bandage Ella had attempted. Luke sat on the bottom step of the stairs, his head lolling in his hands, wracked with exhaustion after trying to drag Cole through the woods. He hadn't made it, calling Rowan, but she already left, her gut telling her something had gone terribly wrong.

"Shit," one of the paramedics hissed as he took over from Ella. He pried Win's bloody sweater out of her trembling fingers, and she hadn't dared let go. He patted her kindly, and she withdrew, sinking next to Luke on the stairs. "Any idea what did this?"

Rowan and Luke shared a glance before he said. "We didn't see."

The paramedics set to work, and Rowan crumpled against the wall, her hands shaking. Win was out there somewhere; she'd taken off, reckless and hot-headed. She watched as they loaded Cole onto a stretcher and strapped him down. Her eyes drawn to the ghastly pool of blood he'd left behind. It was a miracle he was still breathing. Bile burned her gullet as it rose, and she punched her chest. They took him out front. Luke stood, shakily and she caught the back of his shirt.

"What the hell happened?" she hissed, and he turned, his shoulders rising in a defeated shrug.

"It was a huge cat…," he faltered, his lips quivering, and he avoided looking directly at the blood. Rowan guessed his senses must be on overload. It was dense and thick, the outline of the window reflected in its red surface. "Rowan. I think—it was Spencer."

Rowan's lower lip dropped, her breath hitched. "What? That's not possible."

"I know." He leaned closer, making sure no one could hear them. "But it was him. I know it. I could smell him."

"And Win went after him?"

"I couldn't stop her."

Two more vehicles pulled in the drive, and her stomach dropped through the floor. One belonged to her father. The other was a police van with its doors thrown back. Eight officers, armed with shotguns and protective clothing, barrelled out. Rowan leaned weakly against Luke.

"We have to find her."

"I'm going with Cole," he said and brought Rowan back to reality. "I have to. The poor guy is alone. I tried calling his parents, but there was no answer."

Ben ran up the drive, staring open-mouthed at the small army of officers who were piling into the woods. Evan jogged out to meet him on the porch. Rowan could hear him cursing and shouting, and her heart seized. Hadn't this happened before? She shook her head, wishing her memory wasn't so fuzzy. Spencer tried this before.

Spencer.

"I'll go with you," Ella said to Luke, who shook her away.

"No, stay here in case Win comes back. I'll go with Cole. Ben will start freaking out when he knows she's missing and you guys are good for him. I'm not going to be much help. Plus, I just want to vomit—not great for anyone."

Reluctantly, Ella agreed, and Rowan wondered at what point he'd become the take-charge guy. Not that she minded, wrapping him in a half hug and kissing his forehead. "Call me with news on Cole."

Luke passed Ben on the steps, but the older man hardly noticed him as he barrelled through the door, his eyes torn to the blood. He lurched, covered his mouth, and stepped around it. Rowan mentally braced herself for his ire, the look of bitter disappointment she'd become accustomed to as a child.

Instead, he grabbed her and jerked her into his arms. "Thank god." He held her tightly, and her hands hung limp at her sides. "What's happened? Are you alright?"

"I'm fine!" She pushed him away gently. He smelled different. She wrinkled her nose, confused at the oddly familiar scent but guessed it might be a shampoo he was using. "Win is still out there!"

He paled, breathing hard. But he took her shoulders, stroking his thumbs down her arms. "It's okay. Come on. We should clean this before someone skids in it…I'll do it. You and Ella sit down."

"Dad, I should go out there!" Rowan hissed under her breath. He was suggesting she put her feet up and have a coffee while her sister was in danger.

"No, you stay *here*. The forest is crawling with cops right now, and you'll wind up getting shot!"

The ambulance door slammed behind Luke, and the lights whirred to life and sped out of the drive. Ella appeared with a mop and bucket. The pink sweater she wore was stained in Cole's blood. Ben gently took it out of her hands.

"I want you to rest, both of you. Evan and I have got this."

Ben propelled Rowan toward the kitchen, where she sagged into a chair. At the sink, Ella was rinsing off her hands, scrubbing soap into the cracks of her palms. Evan and Ben worked, mopping up the mess. Bleach and disinfectant burned the back of Rowan's nose. Queasy, she put her head on her arms, black spots filtering her vision. Ella handed her a glass of water, and Rowan sipped it, her mouth parched.

Holding her breath, Evan crossed the room with the bucket and emptied the bloody water down the sink. Rowan slapped the table. "I can't just sit here and wait!"

"Yes, you can!" Evan shot back. "Do you want to end up in a net? Because you will, Rowan. These guys aren't messing around now. They'll shoot to kill this thing."

"Spencer," Rowan said. The name echoed around the table. Ella sucked in her breath, followed by a collective gasp.

"What?" Ben fell in a seat.

"It's him," Rowan said. "Luke smelt him."

"How is that possible?" Ben looked at all three women dumbfounded. "He isn't even here…they're all in…." His voice trailed off, his gaze flying to the ceiling as he rubbed his chin and laughed.

"Oh, my god. They're *all* here. All of them. That means...Jake too."

Rowan narrowed her eyes. "*Dad?*"

"We woke them up. It's what she said...." He stared at Evan, who was avoiding looking at him. "That's what she said. We woke them *all* up."

"Dad, seriously? I know this is crazy, but now isn't the time *you* get to lose it. I've been dealing with this shit for years. What the hell are you talking about?"

"Nothing." He stared over the top of Ella's head, straight at Evan. His voice lowered, eyes darkened. "Nothing important right now."

"I think it sounds pretty important!" Rowan insisted, but her voice was silenced by a man shouting her name, over and over. She stiffened. Her first thought was it was a cop, and they'd caught something. Her chest tightened and she rose from her seat. The back porch door clattered open, heavy, labored footsteps padded through the boot room.

"Help! Rowan, I need help!"

All four stood, gasping as Grayson filled the door, cradling Win in his arms. Her head lolled backward, hair matted with blood trailed over his arm. Blood trailed crazily down her legs, through her bare toes. Ben cried out in horror.

"Oh, Win! No!" Ella was the first one to move, crossing the room and helping guide Grayson through the door. "Let's get her upstairs quick!"

"She needs a hospital," Grayson panted. "I don't think this will heal. He tore a chunk out of her."

"No, we can handle this here," Evan dissuaded him, urging him to follow her up the stairs. Rowan followed in a dream-like state, watching as Grayson eased Win onto her bed, her arms and legs flopping like a ragdoll.

They crowded the bed, staring in horror as Evan unwrapped the makeshift tourniquet. Ben covered his mouth as Evan pulled back the ruined hoodie. Win's pale, sliced flesh peeled away from the muscle.

"Oh, god!" Rowan groaned. "He's right. We have to take her to hospital."

Evan's eyes darkened as she flicked them up. "And what happens when they want to investigate how quickly she's healed? Or if she phases from shock? They'll ask questions.We have to deal with this here!"

"It's Therian," Grayson argued. "It won't heal well."

"It's already stopped bleeding, which is good!" Evan insisted. "Trust me. We have to do this here. I can help her, but I'll need assistance."

Grayson threw off his outerwear, flannels, and jacket, tossing them on the back of a chair. Stripped down to his tee-shirt underneath, he knelt on the bed. "I'll do what I can." Rowan's eyes bugged in disbelief. He wasn't supposed to be here, in their home. He cut an oppressive figure against the pretty, crisp backdrop of Win's bedroom.

"Me too," Ella chimed in. She'd swayed on her feet at the sight of Win's injury. "What do you need?"

"Ella—in our room, under the bed, there's a large brown leather suitcase. Bring it here. It's got everything I need. You learn to be prepared when dating a Hickory!"

Ella dashed out of the room. Ben floated around the bed as though he was a casual observer, unable to take in what he was seeing. Rowan perched on the edge of the bed, and at last, Grayson met her gaze.

"You saved her life," she whispered. "Did you see him?"

"Yeah, I saw him." Grayson chewed the inside of his mouth, his eyes rolling back to Win. He lifted her limp hand and kissed it. "I shot him."

"Did you kill him?"

"No, he got away. I told you I wasn't going to let anything happen. I only wish I'd gotten there sooner."

Rowan felt the heat of her father's eyes on her back. When she met them, he was staring at her open-mouthed, flicking his eyes back and forth between Win and Grayson. He pulled out a chair and fell in it as though his back gave out.

"And, who *exactly* are you?"

Rowan sensed the awkwardness in the room, how peculiar Grayson must seem. He didn't look like he belonged anywhere. Grayson cleared his throat, wiping his hand on his pant leg, and held it out across the bed. His daughter's blood dried into the cracks of his palm and stained under the beds of his nails. Weakly, he shook it.

"I'm Grayson Riley, sir," he said. "I'm Win's boyfriend."

"Win doesn't have a boyfriend."

"She does, as of about twenty minutes ago."

Ben didn't argue, only made space for Ella as she ran back into the room armed with the suitcase. "Well…you saved her life. We can discuss this later. Right now, I'm pleased to know you."

Evan flung open the suitcase. Inside it was packed with sutures, gauze, and surgical packing. She pulled out a surgical needle and thread and a pair of gloves. Rowan whistled. "Were you preparing for war? This is a lot of stuff."

"I told you, I'm prepared."

"You mean you expected something like this?"

Evan tensed her shoulders in readiness, snapping on the gloves. "We can talk about it later. Right now, I want *you* out of the room—and Ben. Grayson and Ella, stay."

Rowan's temper flared. "Why us?"

Evan met her eyes defiantly. "Because you are throwing off some chaotic energy, and I need to focus. These guys are the only level-headed ones here. *Please*," she added when Rowan spluttered in protest. "I'll take care of her."

Rowan relented, about to argue but didn't like the look on Evan's face. She was stressed, wired and Rowan knew not to push her. She grabbed her father's arm and dragged him out of the room. They sank to the floor in the hall, legs opposite one another, their backs pressed to the walls. Rowan rested her head against the floral wallpaper and focused on staying calm.

"Do you *know* him?" Ben asked, and Rowan's eyes sprung open.

"Dad, give me a break. He got her here safe, didn't he?"

"I'm not arguing. I wouldn't dare argue with him. He's massive! Like six foot six or something?"

Rowan bobbed her head. "Yup."

"But this is him? The *guy?* The one who…" he didn't want to voice it out loud. "The one she thought was dead?"

"The very same." Rowan closed her eyes, adrenaline coursing under her skin. Right now, she had much to be thankful for. Grayson had gotten Win home to her family. But her gut swelled in anticipation, a storm brewing above the house, threatening to destroy everything Rowan had been trying to keep Win safe from. Win would recover, and then she'd wake up, and there would be a shit storm. Rowan prepared to face her anger and resentment when she learned how she kept Grayson from her all these months.

Ben gasped in shock, clutching the wall, and Rowan's eyes snapped open. Inside the bedroom, Win screamed.

Twenty

Win's eyes fluttered open, her lashes wet, heavy. She hissed in pain, her hands padding the bed. "Grayson?"

"I'm here." His voice floated out of white space. She saw his silhouette backlit against the light from her bedroom window. Licking her cracked lips, she winced, her mouth woolly as cotton.

"You passed out, honey," Rowan said. "About three times."

"It hurts," she whimpered. Under the blanket, her thigh was alight. Tiny needles zapped her skin, hot, swollen, and throbbing. Blinking, she eased onto her elbows but was promptly pushed back into the pillow. Her vision was blurred, hazy, and white. "I have to get up…Spencer!"

"We know," Rowan assured her. Voices were floating out of the haze, like ghosts. Win remembered his bite, teeth sinking into her flesh, leaving a mark that would never fade with time. A scar would brand her for life, a Therian mark.

"Cole," she spluttered. "Is he okay?"

"Luke called from the hospital. He's getting a bus home. Cole is fine. He needed a lot of stitches, and he won't heal as quickly as you, but he'll be fine."

"But, his hand?" Win's cheeks were wet. "He lost…Spencer…"

"Take it easy," Rowan assured her. "You need to focus on yourself."

Win willed her vision to clear, the haze to fade. Her head throbbed, her brain pulsing inside her skull. One by one, she could make out the faces around the bed: Evan, Ella, her father, and Rowan. Grayson stood in the corner, arms folded, pale and exhausted. "Come here," she begged, and he smiled weakly, pushing away with the wall with one foot. He dropped to his knees beside her.

"Rowan is right. Take it easy. Everyone is here, and safe." He took her palm and kissed it. Tears welled up, panic fluttering to her throat.

"Don't go, okay?" she said, tears spilling onto the pillow under her head. She turned to her father. "Dad, *please* don't make him go."

"I won't," Ben agreed with a chuckle. "I'm not sure I could if I tried."

"She needs to rest." Evan stood, stretching. Her floral dress was stained with blood, and she stooped, almost frail, energy drawn out of her. She leaned over Win and kissed her forehead. "Sleep, now! No one is going anywhere. Ben…can we talk downstairs?"

The room emptied, leaving Ella lingering in the door. She rushed to Win's bedside, having waited for her opportunity, and gave her an awkward half embrace. "I'm going to take off. I need to shower off all this blood."

Win folded her hand around Ella's arm. "Are you okay?"

"I'm fine." Ella didn't look fine. She looked wired, jittery. "Can I take the diary? I was really into it before Luke called, and I think I might have thought of something. But I'll come back later?"

"Come back tonight." Win nodded. Right now the mysterious

diary her uncle gave her as bedtime reading, about the furthest thing from her mind.

Ella said goodbye, casting a glance at Grayson, who plucked a book off Win's shelf and settled in a chair by the window, his long legs stretched out in front of him. Ella grinned at Win and gave her a sly wink. Once she'd gone, Rowan lingered in the doorway, wringing her hands, her keen gaze on Grayson. "Grayson…can I have a word? In the hall?"

Grayson's pale gaze snapped up, and he drew up his legs and straightened. "I'm not leaving, Rowan."

"I wasn't asking you to."

"Anything you want to say, you can say right here."

Win's eyes darted back and forth between them, confused. "Is something the matter?"

Rowan smiled brightly, waving away her concern. "Nothing. Get some rest, okay? I'm going to see if the cops have turned up anything."

A deep rumbling shook the room, vibrating the books on the shelves. Rowan gasped as a police chopper whirled by the house, doing a quick swoop before lifting back up. "They've launched an air search," she said.

Win fisted the bedclothes, hauling herself into a sitting position. "They won't find him. He'll hide—something he's pretty good at! Or he'll go home."

"This is insane." Rowan pulled at her hair, breaking into a pace. She nudged Grayson away from the window, staring at the colossal chopper circling their woods. "How can this have happened to him?"

"You forget something," Win piped up, and both of them turned to look at her. "He *survived* the calling. Somehow, he pulled through. And I'd like to know how."

"The same thing is happening to the other kid." Grayson folded his arms. "He won't be far behind, and I'm not sure I like the idea of him being here when it happens. It could be dangerous."

"His name is Luke," she corrected him, rolling her eyes. She recalled Grayson admitted to a touch of jealously over their friendship in the summer. Grayson smirked when their gazes met, his cheeks reddening.

"And it's a bit late in the game to be acting protective," Rowan snapped. "We have this handled."

"If you had it handled, then maybe *this* wouldn't have happened!" He waved his hand at Win's bandaged thigh. Rowan's cheeks pinked, and looked away.

Again Win looked between the two, sensing a tension. Grayson looked away, preferring to gaze out of the window than at Rowan. "What's going on?" she demanded.

"Nothing," they both said at the same time. Exhaustion swept over her. She fell back on the pillow, ignoring the two of them as she closed her eyes. Sleep pulled her into a dull haze. She filtered them out, knowing they were snapping at one another over her bed. Her thigh ached, and her ribs were tender, causing her inhaled breath to twang. She vaguely recalled Evan making her take a painkiller, which dulled the splintering sensation in her back. Spencer had tossed her around like a plush toy. But she'd given him a fair whack—not too bad for her first-time fight. Not that she ever wanted a repeat performance.

Win sensed something peculiar happening under the bandage. Her flesh was knitting but rapidly, a fiery, unstoppable itch spreading over her lacerated skin. She could feel the skin tightening, pulling together and her legs scissored under the covers, eventually, the irritation pulling her out of the sleep she needed. When she sat up, Grayson was sat on the floor under the window, his back to the wall.

He stood fluidly. "You okay?"

Sweat drenched her back; the prickles under the bandage were like a thousand tiny spiders crawling under her skin. "No, this hurts. It's worse than the bite."

He handed her a glass of water and some little yellow pills. "Evan said to take this." He tipped back her head and made her drink. "You've been asleep about an hour."

"Is Luke home?"

"I don't know. I've been up here. He hasn't been up."

Win made a groggy noise of disappointment, wishing she could see him with her own eyes. The last time she saw him, he looked dreadful. Grayson pulled up a chair next to her. She rolled to her good side to face him, gritting her teeth, taking his arm, and pulling it against her.

"Maybe you should sleep some more?"

"I can't. I itch."

He grinned. "Don't go scratching anything. What does it feel like?"

"Like my skin is tingling—zapping." She let out a shaky sigh. "But you can distract me."

He chuckled, leaning across and kissing her forehead. Win recoiled, thinking she must look a sweaty mess, but she wasn't about to let him go anywhere. Having him in this room felt surreal. Unmasked, short, neat hair and ordinary clothes. It was like a dream. She examined his calloused hands linked with hers, his bitten down nails, and she smiled gently. It was still him.

"Don't go getting any ideas," he said, exhaling long and hard through his nose, the pad of his thumb tracing over her knuckles. "I didn't think you wanted to see me at all."

Win settled into the pillow. He'd said this earlier, and she'd been confused. "Why would you think that? Grayson, I thought you were dead. I've spent the last three months…grieving."

Now it was his turn to look confused. He scratched his chin. "But…I told you I was alive?"

Win's sleepy smile dropped. "What…?"

"Look," he said. "After the fire, I had to get away. My mother was dead, and after our fight, I never thought you'd want to see me again. So I took off for a day to clear my head. I'm sorry. I shouldn't have stayed away."

Win's grip on his hand tightened. "I get that. I *don't* get the part where you let me know you were okay…Grayson…I did *not* know!"

They were both shooting strained glances back and forth, both in the dark, believing their truths. Grayson said. "I left you the arrowhead."

"Arrowhead?"

"Yes! Right where your head is now. Under your pillow where I knew you'd find it."

Win bolted upright. "I didn't find it."

"I left more…arrows around the woods, in the yard. I left notes." He pulled his hand away, suddenly embarrassed. "More like begging letters. I hoped you'd come. When you didn't even respond— I gave up. I thought you moved on…and with the guy you're seeing in school…."

"Whoa! Who?" she spluttered. "Cole?"

"I thought you didn't want me in your life— and I don't blame you— after what I did."

"I'm not dating Cole!" Her face was growing hot, her temper rising. "Who told you I was?"

He swallowed, a treacherous look crossing his face. "Your sister."

"*Rowan* told you? When have you even spoken to her?"

"I saw her a couple of days ago. In the woods."

"What?" Win tore off the bedclothes, tried to stand, and then her legs buckled. Grayson caught her under the arms and forced her back to the mattress.

"Don't get upset!"

"I'm more than upset…she knew you were out there and didn't tell me!"

"Calm down!" he growled, his temper growing short. "It doesn't matter now."

Win's eyes filled up. "Yes, it does. She's been lying to me…" her voice trailed away, reality becoming startling clear. There was no way Win would have missed a sign like an arrow. Upon seeing it, she would have guessed it was his mark, his way of letting her know he was okay. He just needed time. She would have accepted anything to know he was alive. But if she never got the sign, if someone was removing them before she even spotted it. Win's heart sank, her shoulders slumped. Rowan wouldn't have done this to her.

But she did.

A bitter taste filled her mouth, she clutched at her chest, willing herself not to cry, and she had to stay mad. Rowan's betrayal stung worse than any bite Spencer could have given her.

"Win…listen…"

"No, you listen!" Her eyes flashed dangerously. "Your little *signs* suck ass! Why not walk through my front door? Come to my window? Rather than leave me cryptic clues and hidden messages. I would have come, Grayson. I never wanted to lose you!"

Grayson held out his palms, and Win knew she was growing hysterical, pain and trauma making her temper flare. "I know. In hindsight, it was stupid!"

"I thought you were dead!"

"I *know*!" he cried, exasperated. "I know! But after the fire—I was terrified. And walking in here after what I'd hidden—my lies—having to face you and your family. It was intimidating. It would have been like shark diving without a cage!" He paced the floor, his heavy boots thudding. "I thought….somehow…if you found the notes, I could talk to you, and it might be like it was before."

"It's never going to be the same!" Win burst. "We are different people now!"

"I'm sorry. I know I've screwed things up again!" He came closer, planting his hands on her upper arms. "I know we have to work things out…but I'll go…if it upsets you."

"No!" She crawled out of bed, flinging her arms around his neck, the tips of her toes barely touching the floor. She buried her face in his hair, drinking in his woody smell she missed, her heart beating against his chest. "You are not going anywhere. You said it yourself— we're together now, and I'm not letting you vanish on me!"

A knock on the door broke them apart; Win fell back to the bed as the door creaked open. Rowan filled the space, arms crossed, her eyes on the floor. "Win, put on a robe. You both should come downstairs."

Win's eyes flashed yellow, her temper rising. "We need to talk, Rowan!"

Rowan chewed the inside of her mouth. "Yeah, I *know*, but not now. Get decent and come down."

"I'm not going anywhere until you explain why you hid Grayson from me!"

Rowan held up her hands. "We'll talk. I promise, but right now, you need to come with me."

"Why?"

Rowan looked skyward as if her day couldn't get much worse. "Jake Fraser is here."

Twenty One

Sickly pale, Win dressed in a robe and let Grayson lift her off the bed. He carried her downstairs, letting her slip to her feet as they reached the bottom step. She didn't want him carrying her into the kitchen, where her entire family plus one uninvited guest were waiting for them around the table. She wanted to walk in, alone, rather than weak and afraid. Dizziness swept over her as she tried to put weight on her injured leg. She found Grayson's arm with splayed fingers.

"I'm here, okay?"

She nodded, nauseous and shaky. Then Luke unlocked the front door, walking in and shaking rainwater off his jacket. His eyes traveled up and found her. He fled across the hall, picking her up in his arms and lifting her off her feet before she could speak.

"You're okay!" He held her tighter. "I've been so worried." He looked down at her bandaged leg, his lower lip quivering. "What did he do to you?"

Win gently pushed him back, nodding to Grayson, who was waiting by the stairs, an unreadable, cold expression on his face. "I'm fine. Well…I'm fine now. Luke…your dad is here."

He nodded. "I saw the car." Luke's eyes were dull, red, and sore, and more than anyone, he looked like he needed twelve hours sleep. Slowly, he registered Grayson standing behind Win, his mouth pursing like he was sucking a lemon. "Hey."

Grayson nodded and replied with a gruff, "Hey."

"Good that you stuck around this time—and didn't leave Win for dead."

Grayson fumed quietly, grinding his teeth. Win punched Luke's arm. "Luke! Don't be a jerk. He saved my life."

"I guess I have bigger problems." He glanced toward the kitchen. "God, I do not want to see him right now."

"Then we go in together." She pressed her hand into his.

Grayson exhaled and trailed in after them. "I can wait upstairs?" he offered, to which Win shook her head fiercely.

"No, way. You're staying with me!"

"Or you can wait in the woods? That's where you usually hang out and stalk people, right?" Luke didn't miss a beat, and Win's face flamed.

Win tugged Luke's hand, giving him a pinch with her nails. "Quit it! He stays." She glanced at Grayson over her shoulder, throwing him a shy smile, reaching behind for his hand. "Ignore him. I don't want you leaving me, ever again." An adorable blush crossed his cheeks, and she squeezed his fingers.

An ominous silence befell the room as the three of them walked into the kitchen, Win clutched Luke's hand, and Grayson trailed behind like a great looming shadow. Grayson slid into a space next to Evan, pulling out his chair and sitting on it backward. Rowan moved along, so Luke and Win could take a seat. But Ben pulled his youngest daughter protectively onto his knee, draping an arm across her lap. Jake sat at the foot of the table, arms folded, his lips pressed together.

"Well, isn't this a lovely family reunion," he quipped, making sure to stare pointedly at his son, who was still clutching Win's pale hand, their fingers interlocked. Jake's eyes rested on them before raking up to Win's face, giving her a slow smile. She looked away, anywhere else but at him.

"It's been a while, Jake," Ben said. "How is life in Hawaii?"

"Well, clearly, I'm not there, Ben. I've been forced back to this shit end town. I thought I'd managed to leave this place behind. But no, it seems, no matter what I do, I end up entangled with Hickorys."

"I think we need to talk about your son, Jake."

Jake clicked his tongue. "You think so?"

"He nearly killed my daughter."

Tension built in the room, Win's stomach was knotted, unsettled, despite Luke's clammy palm in her hand. Jake sucked in his breath, finding her gaze across the table. "I never wanted this to happen— any of it. Are you alright?"

She swallowed, unnerved to have caught his attention. "I'm healing."

"Neat trick you all have," he quipped.

"Not all of us," Ben snapped. "And it could have been worse. The kid wasn't so lucky."

"I'm sorry," Jake said with a long breath. "I'm sorry for all of it."

Ben groaned and rubbed his eyes, resting his elbow on the table. "Why are you here, Jake? Why are you back in town?"

"We had no choice," Jake answered simply.

"Where is Spencer now?" Across the table, Rowan found her voice. Win noticed how her complexion greyed.

"He's laying low—what with the police in the woods and the chopper flying over. He's healing." He flicked his eyes to Win. "You sure gave as good as you got."

"No, that would be me," Grayson growled. "I shot him."

Jake smiled broadly as if noticing him for the first time. "Ah,

I was wondering who you were. You must be the *boyfriend*." He winked at Win, gesturing to his jacket. "Is this the coat guy?"

"Back off, Jake!" Luke snarled, his eyes shifting to a cerulean blue. Win winced, his grip on her hand clamping like a vice. A vein pulsed in Jake's jaw; the rejection stung.

"The name is *Dad*, in case you forgot. And you don't get to speak to me like that! Why exactly is *he* invited to a private family conversation?"

"Because *he* put himself between my daughter and your son. I'm more than happy to let him take up permanent residence if he wanted to," Ben replied, and Win marveled at his calm tone. "And, this isn't your family. It's mine, Jake. It's always been *mine*."

The pointed tone of Ben's words wasn't lost on Win. Awkwardly, she met Luke's eyes and could tell he'd noticed too.

"Why don't we cut all this crap, and you tell us what has been going on?" Rowan cut in. The air was thick with unspoken tension as it was. Jake held court at the head of the table as if he owned it and everyone in the room.

Jake rolled his shoulders, placing both hands palm up on the table in an open gesture. His posture screamed confidence and composure. "I don't know where to begin. But it was about three months ago. My wife, Carla, left about six months before, so it's been Spence and me for a while…"

"Divorced again—there's a shocker," Ben chided, pleased with his quip and Win shook her head at her father. Jake said nothing in response, only ground his jaw.

"So, one night, we were asleep, and our entire house flooded with light. It blazed through the rooms, and I was convinced a plane was about to hit— it was so bright, and everything rumbled. But it was strange— the light was blue, hazy, it crackled. But it soon passed over, and I put it down to a helicopter going low overhead. We said nothing about it the next day."

Win closed her eyes, ashamed. *We woke them all up…*

"A couple of weeks passed, and we never thought anything

of it. But then Spencer started getting sick—painful headaches. A doctor checked him out and gave him a clean bill of health. But not long after, dreams started, and pains in his body. He paced most nights, sweating, delirious, and begged to come home. He said he'd feel better here but couldn't explain why."

Win chewed her lip to a pulp, sharing a look with Rowan.

"I did this," Win admitted, her chin wobbling. Saying it out loud was good, cathartic, a public cleansing. She looked at Luke. "It's my fault— all mine. When we burned the cabin, we set them free, but it touched something in you. It woke you all up, all *three* of you."

Luke squeezed her hand on top of the table, a gesture that didn't go unnoticed by Jake. He stared darkly at their laced fingers. "*We* did this," insisted Luke. "You can't take it all, all the time Win. Save some blame for the rest of us."

"You couldn't have known," Evan assured her.

"What about you?" Grayson's grave tone floated down the table, directed at Jake.

Jake blinked. "What about me?"

"You didn't get sick?"

"Do I look sick?"

Win realized he didn't. She guessed his age to be around forty like her father, but the difference was vast. Jake could have passed for a much younger man; he was bright eyed, dark haired, not a fleck of grey. He looked in perfect, youthful health and handsome in his cold, dark way.

"That doesn't make sense," she said, and Jake snapped his head in her direction. "You didn't get affected?"

"It's because he's too old," Grayson said. All eyes, all attention centered on him, and he blushed, clearly unused to so many people looking at him at once. "What I mean is— I think it's because he's aged out."

Rowan rolled her eyes. "I hate you know so much about us."

"I'm sorry. I know how weird that sounds," Grayson continued. "I was brought up by a man who made it his life's work to learn about Therian. He believed as long as there were Hickorys, there were Rileys to keep them in order."

Win's face flamed with embarrassment. It was becoming startling evident Grayson wasn't a people person. "That's not worrying *at all,"* Luke joked.

"How about we get back to the part where Jake is really old?" Ben added in, his impatience growing.

"I can't help how I was raised. It's true, from what I understand, the process begins in early teens and ends around eighteen. Jake would have bypassed it entirely," Grayson attampeted to explain. "Technically, he's one of you. But whatever happened to Spencer hasn't happened to him."

"But I still get the anti aging benefits?" Jake chortled, running a hand through his hair. "I can live with that. Unlike you Ben. Jeez, what happened to you? Is this what daughters do to a father?"

Ben's expression pinched, about to take the bait but Win waved her hand. "How about we keep the subject on your son?"

"What can I tell you, Winifred? My son has always been—different. You learn to get used to it."

"Can you all *stop*?" It was Evan, who up until now had remained silent, sitting by Grayson. "I want to know how he got through this without harm. Stop bickering!"

"I don't get how this hasn't happened before," Ben thought aloud. "You've lived across the woods for years. Why haven't you ever…?"

"Phased?" Rowan filled in the gap for her father, to which Jake shrugged his shoulders.

Ben struggled for words. "Why now? Why not before all this?"

Win's gaze fell on Evan, not knowing why she expected her to answer, but to her surprise, Evan was staring at the floor, chewing her lip. Again, it was Grayson who answered.

"This is cursed land," he said. "*Hickory* land. Win and Rowan are direct descendants. Their blood is stronger and linked directly to the curse—to John. My guess is Jake lived apart all those years… it just never kicked in, till the blue light woke it."

Win nodded grimly in agreement. "Uncle Willard said something similar."

Ben's forehead creased in a frown. "So…you knew? All these years."

Jake's lips lifted in a wicked smirk. "You aren't the only man here capable of keeping secrets, Ben."

Once again, Luke and Win shared a confused look. Even Rowan seemed dazed by the turn the conversation was taking, the unspoken tension between the two men. Finally, it was her who piped up. "Can we get back on track?"

Jake wafted his hand around, straightening his sweater before continuing. "I was lucky to discover Mercy remained unsold. So I bought it back, and we moved in around a month ago."

"You've been here a month?" Luke fired.

Jake clicked his tongue. "I didn't see it as any of your business."

Luke deflated like a balloon, and Win felt his hand slip out of hers. Jake noticed his reaction, pausing to make sure his comment sunk in before continuing. She wondered how Luke was coping, faced with the man who'd walked out of his life in the summer, seemingly unfazed, unwilling to fight for him. Win wished she could talk to him, even telepathically, but she didn't dare, judging by how that went last time.

"We settled back in, and for a while, Spencer seemed better. The pain was still there, but he was coping. One night, he went out. He was going mad, cooped up in the house and said he'd go into Lincoln for a few drinks at a club he knew."

Win's stomach tightened, his tone darkening.

"Around one in the morning, I heard him come home, but you know him." He looked pointedly at Rowan. "He wasn't alone. So I did what any good father would do and ignored it. He needed to let loose, work out some energy..."

"With a girl?" Ben finished for him, and Win remembered the girl who'd gone missing from Lincoln. "Oh, my god!"

A flicker of guilt crossed his face. "I had no idea what would happen. I heard screaming…."

"Uh, spare the details. We get it!" Luke flared.

"No, you don't!" Jake said. "What I found in his room...."

"Jake, *please.*" Rowan covered her mouth, sickly pale.

"Spencer was gone. Entirely. The thing that was left was a wild animal."

"So, what did you do?" Win asked. "Put him in a cage?"

Jake made a noise in his throat, like a strangled laugh. "Uh, no. I was worried about being next on the menu. Eventually, he calmed down, and he seemed aware of where he was and what happened. Most of the time, he appeared content until the other guy went missing, and I knew he'd gotten out."

"Hold up!" Rowan spat. "What are you talking about? He doesn't turn *back*?"

"No," Jake answered. "He hasn't. He's...kind of stuck."

"As a panther!" Luke laughed, then realized how wrong that sounded. "I bet he's pissed!"

"Well, I have no idea— he can't communicate with me. I've tried. I would imagine he's terrified."

"He's killed two people. And he could have killed Cole today and Win. Why the hell haven't you come to us before?" Ben roared.

Tell your sister I said hello. Win recalled Spencer's words to her before he'd sloped off in pain. He'd not struck her as terrified, not in the least. Something about that made her think Spencer might be living his best life.

Win looked down the table toward Grayson, who lifted his shoulders in a shrug. "I've never heard of this before."

"I have," Rowan said. "Back in my early days, I got stuck for a week. It took a lot of coaxing to bring me back, but I had Grandpa. I don't know what Spencer would need."

"A bolt between the eyes?" Luke chided.

"When we go through the calling, the animal is what our bodies want to be. It takes focus and control to remain human. Spencer sounds completely feral."

"I know he understands me," Jake said. "When I'm feeling brave enough to get close to him. He's still in there."

"Oh, he understands," Win said. "He knew me this morning."

"We can't knowingly let him roam free," Evan said. "He'll kill again. We have to deal with this."

Win listened intently; her thoughts dwelling on the poor girl who'd been Spencer's unwitting first victim, her mouth formed the question pressing in her mind. "What did you do with the girl?"

Jake paled under his tan, and for the first time that afternoon, he genuinely looked ashamed. His throat bobbed. "I buried her."

Inwardly, Win hissed. The thought of him having to bury her alone made her queasy. As much as he irritated her, that must have been heartbreaking, and it tugged on her conscience. But then she frowned. "But…they found her on our property?"

A horrible silence befell the table, and after a few moments, it was Grayson who had the guts to say what they were all thinking out loud. "Spencer dug her up."

He still hates us….he still hates me…. Rowan's voice floated across the table, and Win jerked and stared at her sister, head low, chewing her lip. Win sagged, aghast that she could feel the despair raging through Rowan. After all this time, Spencer was still trying to hurt her.

Ben rubbed at his face, raking his hair back. "Shit… her family. They must be going insane."

"It still doesn't answer how he survived the calling?" Rowan said, bringing them back to the present. "How did he survive what was happening to him?"

"All I know is one minute he was a coherent human being, and then he wasn't," Jake offered, which was rather useless. "I don't pretend to know all about Therians and their inner workings. I've spent most of my life denying you all existed. I just want to help him." His mouth was set in a firm line; eventually, his eyes fell to Luke. "I'm prepared for what this means—if he comes back. He'll have to pay for what he did. For real this time."

Luke choked out a snort. "What jail could he go to?"

"Look. No matter what's happened between us. I don't want to see this happen to you either…to have you both lost…."

I was lost a long time ago.

Win's head snapped up. She'd heard Luke's voice in her head, like a blaring siren. She squeezed his hand harder.

When Luke didn't answer, Jake grew edgy, shifting in his seat uncomfortably. "What can we do? *Please?* Is there any way of pulling him back? I don't want anyone else to get hurt."

No one spoke for a while until finally, Ben straightened in his seat. "What about the bodies? The ones in our yard?"

Jake ground his teeth, a vein pulsing in his temple. "I knew you'd have some issue."

"Of course I do!" Ben laughed, though it wasn't funny. "He brought body parts onto our land, using it as a dumping ground. And now, this family is at the center of a murder investigation. Win and Rowan can't use their own home to phase. I'm wondering if we shouldn't just let the cops deal with him. That poor girl… He needs to pay for what he did. "

"What do you suggest? They shoot him dead?" Jake blasted.

Win felt a cruel smile tugging on the corner of her mouth. There was the favoritism thing again. Perhaps Jake did have a favorite?

"He's a murderer, Jake!" Ben wailed. "Last summer, he tried to kill Rowan after dating her for five years. He shot her out of the sky. Why the hell should we help him?"

Jake opened his mouth, spluttered, and then said something to nudge Win's conscience.

"Because…we're a family," Jake said, looking around the table. "Aren't we? Yeah, maybe a strange one. But, we're blood."

He looked straight at Luke, his steel gaze burning. "I only had a few years with my mother before she died. But I do remember one thing she always used to say. We're a pack…and…."

"The pack runs together," Rowan finished, lifting her eyes. They were wet. "Grandpa used to say the same thing. We are stronger together."

A long silence stretched into minutes, Win clicked her nails on the table, a dull, splintering ache pulsing up her leg, her painkillers were wearing off, and she was growing sleepy. She caught Grayson's worried expression, watching her across the table. Finally, it was Evan who spoke.

"We just want this to all go away," she said. "Jake, we need a little time. But we can think of something. There has to be a way to pull him back to his own body. And in the meantime, he can't hurt anyone else."

Why did Win have an awful suspicion right now Ella had the key to everything? The diary she'd taken home might have a clue about the light cast from the stone in the woods. Win mentally willed her friend back soon. Why hadn't she made time to read it herself? Right then, she cursed herself for all the distractions she'd allowed to get in the way.

Jake stood. "I should leave." He shuffled back into his coat. As he rolled his cuffs under his coat sleeves, he glanced about the kitchen, his gaze attracted to the peeling paint, the faded cupboard doors, smiling as though he found it quaint. Ben stood, arms crossed, practically on his back as he followed him into the hall. Gingerly, Win pushed up from the chair, leaning against Luke as she hobbled out behind, lingering in the door. Jake's eyes cast over her long bare legs, the bandage wound tightly around her thigh.

Then he fumbled in his coat pocket and drew out a black leather wallet. He opened it, pulled out a wad of dollar bills, thrusting it toward her. Win snatched her hand away as if the cash was on fire. "I don't want your money."

"Please," he insisted, prising her palm open and then closing it around the wad. "Take it for college or new clothes…buy yourself a new coat, for god's sake."

Win thrust it back, but he held up both palms, stepping away. "I don't want it!"

"Jake, we don't need your money." Ben stuffed one hand in his pocket, scratching his jaw. "I'm perfectly capable of paying for my daughter's college tuition."

"Oh, come on, Ben, what does a city planner pay these days? Not much, by the looks of this old place."

"I haven't been a city planner since I was twenty-three, Jake!"

"Whatever…clearly your salary isn't enough to keep this place going; what with all the mouths you have to feed, including my son."

"Luke pays his way and is more than welcome here."

Jake huffed. "Take it, please. After what Spencer did to her, it's the least I can do."

Rowan shoved past Win, grabbed the wad of dollars out of her hand, and then stuffed them back in Jake's breast pocket. Riled, his lip curled, but she drew up to her full height, only an inch shorter than him. "I'm the family alpha. And we don't want your money. The *least* you can do is keep your son away from us until we figure out how to make this all go away."

He smiled strangely. Though it was charming, it was snakelike, his eyes boring right into her.

"I think you'll find, Alice Hickory is the family alpha. But who am I to argue, huh?"

Ben planted himself next to Rowan. "Alice *Adler* died a long time ago, Jake. You know that."

Jake chuckled, though it was laced with cruelty. As he walked out the door, he wagged his finger in Ben's direction. "You know, I was always intrigued how you managed that little cover-up, Ben. And I'm sorry, Rowan, you are a poor imitation of your mother. You don't even smell like her."

Rowan winced as if he'd slapped her, and Win recoiled, wanting to rush to her side. But something painful glinted in Rowan's eyes, boiling up like a pressure cooker, and Win didn't dare move.

*He knows something..*Win thought aloud, too late to hide from her sister. Rowan looked sharply in her direction. *He knows something about Mom...it makes sense...he shows up back in town...and she's gone…*

Rowan shook her head wordlessly, on the brink of losing her temper. *Not now, Win!*

"Get *out,"* Rowan seethed through gritted teeth. With a crash of the door, he was gone, and no one breathed till the Mercedes started up in the drive. Ben trembled, reaching out to touch

Rowan's arm, but she dodged him. Shaken and misty-eyed, she darted for the stairs and ran to her room. Win slumped, and Grayson appeared behind her and took her weight. He gave her a nod before lifting her knees from under her.

"Back upstairs," he ordered, then looked sharply at Ben. "If you don't mind?"

"No, no!" Ben was scrubbing his face, anxiously pacing. "Your welcome here, Grayson. I'm sorry, but I hate that guy."

"You aren't alone." Luke followed behind Win and Grayson. Jake had an overwhelming effect on people. She made him stop so she could knock on Rowan's door, but when she got a muffled reply Win knew better to let her cry it out. Rowan had held it together all morning, it was no wonder she was about to erupt like a volcano.

Grayson kicked open her bedroom door using the toe of his boot, then folded Win back into the duvet. Luke lingered in the doorway, watching with a strange expression, his lower lip chewed until it was red.

"So, I guess, we never met properly." He gingerly stepped into the room, and Win tensed in anticipation of what might come out of Luke's mouth. "Sorry I was shitty earlier. It's been a long morning."

Grayson's expression was stern, unreadable, and Win could see him mentally weighing Luke up from top to bottom. Luke was lean compared to him, but Grayson knew Therian, and Win wondered if he was assessing just how big Luke might get. Finally, Grayson's lips twitched into a thin smile.

"It's fine," he said. "I get it."

"What's up with your face?"

Win went hot. "*Luke!*"

"What! I'm only asking?"

Grayson absently scratched the scar running under his ear to his lower lip. "Run in with a wolf a long time ago." He glanced at Win. "I got in his way."

Luke clapped his hands awkwardly. "Well…I'm going to phone the hospital, check on Cole, and then Ella is coming back."

"You're being unusually nice to him," Win said. "You should try being nice more often. Cole seems like a sweet guy, just misunderstood."

Luke shoved his hands in his pockets, backing out the door, his eyes lingering on Grayson, on his arm draped around Win's shoulder. "There's a lot of that going around."

A woman in a stained nightgown edged around the woods. Her fingers trembled as she reached the trunk of a gnarled, ancient oak. Leaning heavily against the damp bark, she let out a ragged breath and sank to her knees, tears spilling out from over her pale lashes.

What are you doing? Go home...go home!

But her legs refused to move. Resting her head against the trunk, she hugged her knees to her chest. Far in the distance, through the woods, she could see the blinking lights of her yard. Her home. Alice wept into her knees, wanting Ben, wanting her babies, missing them so hard she ached. Guilt coursed through her. She knew she must move. But moving was painful, and she was tired. And there would be questions, so many questions to answer. So much to confess. The moment she stepped over that threshold, she would be compelled to answer her daughters.

Weakly, she stood, her fingers digging into the knot of the tree. She looked up at the intricate, twisted heart of the oak. This was *their* tree, the knot hole big enough to hide things inside. Of all the places, she could have stopped. She'd rested here.

A hiding place...*their* hiding place. "No...I can't go back." It was a desperate plea to no one, like a child begging not to have to go to school in the morning.

A noise rustled through the trees, and she jumped, feeling hot eyes on her back. The sound was much farther away, but her hearing was off, piercing sounds distorted and fragmented. But there wasn't anything wrong with her vision, and she saw him appear at the edge of a clearing, hands in pockets, head tilted, watching her—that smile on his face, so charming, compelling. A face so handsome you could lose your breath, but it only made her heart beat faster in panic. Sweat beaded her forehead, and she found the strength she'd been lacking. He held up his hands, creeping closer as she stood, one leg cocked at an angle, ready to flee.

"Alice, you're safe…." His voice was still the same. The voice of a friend—familiar, warm, and like home. They'd been friends once, a long time ago. With him, you were never safe. Alice learned that the hard way, a lifelong friendship destroyed in an act of pure malice.

No…

"If you can't go home to them now— then come home with me."

She blinked back tears. "No, Jake…" she said aloud. His face dropped in misery, that familiar disappointment she couldn't bear. "No."

Alice ran and didn't look back.

Twenty Two

Clouds parted, allowing fragments of sun to dry up the ground as the afternoon crawled toward early evening. Win slept but awoke to find Grayson gone and Ella sitting in a chair by the window, her nose still in the diary. She sat up too quickly, her thigh throbbing. "Where is he?"

Ella smiled. "He went to get food, don't panic."

"Why can't he get food here?"

"I think he wanted a break from the chaos." Ella closed the diary, dark shadows sweeping under her eyes. "He'll be back, don't worry."

Win fell back on the pillow. Her tongue stuck to the roof of her mouth, she grasped for her bedside water glass and sipped it greedily. She looked at Ella over the top of the glass. "Good book?"

Ella made a face. "It's intense."

Win eased herself up in a sitting position and patted the bed beside her. "Tell me."

Ella pressed the diary to her chest as if to protect Win from the information within. "I'm not sure you want to know. But I did read something interesting."

Ella climbed on the bed beside her, rolling onto her side and leaning one elbow on the pillows. "This girl—Mary, your ancestor, was not a good person, Win. Like, not in the slightest."

Win's expression soured as goose bumps erupted over her arms. "Oh."

"There's so much in here about Vivienne, Callum…but that is another story. Mary mentions the stone on more than one occasion. And it sounds like even she didn't know what it was. It does mention one thing that kind of freaked me out. Here…I'll read it."

Ella flipped the diary open, flicked through the crinkly pages, careful not to tear them as she turned them over in her hand. When she found the passage, she ran her finger along the faint text, narrowed her gaze, and read it aloud.

"I walk through the night, but instead of going back to my house, I'm pulled further into the woods, a dull humming filling my head. It calls me, and as I pass through a clearing, I see hazy blue light and a giant stone. A stone with faces carved into the surface, some of them are laughing at me."

Win shifted on the bed, noting the drop in the air temperature in the room. She rubbed her arms.

"This is slightly later…but it reads… *Nobody in my house is talking to me, not Eliza or Louisa. I think they know about me. They know about the strange stone in the woods and how it calls out to me. I feel like it wants to pull me in."*

"That's creepy," Win agreed, instinctively edging closer to Ella. Ella flicked her hair, lifting her chin, and gave Win a grimace.

"Well, this bit is the part I don't like... *The humming called me to the stone in the woods, my legs heavy as it pulled me closer. Blue light surrounded me, filled me up, made me warm, and when I walked through the light, the sun was shining, and it was no longer snowing. I saw two boys playing by the edge of the brook, and they were wearing strange clothes. One saw me. It was fun to follow them home. There are monsters in the air here, loud and bright, and land animals made of shiny tin."*

Win gasped. "Oh, god…she went through time!"

Ella snapped the book closed. The smell of dust still lingered between the pages. "That's what it sounds like. It sounds like she came forward in time…to our time. Shiny, tin monsters?"

"This is insane, but it means I can do this. How, though? Would we need to do what we did before with Iris— call the four corners, ask to communicate with her?"

"Win, by the sounds of your dream—you don't need to do any of that. It sounds as though you've done it already."

Neither spoke. Win stroked the spine of the book with her thumb. Ella finally burst.

"Win, I'm not sure how this helps Luke. This Mary sounds a little unhinged. No offense, but do you really want to reach out to her?"

Win agreed, but Willard gave her this for a reason. He'd said learning about Mary would help Luke. And right now, Win wasn't prepared to lose him, not after what they'd gone through. Spencer survived, so could he. She gripped the edge of the book. "I want to do this." Another thought occurred to her, filled her with hope. "If she knows how to help him...maybe she might know what happened to my mom?"

Ella's features softened, and she nodded. "If it works, it'll be worth it. Let's do this, but I'm staying here. I'll be your anchor in case anything spooky happens."

Win sat up, pushing her hair off her shoulders. "What should I do? Close my eyes?"

"You've done this before. Like you would do when you phased into your memory of the pit, relax, close your eyes and concentrate." Ella hopped off the bed, quickly drew the curtains, and closed the door. Win's eyes widened in alarm.

"*Now?*"

Ella sighed, her expression pensive "Luke is taking me to dinner. We both need a little…."

"Space?" Win filled in the gap, secretly elated he was taking her on a date, even as sick as he was. They needed alone time, and more than anything, Win wanted the same, but with Grayson.

"So, it's now or never."

"Now!" Win agreed.

Wincing, she attempted to cross her legs under the covers. Ella crawled on the bed and mirrored her position. Ella took Win's hands in hers, and they both closed their eyes. The room was heavy with silence. After a moment, Win peeked an eye open, stifling an involuntary nervous giggle, her fear of appearing stupid pushing it out of her mouth.

"Concentrate, Win!" Ella snapped, her lips twitching into a smirk.

They both relaxed, focussing on breathing. When Win first arrived in Cedar Wood, she'd had to be barefoot in the yard to attempt any kind of mediation or phasing, but now her connection was stronger. Now it dwelled in her blood. She found it easy to slip into a relaxed, meditative state, letting her palms relax in Ella's hands. Soon she grew warm, languid, her vision crisping and curling at the corners until she dissolved into a white haze. Win tried to picture her ancestor. She spoke out to her in her mind, rolling her name around in her mouth.

Mary, Mary….Mary Hickory. Win shuddered, her fingertips cold. Her spine tingled, as though a pointed finger ran the length of it, a wisp of breath tickled her neck. Her vision behind her eyes melted, shapes forming into substance.

Come on, Mary…

A black shape moved across her eyes, and Win pulled away, instantly recoiling. Something about the form it took chilled her blood, unnerved her. But it moved, hurtled toward her, chasing through the mist. Win wanted to open her eyes, willing her fingers to squeeze Ella's, but they were leaden, numb. She saw the outline of hair billowing in the breeze and two white spots of light, like eyes watching her from the shadows. Prickles of ice flew up Win's arms, her breath shortened, and she gripped for Ella's hands, her anchor.

I don't like this....this feels....all wrong...

"What the hell is going on? Why is it dark in here?" Luke's voice broke the connection. Win panted, snapping her eyes open.

Ella rolled off the bed and opened the curtains. "Are you okay?"

Win pressed her hands to her chest, disappointed but also oddly relieved. "I'm okay." She shook her shoulders. "It didn't work."

Ella eyed her suspiciously. "Well, something happened."

"It's freezing in here." Luke crossed the room, checking the window, placing his hand on the radiator. Win's vision cleared, and noticed he was carrying a bedroll mattress, one used for camping, and a pillow stuffed under one arm. A shape filled the door, and Grayson wandered in, glancing at the three of them like three naughty kids caught drinking.

"Everything okay here?" He smiled, glanced at Ella, who immediately blushed and looked at her hands. Win gave him a sheepish look.

"We were trying something. I'll explain later."

Grayson stepped past Luke with one long stride. "Well, Rowan wants you to shower, and then Evan needs to check your dressing. They've asked me to get you up."

"She doesn't need help showering," Luke cried. An enormous red wave traveled up his neck, making his skin blotchy. His eyes hit the ground as Ella shot him a puzzled look. Grayson smiled at him evenly.

"I was planning on waiting *outside*." He waved to Win in an up-off-your-ass motion. "Come on, your sister is on a knife-edge already, and I don't want to get in trouble."

"Take no notice of her," Win assured him, rubbing the back of her aching neck. That reminded her, she and Rowan needed to clear the air, or rather her sister owed her a gigantic explanation.

Luke threw the camping roll on the bed. "This is for you to sleep on," he said to Grayson. "Ben says you can stay on the floor."

Win recalled a conversation in which Ben assured her she would *never* have a boy alone in her room. She raked her eyes over him top to bottom, and as appealing as he was, she didn't think she would be able to get up to anything.

Ella tugged Luke out of the room. Win stretched, holding up her arms to him, grinning, the last few moments of contacting Mary forgotten. He smiled and pulled her into his arms, waiting like a gentleman outside the door while she hosed herself down in the shower, avoiding her wound. Wrapped in her robe, she crawled back in bed, clean and dry, and braced herself when Evan came to check her leg.

Grayson crouched in the corner, watching in grim fascination as Evan peeled off the grubby bandage, inspecting it closely. "It looks good." She ran her hands over the smooth skin. The outline was visible but a fraction less raw. "It's the underneath that'll take longer. Hopefully, another twelve hours, and you'll be back on form."

Evan whipped on a new, clean bandage. Her hands paused mid-air, and she stared around the room. An icy blast crossed her arms, and Win saw all the hairs on her arms jump to attention. Evan's brow creased in a frown. She looked directly at Win with her lip curled.

"What have you done in here?"

"What? Nothing!"

Evan shook off the feeling, giving a weary shrug. "Feels odd… is there a window open?"

"No."

Evan stood, retrieving Win's old, bloodied bandage. "Okay, well, you need to sleep. Grayson is here—but no funny business!" she added with a wink in his direction. He laughed shyly, staring down at his linked fingers.

"Is Rowan okay?" Win asked, feeling her sister's absence. Rowan hadn't been in to see her all afternoon, not since Jake's visit.

"She's having a break, Win. All this has her in a mess, what with Spencer too. She'll be in tomorrow to see you when she's back to herself," Evan replied tightly, and Win nodded, knowing Rowan needed time. Jake's words cut like a razor.

Evan left the room, closing the door behind her quietly. Grayson unrolled his bed, lying alongside Win's on the hard, wood floor. He threw her a curious glance, his pale eyes shining in a way that drew a deep, hot blush out of her skin. "So," he began with a grin. "Are you going to tell me what you and Ella were really doing in here?"

Win sat up, hugging her knees, a smile curling on her lips. "We weren't doing anything."

"Liar," he said, tapping her nose. "Tell me."

Win huffed and rolled across, leaving him some room to settle next to her. He pulled up a pillow under his head, smiling as she fiddled with his chain. "We were trying to contact my dead ancestor," she admitted, daring a glance up. He ran his warm hand down her arm, and she shivered as the hairs on her arms stood to attention.

"How'd that go?"

Win huffed, disappointed. "It might have worked if Luke hadn't barged in. But—it was creepy. I'm kind of glad it didn't work."

Grayson's expression darkened in concearn. "So, who is this person?"

In answer, Win fetched the diary stashed under her pillow. Grayson sat straight, huddling her under his arm as she flicked to the page with the most disturbing paragraph, the one mentioning tin monsters. Happy to sprawl out next to him, she gazed up, following his expression as he read, his mouth twitched into a grimace. "Hmm," he said after a short while. "That's—strange."

"I know. It's as creepy as hell."

"No, I mean…." He scratched his chin, deep in thought. "I feel like…I know this."

Win sat up in alarm. "Know what?"

Grayson took a breath, studying her worried expression, before admitting a short laugh. "You'll think I'm crazy."

"Trust me. I won't."

He closed the diary but kept it on his lap. "When I was a kid, my brother and I took a boat out on the river. My brother—Henry—hated the woods. He was always weird about being out alone. This one day, he said he saw a girl watching us in the woods. And she followed us home. But I never saw anything."

Win's stomach dropped, and a cold chill tickled her neck. Grayson carried on, unaware of her reaction. "See—Henry was a hard-faced kid. He never got scared, but this shook the crap out of him. And the odd thing was, it wasn't the first time he'd seen her. She'd followed us before."

Win rubbed her arms briskly, having broken out in goosebumps. "That's so creepy. And you never saw her?"

"Never." He pulled her against his shoulder, his fingertips trailing down her arm. "I forgot all about it." He clutched the diary, folding his arms around it, as if to shield her from its contents. "I don't like this, Win. Don't try and contact whoever this was. I don't think…she's good."

"I won't!" she promised as he snaked out of her grip. "Why don't we change the subject? You can tell me about everything since we last saw one another."

A sense of dread filled her gut, and she couldn't shake the feeling of eyes on her back and the horrible sensation of cold infiltrating the room. She was keen to get her mind off Mary Hickory, and she wanted to know everything Grayson had been doing. She'd missed months of his life. They talked for hours, holding hands across the bed, till it grew dark outside and she heard Luke arrive home. Ben came to say goodnight, shooting Grayson a grateful smile as he closed the door. When they were alone, Grayson stood, kicking out his bedroll.

Win bit her lip, watching as he hauled his shirt over his head, remaining in his thin vest and pants, his sliver chain glinting around his neck. He caught her eyeing him and cast her a wearied glance. "Before you say anything, the answer is no."

She'd gone hot all over, rolling to her good side to face him as he crawled inside the bedroll. She pursed her lips. "It looks uncomfortable down there."

"I've had worse."

"Don't you think you'd be better off sleeping in here with me?" she teased, watching as he rolled to face the wall, his shoulder stiffening.

"That wouldn't be a good idea. You're supposed to be resting."

"Shame." She spread out in her bed, sleep tugging at her eyes. It was still surreal; to have him in her room, inches from her, accessible and real. And alive. "I missed you so much." Her throat clogged with tears. He closed the gap between them, kissing her mouth, cupping the back of her neck. His mouth was warm, soft, and familiar; she made a happy noise against his lips. When she tried to tug him nearer, a kiss not enough to satisfy her, he pulled away with a mischievous grin. "Go to bed!"

Win laughed, content for once in her life to do as she was told. Her skin still ached under the bandage. It took a while to drift off, the events of the day unrolling in her mind. She thought about Spencer prowling around the Mercy estate somewhere, trapped in his animal form. She thought of Rowan, Luke and Cole alone in the hospital while listening to Grayson's breathing, which quickly became a soft snore.

Win bolted awake. Skin covered in goosebumps, a draft billowed over her bare legs, all the sheets and covers gone as though yanked from her body. She had no idea what time it was; only it felt like seconds ago she drifted off. She sat up, pain-free, bone-cold, and the odd sensation of time having slowed to a crawl.

A girl stood at the end of her bed. Win recoiled, opening her mouth to scream, but it wouldn't form. Her voice was no more than a whisper, and next to her on the floor, Grayson was blissfully unaware. The girl tilted her head, regarding her closely; stringy, lank dark hair framed a pale, oval face. Win gasped. The girl's tattered white gown floated as she moved, and her eyes— what was wrong with her eyes? They were dense, black orbs.

"Gr-Grayson?" Win found her voice, but it drifted into a void, nothing. The girl smiled, revealing small uneven teeth. She couldn't have been more than thirteen years old.

She stepped closer. "I heard you wanted to speak with me."

Twenty Three

This has got to be a dream…she's not here…

But the girl standing at the foot of her bed was real, human, and vivid, which in itself was frightening. Her black gaze found Grayson on the floor. Soundly and deeply asleep, Grayson turned on the thin camp roll, his arm flung over his eyes. Mary tilted her head, mildly fascinated as she watched him sleep. Win growled, "Don't look at him."

Mary's eyes snapped back, and Win recoiled. She turned her head, panic-stricken. "Grayson, wake up!"

"He won't hear you. He's asleep. And so are you!"

"I'm not!"

Win had the sensation of falling, light and helpless. She gasped, catching herself, and jumped from the bed. But she was still in the bed. At least that was what her eyes told her. She stood on the rug, barefoot, bearing weight on the leg Spencer damaged only hours ago, and yet she saw herself sleeping soundly in the bed, her hair splayed out on her pillow like a red halo. Her arm hung over the side toward Grayson; she stretched and rolled, turning to face him. Win opened her mouth, unable to believe what she saw.

Mary was standing too close to her. She'd moved with deadly silence, and Win jumped, holding up her hands. "What the hell is this?"

"You're phasing, and so am I. I heard you calling me. I hear everything. I'm always…around."

"Around, where?"

Mary's gaze flicked to the window, the walls, the bed. "I'm everywhere. I lived here a long time ago. I'm in the walls, the old wood. We all are. This was my sister's room, you know. Funny, I can still see her here."

Win shivered, but it wasn't real. Her skin didn't react. "Which sister?"

"Eliza," she said, her voice far away. "She was kind, the only one who ever was. I'm glad she outlived us all in the end."

Win swallowed, the enormity of her words weighing heavily. "Okay, so…I kind of needed to talk to you."

Mary nodded. "That's why I came."

"You're like me. The last of your line, or the youngest. Is it true, we have power in our blood?"

"If I had any real power, maybe I would have lived a little longer."

Win slumped, disappointed. "Okay, but you know something about the stone?"

Mary's brows were like two dark brush strokes; they pulled together in confusion. "Do you mean the door?"

The door? Shit…it's a door? If Win's limbs weren't so heavy, she would have palm slapped her forehead. A whisper of a smile crossed the young girl's mouth.

"Yes, it's a door."

"Through time?"

"Time, yes. It's powerful and old. It's always been there. Long before this town, before there was woods or anything here but dirt."

"And it's the source of our curse— it's what caused this to happen?"

"No."

Win drew back, confused, wishing this girl would open up. She glanced across at her sleeping form in the bed. "Can you show me at least?"

Mary turned and headed to the bedroom door; she glanced back over her shoulder. "Of course, that's why you called me? You want to learn more about your power."

"Only because…" Win started and bit her tongue. There was a cold glint buried in Mary's gaze, something feral about her curled lip. Win was rooted to the wooden boards, terrified to move outside of this room. What if she couldn't get back?

"You'll return here," Mary assured her, the door swinging open. She moved like a specter, her dirty feet bare against the floor, and her footfalls were silent. Darting a glance at Grayson, Win reluctantly followed, her step light and airy, like she no longer had weight or presence. She followed Mary outside into the moonlit yard. The sphere beaming down at them reflected in the puddles, casting a glow on Mary's bone-white skin. Wordlessly she held out her hand.

Win stared down at the girl's outstretched hand, long cold fingers inching toward her. "Do we have to hold hands?"

Mary's smile slipped away, something in her expression resigned and hurt. "If you want to stay here, don't take it. But, that'll be a waste, won't it? And you won't get what you want."

Gingerly, Win placed her hand in Mary's, her grip strong for a child who appeared so frail. Mary's eyes shone, and the world lit up around them. There was a flash of white, like a camera popping, and Win squinted, opening her eyes to find herself standing in a very different yard.

It was twilight. The ground was hard and cold and covered in long grass. There were animal pens spotted around and the familiar old black-clad hay barn in the distance. A dusky haze drew in, but when Win whirled around, her grandpa's engines and trucks were gone. Her eyes widened as she turned back toward the main house.

"Oh, my…what happened to the house?" she croaked, unable to believe what she was seeing. It was Hickory House, the same washed-out cladding and wrap-around porch, but it was twice the size, sprawling with wings added either side— and there was a third floor. "It's so big! Where'd it all go?"

"A fire, I believe," Mary stated, interested in Win's fascination. "In the late 1800s, long after my time. But this was a house built for a captain and his family. It was one of the finest in the town. We also owned more land until it was sold away to pay for debts. But this isn't why we're here. Come on."

"Where are we going?"

"To a place you've been before. But this time, you'll see things differently."

Win didn't dare ask as she followed Mary across the yard and through the treeline, a route she'd walked many times before. But the trees were younger, greener. It was so strange; Win could feel the new life in them, the energy rippling from the ground, a gentle hum filling her head. They walked into a shadowy clearing, where the tree roots knotted and bent, appearing to form a gnarled arch. Mary walked through, waving her arm to usher Win to wait in the safety of the trees. There was a group of people chanting, and Win was overwhelmed with a startling sense of familiarity. She'd been here before.

The stone was in the center of the clearing, and there were muffled voices as two cloaked men dragged a prisoner and tied him to it with cords. She was aghast. "I know what happens here!"

Mary shook her head, not turning her head away. "No, you don't."

"I do. This is the night…they hurt…."

"My father, yes. I know."

Mary was taking no precaution to stay hidden. "They won't see us here," she assured her aloud. Win was quickly getting the sense Mary was reading her mind before she'd even had time to form a thought. "We're in the spirit plane."

The frenzied chanting began, and Win closed her eyes. She didn't want to see this again, but she couldn't unhear what was happening. As he was sliced open, Joseph's shrill scream was enough to pierce her skull, forcing her eyes open to watch. The woman with the cloak rose from the ground holding up the thing she'd cut from his body. Win shuddered.

"So, what *was* that?"

"His liver."

Win gagged, bile burning her gullet. "And he *lived*?"

Mary looked thoughtful. "We were cursed by magic. It was his bodily sacrifice to their god. He lived after, but it bled sometimes. It served as his reminder of what he'd brought down upon us all."

"So, I was right? The stone…is what cast the curse?"

"No." She seemed disappointed, and Win wondered if she'd missed some vital moment while she'd had her eyes closed. "It wasn't the door. It was the one who opened it."

"But…" Win shut her mouth as the scene shifted, and out of the darkness, she saw *herself* peel out of the shadows, darting to where Joseph lay injured. Like watching a movie reel, she stared open-mouthed, seeing herself ripping off her nightgown hem, trying to keep him talking. "This is insane. How could I have been here?"

"You can open the door. Your blood is the purest of your family line."

"No, that doesn't make sense. I'm here now with you, in the *spirit plane.* But how can I have got *there*, able to touch him, help him? He had the end of my nightgown in a box. I was here in corporeal form. Can you explain that?"

Mary blanched, looked away. "I see your confusion."

"Do you?" Win grew more frustrated. "I don't get this. That night, I saw my mom—at least I thought I did."

"She wasn't there. That was your mind casting shadows,

playing tricks. It's possible you were in a dream like state. When the stone calls to us, everything becomes disjointed, confusing. You slept walked through the forest and passed through the door."

"It's a door that only I can open. I can walk through it?"

"Yes." Mary looked doubtful. Win doubted even she had the answers.

"Can *you?*"

"Not now, I'm dead," Mary admitted. "Once I could. However, I had no idea what I was doing or where I'd end up. The door called to me, something in my blood understood its power, something dark…."

Win didn't like that word, or what it implied. "Dark?"

"I don't have any other way to describe it. It always felt wrong, dark, and evil. But it pulled me in. It's always been that way. The door appears when it's needed. Blood opens the door, and blood closes it. The ones who cursed our family were only ever wielders of power. Borrowers—thieves. There is no good magic, not in this world."

"What did they create?"

Mary smiled unevenly. "Us."

Win watched as men with torches flooded the clearing, hauling up Joseph from where he lay and carrying him back through the forest. She turned to Mary, who watched it all as though it was a television special. "Who are *they*? The ones you're talking about?" Win asked.

Mary nodded. "Follow me." She took Win's hand without warning, and a bolt of light shot through the clearing. Win cried out, covering her eyes, and when she opened them, she squinted away dots. It seemed darker now, colder, and Mary was hurrying away through the trees. Not wanting to be left behind, Win caught up with her, watching as Mary's filthy feet stepped through the long grass.

"Where are we going now?"

There was laughter up ahead, and Win stopped to listen. It was girlish laughter. The kind friends shared when they were misbehaving. Mary seemed uncomfortable, holding Win back with her arm as out of the trees, four women appeared, cloaked and giggling and chatting together, all holding candles. Mary signaled to follow them and Win grimaced, trailing behind the women as they jogged through the trees, all holding up their gowns in case they tripped.

Win gasped. "Are they..?"

"My sisters," Mary said sadly. "Come along."

Win panted as she trotted along behind Mary until she finally recognized the path, though it was weedy and overgrown. Mercy rose out of the pink twilight, looming and oppressive, much as it remained today, and Win nearly lost sight of Mary, distracted by the buildings foreboding shadow. A torch-lit path burned through the path ahead, and there was laughter in the air. It was a party, held outdoors, not dissimilar to the bonfire she'd attended at Luke's earlier this year. That hadn't ended well, Win recalled, a sense of apprehension growing in the pit of her belly.

"It's Samhain night," Mary answered before Win asked.

"Samhain…you mean Halloween?"

"We called it something different back then.."

"This is so weird." Win looked around, feeling like she'd wandered onto a costume drama movie set. Everyone was dressed in 18th-century attire, the women in laced bodices, cloaks, and bonnets. The men wore short pants fastening with stays and heeled leather boots, their beards long while the children wore their hair under mop caps. Hugging her arms around her, she looked around, sensing dread in the air. A bonfire raged in the distance, and a wooden stage was built in front of it. Her stomach turned. What was that for?

Although the figures jostling around her looked quaint, like something she'd seen in a history book, there was a sense of foreboding in the air. Children laughed and scampered between their mother's skirts, climbing and jumping from hay bales. Win stilled herself in preparation. Something was going to happen. But she realized that was why Mary brought her here.

"You'll see shortly," Mary said, and Win shivered. She wished she would stop reading her thoughts. The laughter and music died away, and a tall, lean man with flattened black hair and a hooked nose climbed onto the stage. As he addressed the crowd, it was clear he was a reverend or someone in authority. He spat when he spoke, and, with the eccentric glint in his eye, he reminded Win strangely of old Robert Fraser, Luke's grandfather.

"Is that…Jacob Fraser?" she choked. Mary was staring at him with a strange look on her face, one of wonder, awe, and longing. "Did you know him?"

"Yes." She swallowed. "I knew him. More intimately than I wanted to."

Win jolted, alarmed at her admission. Eyes boring into Mary's profile, the younger girl refused to speak until finally, she said. "You don't always need a weapon to destroy someone."

"Mary?"

"Just watch!"

Win tore her eyes back to the stage, and now a hushed murmur seeped through the crowd. People cried out in alarm as a woman was dragged on the stage. Cries of despair floated around the sea of people. Confused, scared, and in a dream-like state, Win stepped forward into the crowd, Mary close behind her.

"What's going to happen to her?" Win squinted, the light of the fire in her eyes. She could make out the shape of the woman's bare shoulders, her long swathes of dark, smooth hair. Win froze.

"We must mark those among us—who present a danger to our younger members of the town, those vulnerable and easily led." The reverend spoke to the shocked crowd, but Win barely heard him. All she saw was the face of the woman on stage, the terror gleaming in her eyes. She knew those eyes.

"No," Win whispered, pushing her way through the crowd, but it was like walking in the ocean, the sand dragging under her feet. "Don't hurt her…please don't hurt her!"

"Do you deny the hideous acts of your sister?" he demanded of her, spitting saliva in her face. He was black-eyed, working himself into a frenzy, as the guard behind her yanked her head back so hard it exposed the pale column of her throat. Win's eyes filled up with hot tears.

"No! she screamed. "*Evan!* No!"

"They can't hear you," Mary cackled behind her. She was grinning, shaking, nearly drooling with excitement, and Win cast her glare of disgust and horror.

"Help her, *please!*"

"We can't…this has already happened. Don't you understand, you idiot? You've a fox in your henhouse!"

Evan…Evan was here. Alive in *this* time. How was this possible? Win's mind broke, unable to see anything but Evan bound tight, while behind her, a bonfire roared. The guards forced her around, with her back to the crowd. They busted open her corset while she choked and sobbed. Win's knees buckled, unable to look away, as the reverend took a flaming, red hot poker and forced it against her skin.

Win shrieked, and Evan's skin burned, sizzled, and she collapsed onto her knees, moaning into her long skirts. The crowd yelled in fury, children crying, and women fled the meadow. Blood drained from Win's legs, hardly able to stand and watch a second longer.

The reverend jeered at the crowd. "I have branded Eunice Varga in the name of our Lord. May she cast aside the devil."

Evan was dragged off stage by her arms, limp as a ragdoll. Win tried to run, but her legs wouldn't work, she gasped, turning to Mary. "I have to go to her."

Mary laughed acidly. "You still don't see!"

She grabbed both of Win's hands, and immediately the light enveloped them. The crowds were gone, and the two of them floated in a sea of mist. Mary presented Win with visions—time-lapses of the past, and Win held her breath.

She saw a vision of Evan in the Varga house, painting the mosaic pattern on the back tile of the fireplace. Her deft, gliding brushstrokes as she drew faces, a wolf, birds, cats…an eagle.

"No, this isn't real," Win sobbed.

Sickened, Win tried to block out the images. She saw Evan leaning over a workbench, crumbling up herbs, crunching them to dust under a pestle. Another woman carved up a man tied to a table, removing organs and placing them in jars, while the man wept and begged for his wife. More men met the same fate.

A woman's feet dangled above ground, swollen and bloated as she hung from a noose. A crowd jeered as her neck snapped.

"No, please."

"You have to see this!"

"I don't want to!"

The last one, Evan was there, that night in the clearing. Her sister, Vecula, held up Joseph's body part over her head, a sacrifice to the stone. The clearing filled with hazy, blue light, and her hand was empty, blood trickling through her fingers.

Mary released Win's hands, and the pale white light faded. They were back in the clearing, and Win was sobbing on her hands and knees. Her lungs were tight, ached as she tried to stand.

"This can't be true," she wept, wiping her muddy hands as she stood. "Tell me this is a dream, please."

Mary cast her a strange look, confused and in awe of Win's naivety. "You've always known. Admit it! You knew there was something wrong with her from the beginning. They opened the door. They *opened* the door!"

"But—we love her. She's part of our family," Win resisted. "They were witches? It was never to do with the Atoloa?"

"The Atoloa were pawns in a game. A much nastier one."

"But I don't understand...."

"Maybe you are blind?" Mary said. "Blind to so many things. You are so wrapped up in yourself you only see what you want."

"What do you mean?"

"I know why you wanted my help. You want to save *him*. He's a Fraser—they aren't worth saving."

Win spluttered. What did that have to do with anything? "In

my time, things are different. Luke won't pay with his life for this stupid fued."

Mary didn't seem to hear. "You want him to live?"

"Of course I do!"

"Why?"

"He's my family…he's my blood."

"And?"

"And *nothing!*" Win spat, furious, her cheeks red and sore. "You've not helped me at all. I still don't know how to help him. I could still lose him!"

"You know everything you need to know. I've shown you everything. He's in here." She tapped Win's chest with her bony fingers. "And when the time comes, you'll know what to do."

"That's not good enough!" She was bawling now, hot tears streaking down her face. "I can't have come this far to go home with nothing. I can't live in a world he *isn't* a part of."

"Why?"

"Because he's my friend!"

"*Why*, Win?"

"Because I *love* him!"

As soon as the words hit the air, it played on repeat, as if to taunt her. Filled with shame and loathing, she shook her head, her hair damp and sticking to her face. "You made me say that."

Mary smiled, triumphant. "I didn't make you say anything."

"It doesn't matter what I feel. I still don't know what to do."

Her admittance left her raw. Nothing mattered now. He couldn't ever belong with her, not in the romantic sense. But she would die before she let anything happen to him.

"You know everything, Win." Mary cocked her head. A delighted grin split her face, revealing a set of narrow, sharp teeth. Win gasped in alarm. "Well—maybe there is one last thing you should see."

Mary held out her hand, and Win looked at it, unappealing as a dead fish. She didn't dare take it, not after everything she'd already seen tonight. And something strange was happening. Her vision crisped on the outer edges, she was warm, a drawing sensation tingling in her legs. Her walk in the spirit plane was fading, and quickly. Panic filled her, and she grabbed Mary's hand. White light flashed, and when Win opened her eyes, they were still in the same damn clearing.

"For god's sake," Win muttered, exhausted. Mary nodded toward the space lined with trees when a gentle pulsing shook the ground. The stone appeared in a haze of blue light, and Win's terror rose as Evan wandered into the clearing. Only this was recent; from her own time, she recognized Evan's clothing. Evan knelt before the stone, chanting, holding out her arms, and commanding the light between her palms. The energy fizzled and cracked around her.

Win's mouth dropped open. "What is she doing?"

Mary didn't answer. Evan shook, groaned, and writhed, throwing back her head as she offered up her arms. Out of the darkness, the falcon flew into the beam of light. Win wobbled, stepping forward, knowing nothing she did or said would matter. "Mom? *Mom!*"

The falcon panicked, caught in the beam, where it sizzled and fried. With a great wave of light, it burned into dust, and Win screamed.

"Oh, don't look away now!" Mary said. "This is the best part."

The dust settled, and what remained on the ground was a shaking creature cowering under a mane of dirty yellow hair. Win cried out. "Mom? What did she do to her?"

"She gave her back to you."

"But…" Tears stung her face. "How could she do this? And not tell us?"

"Something I've no doubt you'll ask her."

The scene darkened and faded. Alice's sobs echoed on the night breeze as it all misted into nothing, faded to black like the end of a movie. Win trembled, hardly able to process what she witnessed. "I need to go home."

She glanced at Mary, who was looking down at her feet. A dark stain spread across the girl's white neck, red, thick blood welling up out of a wound that appeared from nowhere. Win tried to step forward, but it was like being trapped in a bubble.

"What's happening to you?"

"I have to go now." Mary's face paled, her life draining away. "I have to go back."

"Go, where?"

"To where I died." She waved her hand when Win tried to ask more. "No more questions now. It's always this way. I have to go back to him, and I die."

"Him?"

Mary evaporated, growing misty and trickling away. She clutched at her throat as if that would hold back time, give her a few more seconds of life. Blood dripped through her fingers.

"Mary…I want to help you."

"I have to go to him now. It's always the same. I always die this way."

"Who? Who hurts you?"

"Blood opens the door, and blood closes it. Go *home*, Win."

Win stumbled, the ground fading from under her feet. Thrust back in time, there were voices in her head demanding answers. Mary vanished, leaving no trace, and without warning, Win was jerked back into her own sleeping body.

She bolted awake, Grayson's face inches from her own. Drenched in sweat, she writhed in fright, pain exploding up her leg. He held her shoulders steady. "Win, can you hear me?"

She scrambled up the bed, pushing out of his arms. Rowan was there, and in her stricken state, she flicked on the light. It blinded Win, and she squinted, her eyes wild, pinpricks of black in a yellow orb.

"Win, what's wrong?" Rowan shook her. "Tell us what happened! Was it a dream?"

The bedroom door flung open, and chaos erupted. There were too many voices filling her head, demanding answers, afraid, confused. Luke was there, and her father was too. Her pupils narrowed as Evan stood at the end of the bed, her hair swept off her neck, fear rippling off her in waves.

Win's fangs elongated, and she leaped from the sheets. Despite her injured leg, she caught Evan's neck with her hand, forcing her back with such ferocity her feet didn't hit the floor. Win cracked Evan's skull against the closet door. Evan gasped as she kicked her feet. "Win…please!"

"Win, get the hell off her!" Rowan grappled with Win's clawed fingers until she loosened her grip, and Evan landed on the floor. Evan crawled away, choking, gasping for air. Rowan attempted to fling Win away, but she held fast, like an immovable rock.

Win loomed over Evan, yellow cat eyes boring down at her. "You did this to us."

"What are you talking about?" Rowan yelled, grabbing at her limbs, trying to keep her back. "What's going on?"

"You!" Win stood over her, tears filling her eyes. *"Where is our mother?"*

Twenty Four

A hush fell across the room. Evan's golden skin blanched as she crouched at Win's feet. She held up a hand, her eyes finding Rowan, whose mouth hung open. Ben hissed and swore under his breath, padding into the room, tightening his robe, and flicking on a light so everyone startled awake.

Win repeated the question, but this time, her voice shook. "Where is our mother?"

"Win, what the hell is going on?" Rowan demanded. She planted herself between them and helped Evan to her feet. Evan shook; a fine sheen of sweat had broken out across her brow.

"Win, was this another dream?" Rowan asked.

Win narrowed her eyes at her sister, angry yet again she didn't believe her. "Ask your girlfriend!" she spat.

Win felt a body at her back, Grayson's hands on her shoulders. "Win, calm down—you're freezing!"

She shook him away, and he lifted both palms in motion of surrender. But she stopped, held her breath, and mentally forced herself to relax. "Evan." Win's voice grew wobbly. "Tell her the truth."

Evan spluttered and wrung her hands, peering at Ben over the heads of people who were now hotly eyeballing her. Ben puffed, and pushed past Luke, and stood at Evan's side. Win's mouth dropped open.

"Dad, *no!*"

"What's going on?" Rowan faltered, jumping away from them. Ben rubbed his eyes.

"Don't be too hard on her. We've both been hiding something." He looked at his strange audience, eyes keen on him. "Girls…Evan brought back your mother."

"What? When?" Rowan babbled.

"How?" Win asked.

Ben held up his palms. "Wait! *Listen* before you start firing questions at us both. Evan came to me about six weeks ago and told me what she had done. We kept Alice in her apartment as she was in no fit state to be seen by anyone. And we made the decision, *together* to let her recover and try and get back to normal before we brought her home."

Rowan's eyes were wide, tear-filled. "Get back to normal? Do you have any idea what you've done? You can't just bring her back. She would have been wild…not the woman we knew."

"We know that now," Ben threw back at her, frustration building in his tone. "Believe me. We didn't want to upset her any more than she already was. We were making progress. She seemed better…."

Rowan smiled, hopefully. "So, where is she? Can we go see her?"

"Uh, no." Ben looked at his feet. "She ran away. Yesterday. We thought she might be heading here, but it seems she's taken off."

"You should have told us!" Win barked. "We could have helped."

"Win, there was too much happening, and we didn't want to bring her into it. Call it horrible timing. But we'll find her…it's just been a bit chaotic."

Rowan stared at Evan's profile. Evan recoiled inwardly, bowing her head. Win willed herself to calm down; the adrenaline that had flooded her body slowly ebbed away. She saw Evan quivering, her hands shaking, and regretted her outburst. This was a woman who'd stood beside her all summer, comforted her. She deserved to be heard.

"How could you not tell me?" Rowan asked her. Win could see Rowan's confusion. Evan's betrayal cut like a dagger, and all could be lost if Rowan exploded. Evan might leave, and then where would they be? Win needed her. So did Luke.

"Rowan, we should listen to her."

Rowan ignored her and whirled back to Evan. "How did you even do this? How can you have power?"

"She's a witch, Rowan," Win said. "A healer…doesn't even come close to what she can do."

Evan's eyes widened. "That's not true. I am a healer!"

"How did you bring her back?"

"A reversal incantation," Evan tried to explain. "Using the stone's light. I used the power to reverse the falcon's hold on Alice's human form. I did it to help—I swear to you. I'm not a…."

When Evan looked around the room frantically, weighing up any way she could escape, Win let her frustration get the better of her. "Show them your scar!" she said.

Evan's gaze darted around the room for any support she could find, but when no one spoke, she relented miserably and hauled up her vest, revealing a faded, shiny mark carefully hidden under her bra line. It marred Evan's unblemished skin but was flat and smooth and barely resembled the cross it had been two hundred years ago. Rowan threw up her hands, exasperated.

"What is that, Win? A birthmark? I've seen it before, many times."

"It's a brand!" Win yelled, wishing she could throttle her sister. "She was branded at a Halloween gathering on the Fraser property. Her name isn't Evan either. It's Eunice." She caught Luke's attention. "Your ancestor was a *real* asshole."

Luke seemed resigned. "We know how to throw a party," he muttered, perching on the edge of the bed.

"Evan—tell me the truth," Rowan pleaded.

"It's true," she whispered. "It's all true. My name was Eunice Varga—a long time ago. But I'm not that person, and I haven't been for many years. Once my sister was executed, I was free, and I escaped and didn't come back to Cedar Wood for over a century."

"What are you saying?" Rowan stuttered. She shrank away, her hands finding the wall for support. "You're not old…you've been alive since…."

"Since the curse was cast," Win finished. "She was there."

"No, you have to understand!" Evan cut in. "I was a healer. I never harmed anyone. Vecula was the one with the power. I was bound to her. I couldn't leave. Until one day she got caught, and I finally had my chance."

Luke stood, straightening his glasses, shoving his hands in his pockets. "The Varga house? All those men who died? That was you?"

"It was Vecula, not me!"

"How *old* are you?"

Evan covered her eyes in despair. Win grabbed her phone from the nightstand, thumbing through the photos on her phone until she found one of the tiles at the back of the fireplace. Luke leaned over her shoulder and peered down at the screen. Win held up the phone.

"What do these mean, Evan? These paintings? I saw you painting them…what do they have to do with the door?"

Luke cocked a brow, puzzled. "Door?"

"Stone," Win corrected herself. Evan darted a nervous look toward the photo.

"They're Mesoamerican," Luke said, and five pairs of eyes turned to him, surprised he would know something important. He shrugged, holding out his hands. "It wasn't *me* who noticed. It was Ella. She's got a thing about history. She was looking at them the day we were in Mickleford, babbling on about how weird it was to see ancient art painted in the fireplace of an 18th-century house in Massachusetts. You know I don't listen most of the time."

Ben, eyed Evan sideways. "That would be impossible. You'd be ancient."

"I don't even know how old I am." Evan found Win's chair and collapsed into it. A murmur floated around the room. "I was a healer. Only, a healer."

"But you were there that night." Win stepped toward her. "You cast our curse with her."

Evan dared to meet her gaze. "I was trapped with her. I don't expect you to understand—she was my sister. But after she got caught—I ran."

"Why did you curse us?" Win asked. Something vulnerable and innocent lurked in Evan's eyes. Win's initial temper dwindled, finding it impossible to stay angry, recalling the night she got that scar, and it sickened her.

"I didn't cast the curse, at least not me, alone. Vecula was obsessed with the stone, she wanted to return home to her god, and she believed she could cross if we opened the door. Only for that kind of magic, you need more than one person. You need unity—energy—a coven."

A pack...Win thought, wondering if their unity was responsible for calling the stone out of the shadows on the night they raised Iris.

"Vecula grew friendly with the women in the village, and some of the Atoloa women left behind. With some gentle whispers, she created disharmony. It seemed Joseph Hickory wasn't a popular man in the town, and many agreed he should pay for his crimes.

He was the perfect target—a sacrifice. The curse— his punishment was a rouse for a much bigger plan. Vecula wanted to open a channel and go home. Only…it didn't work."

"But instead, you created...us?" Win finished, and Evan nodded grimly.

"Yes."

"So, it was nothing to do with the shaman women of the tribe?" Luke pressed. "You were witches for hire?"

Evan nodded, her chin trembling. She steadied herself, her hand on the back of the chair. "I was born a long time ago, Win, in a place a long way from here, where it was hot and dangerous, and you had to be strong to survive. There were four of us, me, my older sister Vecula and my brothers Isaac and Wolfric. We were all gifted. We all had a different kind of power. My power always came from the earth. Plants, flowers, spells. I used them to heal."

"You had brothers too?" Win asked, and weakly Evan nodded. "Is Eunice your real name? Issac and Wolfric don't sound like ancient names?"

At the mere mention of her family names, Win shuddered, a cold chill erupting from deep within. Evan seemed to notice. "We've had many names. I don't even remember my real name." She breathed out deeply. "I'm sorry, this is hard to hear. It's hard for me to say it out loud. Vecula was…" her eyes darkened with a terrible memory. "She was the most powerful. She had a born talent for dark magic, with her spells and incantations, but in our village, she was feared. She was spiteful and wanted more than to heal, and she quickly discovered the corruption that came from taking life—blood power. Isaac was a warrior. He was strong, a fighter, and Wolfric was the youngest." Her voice trailed away, leaving a heavy silence in the air, everyone rapt with attention. Something painful crossed her eyes, a memory. "One-night, Vecula came to all of us, her mouth covered in blood, and said she had given herself to god Nassau. The killings began, and before long, we were running for our lives. Everywhere we went, we ended up running. We were cast out of our home, but our blood tied us to her. She'd cast a curse on us all. Life eternal."

She revealed the underside of her wrist, upturning her pale skin, where the tattoo of a square with a dot in the center etched into her skin, with jet black ink. "My binding. She did this to us all," she explained, running the pad of her thumb over the mark as though it stung.

Rowan swallowed audibly. "You said it meant family. When we first met, I asked you what it meant…."

Evan kept her eyes low. "It kind of does."

"You lied. What happened to your brothers?" Rowan asked. "Weren't they…immortal?" Saying the word immortal out loud was bizarre.

"Immortal, but not invincible, much like you. Isaac died in a siege in Poland a long time ago, and crowds killed Wolfric in Iceland. Soon it was just Vecula and me. We traveled everywhere, setting up in new towns and offering our services wherever we went. It would be good for a time. She would promise it would be different. We would try to blend in, set up a home, even find partners, but eventually, Vecula would ruin it. She would step out of line. She always went too far, craved more blood. We were run out of the villages, lucky to escape with our lives, sometimes. She was obsessed with traveling here, to the new world, and finding that stone. She longed to cross realms, to be joined with her beloved god." Her eyes lowered. "Because by now, you know what it is, don't you?"

"It's a door." Win confirmed. In the whole time Evan had spoken, no one moved.

"Yes, it's a door."

"A door to where?" Win pressed.

"A door through time," Evan whispered. "Vecula believed it would take her home."

Blood opens the door… Mary could open the door. So could Win, but right now, she pressed her mouth closed. Feelings were too raw, and everyone was on edge. Rowan was furious, and Win knew one wrong word, and she could lose her temper entirely, and she didn't want Evan anywhere but in this house.

Rowan shuddered. "This doesn't change anything. You still lied. You still brought back our mother and never told us. She's out there somewhere, alone and terrified because of you. You meddled in our family!"

Evan stood abruptly, her hands pressing together in prayer. "I only wanted to help you. I wanted to give back, restore what had been taken from you. I've never meant you any harm. I've spent the last century trying to repair the damage my sister caused, and I know how important family is. I lost two brothers because of what she did."

Ben crossed the room and took Evan by the shoulders. "Why don't you wait downstairs? I need to talk with Rowan and Win, alone."

"I never lied about how I feel Rowan. Never." Meekly, Evan agreed to leave, scuttling out of the room, throwing Rowan a long look.

Rowan blew air through her nose and looked away as if the sight of her was painful. Evan closed the door behind her, and Grayson awkwardly stood, brushing Win's shoulder as he passed. "I'll be downstairs," he whispered as he passed.

###

It was only Ben, Rowan, Win, and Luke left. When Luke rose from the bed, Ben waved him back. "Stay, you're family."

He slumped back down, and Win perched next to him. Ben paced, walking the rug so hard it gathered at the edges. "I know, before you say anything…I've screwed up."

"Dad, how could you not tell us?" Rowan cried. "Where is she?"

Ben held out his palms. "I have no idea! Honestly, I thought she'd come home. She escaped the moment my back was turned."

"Escaped?" That didn't sound good. Win wondered at what

condition her mother's mind was in if she felt the need to escape, inwardly she sagged.

"It sounds like we were holding her hostage." Ben rubbed his eyes, he was tired, and it was still only two in the morning. "It wasn't like that."

"What did you expect from her?" Rowan threw up her hands. "You pull her out of her animal body, a place she'd been safe for years…she can't just pretend it didn't happen. She can't be normal."

"Not me! Evan! I never dreamed this was possible. But I'm not going to lie…having her home was incredible, even for the few times she was lucid."

Lucid? Win groaned, falling forward, propping her elbows on her knees. It sounded like Alice was in no condition to be around anyone. Luke's palm was warm between her shoulder blades; she straightened, giving him a thin smile. Under the garish yellow of the bedroom light, a grey tinge colored his lips, his skin clammy.

Are you okay?

He looked at her abruptly and half-smiled. *A headache, that's all.*

Go to bed. You need to rest.

Wordlessly, he shook his head, lifting his fingers to his lips as if pressing back the urge to vomit. Whatever was happening to him was happening fast. And talking telepathically wore him into the ground, Win made herself promise not to do it until he was healthier.

"I should go out there and start looking," Rowan said. Win could sense her edginess, her need to flee, and thought Rowan would rather be doing anything other than dealing with her girlfriend.

"You have no idea where she'll go, Rowan. Maybe she needs space?"

I need space, she thought, lowering her gaze, and next to her, Luke smiled. She'd not intended for him to hear, but right now, she was too wired to hide her thoughts.

"Rowan, right now, the only thing you need to do is deal with Evan…and stay in this house. Don't forget we still have Spencer prowling around somewhere out there," Ben said.

"And how do I deal with Evan, Dad? Enlighten me. She's been lying to me for weeks—so have you!"

"I did my best," he argued. "What was I supposed to do? I couldn't bring her home. If you'd seen her, what she was like…."

"Which is why I want to find her!" Rowan yelled.

"She doesn't want to be found!" Luke barked, impatience clouding his voice. Rowan and Ben stared at him, and he inched a little behind Win. "*Clearly*, she wants space. Give her that. It's not like she doesn't know where you are!"

When nobody spoke, Win seized the opportunity she'd been waiting for. "I saw Mary Hickory in my dream."

Rowan narrowed her eyes. "What?"

"I saw her, well, more like she came here. Ella and I called her earlier, and it didn't work, but after I went to sleep, she showed up. She showed me everything, things that happened in the past, Evan's past. Rowan— it was horrible. She was branded in front of a crowd. I know she lied to us, but I don't believe she's here to harm anyone."

Rowan pushed back her hair, going to the window and leaning on the edge. "What else did you see?"

"I wanted to ask for help…how the power we share can help Luke get through the calling…."

"And what did she tell you?"

Win flushed, her stomach sinking. "It was fairly cryptic. I already have the answer. Or so she told me."

"How helpful," Rowan quipped, and Win stared at her hands, stung.

Thanks anyway… Luke nudged her shoulder with his; she met his eyes and couldn't look away, only managing to do so when a lump knotted in her throat.

"Rowan, go talk to Evan," Ben urged. "Don't leave it like this."

"I wish she would just go."

Win stood, stumbled as she tried to put weight on her leg, and hobbled across to the chair Evan occupied only moments ago. "You don't mean that. I know you're angry. Do you remember the awful argument we had in the summer? I was convinced Evan wasn't trustworthy."

"And *guess* what, you were right! How did I know you'd bring that up to throw in my face?"

Win told herself to keep calm. Rowan was wounded, hurt, and now was losing control of everything she tried so desperately to keep together.

"I'm not throwing it in your face," Win continued. "Even though I thought those things, she proved me wrong. She *loves* us. I feel it. And I believe she was trying to help us, to give us back our mother. Okay, so it's massively backfired. But Mom will come home. Evan deserves a second chance. I'm prepared to forgive Grayson for what he did…and I'd forgive you too."

Rowan's yellow eyes flashed angrily, her lip curled, and Win sensed her blunder.

"How generous of you, Win. I'm so happy you'll forgive me for protecting you from the masked hunter who stalked our family and nearly got you killed!" Her tone was acidic, laced with venom, and Win stepped back, her thigh tugging, a reminder of the danger still lurking outside.

"Rowan, I'm not going to fight with you. You *lied* to me. You let me believe he was dead!"

"He is dangerous, Win!"

Win lost her temper. "He isn't *Spencer*!" she yelled, her growl erupting from her chest.

"Okay, enough!" Ben stepped between them, pushing them back with a hand on each shoulder. "Rowan, this thing you have with Grayson, *drop it.* Drop it right now!"

Rowan's lower lip shook. "But Dad…!"

"I mean it! You might be the alpha, but I'm your father. The guy might not be my first choice for a boyfriend for Win, but I feel safer with him in the building right now. Shelve it until after this is over."

Rowan's teeth bared. "It's a bit late to be playing the patriarch card, Dad. Where were you five years ago? You have no idea what Win needs!"

Ben shuddered and stepped back, exhaling deeply, his daughter's venom enough to render him into silence. With his head lowered, Win jumped in, knowing how deep that remark would have cut him.

"Rowan, you have to stop this! You can't be everything to everyone all the time!"

"But that's my job. To keep you safe?"

Win cocked a brow. "Keep me safe? Or keep me in line?"

"Win, don't…." Luke warned, but it was too late. Rowan's eyes blurred with hot tears.

"Keep you in line? Win, I want you to fly. To leave this place and have some kind of life. And that guy will only hold you back!"

"But it's *my* choice! *My* failure if it goes wrong. You can't be my alpha, my sister, and my mother too!"

"But look what he did to you!" Rowan yelled, her voice shattering around Win's bedroom, still untidy, bedclothes crumpled on the floor. Rowan broke, tears clinging to her lower lashes. She was gaping at Win's bandaged thigh.

Win hobbled closer and put her arms around her. "Rowan… Spencer did this. Grayson wouldn't hurt me."

Rowan eased away, wiping her eyes, turning her back on them all. It was an age before she managed to speak, and when she did, it was peppered with sobs. "On my watch. Spencer did this on *my* watch. I should have *felt* him…stopped him. I've been so blind to all of it."

Luke hopped off the bed, wrapping one arm around her, pulling her against him for a hug. "Rowan— he's my brother. *You* should have felt him? What about me? I'm equally responsible."

"No one is responsible!" Ben cut in. "No one is to blame for Spencer's actions. Not even Jake, as much as it pains me to admit. He's a grown man and acted alone."

Rowan put her head weakly on Luke's shoulder, sniffing and wiping her nose. "It still doesn't help me with Evan. I don't know if I could trust her again."

"Then you have to be equally as angry with me," Ben said. "I told her to keep it from you. Be angry with me, not her."

Luke sighed. "You're angry with Ben most of the time anyway—may as well add it to the dad fail list, like I do."

Win's lips twitched into a reluctant grin, the tension dripping away. Rowan smirked, batting him in the stomach.

"Give her a chance, Rowan," Ben urged.

Rowan wrung her hands, miserable, and Win hopped back to the bed.

Ben opened the door and motioned for Luke and Rowan to follow him. "I think we've all had enough for one night, and we can thrash this all out in the morning. Bed!"

Heavy footsteps thudded up the stairs, and Grayson appeared in the frame of the door, pushing it open with his fingertips. Win noticed Rowan huff and push past him. She rolled her eyes, knowing if Rowan could have gut-punched him right then, she would have.

Win crawled back under the covers when they were alone, pulling the duvet up to her chest. Grayson paused, giving her a sad smile as he reached for his pillow. Win held out her arms, shooting him with pleading eyes and pout to match. Huffing, he snatched up his pillow and motioned for her to scoot over. "I take up a lot of room," he warned, falling into bed beside her, but she didn't care, nestling into his back, wrapping her arms under his.

It took her a while to drift off again. Finding his hands in the dark, they linked fingers, and she felt marginally safer. Every time her lids fluttered closed, she saw Mary, her bleak, haunted face and the blood dripping from her neck.

I'm in the walls…I'm everywhere…

Win shuddered, forcing it away and trying to ignore the creeping sensation that someone watched her as she slept.

Twenty Five

Win woke early. It was still dark outside, and every part of her wanted to stay curled into Grayson's back. She was warm, her arm dangled over his hip, her cheekbone pressed against his shoulder blade. But there was an insistent tugging on her foot, and she struggled awake, finding Rowan standing over the bed.

"We have to go out," Rowan reminded her curtly, her expression stony. "So you can phase?"

"Uh." Win tried to sit and rubbed her eyes. Next to her, Grayson stirred wake, instantly alert, like a cat sleeping on a ledge.

"I'll take her," he suggested, rubbing his eyes and raking his hands through his mussed hair.

Rowan sniffed and shook her head. "No, it's fine."

"I'm happy to." Grayson unfolded his legs, stretching.

Rowan huffed. "Grayson…"

"I'll take her. Let me help out, Rowan. Please!" Grayson was already on his feet, pulling on his pants and shirt.

Rowan relented, stalking out of the room as Grayson snorted, leaning on the edge of the bed to fasten his boots. "She *really* doesn't like me."

Win threw her arms around his neck from behind, kissing his face. "Give her time. She's having her own crisis. Stuff she needs to work through with Evan."

Once they were ready, they crept outside, bundled up in heavy coats and scarves. Police vans and cars were parked along both sides of the Hickory drive, and Win wondered if they were still out searching for Spencer. Grayson started the truck, and they drove in silence to West point, where he parked behind some dunes and then ushered her out of the cab.

He averted his gaze when she started to strip off, her teeth chattering.

"You're blushing, Grayson," she teased, whipping off her shirt and hopping down to the sand.

"Don't know how you can tell in the dark," he muttered, throwing her a wry grin and blowing into his hands.

"Good eyes, remember?"

Win sprinted down to the beach, hiding in the long grass where she could change in safety. The waves crashing against the shore washed out her anguished cries. She had forgotten about her injury, and phasing was an eye-watering reminder.

She wasn't gone long. Long enough to let the animal free for an hour, to run the sand, letting the wet grains seep between her claws, ducking in and out of the waves, playing in the spray. In the distance, the lights of the tiny harbor town glimmered, the sun still struggling to rise. Her hind leg stung, the scar stretched taught in her jaguar form, and it throbbed when she tried to gain any speed. Deflated and tired, she hobbled back, and when she was back in her own body, she wrapped herself in the blanket he'd left her and limped to the truck.

Sitting in the back, propped against the side rail, he tossed her jeans and underwear. Win ignored them, letting them fall onto the grassy sand. She climbed on the truck and straddled his lap, taking him by surprise. "Win," he groaned as she kissed his jaw. "We can't do this now."

She ignored his agony, opening the blanket, nestling against him, and wrapping it around them both. Smiling to herself, she planted kisses up to his lower lip. "Why not? When will we get a chance to be alone?"

He shivered, finding her mouth with his, kissing her long and hard before gently pushing her back. "Because, if we do this, your sister will know…and that's weird." When she pouted, he grinned, kissing her. "It's not that I don't want to! I do, trust me."

Grumbling, she rolled away, putting her head on his shoulder. "You're right," she agreed, pouting. "Aren't you just a perfect gentleman?"

"It's about time," he quipped, wrapping a massive arm around her and pulling her close. Staring up at the inky, star-speckled sky, their breath fogged on the cold air, Win's stomach lurched at the conversation brewing with her sister and Rowan's lack of apology.

"Don't be too hard on her," Grayson said as if reading her thoughts, his fingers tangling in her unruly hair as he brushed it. "She wanted to keep you safe."

Win smiled gently, relenting. "I know."

"Anyone can tell she's finding this tough. I'm an extra thorn in her side, and she needs time and space."

Win stared up at him, alarmed and glassy-eyed. "You aren't going to bale on me, are you?" She sat up, forcing him to look at her by crawling into his lap. "Because I don't want time—or space. I've had as much of that as I can take. Rowan and I will be okay. I don't want you to leave."

In the dark, he gazed down at her and kissed her mouth softly, causing a ripple of heat to rush up her spine. "I'm yours, Win."

The roads were dark and frosty, and Grayson drove slowly as they approached the house. Win's eyes keenly scanned the tree line as they pulled in. For a split second, she saw a flash of movement, wisps of blonde hair glittering among the glistening brambles.

"Wait! Stop the truck!" she gasped and jolted as Grayson stamped on the brake. Win flung open the door, greeted by cold air as she stepped into the woodland surrounding their home entrance. Thick masses of trees beckoned her in, and she stood in the mud, staring. "Mom? Is that you?"

Win didn't know what she had seen, and maybe it was her imagination? But for a fleeting moment, she'd sworn she saw a figure in the trees. It was too quick, and Win wondered if she conjured the ghostly apparition in her mind, missing her mother, knowing she was somewhere out there alone and afraid. From the cab, Grayson called out to her, the interior light blinking. "What is it?"

Win sniffed but smelled pines and nothing more. She deflated. "Nothing." Whatever, or whoever had vanished.

They crept into the quiet house when they arrived back; everyone was still fast asleep. Grayson dived straight back in bed while Win lay next to him, her thoughts in turmoil, nails digging into her palms as she stared at the ceiling fan.

She had a foreboding sense of dread like time was running out. Last night, Luke looked awful, sick as a dog and trying to hide the slight tremors in his hands. Mary had given her information overload, but none of it made sense. Spencer survived, so Win prayed Luke could too. But Willard's warning still rippled in her memory. The calling was shredding him from the inside out. When the time came, she was still in the dark. Evan and Rowan were asleep in the next room, and Win wondered how long their truce would last. Rowan was in a fighting mood. She was moody and wounded and was likely to lash out at someone.

Win hoped that Rowan gave Evan a fair chance. No matter what lies Evan told, her intent had been genuine. And despite doing her best to wash it away, Win couldn't forget what happened to Evan at the Fraser Samhain gathering. It made her heart wrench. The humiliation, the fear Evan must have felt, made her wish she'd never seen it. And Mary, so strange, so utterly devoid of feeling. How could they be related to someone so heartless?

Win quickly discovered that Grayson was a duvet hog. Not only that, he crowded the whole bed, so she snaked her arms under his, melting into his broad shoulders as she forced herself to sleep.

Win had the same plan as Luke. Waking a couple of hours later, she couldn't stand lying in bed a moment longer. Her back ached, her leg needed stretching, and Grayson was too warm, even for her. After dressing and kissing Grayson on the temple, leaving him sprawled across her bed, she struggled downstairs and found Luke eating in the kitchen.

He gazed at her like he'd not seen her for a week. Then he looked away, stuffing his mouth full of cereal. "You're up early," he said. She sensed an awkward tension, and she wondered what he was thinking. Part of her felt compelled to confess that last night, Grayson slept by her side, and nothing happened. She wondered if it might wipe that painful, longing look off his face. But she reminded herself that she had to keep Luke at arm's length, no matter how weird things got between them.

Win shifted her bottom into the seat opposite. "I was going to drive to the hospital this morning. See how Cole is," she revealed her plan, and Luke's eyes brightened.

"Me, too!" He smiled. "I'll drive you." He looked at her thigh under the table. "I don't think you're in a fit condition to drive anywhere. How's it feeling?"

Win shuddered as a sharp tingling sensation rose under her jeans and a constant reminder of her wound. "It's a little better. Stings like hell."

Luke's face fell, shaking his head. "I could kill him, and I *would* kill him if I weren't so pathetic right now."

Win smiled, grateful for the gallant offer, even if she noticed the dark circles under his bloodshot eyes. She wrote a quick note for Rowan and met him out on the drive. The sky was thick with white clouds, and Win wondered if it might snow. Luke cursed, turning the engine over and over, but it choked and spluttered. He got out and slammed the door.

"It's dead," he snapped, rubbing his eyes, and Win groaned in disappointment. The truck had been a birthday gift from her grandpa, and she recalled her father being wary about its age at the time.

"We could take it to a mechanic?" she suggested, not wanting to admit she knew nothing about cars. Despite spending hours being her grandpa's assistant, she managed to hand him a tool when he needed one, but that was it.

"What's going on?" a voice came from behind, and Win whirled to see Grayson standing there, hands-on-hips, still in the vest and open shirt he'd slept in. Win blushed, feeling guilt creep up her neck.

"The truck's dead." She waved her hand to the hood that Luke pried open. Luke peeked a look at Grayson over his arm. She saw him roll his eyes and look away, sensing that his mood had gone from good to abysmal in seconds. "We were heading to the hospital to see Cole."

Grayson barrelled up beside Luke, peering over his shoulder. He folded his arms. "I can take a look if you like?"

Luke's attempt at a smile didn't quite reach his eyes. "I'm good, thanks."

"Well, you're looking in the wrong place," Grayson was curt, nudging him aside. "I'm good with engines. Let me fix it for you."

Win beamed. "Really?"

Grayson threw her a charming smile, snaking his arm around her waist. "I wouldn't mind getting out of the house. I woke up to the sound of quite a heated discussion coming from your sister's room."

Win's face dropped. "Ah, yeah, I can only imagine how that conversation is going."

Grayson looked over to her grandfather's workshop, nestled in the treeline. "Mind if I go in there? Find some tools?"

"No..." she said, happy he was helping. "Help yourself! Perhaps we can get the bus to the hospital or something?"

Several officers barrelled out of the woods, heavily armed, walking across the gravel to the van parked along the grassy verge. One of them was Noah, and he flashed a short smile. "Did you say you were going to the hospital?"

Win shoved her hands in her pockets, her shoulder bumping Luke's as he appeared beside her. "Yeah, we wanted to visit our friend, Cole. The guy who was injured yesterday."

"That's where I'm heading now. I wanted to see if he was up and ready to talk. Can I give you a lift?"

Luke threw Win a look which read he'd rather go by tandem than go in the back of a cop car. But Win ignored him, nudging his ribs. "Thank you. That's kind of you!"

Noah waved off her comment. "It's the least I can do. We've taken over your yard, cops everywhere. I'm leaving in five, okay?"

Noah flashed Grayson a quick look, once over up and down, assessing him, which unnerved her. Probably as he'd not seen him before, she told herself, watching as he jogged across to the van, where the other officers were stripping off their protective gear.

"That works out well." Grayson scooped her off her feet and kissed her cold nose. "Hopefully, I'll have this fixed by the time you get home. There's probably sand in the engine from this morning." He seemed uncertain for a moment. "Your sister won't tear me out, will she? If I go looking through your grandpa's workshop? I kind of get the impression she hates my guts."

"Grayson!" Win laughed. "You have my permission to use whatever you want in there. I'll let her know. Don't be so worried."

"Yeah, she kind of has bigger problems!" Luke quipped.

Minutes later, they were fastening their belts in the back of Noah's car. It smelled of a clean, new car and was immaculate inside, unlike the inside of her rickety truck. Noah commented about buckling up, and Luke and Win shared a grin. It was like they were kids on a memorable ride-along morning with a police officer. As they drove away, Win watched Grayson dive under the hood, and despite the cold, he stripped off his shirt, revealing his large, toned upper arms. Win allowed herself a moment to bask in his male beauty, her chest flushing, as she imagined getting him alone at last. She wished he'd not turned her away this morning; she was pent up and edgy.

Beside her Luke, chuckled, clearly finding something amusing, and Win shot him an indignant glare.

"What?"

"Nothing." He bit his lip, making a face, lowering his voice, so Noah didn't hear. "Your heart just sped up. What could you *possibly* be thinking about?"

Win flashed him a baffled smile. "You hear that?"

"Uh-huh," he answered, looking away forlorn. "Keep it down, will you?"

He wound down the window and stuck his head out, sucking in the air. Beside him, she cringed. She had no idea it would be this strong for Luke, that he was rapidly picking up on her senses as well, reading her body language. It was weirdly voyeuristic.

"Sorry, I'll try not to…think about anything," she said, but he didn't return her smile. Sighing, she looked to the front of the car, spying Noah watching them with his soft, brown eyes in the rear-view mirror.

"Did you find anything out there?" She changed the subject, keenly aware he was listening to them. Wearily, he shook his head.

"It's like the damn thing vanishes into thin air," Noah admitted. "We've baited the area, but it doesn't seem to want to bite. By the way, you were up early this morning? You and the big guy you were with?"

Next to her, Luke stiffened. Win had no idea she and Grayson had been spotted. "Ah, we went running."

Noah's thick brow arched. "Kind of early for a run? Five in the morning?"

"He likes to get out before the sun comes up." Win smiled, keeping her gaze firmly locked on Noah's in the mirror, hoping that he'd accept her blatant lie.

Noah shrugged. "Not seen him around town. Is he living with you?"

"No." She fidgeted with her hands. "He's only staying a few days."

"What's his name?" Noah pressed, and beside her, she sensed Luke's heart speed up.

"Um, Grayson." Her tongue felt like sandpaper.

"Ah…okay. I don't know him. You don't mind a good-looking guy hanging out with your girlfriend?" The last question was aimed at Luke, who leaned his head in from the open window, his hair blasted back from the wind.

For a moment, both Luke and Win shared a confused glance. She groaned inwardly, recalling the whopper he'd told Noah the night they first discovered the zoologist in the woods—that they were dating.

Don't say too much, Win warned him. He ignored her.

Luke's smile dropped, his brow arching. "Good looking? *Really?*"

"Well, you know he's a big guy, and even with the face thing…."

Luke snorted. "I don't see it personally. But maybe *you* should ask him out?"

Win died inside, throwing back her head on the rest behind her. She and Grayson should have been more careful. Noah clicked his tongue and said nothing, and they arrived at Meadowford General after twenty minutes of stony silence.

The hospital was airy, light, and the emergency ward packed as they wandered after Noah, who appeared to have a free hall pass wherever he went.

He tossed them a look over his shoulder. "Cole is on Phoenix Ward," he said as they lagged behind him. He paused, his eyes resting on Luke's face, which had gone from light tan to sharkskin grey. "Are you alright?"

Luke's mouth watered, and he wiped it on his sleeve. "Fine," he muttered, swallowing. Win understood, knew his stomach must be swirling. It was an assault on the senses, the smell of antibacterial floor cleaner, the bright, flashy lights, their shoes squeaking across the polished floor. Darting in an elevator, they traveled up four floors; the bell pinged and opened onto a kid's ward. Cole was still technically underage.

A nurse let them in, and they wandered through aisles of beds, walls covered with bright, cheery kid's art and patient photos. Cole's room was down a long, narrow corridor that sprang from the ward's busier end. He straightened in his bed the moment Win peeked her head around the corner. She beamed, suddenly emotional.

"Hey!" She threw her arms around his neck, hugging him as gently as she could. "You look good!"

Cole rolled his eyes, holding up his damaged hand, tightly wound in a bandage. "I don't think I'll have that basketball scholarship to fall back on. I might have to study this semester."

Luke lurked in the doorway as Win climbed up onto the side of Cole's bed. In the corner sat a woman with short blonde hair. She smiled awkwardly, rising out of her seat, and Win guessed it was Cole's mother. She gave them all a wave, taking out her book and her handbag, and headed for the door.

"I'll give you guys some time," she said, nearly bumping into Noah as he entered the room. Noah scraped up a chair, sitting by the side of Cole's bed.

Win's heart ached for Cole. He was beaten, bruised, and swollen, both eyes nearly welded shut, scrapes and cuts zigzagging his shaved head. She held his hand. "How are you doing?"

Cole shifted, allowing her some more space. "I'm okay. The bite was deep but, thankfully, avoided anything I'm going to need in the future. It's just my hand that sucks."

Her eyes filled up. "I'm sorry."

Cole shook his head. "Are you kidding me? You saved my life!"

He glanced at Luke, leaning heavily in the door. "Both of you. You dragged me back to the house. That thing would have eaten me!"

Noah cleared his throat, signalling his presence in the room, shifting his chair forward.

"Do you feel up to me asking you a few questions?"

"Sure." Cole nodded, solemn. "I mean, I can't remember much."

"Can you describe it?"

Cole looked skyward, his eyes filmy. "Uh, really big. It was sort of silver, like a mauve tone, and huge, yellow eyes. Its paws were enormous!"

Noah nodded. "How big, exactly? It's just that from all the checks we've run, a cat that large doesn't exist in any file we've studied. You think it was a panther?"

"I mean, I'm not an expert. I didn't have a good long look before it chased me down. I was kind of facing the other way—running to save my ass," Cole stuttered out laughter. "I don't know the difference, panther, lynx…leopard. It was a big cat."

Noah appeared thoughtful, standing and straightening his belt. "But, roughly how large? How tall? If you could measure from the floor?"

Cole blinked, confused, and Win felt heat rising under her shirt. She wasn't sure where Noah was headed with his questions. Cole looked at the floor and pointed at Noah's hip. "I would say from the floor, to where your holster is…that would be my guess… but it's vague."

Noah narrowed his eyes, mentally assessing the height with his palm. "That's roughly over four feet then." He made a note, scribbling it in a small notebook he pulled from his breast pocket. He looked skyward. "Are you sure?"

"Kind of." Cole didn't look in the least bit sure.

"That's larger than a Tiger."

"I don't know what to tell you."

"Are you sure it *wasn't* a Tiger?"

Cole gaped at the officer. "Why would a Tiger be in the woods?"

"Well, some rich people have a thing for buying exotic pets, and then when they can't cope, they set them free," Noah explained, and Win let out a slow breath. That sounded like the best explanation she'd ever heard—a crazy, wealthy pet owner, and all these years and her family never came up with that perfect excuse.

"Look, it was big, but I don't think it was a Tiger." Cole's shoulders rolled in a deep shudder.

"And did it spring out at you? Chase you down?"

Cole paled. If it was possible to go whiter under these hospital lights, he did. "Uh, it dropped. Dropped out of the trees." He sucked in air, visualizing a memory. "It was just there."

Noah's eyes flew wide, a grin cracking his mouth. He clapped Cole on the shoulder. "That's awesome, Cole. Thank you! I'll call that in right now. We've been looking on the ground all this time, and it's probably in the goddamn trees!"

Noah marched out of the room, flipping out his phone and sliding it open. Win squeezed Cole's good hand. "Well done. It's not nice having to relive that."

Cole swallowed sickly, and by this time, Luke took up the chair Noah vacated.

"You guys are so brave." Cole looked at Win, fixing her with a hard stare. "You ran after it? I remember you leaving?"

"Oh..." Win panicked, her lie about to stick in her throat. "I was with you the whole time."

Cole looked confused, shaking his head wearily. "It's weird. I don't remember that. But then I just described a four-foot panther to a cop, so guess I must be pretty out of it, huh?"

Another shape filled the door, and Ella breezed in. Win jumped off the bed, rushing to hug her friend. "I didn't know you were coming."

"Luke messaged and told me you guys were here, and you'd need a ride home," she explained, after crossing the room and hugging Cole and then presenting him with a box of pink donuts. His eyes went wide.

"You are an angel!" He wolfed one down, licking his lips. They chatted for a few minutes, uncharacteristically; Luke was friendly, talking to Cole, discussing the next few games and how he could still play despite his injury. Win eyed Ella and shooed her out into the hall.

Ella leaned against the wall. "What is it?"

"It worked," Win told her. "After you left, Mary visited me, in my dream!"

Ella's eyes rounded as Win made quick work of the night's events. By the end, her mouth was hanging open. "And your mom is out there? Somewhere?"

"Yes!"

"That's kind of dangerous, what with Spencer on the loose," Ella said, crossing her arms. "Perhaps it's better if she does stay away?"

A nurse arrived to take Cole's vitals, and it seemed like an excellent opportunity to leave him to rest. Luke went green when the nurse flashed a needle and dashed for the bathroom along the corridor, his shoes squeaking after him. The sight and smell of blood provoking a nasty reaction. Ella exhaled. "Oh, gosh."

"You better go after him," Win urged, forcing herself not to tailgate him, even though she wanted to. Ella made a face and followed him into the bathroom.

Win waved goodbye to Cole and wandered down the corridor; as she pushed back the heavy, ward door with her hand, she ran into Jake Fraser. She gasped, staring up at him in mild horror, bouncing off his shoulder.

He staggered back, surprised, straightening his sweater. He looked good, fresh from the shower, clean hair, bright-eyed, and healthy compared to Luke. "Win! I wasn't expecting to see you."

She could have said the same; awkwardly, she lingered in the door. "Why are you here?"

"Visiting a friend," he told her nonchalantly.

"It's a kid's ward, Jake."

He smiled, revealing white teeth. "You look better. How are you feeling?"

Her shoulders dipped, weighted with frustration. Talking to him was like chatting to a blank wall. But instead of showing him her annoyance, she lifted her chin and blasted him with a pretty smile. "I'm better. No thanks to your son."

He shoved his hands in his pockets, eyeing her casually. "As much as I'd love to continue this scintillating conversation, I need to get going—a word to the wise. The cops are crawling all over my land and yours. You should keep out of our way."

"Oh, don't worry, we will!" She wished she could think of something better. "As long as you keep Spencer away from us."

Jake's smile dropped. "And what do you suggest, Win? Chain him up? He'd likely kill me."

"I'm willing to risk it." She crossed her arms, pleased to see the smirk melt off his face.

"Now, there was me thinking how lucky I was to find I have not one but two nieces to spoil. Guess I'm off the Christmas card list, huh?"

"We aren't your nieces, not really. Again, you don't have to worry about us. We do just fine and don't need spoiling or *anything* you'd be willing to offer."

"Oh, come on. I can't take back what Spencer did. But I *can* take you shopping!"

Win's lips twitched, but she was determined not to laugh. It irked her to admit; he was wearing her down. There was something about him, a charm that, despite everything she felt, drew her in. But, she supposed that was why he'd been married so many times.

"Money doesn't buy love, Jake," she said at last. Why was she falling into this bottomless pit with him? He loved bantering with her, basking in her discomfort. She felt her cheeks burn, and he snickered. She added something that made his smile drop. "And it's not me you need to buy. You need to make things right with Luke."

Jake breathed through his nose. "And what makes you think I haven't tried?"

"He would have said…he would have told me!"

"Would he? Well, guess what? You're wrong, red. After we met at the house, he had me worried. He looked awful, and it *tickled* my conscience, so I called him several times. He hasn't returned them."

Win looked at the floor, surprised Luke hadn't mentioned it. When she glanced up, he was smirking, glad to have wiped the floor with her superiority. Part of her was elated he'd tried, that somehow, her berating may have gotten to him—a bit.

"I do love these little chats, Win." He strolled away, pushing open the door. "I look forward to many more as we get to know one another."

Several expletives came to mind, but she bit her tongue as Noah rounded the corner. He flashed Jake a glance before leaning on the wall next to her. "Was that Jake Fraser?"

"Yes." She ground her teeth.

"Ha! I thought so. How do you know him?"

God, Noah was so damn nosey. Win exhaled, knowing it was fruitless lying. "He's my weird, creepy distant uncle."

Noah chuckled. "Huh? That's crazy. I didn't know you guys were all related?"

Win groaned. "Yeah, well, unfortunately, it goes back a couple of generations. We only found out this summer."

Noah stared at her, mulling something over. "So, I know Rowan denied it, but I'm fairly sure she and Spencer dated all through high school...and didn't you say you were dating his brother?"

Win's face flamed. *Oh…crap!* "Uh…"

Noah held up his hands. "You know what? None of my business. I need to take off—do you think you'll be okay getting home?"

Win nodded, wanting to disperse into the ground. She wondered what kept Ella and Luke, willing them out of the bathroom to rescue her from Noah's quizzical stare and constant questions. There was a glint in his eyes, and she couldn't quite place it. But she felt odd like he was sizing her up. And after that little tidbit, she'd just revealed, they must sound like the craziest family in Cedar Wood.

I'm onto you, his gaze read. He was already suspicious about Grayson and he'd questioned Cole about the panther in a way that sent alarm bells ringing. He knew their history. Win's guts churned, watching him walk away. Abruptly, he stopped and turned back. "One more thing…." He scratched his chin, turning on his heels.

Oh, damn…

"How does Jake Fraser know Cole Ward?"

"What?" Win folded her arms, suddenly tired of all the questions.

"Is he another relative? Or a mentor or something?"

She bristled, searching for an answer but came up with the truth. "He doesn't know him, not that I'm aware."

"Oh." Cole looked thoughtful. "Interesting, he must have a white knight complex."

Win became increasingly annoyed the longer she looked at him. Clenching her teeth, she attempted to smile. He was toying with her, not unlike Jake, and she hated it. "What do you mean, Noah?"

Noah stood back, hands in his pockets. "Mrs. Ward wanted to thank him. He just cleared all of his medical bills."

She gaped at him, her bottom lip dropping. "He did?"

Noah grinned. "Maybe he isn't so weird and creepy after all?"

Twenty Six

Rowan gritted her teeth, staring at the interloper in the yard below. The clanging of metal grated her nerves as Grayson rattled with the broken engine. Crossing her arms over her chest, she turned away from the window, not wanting to look at him a second longer. Weary, she trudged to her room, a place that up until last night had been a blissful shared space with Evan. Their room was bright, with pretty linens and drapes. Evan's signature look all over the room. Rowan's stomach churned. She pushed open the door with the tips of her fingers, and Evan sat in the corner, her feet up on a chair, biting at her nails.

The moment she spotted her, Evan straightened, her gaze hopeful, expectant, her long hair falling in waves across her shoulders as she stood up. "Hey," she said. "Are you ever going to talk to me?"

Rowan crossed the room, opening and closing drawers in her dresser, folding away a pile of their shared laundry, sorting the underwear, and pretending she couldn't hear. Evan stepped up beside her, taking her shoulders as she turned away.

"Rowan, please!"

"Would you give me anything real if I did talk to you?" She was irritable, her nerves jangled, having spent most of the night sleeping on the far edge of the bed. Finally admitting defeat she'd ended up on the couch. Her neck ached, and her limbs were stiff.

Evan grasped her hands and pulled her to the bed, where she sat, and Rowan knelt at her feet. Evan ran her hand over Rowan's cheek, stroking the pad of her thumb along her brow. Rowan closed her eyes, the movement so soothing she could have fallen asleep in her arms right then.

"Ask me anything," Evan offered.

Rowan cocked a brow, not knowing where to begin, the questions running through her mind all night, now a jumbled mess. "Where were you born?"

Evan exhaled, pushing a strand of hair out of her dark eyes. "We were from a village in South America, near the Guatemala borders, though I don't think that place exists now."

Rowan sucked in her breath. "And when *exactly* was that?"

Evan ducked her eyes to her hands folded in her lap. "Does age really matter?" Rowan burst out laughing, but it wasn't funny.

"It matters to me!" she spat. "One hundred years ago? *Two hundred?*"

Evan met her gaze darkly, and Rowan gaped.

"Five hundred? *Eight?*"

Evan bit her lip and refused to answer, and Rowan threw up her hands in despair, raking her hands through her curls. "Holy shit, Evan !"

"I'm sorry!"

"What's your name? Your real one—because it sure as hell isn't *Eunice*."

Evan exhaled gently. "I don't even remember, but you're right. Those were adopted names. Over the years, I've had many.

Eunice...Isaac...those were European names we chose to blend in at the time."

"So your Atoloa family was a pack of lies. You've never been one of them?"

"Kind of," she answered, her eyes darting up nervously, wary of Rowan's fragile temper. "I lived with a tribe there once."

"Ha! Like two hundred years ago? And your grandma—you told me she was sick."

"Rowan…"

"It was lies! You were covering up so you could leave and see to my mother."

Evan looked desperate. "I had to tell you something!"

"You told me you were drawn here—that you were here to help Win? Was that a lie?"

Evan's head jerked up, tears lurking in her dark eyes. "No, that's true. I'm here to help. I swear to you!"

Rowan stood up, hands-on-hips facing her down. "What's coming, Evan? What's so important you needed to wrench my mother out of a life she was happy in?"

"Aren't you pleased? That I brought her back?"

"Of course I am—but she was complete. Do you know how hard this is on us? We're stuck between forms, and we live knowing that we could revert to the animal inside if we lose control. My mother was done! She was free, even at the cost of losing us. So, what is so important that you felt she needed to be here?"

Evan covered her eyes with cupped palms, but angrily Rowan tore them away, and she stared up at her in alarm. "You aren't ready, Rowan."

Rowan's nostrils flared angrily. "What do you mean?"

"You aren't the true alpha of this family! Not yet."

Her words stung like a slap to the face, and Rowan staggered. When she didn't speak, Evan continued. "You are the acting alpha, and you *have* power. But its like being second in command. Spencer wouldn't stand a chance against you if you were a full alpha."

Rowan was dizzy, filled with a strange mix of emotions. Hearing that out loud should be a relief, but instead, she just felt like a failure, another thing ripped from her grasp. “Do you mean I’m not good enough?”

“No!” Evan stood, taking her gently by the shoulders. “But it’s not *your* time. It’s Alice’s role, now that she’s human. There are wounds here, buried in this family, so deep even you don’t know about them. Your mother understood the curse, and she sacrificed her human life for it. Alice Hickory is John’s heir and the natural alpha. She has to be the one to unite you all, to bridge the gap between you—so you can stand together.”

Rowan went cold all over. “Stand together for what?”

Evan backed away. She wrapped her arms around her waist. “Spencer will come for Win. Again and again, no matter what we do. He wants to end the line.”

End the line…Why did that ring so familiar? It made the hairs on her arms stand on end. She whispered. “Win…”

“Is the last of you,” Evan filled in the gap. “She could end the curse, and you’d be free. The eldest Therian takes the role of alpha, a born leader. The youngest continues the line, their blood bound to the curse.”

Rowan let that sink in, breathing hard. To be free…to walk in other places, travel far enough away that she could disappear into thin air. To be released from this place seemed unthinkable, and she’d come to terms with her fate long ago. “You mean last summer—he wanted to kill her because her death would end this curse?”

Evan dropped her head between her shoulder blades as if the truth was a relief. “Yes. But it wouldn’t have worked if he had succeeded.”

Rowan sat back, confused. “Why?”

“Win wasn’t full Therian then. It was the same for Mary Hickory all those years ago. She died before she ever went through her calling. So the line continued with her sisters.”

It was never about me…It was never about the family fued…

"But how could he know any of this?"

Evan shook her head. "I don't know. And you have to believe me! If I knew who wanted to hurt her, don't you think I'd tell you? I only want her to be safe. But I know this—everything he ever did to you was *always* about getting to her. So he could be rid of the curse."

There's a fox in our henhouse…

Rowan shook away the odd thought that popped into her head, not knowing where or how that infiltrated her mind. "And he won't stop?"

"No. Never. No matter what you do."

Rowan shook her head in disbelief, eyeing her closely. "There's more. I know you, and I think you're holding something back."

"I'm not!"

"How can I trust you? Was any of this real? You and me?"

Evan crossed the room, throwing her arms around her neck, kissing the side of her face. "It is real. I'm not lying, and I know how bad this looks. But I love you, Rowan…I swear to you."

Hot tears streaked down Evan's lovely face, but Rowan pushed out of her arms as much as she wanted to remain encased within them. Empty words. Her heart beat faster. Empty words, so easy to slip off the tongue. Hadn't she known this before? Hadn't Spencer said the very same thing?

Rowan left the room, stalking downstairs, her nerves raw, and the moment her feet hit the bottom step, she spotted Grayson lurking in the kitchen. He was bent double, peering into the lower cabinets, but straightened the second he heard her footfalls. He looked at the floor, and for a moment, Rowan hated herself for having caused that reaction.

"Can I get you something?" she snapped.

"Uh, I was getting a drink." He scratched his head, his expression pensive as she squeezed past him like he didn't know where to place himself.

"I'll bring it out to you. Don't go through our stuff!"

The instant the remark was out of her mouth, she regretted it, rubbing her eyes and then plastering a thin smile across her lips. He was edgy around her, and she didn't know why that hurt. She sucked in her ribs, grabbing a can of soda from the fridge, watching as he walked out the front door.

Be nice, be nice, she reminded herself. It wasn't his fault, and he'd saved Win's life. She jogged outside, whistled, and then tossed him the can. He caught it reflexively, and she was impressed.

Grayson went to open his mouth to speak but then seemed to change his mind. Irritated, Rowan turned and stalked away. It wasn't him she was mad at.

He was making her feel sad, and she didn't want to feel anything toward him. Her feet itched, skin scratchy, and she remembered she hadn't had a chance to phase, having spent most of the morning arguing with her girlfriend. The wings hidden under her skin longed to stretch. Stalking off around back, she ignored all the warnings in her head. Too many thoughts, information loaded onto her shoulders, she ached to be free. And somewhere out here, her mother was wandering around alone. She may not be the real alpha, but she could be useful.

The next best thing…The thought trailed into her head, and she wiped at the corners of her eyes.

"Where are you going?" his gruff voice called her back, and she paused, tossing him a sneer across her shoulder. He was standing behind her, his feet quiet for a man his size.

"I'm going to scout around and look for my mother."

"You should stay here…the cops…."

She shot him a look which made him stop mid-sentence.

"I'm fine, Grayson," she threw back, haughty and aloof. "You can take your concern and shove it up your ass."

Twenty Seven

By the time Ella pulled the car into the drive, a few lonely flakes of snow started to fall, settling on the roof of the workshop. Win craned her neck as she slid out of the car and spotted Grayson's legs sticking out from under the truck. An odd fluttering sensation settled in her chest, seeing the workshop lights on for the first time since her grandfather passed. Upon hearing the car arrive, he rolled out from under, stretching, sweaty, and covered in oil.

Win sprinted across the yard, flinging herself into his arms. He managed to catch her mid-air, planting his arms under her bottom as she wrapped her legs around his waist. She kissed him longingly, having missed him while she was gone.

"Any luck?" she asked. Grayson let her slide down his body to her feet.

"I had to go into town for a part. I think I'm nearly there, but I could do with some help, someone to read out the manual. At least your grandpa kept them all!"

"I can help," she said, casting a glance around. A police van parked up on the grassy verge and alongside it Noah's car. The yard seemed oddly quiet. She cast her eyes skyward. "Is Rowan around?"

Grayson made a face. "Uh, no. She took off about two hours ago."

Luke rocked up beside them, followed by Ella. "Took off? You mean literally?"

Grayson looked grim. "I did say she should stay here. But she didn't take kindly to that suggestion. She wanted to look for your mother."

Win groaned and rubbed her eyes, feeling the warmth of Ella's hand on her shoulder. "What about Evan?"

"She's been inside most of the day, and now I think she's intent on making dinner tonight."

Luke smirked. "Well, that won't be awkward."

Win scraped her hands through her hair, pacing the gravel. She stared miserably at the trucks, at the darkened woodland flanking them on all sides. Couldn't Rowan have waited five minutes? She had to strike off alone. A sense of foreboding tugged at her insides, and she exhaled sharply.

"I'll take a walk, see if I can find her?"

"No!" Ella, Luke, and Grayson barked in unison. Grayson threw down an oily cloth after wiping his hands.

"That's not happening! Not without me."

"I'm not dragging you out there," she protested, stalking away, wringing her hands as she walked around back, staring hard at the treeline. Grayson caught up with her, catching her shoulder with a light touch.

"Please, Win." He turned her around. "She decided to go. If you go, then I'm coming, and you can't phase anyway…."

"Alright!" Win genuinely lost her temper, saw his crushed expression, and then instantly regretted it. She touched his arm. "I'm sorry."

"No, I'm overstepping," he admitted, keeping his eyes down. "I can't just waltz in and tell you what to do!"

She smiled and wound her arms around his waist. "Overstep, please. I don't mind. I wish…."

Footsteps on the ground behind her made her pause mid-sentence, and she flung around, finding Rowan standing behind them, her red mane of hair disheveled from her outing. Win sighed in relief. "Thank god!"

"You wish what?" Rowan asked. Win strolled toward her, trying to keep her face neutral, she wasn't about to test her, and Rowan was already on edge, tired and anxious.

"Nothing." Win wrapped her in a hug, feeling her sister's arms slide around her. "I'm glad you're home."

Rowan pulled away, blinking back tears. "I smelled her, Win. I recognized the scent. I smelled it on Dad yesterday, and now I found it out there. She's *been* here."

"And she didn't come home?"

"It means she's terrified." Rowan waved her hand at the skies above. "It's starting to snow, and I can't stand to think that she's on her own, lost…."

"She's not lost!" Win assured her. "She just needs time."

Rowan wiped at her eyes with the heels of her hands, sniffing. "Evan is talking about everything like it's normal, and I can't even look at her…."

Win hugged her hard, sensing her sister's vulnerability, how fragile she was for the first time. Miserably, Rowan trudged indoors, and Win found Grayson, linking her fingers with his as they went back to the truck.

The remainder of the afternoon passed in a haze. Ella volunteered to be manual reader, and as the light started to fade, she held up a torch for Grayson under the truck. Win watched from the porch, huddled next to Luke, as more and more snow drifted from the sky. The police team inside the woods all day pulled out and was replaced by a new team of cops.

Noah made a few appearances, and Win made sure to avoid eye contact, his probing, inquisitive eyes, having stomached enough of him for one day. Under the hood, Ella looked over, beaming, and Win giggled, reading her thoughts. Ella was clearly enjoying getting to know Grayson at last.

Grayson got behind the wheel, and then by a miracle, it roared to life. Ella whooped for joy and attempted to high-five him, which he returned with reluctance.

Luke howled with laughter. "He really has lived under a rock his whole life."

Win wrapped her arms around her knees as she stared at his profile. A worrying blue tinge framed his lips. "I saw your dad at the hospital. He paid all Cole's bills."

It was something she'd mulled over telling him all afternoon, knowledge of Jake's generosity burning her conscience. She couldn't help the feeling that in his odd, backward way, Jake was trying to reach out, make amends. When Luke only picked at his nails, Win prodded him. "And you never said he called you?"

Luke shifted uncomfortably. "I don't tell you everything, you know. Besides, you were a little wrapped up."

He meant with Grayson, and it stung. Win glanced over at Ella and Grayson still talking. She was grateful her friend was making an effort but sick with the thought that Luke harbored feelings he shouldn't. "Don't make it about him," Win said. "I think you should talk to your dad. After everything that's happened, don't you believe in second chances?"

Luke kicked at the stones with his toe. "Try fourth chances, fifth chances? He's run out of chances, and he doesn't care."

"I think he does!"

Luke flashed her an angry look. "You don't know him, Win. He could charm the underwear off a nun. He looks genuine, and money is the way he shows affection. But I know him—how he lies."

Ella peered around Grayson's arm, alerted by Luke's sudden

change in tone. Win's stomach went over. "Alright, fine," she shushed him. "I won't say anymore."

Luke's eyes filled up, and this made her anxiety worse. He was emotional and running on empty. "I do love him, Win. I'm not *cold*. Don't think that of me. When I was a kid, I adored him. He isn't all bad—but after my mom died and Spencer moved back in..."

Win's eyes went wide. "Whoa! *What?*"

Luke looked confused, cocking a brow. "What?"

"You just said…when my mom *died!*"

He shook his head, laughing and scratching his chin. "I meant left."

Her heart sped up, her fingers curled around the edge of his shirt. "Luke!"

"I meant left," he insisted, his hands tremoring. "I'm not feeling good, that's all."

Win cast another look over to where Grayson and Ella were talking, deep in conversation. Ella was chatting, waving her hands around, and Grayson studied her with rapt attention, clearly trying to keep up with Ella's speed. Win breathed a sigh of relief that neither heard. When she turned to Luke, he twisted toward her, his gaze expectant, longing, and Win inched back nervously.

"I need to say something," he announced, and Win's stomach dropped. "When we get five minutes alone."

Win broke out into a light sweat despite the cold, she laughed nervously. "Can't you say it now?"

"No." He blushed. "It's private."

Oh god, not now…not this!

"Tell me!" she insisted, knowing full well he couldn't. Not with Ella standing ten feet away. Win's neck tingled with treachery.

Luke looked away. "You know it's funny, all these months, and it's been just you and me, alone. Living together. And now I can't seem to get near you."

Win knew what brought this on. He was edgy, filled up with

strange hormones and emotions. And perhaps some part of him suspected he wasn't going to make it. Win remembered how she felt, how lost, set apart from the ordinary world, like a lonely outsider. She squeezed his shoulder.

"You're near me now. You always are. Listen, we can talk…."

"Is everything okay?" Ella interrupted. She stood over them, watching them both anxiously. Win took the opportunity to jump to her feet and spring away. Luke smiled shakily.

"Luke isn't feeling too hot," Win said, not a complete lie.

"Well, I was going to take off." Ella glanced at them both, cagily and Win hoped she hadn't heard any of that. "Unless...you want me to stay, Luke?"

He glanced up at her through watery eyes, and by sheer willpower, threw her a smile masking whatever had been going on in his head. "I'm good, Ella, I promise."

Win felt like the word liar was stamped right on her forehead in garish red letters. She hugged her friend, and Luke shuffled to his feet and walked her to her car. Before she left, Win jogged to the car to say goodbye, and she grinned through Ella's driver's window.

"Thank you for being so nice to Grayson!" She reached in and squeezed her friend's shoulder. Ella beamed happily.

"He's so cute, Win!" she squealed. "I'm so happy for you.." Her voice trailed off, her eyes following Luke, who wandered toward the house. "He looks terrible…you will call me if he needs me, right?"

Win's smile dropped. "Of course."

"I feel like he's pushing me away," she said the words out loud. Win faltered, about to fill in the silence with a myriad of excuses when Ella said. "I know he doesn't want to hurt me. Or to see him like this. You'll look after him, right?"

Win's words dried up. Ella's expression changed. It was subtle, tension clouding her eyes. "You will look after him, won't you?"

Finally, Win said. "Of course. You know I will."

After her car rolled away, Rowan appeared on the porch and

tightly announced that Evan made lasagne. Luke walked back, hands in pockets, and cocked a smile. "This is going to be weird."

"I can take off too?" Grayson offered when Rowan flung him a look that suggested he'd been on the property for too long. But Ben appeared beside her.

"No, Grayson should stay. I'd feel much better knowing he was here."

No one argued. It did seem illogical to kick out the guy with the crossbow, someone valuable and competent. Grayson might not be Therian, but he understood them, and he'd already spent a good deal of time tracking Spencer, managing to avoid being eaten.

Inside, Evan set the table, her pretty hair piled up, her eyes shining, and her smile fixed. She cast Rowan a wary glance as the tall, redhead slid into a chair at the table. Rowan looked utterly miserable, and Win sensed her disillusion as she sank into her chair. Grayson scraped up one beside her, his bulk filling so much space that Luke shifted several inches.

"Well, this looks great," Ben gushed, unscrewing a wine cap and emptying himself a glass of red. Win was amazed at how well he could pretend things were fine. He'd been lying to them for months, concealing the whereabouts of their mother, and yet he was cheerful, his smile laced with the anxiety hidden underneath.

Perhaps they were all good at pretending. No one spoke at the table, knives and forks clattered on plates, and strained swallowing noises filled the small kitchen. Outside, the sun faded entirely, and it was black. The atmosphere in the room was oppressive, and inch by inch, Win could feel herself slipping down her chair. Evan made several attempts at conversation starters with Grayson, who seemed unsure how to answer. He gazed uncertainly over at Rowan, who looked like at any moment, she would reach across the table and throttle him. Next to her, Rowan's skin burned, Win could tell she was boiling.

Under the table, Luke nudged her toe. *This is as awkward as shit…*

Ben downed his glass and was already pouring another. Win flicked her eyes in Luke's direction.

I wish this was over.

Luke pressed his lips together, avoiding looking at her directly.

It'll go down as one of the most interesting Hickory family dinners. Evan's in denial, and Rowan is having some kind of breakdown. Grayson is practically monosyllabic, and your dad is getting wasted. I can't wait till Christmas!

Win did her best to conceal her laugh, bringing her napkin to her lips and hiding her smile. Rowan slapped the table with such a thud that the crockery leaped in the air. She threw them both an icy glare, wagging her finger between them. "Are you two… *talking?*"

"What! No!" Luke spluttered.

"You are! I can tell…*stop* it now!"

"We weren't doing anything." Win didn't manage to sell her lie, for Rowan's eyes flashed with anger. And across the way, Luke looked like a naughty toddler who'd been told off.

"Rowan, calm down!" Ben reached for her shoulder, but she shot out of her chair. Tears streaked her face, and she pressed her palms to her eyes.

"I can't do this," she sobbed. "I *can't* do this anymore."

Evan started to rise from her seat, her eyes creased with worry. "Rowan, please calm down!"

"This is what families go through sometimes!" Ben chimed in.

"No!" she spat. "I can't be the alpha, the head of this crazy family. It's all gone so wrong. I've failed miserably at everything I was supposed to do, and now our mother is out there somewhere and won't come home! You and Evan have been lying to us. Luke looks like he's dying, and I've had to put up with *him* all day!" Rowan gestured to Grayson, who slowly gulped his mouthful of food and ground his teeth.

Win's face flamed, rocketing out of her chair. "Rowan, you are so out of line!"

Grayson's shoulders slumped; he stared at his dinner plate, not knowing where to look. "I'm going to make life easier for you, Rowan. I'll leave."

"No!" Ben and Win both yelled in unison. Win growled in frustration.

"You are so rude, Rowan!"

Tempers rose around the table. Rowan burst into frustrated tears, pushing Evan away as she reached for her. A heavy silence thickened the air. Rowan sniffed and wiped her eyes, but Win, however, was defiant. "He isn't leaving, Rowan. And if you make him go, then I'll leave too."

They met eyes, Win projected as much ferocity into her glare as she could muster, but it wasn't easy, faced with Rowan's tear-streaked face. Slowly, her older sister nodded. "I know."

"I'll do it."

Rowan's lip quivered and curled into a smile as she darted a look at Grayson, her expression resigned. "I believe you. I'd do the same."

Win crossed around the table, wrapping her arms around Grayson's neck. He smiled tentatively and stood as Rowan approached, placing a hand on his shoulder.

"I'm sorry." She wiped her nose, her eyes still streaming. "I'm sorry I've been such a bitch. It's going to take me a while to get used to you around here. And you do take up *so* much space."

Looking up at her, eventually, he smiled shyly. Shrugging, he said. "Okay. Truce?"

She shook his hand. "Truce. Unless you secretly plan on embalming my sister?"

Grayson huffed and sat again, letting Win crawl onto his lap protectively. Luke snorted out a laugh, and even Ben laughed into his napkin. "Oh, Rowan, leave him alone," Win moaned.

Grayson shook his head, smiling. "No, it's fine. I can take whatever mud she throws. I grew up with far worse."

The ground shook, rendering them all silent. A deafening roar rushed over the top of the house.

Win jumped, finding Grayson's hand as lights flashed through the windows, filling up every dark corner. Instinctively Rowan pulled Evan to the floor, and Win ducked to her knees, covering her ears. The drapes blew back, and the floor shook, as two large choppers swooped low over the house.

Luke bounded to the back porch, flinging open the door, staring after the light trail the helicopters blazed through the night sky, his mouth hanging open as they circled over the Mercy estate. The police chopper circled, their beams shining down over the forest. Win drew up beside him as a crack of a bullet sliced through the dark, then another one, and one more. Her fingers dug into his shoulder.

"Luke…they're firing over Mercy," she gasped as Rowan ran past them into the yard, waving her hand for them to follow.

Luke grabbed her hand. "Win…I have to find my dad!"

Twenty Eight

Luke ran, his sneakers slapping through the mud. Win bounded after him, still struggling on her injured leg. It throbbed wildly, but when she caught him, she panted and bent double.

"Wait a minute!" she begged. He was sweating despite it being below zero. The ground was glistening with the frost.

Rowan caught up with them, Evan, Ben lagging behind. Grayson caught up; he'd ducked back inside to fetch his crossbow, no time to suit up before strapping it across his chest.

On the edge of the forest, they listened as shots firing tore through the air. Something else filled the night, a howling scream.

Luke paled. "That's not Spencer."

A roar whirred overhead, another chopper hovering nearby, the velocity caused by its propellers thrashed through the yard, puddles emptied back from their rivets, and trees bent double. It landed in the tall grass. Covering her head, Win squinted against flying dirt and mud as the chopper touched down and powered off.

The doors flung back, and two air paramedics jumped out.

"It's an air ambulance," she called over her shoulder. There was a commotion in the trees, and men staggered toward the yard. There were four of them, and two were severely injured, one hobbled on a slashed leg, his pant torn away from his calf. The other was dragged along under the arms, and it was too dark to see what happened. He was the one who needed the stretcher and who the paramedics were keen to get on board. Rowan shoved her way past, waving as Noah wandered out of the woods. He was dazed, limping, and covered in mud.

He caught sight of her, pausing for breath by a worn-out tire, collapsing down on it. Rowan jogged toward him. "What's going on?"

Noah took off his hat, his shotgun at his feet. He was banged up, bleeding and sweaty, mopping his brow with the back of his hand. "The animal attacked them. It's the biggest thing I've ever seen."

"Did you shoot him?" Luke cried.

"We tried, but it's so fast. One of my guys thinks he caught it in the left flank. But it keeps vanishing," Noah puffed through his nose. "Say…we tried calling at your old place. Do you know the whereabouts of your dad?"

Luke's chin dropped. "My dad? No—he should be there."

"We found the place wide open, unlocked. It looks like he left in a hurry, and even his dinner was still on the table. We want to make sure he isn't out here somewhere."

The injured officers were loaded into the back of the chopper, the doors slammed shut, and it powered back up, sending Win's hair flying in streams as it lifted into the air. As the roar dwindled, everyone looked to Noah, staggering to his feet. Rowan steadied him.

"You need a hospital," she said, but he shook his head, bending to retrieve his shotgun.

"No, need to get back out there." He looked at all of them.

"You shouldn't be out here. Whatever that thing is—it's not like any cat I've ever seen. We never saw it coming."

Rowan walked with him to the front yard, where he'd parked his vehicle. Win turned to Luke, who was staring into the woods.

"What are you thinking?" she asked, not liking the expression on his face. Luke's profile was stony, calm. Win didn't like the way his skin pulled tight over his cheekbones, making him look emancipated, his lips thin.

"My dad…I'm worried."

"Me too." As much as Jake confused her, he was Luke's father, and she thought of Mercy abandoned, left open, and desolate. Luke held out his hand.

"Come with me," he said. "I need to see for myself."

"Whoa!" Grayson stepped up beside them. "If you two go, I'm coming!"

Luke tossed him a half-hearted smile. "Sure. I'd be happy to have a guy with a crossbow."

Rowan appeared, sidling up beside Evan and her father. "Noah is heading to the hospital. They are sending in more men. But they won't find him."

"What are you saying?" Ben cried. "You want to go after him?"

Rowan looked at each member of her family helplessly. "They'll get killed, all of them. If Spencer is wounded, he'll be angry, and we have more chance of finding him than they do."

"Then let's go!" Luke snapped. "I want this over!"

Grimly, Rowan nodded. "Luke, Win, and Grayson, you go and see if you can find out what happened to Jake. Evan and I will scout out the woods…and Dad, you should..."

"Don't you dare bench me!" Ben snapped. "I'm not sitting indoors waiting for a phone call."

The tension in Rowan's expression broke with a small smile. "I was going to say you stay with us. If I have to go up, you can stay with Evan." Rowan tossed her girlfriend a conspiratorial grin. "I'm assuming after centuries of life on earth, you haven't survived by looks alone?"

Evan rolled back her sleeves, opening the palms of her hands and revealing a small, lilac coloured blaze of light trickling between her two palms. She tossed it back and forth like it was a ball. When Rowan's mouth dropped open, Evan had the decency to look sheepish.

"I'm not a fighter Rowan, but I do come in handy if you get hurt."

"Don't let Dad get himself killed," Win begged them both imploringly.

Aghast at both his daughter's lack of faith in him, Ben exhaled long and hard.

"Here." Grayson tossed him the handle end of a knife from his belt, which Ben dropped on the ground like it was a hot poker. He scrambled to retrieve it and tucked it in the waistband of his jeans. He stared dismally at his slippers.

"Maybe I better change?"

Rowan groaned. "Fine, go!" She looked at Win, crossed the gap, and kissed her forehead roughly. "You guys go. We'll catch up once Dad has changed his shoes!"

Win smiled at her, thinking at that moment how much she was the perfect alpha, despite her earlier outburst. Rowan surprised her by catching her arm and pulling her back.

"I'm sorry." She whispered into Win's hair. "I'm sorry I lied and for everything. And for what it's worth...he's growing on me. But you'll never have to choose. Never. It's you and me, always."

"It's okay." Win's eyes shone. "Let's talk later when this is all over. You and me."

Win jogged and caught up with Grayson and Luke, the three of them headed into the perimeter woods on the long walk to Mercy.

On high alert, the three of them tracked through the forest. It was muddy, cold, and on the air, their breath fogged like ethereal wisps. Luke shuddered, folding his arms around his chest. He was wearing nothing but a tee shirt and loose sweat pants, and Win shot him an exasperated look. He looked freezing. Luckily she wasn't suffering, even though it was bitingly cold, the ground hard below their feet.

Up ahead, Grayson plowed through, and Win was grateful he knew the woods, having spent all of his life hiding out in it. He'd had sense to pull on a sweater and jacket, his crossbow cocked and held high on his chest, his elbows locked.

"Do you think Captain America will give Spencer half a second before he shoots him?"

Win balked. "I'm sure he'll shoot to wound rather than kill him. I wasn't sure you'd be so lenient?"

Luke scoffed. "He's my brother, Win. I'd rather see him alive in jail than dead in the ground."

Win understood though she kept her lips pressed tight. They weren't supposed to be talking at all, keeping their heads down in case they were spotted by the cops stalking the woods.

"And besides." Luke leaned closer, whispering. "He's my family, and we're all doing the forgiveness thing…he's all I have."

Win shot him a look. "You have me!"

Luke half-smiled. "Not for much longer." In the dark, her brows rose skywards, feeling him pull away from her, inch by inch.

"That's not true. You'll always have me." She reached across, squeezed his shoulder. "You aren't going anywhere."

"Will you two stop *whispering*?" Grayson turned abruptly, aiming his crossbow upward so as not to point it directly at them. "If I can hear you, the cops will!"

The trees parted ahead, and a small clearing opened up to Luke's old yard, the Mercy perimeter woods, and the large iron gates visible in the distance. Luke stomped ahead of Grayson, trailing around back and finding the small iron gate. The three of them ran across the gravel, the old servant's door unlocked. Luke barged it open with his shoulder, the jamb squeaking, his sneakers slapped up the stone steps.

Flicking on lights as they went, illuminating the large kitchen, the shiny chrome surfaces beaming light around the room. Like Noah described, there was a glass of red wine abandoned on the counter, an open newspaper, and a set of keys. The remains of a microwave dinner grew cold and congealed. Win sniffed, Jake wasn't here, but something smelled off. She stalked toward the fridge and hauled it open, nearly gagging. It was full of meat packets, joints, shanks, and steaks piled up to the roof. Some of it was already spoiling. This was Jake's attempt at feeding Spencer.

Trying to keep him away from us. It struck her as a lonely existence, her eyes drawn back to the miserable dinner for one. Win gazed around, this vast place, lofty and cold, and Jake alone, rattling around inside.

Grayson poked his head around the doors. "Is this all there is?"

"No." Luke jogged up the narrow corridor. "This is just my dad's wing."

Grayson met Win's gaze and whistled through his teeth, and she guessed what he was thinking. The extravagant furnishings, everything bright, gleaming, and new, as opulent as it was to her, to someone like Grayson, this place was palatial. Keeping up with Luke, they trailed behind him as he opened the door to the main house. The grand sweeping staircase loomed out of the dark, a chill in the air.

"Dad, are you here?" Luke called into the echoey hall. *"Dad!"*

His voice rose to the lofty heights of the upper floor, lamps flickering in the windows, the drapes moved like they breathed. Win hated this place; it was ghostly, like a museum. Grayson looked around, stepped forward, skidded, his shoes squeaking on something wet. Win smelled it before she saw it, her eyes drawn to a pool of blood seeping into the hallway runner. Luke gagged and covered his nose.

"Dad!" he called, panic-stricken. *"Dad!"*

"The blood goes up the stairs," Grayson pointed out, and Luke shot him a glare.

"I can see that, Sherlock!" he snapped, and Grayson grumbled, ignoring him as he dashed past, following the gory trail. Someone had been bleeding heavily and dragged upstairs. She quivered sickly, hoping they wouldn't find a dead cop, or worse, a dead Jake.

Grayson's boots thundered on the stairs, his bow up as he ran. Luke attempted to keep up, holding the railing for support, but Win saw his pallor, ghostly white, and how fast he was fading.

"Dad!" Luke shouted as he reached the first floor.

"In here."

They all gasped, heads snapping to a half-open door down the hall, a lamp on inside the room, casting shadows across the ceiling. Luke wilted, his legs buckling, and Win caught him, but it was Grayson who slipped his arm under his shoulders, steadying him. Luke's skin was clammy, and he appeared annoyed at having to lean on either of them.

"Take it easy," Grayson warned him. "You look like shit."

Win rolled her eyes at him but placed a hand on Luke's waist. "Let's just get in the room."

Grayson kicked open the door, and the smell was overpowering. Win willed down nausea, blood, sweat, and animal feces filling her nose. But what lay on the bed, neither of them would be able to forget.

Twenty Nine

On the bed, lay a half man, a creature she could have only imagined in her nightmares. Her eyes rounded, not able to process what she was seeing. It was Spencer, but he was stuck between forms. Immediately she was brought back to Uncle Willard the day she'd seen him at his house. He'd gotten stuck, half, and half, and this was happening to Spencer.

Jake sagged on the ottoman in the corner, his shirt blood-soaked, his hair slick with sweat, and Win guessed he dragged Spencer up here by himself. "I don't know what to do," he moaned. "He's been shot. What the hell is *wrong* with him?"

Win stood over Spencer's sleeping form, eyes trailing him top to bottom. From his long, sandy hair down to his marred, scratched torso, her gaze paused at the juncture between his thighs, where there was nothing but fur sprouting up across his abdomen. His legs were covered in thick, soft fur. Powerful, lean legs finished with two massive cat-like paws. His clawed hands fisted the covers, and his visible skin gleamed with sweat. Pale, rosette markings in flecked silver covered his bare chest and abdomen, swirling up his arms. Blood seeped out of his bandaged calf. Win studied his face, the soft expression he wore, angelic, innocent while he slept, a handsome face masking cruelty. His exposed fangs indented his chin, and Win shuddered.

Luke fell onto the ottoman next to Jake. "Are you alright?" Jake gave him a sharp look of surprise.

"I'm okay. I heard the shots in the woods and went in after him. But it nearly killed me dragging him up here. He weighs a ton. You don't look so hot, Luke?"

Weakly, Luke grimaced. "I'm a little nose sensitive—it smells like a zoo in here."

"And you have a well-stocked supply of spoiling meat," Win reminded him, her stomach rolling.

"You said to keep him away from you all. This was the only thing I could think of."

Relenting, she smiled weakly. "I think you did your best."

"What's wrong with him?" Grayson circled back to Jake's question. "Why does he look like that?"

"I've seen this before. My uncle in Lincoln was the same. It's like being stuck half and half, and my guess is he reverted when he was shot." She hoped her vague explanation made some sense.

"We can't let the police find him, not like this." Jake stood, pacing the rug. For the first time, Win sensed his panic, his vulnerability. "What will they do to him?"

"Probably crack him open like a science experiment," Luke made a bad joke, and Jake gritted his teeth and said nothing. Win took out her phone and tapped a message to her father, hoping he'd remembered to pick up his cell. *We've got Spencer. Go home before anyone gets hurt!*

Jake crossed the room, his tan faded, leaving a stark, greyish pallor, grabbing Win's hands before she could sidestep. "I don't want to lose him, Win. If there's any way, we can help him…."

She wriggled her hands out of his grip, instead taking him firmly by the upper arms. He was hot and sweating through his shirt. “We have Evan. She’s a healer. I’m sure there’s something we can do. But Jake… he has to answer for what he’s done.”

Jake looked down, her bandaged, injured leg covered by her jeans. “I don’t think he knows what he’s doing.”

Luke huffed out loud. “Dad, seriously, all these years…you still believe that?”

Jake paced frantically, raking his hands through his hair. “I want this over. I want my son back.” He glanced at Luke. “I want you *both* back.”

A yawning silence fell across the room. Win’s gaze drawn back to the pitiful, mutated creature on the bed, searching her heart and trying to find space for sympathy. But every time she looked at him, she saw him the night of the bonfire. He drugged Rowan, stalked them, and then with no regrets, shot her sister. Such planning, calculation, and deceit, hidden in an appealing, unassuming package. His lip twitched, and Win startled as his lashes flickered against his cheeks. Her fingers found Jake’s shirt, but it was too late.

The bedclothes rippled, and Spencer leaped from the bed, an eruption of snarls, gnashing teeth, and claws. He collided with Win, and the force threw her backward, rolling and taking Jake with her. On her knees, she had time to see him leap past Grayson, slashing him down his center. Blood spilled from the gash, and Grayson bent double.

Spencer cast one look back, his eyes glassy, white, and filmy, those of an animal in pain. He was gone, feet thundering down the stairs. Downstairs, doors crashed open, and Grayson was up, clutching his torso.

“Are you okay?” Win stammered, her backside throbbing from her tumble. He hissed and eased her away.

“It’s a surface wound. I’m fine,” he said with a clenched jaw. “We have to find him before he kills someone.”

Luke staggered to his feet, but Grayson waved him back. “Not you, Luke. You look terrible.”

His words hung heavy in the air. “He comes with me,” Win said. She wasn’t about to leave him behind, his pride in the gutter. “You stay with Jake!”

They all ran down the stairs, finding the open door wide open, wild, freezing air billowing inward. Win ran out into the dark, her eyes narrowing, her night vision kicking in, shapes and sounds were muffled around her, but Spencer’s trail was hot. She could smell him.

Grayson caught her, hissing in her ear. “Be careful.” He leaned and kissed her hard. “Keep Luke close. He doesn’t look good.”

She stood on tiptoe and kissed him back; when she pulled away, she caught Luke watching them with a strange expression before he glanced away. “Don’t you think you should change?” Grayson prompted, but Win disagreed.

“I don’t want to end up in another fight to the death,” she said. “At least this way, I can reason with him.”

“Reason with him?” He ducked closer so only she could hear. “You know I’ll kill him, right? If he comes near you…If I think I can get a shot.”

Grimly, she tried to smile, casting a wary look over her shoulder at Luke, who was stamping his feet and blowing warm air through his hands. “I know. Try not to…but if it comes down to it….”

“Here,” Jake bellowed from the door, a pile of coats over his forearm. He tossed Luke an old jacket, covered in bright collector’s pins. Luke looked horrified.

“Dad, I haven’t worn this since I was twelve.”

Jake huffed, snatching it back and replacing it with a larger denim jacket with flannel lining, then threw Win a sweater. Gratefully, she wriggled into it and then jogged back toward the woods.

Spencer's scent blazed a trail so vivid she could practically see it. "Come on. We'll lose him if we keep standing around."

Ducking low through the trees, Win sprinted ahead, the cold air burning her lungs; it was deathly silent, eerie, and the sky inky black and void of stars. She followed Spencer's trail with her nose, half expecting him to bolt from the bushes, but nothing even rustled. A pregnant silence fell upon them; Win hunched her shoulders, mentally preparing for him to appear. Then his scent tailed off as though he'd vanished into nothing. She recalled what Noah said—he kept disappearing. A cat that large couldn't stay hidden for long.

"I've lost the trail." Grayson was up ahead, returning from scouting through the undergrowth. "How about I take Jake, and we split up?"

Win nodded, eyeing Luke shuffling behind her, every step he took seemed to get heavier, and there was a raspy quality to his breathing she didn't like. Grayson motioned for Jake to keep close, and the older man shot him a look of disdain, unused to being ordered around. But he went, which Win supposed was good. At least he was trying. She watched them go and wished them safe.

Cagily, she turned in Luke's direction and found him leaning against a tree. She marched across and touched his forehead, hissing in desperation as he batted her away. Despair clouded her voice. "You shouldn't be here."

His eyes, like the color of faded denim, found hers in the dark. "Don't say that."

Win tucked an arm under his shoulders. "Just lean on me, okay? I'm stronger than I look."

The throbbing in her leg was a vague memory, it still hurt, but she would run if she had to. Why did she have the awful feeling she'd have to? Her eyes scanned the trees, wondering if Rowan was circling above, but then she guessed her sister would lay low. Spencer wouldn't show if he knew he was being hunted, and she already risked getting shot by a trigger-happy cop.

Shuffling along, Win started to sweat, his weight pushing her sideways, her spine at an odd angle. Something rustled in the bushes, and she panicked, yanking him down beside her. When he tried to peek out, she silenced him with her finger. Two armed officers padded right by them, their shotguns held at chest height. Win held her breath, closed her eyes, praying they'd pass. When they walked on by, leaves crunching in their wake, she let it out slowly and motioned for Luke to stand. But weakly, he shook his head.

"No."

"What do you mean, no?" Win snapped, tugging his bicep. "Come on, up! I can support you."

"I mean no. I can't." His laugh was soft, defeated. "I can't take one more step, Win."

Panic exploded like fluttery wings in her chest, and she ducked to her knees beside him. "Come on, please. You can do this."

"I feel like…." His eyes were filmy and wet. "Like, I'm dying."

"Don't be insane. You aren't going to die!"

"I think…I might." He shuffled back, peeling off his jacket, then hoodie, revealing his sweat-soaked shirt underneath. There was a bolder, a few inches away, and he backed up against it, hissing as his hot skin touched the cool surface. Win crawled toward him, settling on her knees, willing down the lump in her throat.

"Luke, you're not dying. You are strong enough to beat this. Spencer did!"

Luke was resigned. "But Spencer…he was always stronger than me. When we were kids, he was just better than me, and he was so fierce, so good at everything."

"Don't mistake that for courage, Luke. You were brave, the night of the fire." She looked away, chewing her lip, fearing the bawling would start. "This is my fault. I shouldn't have asked you to come with me that night."

He smiled sleepily, his eyelids half-closed. "You know I'd go anywhere with you, right?"

In the dark, she flushed. "Maybe you should rest, not say anymore?"

"I want to tell you something."

Oh …damn, not now, Luke! Her heart sped up, a sick feeling exploding in her tummy. "Try to rest." She grabbed her phone from her pocket, thumbed a text to her father, then one to Rowan. *You need to find us. Luke isn't good!*

They had to be out here somewhere. Luke didn't need to be out in this temperature a moment longer; her fingers trembled as she typed. To her relief, her phone flashed in reply, but the signal was abysmal in the dense woodland. *Where are you?*

"Win, will you just look at me?" he begged, and she refused, staring intently at the screen, watching as the signal bars dropped away, her reply refusing to send. "Win?"

"Shut up, Luke!" she snapped. "Why do you have to be a pain? Stop talking and rest!"

He licked his dry lips, cracking from dehydration like he was boiling from inside out. "Win…"

"No!" She met his eyes furiously. "Don't you dare say what I think you're going to say. If you say it, then it means you've given up. And I'm not giving up!"

"I have feelings for you."

Win cursed and covered her ears. Then she lifted her chin. "No, you don't."

"Uh, yes. Yes, I do."

Win could feel the conversation spiraling out of control. "You're confused and vulnerable right now. Of course, you think you have feelings for me. You told me once you'd never been in love."

He frowned at her, recalling the same memory. Their epic spat in the yard, where she'd nearly torn his head off, for the way he was treating Ella at the time. "I did say that, didn't I? Well, that was true back then. I know what it means, now."

Win shook his words away. "No, no, don't do this now! Not tonight. You're only saying this because you think you're about to die. You don't mean it!"

He attempted to lean forward, lost his balance, and then

retreated to the bolder. "I do mean it Win. I've tried to ignore it, push it away, for so long. And I know it's wrong. But I'm completely…."

"Luke, please!"

"...insanely in love with you. I can't help it. But what does it matter? If I'm about to die anyway, I'd rather you know."

Win's lip trembled; a tear escaped and fell onto her shirt, leaving a damp spot. "But, what about Ella?"

He looked away. "I care about her—but I can't help how I feel."

"Don't say that. Luke, she adores you."

"I know." He punched his chest. "Don't you think I feel like a complete asshole? I know it's going to hurt her, but I can't live this lie anymore."

Win panicked, holding up both hands. "Whoa, wait, you're *not* telling her! You aren't going to break up with her?"

"If I live through this, I will. I'm only hurting her more this way."

Win's eyes bugged, her vision whited, like a mist descending. "No, I'm not letting you do that, not for me. God, you *know* I don't feel that way about you! I love Grayson."

"I know." He was staring at her, longingly, so pale it made her ache. "But I can't ignore how I feel, even if you don't feel the same." He stretched out his fingers, clasping her hand, running the pad of his thumb over her palm. "You're beautiful and strong, and I love you. I don't know how else to say it. I wish you felt the same, and sometimes, I convinced myself you did. I know this thing is wrong. I know, but I can't stop."

She was trying to ignore the heat running up her arm, resisting the urge to wrap her arms around him; he looked so frail, so different from the boy she'd met all those months ago. Cocky, arrogant, but sweet, and utterly loveable. Tears sprang up in her eyes. "If you break up with her, then I can't stand by you— not if you hurt her. The three of us are a team. I don't want to lose that, and neither do you, not really. Besides…I drive you insane."

"I like being driven insane." He wasn't listening.

"We fight all the time!"

He smiled. "It's the best part of my day, fighting with you. Don't you have this feeling…it's weird…like it's bred into us?"

"Exactly…it's not…."

"Don't tell me it's not real. *Don't!"* he warned. "I know what I feel. And I know…you feel something too."

"I don't." She didn't dare lookup.

Heat rushed through her, thoughts spiraling. She couldn't ignore it, the stark truth blinding her. The day she'd first laid eyes on him, in the bar, she'd felt *something*. Energy continually pulled them together, an invisible cord binding them. But it wasn't love, not romantic love.

"Luke," she breathed out, and for a moment, he gazed up hopefully. "We can't be together, not that way. I do love you—so much. But not like that. We're family, and that means *everything* to me. I don't want to lose you, ever. And this will destroy Ella if you say anything."

His mouth curled down as he said, "I know. I've tried to stop. But how can I keep lying to her?"

Win scrubbed at her eyes, wishing this conversation had never happened. But it was out. His words live in the world and refusing to be ignored. "Oh, why did you have to tell me?"

"I'm going insane, Win. And I tell you everything! How could I not tell you this?"

"I don't know...suffer in silence!" Win snapped, suddenly irritable, the temperature around the woods plummeting, her neck hairs stood up. "You have the worst timing, Luke!"

"Well, if Grayson wasn't always lurking around, I might have got a chance to tell you!"

At that, Win sniffed then giggled. "Grayson doesn't lurk. He... broods."

Luke folded his arms, breath fogging on the air. "Lurks, stalks—broods. What's the difference? I know you're crazy about him, and this has no mileage, and we can't be anything more. But if I'm going to die...."

"You're not!"

"If I die, then you need to know how I feel...that I love...."

"Do not say it!" She held up her palm. "Please. I know, okay? I know."

She wouldn't lie to him, not now. She wouldn't give him hope for a future together. He had to live first, it was all she cared about. Abruptly she stood, looking left and right, then held out her hand.

"Up," she said. "We're getting you home." When he didn't budge, she clenched her teeth and hauled him up under his arms. He winced.

"Easy!"

She supported his weight, one hand on his chest, pushing him forward. "I'm not leaving you out here a moment longer."

He gave her a lazy, lopsided grin. "Cause you love me, right?"

"No, because you're holding me back," she retorted, stumbling forward, his breath short, scratchy. They hadn't gone more than four steps when Win lifted her nose.

She saw the yellow eyes moments before the rest of the cat exploded out of the brambles, a high pitch snarl slicing the air. Win screamed and pushed Luke away from her, so he fell onto the dirt, seconds before Spencer pounced, all four of his paws hitting her squarely in the abdomen. Air whooshed through her teeth as she flew back, cracking her skull, feeling it split and open on a jagged rock below.

Stars danced in her vision as the giant cat snarled, then leaped. Win curled up her knees, the flats of her heels smacking his chest as he landed, forcing him upward with such velocity he screeched in surprise. Win was on her feet, stumbling and tripping as she grabbed rocks, pelting them in his direction.

Luke fell on him without warning, grappling his waist, holding tight as the cat snapped and gnashed, then finally kicking him away with his back legs. Luke crumpled to the ground as the animal circled him like a shark, his eyes milky, dead, powering up for a death blow.

Win sensed what it would do before it plunged, and in those moments, she knew she was too late, her strength evaporating. She would always be too late.

Spencer lunged for Luke and sank his teeth into his throat.

Thirty

Anger descended in a fine, red mist, and Win ran at the panther. Using every inch of power she possessed, she barrelled into the cat, knocking him left. He landed awkwardly on his injured leg. Win bared her teeth, blinded by fury, and bent to snatch up a gnarled log. Gripping it tightly, she pelted him around his muzzle before the cat recovered, and he yelped and pawed at his nose. Win whacked him again, striking hard with a sickening dull thud until he cowered beneath her. Whimpering, he skirted away, his tail slithering into the bush, vanishing into the dark.

Shaking, Win dropped the log, crawling on her hands and knees toward Luke, who clutched his punctured jugular, blood spilling out between his fingers. Win cradled his head in her lap, trying to keep him calm, pressing her hands over the wound.

Her eyes stung as she wept. "Hold on, okay?" Her heart hammered, she stroked his hair. "Hold on. We can fix this."

But his wide-eyed expression, gasping for breath and life, told her he was done holding on; he was latched on by his fingertips at best. Win broke. "Oh, please, no! Don't die on me now."

He juddered in her arms, his body scorching, dry, blistering heat rising off him in waves, like his skin cooked from within. When Win gazed down his body, her breath hitched, catching sight of his hands and the long claws erupting from his nail beds. She gasped.

No, this is happening now!

She eased herself out from under him, letting him nestle against her as she ripped his shirt free with her nails. Blood was slowly rising to the surface of his skin, a hazy blue glow rippling across his torso, making him writhe and contort, his spine arching away from the dirt ground.

"Luke!" This was real. This was happening. She squeezed her eyes shut.

Rowan! Please, you have to come!

She knelt by his side, taking his face between her palms, looking into his bloodshot eyes, and for one moment, he stilled. She wept above him. "I'm sorry," she cried. "I'm so sorry...." She would tell him if this was it; if he was going to die now, she'd tell him anything he wanted to hear. "I do love you. I do. I'm so sorry."

He choked, gurgled, rolling sideways, and threw up chunks of blood, something thick swirling in it, like his insides coming out of his mouth. He rolled, spitting up, spraying her sweater with whatever was dissolving inside him. Win's steel resolve melted, conscious of how alone they were in the dark. She didn't know what else to do. The wound at his neck wept blood slowly, but blue light crackled around him, the act of his calling keeping him on the edge of death.

She closed her eyes and screamed. *Rowan, please hear me!* Then she thought of someone else, the only other Therian in this vicinity who might hear her cry. *Jake! Jake! Please help me!*

She fell to the ground beside him, where his head lolled to one side, his eyes empty.

Jake! She screamed. God, someone had to hear her! It was unbearable, the bile in her stomach swirled, and she crawled away, throwing up pale liquid into the muddied grass. Eyes watering, she crawled back to where he lay, sobbing, her chest heaving. Spluttering, she found her voice. "Grayson! Rowan...please!"

Rowan! Jake!

She lay down next to him, determined to give him something to hold onto, she reached for his cold hands and squeezed. Luke's eyes fluttered open. He jerked into a sitting position and then choked. Desperately, she tried to turn him sideways, beating his back with her fist. He writhed and gagged, choking up clots of congealed blood and something else, something long, slippery, and wet. His eyes bugged until he finally retched it up on the ground. Win's senses blurred. She couldn't see straight.

God, she remembered this. *The world ending.* One way or another, Luke was dying tonight.

"Win?" a voice yelled across the clearing, and to her relief, she saw Jake running toward her, closely followed by Grayson. The moment he stepped into the clearing he dropped to his knees beside them, his mouth dropping at the ghastly sight on the ground.

"He's bleeding out," he said, reaching for her shoulder, giving her something to lean on.

"It's too late," she sobbed, the inevitable becoming startlingly clear. "He's dying, Jake."

"No, we have to try." Ashen, Jake hauled Luke across his knees, blood dribbled from his eyes, tear ducts filling with scarlet. "Luke, hold on!"

"I don't know what to do!" She shot Grayson an imploring look. "I don't know what to do for him."

The bushes rustled, feet stampeding over dead leaves, and Win saw her sister, Evan, and her father. All of them gathered around, making a circle, but Evan pushed her way through, taking Win's hands, smoothing away her hair.

"Win, you've done enough," she said quietly. "There's nothing more you can do now."

"Please help him, Evan," she begged. "Do *something!*"

Win staggered back, allowing Evan room, as she crawled over

Luke's prone form. Holding out her hands, a pale lilac light emitting from both her open palms. She steadied herself, bracing her body as she erupted with energy, trying to take the pain from him, pulling it from him with her fingertips. Finally, she sagged to her knees. Luke's eyes rolled, and he passed out. When Win chanced a look over Evan's shoulder, the puncture wounds were sealed. Hope lifted her heart, but Evan's words smashed it right out.

"He's lost too much blood," she cried, her lips quivering. "He won't survive this without blood."

"How can we get him blood? The hospital is miles away. We have no time!" Jake's voice rose in pitch, terrified.

"His insides are liquefying....there's nothing more we can do!"

Win broke in. "No, I'm not giving up...he can't die here." She stared up at Grayson, who was watching the whole scene with abject horror scrawled on his face. Perhaps he was thinking about her change, the night he'd run from this moment. Win wasn't running.

"No!" Jake yelled, his pupils narrowed, his teeth bared. "It's not over...I'm not giving up on him!"

Jake grasped Luke's chin, jerking it back so he could breathe air into his lungs. He covered Luke's nose and gave three deep breaths. Luke coughed and spat out bile.

"It won't work," Evan cried. "His lungs are collapsing. It's over...Win, I'm so sorry."

No, this isn't real....

"He's lost too much blood," Evan gasped as Rowan crouched by her side. The wash of blue light rippled off Luke in waves, growing dim, fading with him.

"You know everything you need to know. I've shown you everything. He is in here."

Accept, she hadn't. Mary hadn't shown her a damn thing. Her train of thought railroaded. She couldn't think straight, and she could barely see. She could feel her father behind her, his solid hands on her shoulders, but she was numb, her fingers digging into Jake's shirt, unwilling to budge.

All she saw was blood, thick and full of Luke, his life dribbling away, sinking into the forest floor. The ground would absorb the matter, the animals would feast, and the forest would hide this terrible secret, but she would never forget. And she wouldn't leave him now. Out here, somewhere she was buried too, her human remains, recalling the night he'd covered her over with dead leaves. There was so much blood. Win blinked as the haze parted. Blood…

Blood is the strongest link we have.

Win's eyes opened, sparks of hope igniting. Thoughts like splinters of glass tried to form a complete puzzle. It was there, in reach, if only she could force it all to fit.

"Your blood is the purest of your family line."

Yes, it was coming. It was rushing at her like a tidal wave. She knew the answer all along; her uncle had told her, Mary all but spelled it out. Meanwhile, Jake rocked his son, talking to him, willing him awake.

Spencer hadn't survived because he was strong. Or because he was superior, better than Luke. He'd drank blood! He'd lived off humans, forcing him through his calling, giving him the power to surge through it. Vecula cast this curse— she was a blood drinker.

Holding her breath, she stared down at Luke, filled with love and despair. There was no world she could live in that didn't hold him to.

Win's mist parted, remembering what he'd said only moments ago.

"Don't you have this feeling …like it's bred into us?"

Yes! She could do this. She was the last Hickory. Her line was the purest, and as much as she didn't like it, she was linked to Mary, bound to the curse. If anyone's blood could pull him through this last, final hurdle, it was hers.

"I can do this!" she cried, shoving Evan aside. She was pulling off her sweater, rolling up her sleeves. "It's me," she gasped. "Rowan…Jake! He needs to drink blood!"

Rowan watched in horror as Win turned up her sleeves. "I need a knife!"

"What the hell are you doing?"

"He needs blood, *my* blood." Desperatly, she looked about for a sharp-edged rock or anything that would slice her skin. Jake stared at her in horror, but something about his expression signified he understood.

"If he needs blood, then let me," Jake said, nudging her aside. "I'm his father. You shouldn't have to do this!"

Win gazed at him, dumbfounded and deeply touched, watching as he rolled up his shirt sleeve, but she stopped him, placing a hand on his shoulder. "No, Jake. My blood is the purest here, and I'm the last Hickory. It has to be me! He's too far gone."

It has to work...it's got to work...

Win caught Jake's hand, her fingers circling his thick wrist. "Jake, believe me!" she begged. "You know I'm right about this. I have to give him my blood!"

Evan looked unconvinced, but the tension in the small, secluded spot they all shared ramped up ten notches. "Win, I don't know about this!"

"Let me try!" she begged. "I *have* to try!"

Grayson was the one who stepped forward, crouching next to Luke; he grabbed her wrist and pulled it toward him, producing a long, buck knife from his belt. Rowan yelled and shoved him sideways.

"No way!" she erupted. "Don't you even think about it! Let him go, Win, this won't work!"

"You don't know that!" Grayson warned her off with his pale glare. "Listen to her, and let her try!"

Win could have kissed him right then from gratitude. Flexing out her wrist, she upturned it, exposing the creamy underside, her pulse throbbing. He placed the sharp end of the knife against her skin. "Do it, now!"

"Wait! Don't cut too deep!" Ben cried, clutching his hair, and Grayson gave him a sound nod.

"I've done this before, on animals." It was meant to be reassuring, but Jake, next to her on the ground, choked.

"That's not worrying, in the least," he quipped, breathing hard.

Win closed her eyes, bracing herself for the pain. Jake wound an arm around her shoulders; she turned into his neck as the knife's edge tickled her skin. She gasped and yelped, the dull slice of a razor-sharp blade dragged across her wrist, opening her flesh.

She grabbed her arm, cradling it to her chest as blood oozed out of the deep cut. It hurt, a dull, biting sting, but she shuffled over Luke's unconscious form, pinching his hollowed-out cheeks, slapping him awake. "Luke come on…*wake up*…you have to drink!"

Her breath stilled. For a moment she wondered if he'd slipped away, her heart clenching as she patted his face. His lids fluttered, revealing bloodshot eyes. "Come on, *please*," she begged. Pressing her wrist to his mouth, she waited, biting her lip, her blood trickling down over his chin. When he didn't respond, lolling his head away, she slapped him hard.

"Wake up!" she screamed, her voice cracking. Jake shook him hard enough his body jolted off the dirt, then his eyes went wide, sucking in his breath, his mouth hot on her skin.

She smiled in relief. "Come on…don't hold back!" He was drinking it slowly. She felt the veins tug, a dull, unpleasant sensation as his eyes rolled back, lapping at the exposed wound. Luke grabbed her wrist, holding it there, panting through his nose like he was drinking ice water on a hot day. She shivered, her stomach clenched in anticipation as around her, her entire family watched the grizzly sight.

"Don't let him take too much," Evan warned, massaging Win's shoulder in encouragement. "Hold on."

Her veins burned, mild pain increasing, and dizziness washed over her. *Please work, please let me be right...* Win stiffened and closed her eyes when suddenly she felt the sharp sting of teeth sinking into her flesh. She shrieked.

Luke's eyes were wide and yellow with two split pupils, boring up at her. His canines sank into her arm, yanking her down on top of him. She braced herself with one hand on the ground against the impact.

"Stop biting me!" she cried. Luke grabbed her neck, pulling her down, so she covered him with half her body. It was a strange, intimate embrace. "Luke, *let go.*"

I can't stop… She heard his voice, weak, scared, but he was there.

Slow up...you'll drain me!

The blue light, which dwindled to a haze moments ago, suddenly fired up again with renewed vigor. The sparks crackled and fizzed against her skin. It was working!

I think you've had enough now…please work...please live…

The light buzzed and seared, lifting Luke's spine off the ground. He arched, his muscles lacerated under his skin, and Win wept.

This has to work…I'm not letting you go.

It is real...it is real for me.

A sob pulled from deep in her chest. She couldn't withstand much longer. She lifted away, the blue energy surging through her, filling every space in her body, shining through her eyes. Whatever was surging through him pushed into her. Her eyes opened her face inches from his. She smiled with love. Bracing herself for pain, she had to let him do this last part alone.

Rolling out of the path of the light, she fell at her father's feet, sobbing while on the ground Luke's body cracked and came apart. Tears squeezed out of her eyes, she turned her face into her father's jeans, his hands tangling in her hair.

Grayson held out his arms, and she crawled toward him. "You did everything you could." She held her injured arm tight to her breast.

Luke writhed on the ground like he was being electrocuted, the blue light burned off him, and Win had the startling realization of how this looked from the outside. As Luke's body dissolved, she didn't blame Grayson for running that night. Rowan grabbed her shoulders, pulling her hard against her.

"Don't look, Win," she whispered hard. "Don't look!"

The light waned, pulsed, and then exploded, careering through the small area. Everyone turned away, shielding their eyes.

Win opened her eyes, swathes of blue dust falling from the sky like snowflakes. The mist parted, her eyes desperately tried to regain focus.

A howl erupted through the forest. Whirling in the direction of the noise, she saw a great, black wolf with bright blue eyes in the distance. She staggered to her feet but stopped when he lifted his head and howled.

Don't come after me. I'm ending this now.

"Luke…" But it was too late. He was gone, his shadow vanishing over the brow of the hill.

Win's mind went blank, staggering backward, and wished she'd not glanced behind her—at the corpse on the ground. There was nothing left of him. And lying beside it were his glasses, cracked beyond repair.

Win opened her mouth and screamed.

Thirty One

He could smell the droplets of blood in the air, snuffling his nose, stinging like hot metal. Above him, the sky was thick and dark, the tiniest flakes of snow floating down toward his lifted muzzle. He stuck out his tongue and lapped them up. Snow still tasted the same, no matter if you were human or not.

He wasn't human anymore.

Don't think about that now.

He knew he should be traumatized; the human part of him longed to crawl in his bed and sob for what just happened. But the fire in his limbs burned, he had a purpose, focus, and he knew what to do next for the first time in his life. And that was finding his murdering, asshole brother and ripping his throat out.

His paws danced over the hard ground. He was light, so agile, darting left to right, flying across the woods like he'd been born to do this his whole life. As the snow fell thicker, settling on the trees, he passed an iced puddle, his reflection gazing back up at him.

Holy, shit…I'm enormous! He laughed but came out a gurgled, growly snort. His elongated, shiny snout sniffed the ice, peering closely at the two bright blue eyes with split pupils, his mane, thick, dense and matte, sticking up away from his body as though he needed a good groom. Like he'd been electrified—cooked from the inside out.

He picked up speed, snow melting off his fur as he ran, concentrating on picking up Spencer's scent, the blood leaving behind a trail of malice to follow. Luke remembered dying the moment his heart finally gave out, and he'd tried so hard to fight, held on with his fingertips, but the light phased through him, and like falling into a void, he'd let go. He remembered Win's face as she stared down at him, tears clinging to her bottom lashes.

She told him she loved him. He wished it were true, hoped with everything she meant it. But she didn't, not really. Not while that blonde giant was in the way. Luke did his best to try and hate him too, steel his resolve, wishing he'd perished in the fire. But he couldn't hate him either, the socially awkward weirdo.

Maybe I'm going soft. That's what she's done to me. I never used to be like this. Once, he'd been as cold as steel, walled off like a glacier, but she'd chipped away at him, gradually, over time, with her laugh, her smile, and her big heart. He saw her like a blazing sun, with fire in her hair, loving every molecule of her, even the way she bit nervously at her nails or stole his clothes. Even that drove him crazy, her persistence in invading his space, fusing with him like she wanted to be a part of him in some small way. Seeing her every day was blissful torture. Sitting on the edge of the bath, painting her toenails, brushing out her hair, counting freckles on her back as he'd impatiently stood behind her in the bathroom mirror. Win forced on a brave face, knowing he and Ella would eventually leave her behind, it heavied her heart, and that made him ache. He was in *big* trouble.

And now, she was inside him, her blood running thickly through his veins, blood she willingly gave in a last, desperate attempt to save him. He'd never be free now, and he never wanted to be.

He wished she loved him, then what he had to do would be so much easier because he wouldn't be alone when he let Ella go. He must let her go.

Luke crossed through a thicket of cedar pines, their leaves providing shelter while it rained down with thick, cold snow. In moments his paws were buried, resting back on his hind legs. He waited, sniffing the cool air.

I know you're here…

Luke sensed the deep, guttural growl, lifting his eyes skywards to the trees. Spencer was here somewhere, bleeding and angry. A drop of scarlet bloomed across the pure white carpet, then another. Luke growled, hunching back as it dropped from the trees, landing on two large paws, standing upright, a strange half-man, half-beast.

Spencer was beaten to hell. Win struck him twice, nearly three times with a heavy log, and his nose was busted, his jaw swollen and purple. His once neatly cropped, sandy blonde hair hung long, dirty, hanging in swathes around his ears. Faint panther rosettes traveled up his torso, right up to his neck like tattoos.

What the hell happened to you? You look like crap.

Spencer favored one leg, the one shot by the cops. His chest heaved with every breath he took. He was tired. "I could ask the same of you, Luke."

Well, I think it's pretty obvious.

Spencer leaned against a tree. "You look good."

I wish I could say the same for you!

Spencer sniggered, running a clawed hand through his dirty mane. "Yeah, I do look a bit monster of the week. It's insane. The power?"

Luke opened his long jaw, puffing out air. *How'd you get like this?*

He ignored his question. "Don't you feel strong?"

Luke cocked his head, narrowing his pin-prick eyes. *I guess. I don't want to end up looking like you. You can't win, Spencer, and I can't let you hurt anyone else. You've killed people…*

Spencer's teeth gleamed, reflected off the snow, two visible fangs crowding his mouth. Luke shuddered, remembering what his brother had been, how handsome and smart. Too smart. Leaving Luke trailing behind in his wake, the endless, depressing comparisons, the lifelong battle of keeping up with Spencer. Until one day, he couldn't fight anymore and became the person everyone expected him to be. Luke Fraser: cute, rich, cold, and a classic underachiever. Good at sports but unable to focus in class, good job he had his father's business and connections to fall back on. While Spencer was the good brother, the one who would go places. But no one knew what lay beneath his charming smile.

Spencer…you have to turn yourself in!

This only seemed to make his brother angry. He rolled his jaw, his tongue dabbing at the sharp canines, raw heat rising off him. "I'm not going back."

You'll hurt more people…people I care about!

"Those dumb idiots you live with, you mean?" he taunted him, acid boiling in his laugh. "They have no idea…."

Luke twitched. *No idea of what?*

Spencer licked his teeth, an odd, disturbing habit. "Of what they're capable of. I know what we can do."

Well, you would! You murdering psychopath. Spencer's face dropped, eyeballing Luke hotly.

"You could be strong, Luke. You have her blood inside you, don't you feel it? We could do so much together!"

They were circling one another around the trees, Luke watching him as he ducked between the branches, only yards apart. The snow was blinding, falling in heavy throes, and he didn't want to test out his new strength. He felt wobbly, unnerved, and Spencer was unpredictable. He wouldn't hold back if he turned back into the panther.

"You're so transparent, Luke," Spencer accused with a cackle, and Luke drew his brows together.

Huh?

"All that you've been given, all this power—and all you think about is sex!"

Excuse me? If he could have blushed, he would have. Heat rose off his mane.

"I know what holds you back. It's the same thing that held me back for years. It's her."

I don't know what you're talking about.

"I'm talking about Win, you moron. She's all over you, in your hair, your skin. I can smell her!"

I just drank her blood, so yeah, that's a given.

"No, it's more, and you know it. Don't pretend. You know I always see right through you, and I always have. You're in love with her!"

Luke sighed. *So, what if I am?*

Spencer stopped pacing, so they stared at one another through the trees, each one second-guessing the other. Who would attack first? Nastily, Spencer laughed. "*So* it's not real. How about that?"

Feels pretty real to me.

"It's not. Nothing real about it. It's pre-programming, genetically coded into our DNA, from the beginning. That's not real love. It's just chemicals."

Ha! Is that what you've told yourself to alleviate your guilt over Rowan?

Spencer's smile dropped, which was more terrifying than his manic laughter. "I don't feel guilty. Grandfather told me the way of it, how they work, how they steal into your thoughts, trap you…."

Our grandmother was Therian, and he locked her in an attic and let her die!

"He did what he had to, and he knew one day it would boil down to this! And funny…they have no idea what they can do. They hide the animal—force it away! This is how we were meant to be!"

It sounds like you're enjoying yourself a little too much! I thought you wanted them gone.

"Not you, Luke! We could be rid of them and create a whole new race of Therian, the way it was destined to be. Primal, wild…powerful!"

You're sick, Spencer…you've always been sick. And I have no idea how you got like this…

"Don't you?" Spencer laughed, wincing as he fell lightly on his injured leg, his breath coming in short pants. "Don't you? You are as dumb as shit, Luke. No surprises there."

Luke jerked, his thoughts clarifying, the scarlet trail Spencer left around the trees…the liquid power in Win's blood.

This is because you drank human blood? This is what it did to you?

"Got there in the end! God, you are a moron….no better than the wet blanket of a mother who gave birth to you!"

His remark sliced deep, and the wolf bowed his head, eyes on the snow. He remembered his slip up earlier to Win. At six years old, Luke woke up one morning, and the soft, pretty, blonde-haired lady he loved packed her bags and left. The taillights of her car faded as she drove into the mist. A caustic burn scorched his gut— she was never coming back. Like a death in the family, her memory, clothes, and belongings were packed away as if she'd never existed.

"I can see what you're thinking."

I highly doubt it…

"If you think I'll stay away from your girlfriend, then you'll have to end me yourself. And you don't have the balls."

Luke lifted his head. *What do you want from her? Why can't you leave them alone?*

The air grew eerily quiet. Nothing stirred, the snow rose up his back legs, penetrating cold. Spencer snarled. "How do you think you survived the calling, Luke? By sheer willpower? You aren't strong enough, and you have never been. If it hadn't been for her, you would be dead in the snow right now."

Dead in the snow…

"Rowan is blind. None of them have any idea, not even the old man-wolf knew. Why'd you think I tried to *end* her last summer?"

End the line…?

Spencer smiled, his teeth shining with saliva. "That's right! She's the one. If she's *dead*, then this all goes away!"

Win's the last Hickory…the end of the line…she'll break the curse.

"You have it. She's the end…but sadly, it means the end of her too! Once she's gone, no more Therian will be born, … except us. We go on, and we'll be the last and the most lethal. A better line."

It ends? But we'll still be…afflicted? It won't go away.

"Why would you even want it to go away? Isn't it incredible?"

I don't want this, none of us do. You mean…we'll be free? Free to leave this place?

"That's right—only we get to keep the added benefits. I quite like my new look, don't you?"

Spencer howled with chilling laughter as he gestured to his mutated body, while inside Luke boiled. How had he gotten so messed up?

If you kill Win…Rowan will come for you. Luke had the pleasure of seeing his brother's expression drop, the grin slide from his face.

"Not if I get her first."

*Not to mention what I'll do to you…and…*he just about choked out the words with grudging respect…*Grayson. You wouldn't have lasted five seconds against him as a human.*

"But we aren't, human. That's the best part."

No…I won't let you…how do you even know any of this? You're smart, but not that smart! Who told you this?

"Hmm, let's just say someone wants this over as badly as I do. Blood opens the door, and when it stops flowing, the curse ends. That means her, dead."

No, Spencer!

"Luke, this could be over! We would be unstoppable together… she'd never see you coming."

If you think I'd kill her…then you're insane…chemicals or not, I don't care. I wouldn't lay a hand on her, and I'll die before I let you hurt her.

Luke's keen eyes locked on his brother, who stalked closer, shrinking, melding into the panther right in front of him.

The panther roared, shrill, high pitch, and bone-shaking, rearing back on his hind legs. In his whole short life, Luke had been in a total of one or two fistfights, one in the schoolyard and one on the court when a game got rough, plus his fight with Win in the summer. How many times had Spencer hurt him over the years? Abrupt acts of violence were laughed off as brotherly quarrels. Luke remembered the bruises, arms twisted up his back so hard his eyes watered, and not once did he ever fight back. Because that was what brothers did, right? They fought, hurt one another, a few fat lips, a tooth knocked out, didn't count.

But right now, Spencer wanted to kill him, nestling back on his hind legs, ready to strike. There was no turning back. Luke had to walk away from this. Even if Win couldn't or wouldn't let herself want him. He would go back. Always. He growled, and the sound terrified him, deep, low in his chest, his fangs bared.

You are so dead, Spencer.

Right then, if that's your answer. Spencer readied himself to leap. *Let's get to it.*

Thirty Two

The night was lifting, snow drifted through the forests, white light disappearing behind maple trees, casting a burnt orange glow. The sky was thick, the cold biting hard. The search for Luke was two hours in, and it was nearly morning. When they met back at the clearing, Win saw the remains of drying blood crisping on the ground, ice forming. She didn't ask her father what they had done with Luke's body. She couldn't stand to look at Ben's face, his complexion aged, sunken. But she knew he had taken care of it.

Rowan landed on the ground, hopping across the forming ice. *Nothing.*

Win tore her fingers through her hair. "He can't have vanished."

Good thing is the cops have cleared out, one less thing to worry about.

"We'll find him," Evan called as she jogged back into the clearing. "But it's going to get light in an hour, and we've been out here all night."

Ben stamped his feet, his teeth chattering. "The snow is coming down fast, and it's covering any tracks he may have left."

Win's gut ached, her body sore and stiff, blood drying on the back of her head where she'd fallen and split it on a rock. But as exhausted as she was, she wouldn't budge. "It's freezing, Win." Ben touched her shoulder, and she flinched, jerking out of her train of thought. "We can't stay out here all day…you lost a lot of blood."

"I'm fine," Win sniffed, her nose running, her cheeks stung from the cold. "I'll keep looking."

She was not going to contemplate leaving him out here. She knew he'd be confused, in shock, and afraid. "You go home." She turned to her father. "You're all exhausted, and I can keep going."

Jake wandered into the clearing, hands firmly shoved in his pockets. "Me, too."

Rowan hopped across a few snow covered branches, where Ben stood. *Tell him we'll keep looking. He looks like he's about to turn blue. Besides…Mom could be heading home and the house is empty.*

Win smiled despite everything. "Rowan says, go home. And keep watch for Mom."

"That settles it." Jake was at her side. "We'll keep looking. I'm not going home without him."

Evan nodded. "And me. Where's Grayson?"

Grayson pushed through some brambles as if on demand, jerking his arm free of a patch catching his sleeve. Win smiled at him gratefully.

"Snowy tracks should make things easier." He lifted his bow, strapping it to his back. "But it's coming down thick."

Win nodded, rubbing her cold arms. "You stay with Evan, and I'll stay with Jake and Rowan…."

Rowan took off, vanishing into a heavy cloud. Grayson caught Win's shoulder, planting a warm kiss on her mouth; his nose was cold and his cheeks ruddy. Win wished she could be anywhere else with him, rather than this storm. He pinched her chin.

"See you later, wildcat. Scream loud if you need me!" He

winked, and she hugged him around the waist. Despite light-headedness from the lack of blood pumping through her body, she wound her arms around his neck and kissed him. She was grateful he was here, and most of all, he hadn't tried to force her to leave Luke behind. Ben trudged back through the snow, and Rowan assured Win she'd get him home from above.

Win stalked into the woods, and Jake caught up with her. "Wildcat? That's a cute nickname." He was rolling his eyes, his smirk annoying, and she stopped, shoving him in the shoulder.

"You know, second thoughts—I'll be fine by myself. We can split up!"

She didn't give him time to answer; instead, she jogged into the trees out of sight, leaving him throwing his hands in the air.

She started again, plunging through the woods, trying to ignore the chill nipping through her sneakers. Her wrist ached, still sore from Luke's bite. Rolling up her sleeves, she squatted against a log, surveying the four puncture wounds—two scars from two brothers. Her thigh twanged painfully as a reminder.

She walked for an hour, her throat growing hoarse, calling out for him, and sniffing the air. She didn't think she could shift yet. Her body was cold, exhausted, and the dirt hardened underfoot. Another hour or so, and she could try. Luke's scent lingered, and she followed it, her spirits lifting. As soon as she thought she was onto something—it drifted away.

The morning was coming, light lifting like a curtain. With frayed nerves, back aching, she rounded a bend, through some thick pines once more picking up on his smell. Encouraged, she flew after it, just one more hill, more trees, another clearing, then to her horror, she ran straight into Jake.

"Oh...*damn!*" She moaned aloud, looking skywards. "Please don't tell me it's you I've been tracking!"

He puffed, out of breath and cold, sagging against a tree. "I thought I was tracking him too...but it's all so confusing out here."

Win took a wide step toward him, near enough to sniff his neck. He balked, alarmed at her closeness. "Shit!" she cursed.

"What?"

"You smell…like Luke." Defeated, she bent double, a stitch forming under her ribs.

He scratched his head. "It's Hugo Boss, actually."

Win nearly stamped in frustration. "No…it's him, it's you. You smell the same."

He rubbed his chin, sniffing his coat. "I had no idea…but wait!"

To Win's dismay, he tugged her close and gave her neck a deep sniff. She shivered and stepped out of reach. Puzzled, he frowned. "*You* smell like him."

Win stared down at her blood-splattered clothes, Luke's blood and bile dotting her sweater. "I guess it makes sense…and you aren't as attuned as me. I smell like him because he's *on* me." She gestured to the macabre display, and he looked away, throat bobbing.

"So, do you mean to tell me I've been walking this damn forest for the last hour—following you?"

Win's shoulders slumped. "I guess."

Wasn't it bad enough that he looked like him, sounded like him, shared mannerisms, and even smelled the same? When she first arrived in Cedar Wood, Luke's clean scent had been one she could stomach. Most boys her age smelled like sweat and cheese. Jake had stolen him away, replaced *her* Luke with this older, smarter version, who was twice as devious. It made her want to scream.

"I guess you're stuck with me then." He flapped his hands against his long coat, gave her a low bow, holding out his arm. "After you."

Win moaned and walked away, with him trailing behind. She tossed him a look over her shoulder.

"So, you're not totally useless then? You can track?"

"Ha, that's not very polite. But yes, sort of. Lucky me, huh?"

Win ignored his sarcasm. "Did you ever wonder what you'd be?"

He caught up with her, shoulder to shoulder; she was a good foot shorter. He gave her a sideways grin. "Excuse me?"

"You know if you hadn't gotten so *old* and aged out. Did you think about what you'd have been?"

He made an affronted noise. "I'm sorry…are you giving me a hard time?"

"No, I'm interested," she insisted. "Do you think a rat…or a snake?"

"I feel like you're trying to goad me. And I don't know why. I'm here, *with you*, looking for my son."

Hands in her pockets, she glared up at him. "Well, you're here *now*. But you're a few years too late."

He caught her shoulder, making her jolt to a stop. "Win. Say what you want to say. None of this bullshit!"

Her cheeks fired up, her feet wedged in thick snow. "Okay, fine. Why'd you let him leave? Why didn't you do what any decent father would have—fight to keep him in your life?"

He looked away, at the trees, the sky, anywhere but at her, grinding his white teeth. Win could see his inner workings, his struggle to hide, there was a secret buried deep, but like the carcass of an animal, she could sniff it out. Her eyes rounded. "Is it because of his mother? Did something happen to her?"

Guilt rolled off him in waves, and she had no idea why she felt this, something sorrowful, shameful locked away, like Iris in the attic. Something he wanted to forget. As guarded as he was, as stony and evasive, if she looked into his eyes, she saw everything he was. He *wanted* her to know.

"Did she…die?" She found his hand, but he jerked it away. "Does Luke know?"

His wall went up, his eyes dull and cold. "You're wrong."

"I don't think so. Is this….because of Spencer?"

Oh my god, it is. How could I not have guessed?

Her blinkeredness struck hard. How did she not see this before? Spirals of thought tried to fuse. Jake hadn't fought the emancipation. He *wanted* Luke gone, out of the picture. But not because he didn't care.

He wants to protect him.

"You're wrong. She isn't dead," he admitted painfully. Win cocked a brow.

"Then where is she?"

"Somewhere safe."

Fragments joined and fused, and Win felt the fog clear. She was right. Something in his eyes betrayed him. He'd sent her away...to save her life. But any sympathy she felt for him plummeted after the next thing he said, his gaze calm and cruel.

"If you want to talk about crappy parenting… we could always look at your mother."

His words sliced deep, Win's shoulders rose as she whirled in his direction. "What?"

"You heard me fine." His smile was laced with venom, and Win knew he was throwing rocks, intending to bruise her ego after she'd found him out. She shook her head in dismay.

"Why would you say that?"

He shrugged. "Well…*where* is she?"

"She's…" Win fought for answers, even though nothing useful sprang to her lips. "She's scared and afraid." How the hell did he even know she was alive? How much did he know about their mother?

"…and nowhere to be seen."

"She'll come back."

"Perhaps she doesn't want to? Perhaps being a Hickory is just too damn hard."

"You don't know her!"

He cackled laughter, drawing up to his full height. "Oh, please. I knew her better than you ever did. Something, I'm guessing, your father *failed* to mention. And I know, she chose to stay lost rather than come home to her precious family."

His smile faded, genuine regret flashing across his eyes as he saw her bottom lip drop and her eyes fill. Win was too tired to fight it, the treacherous thoughts she harbored, the nagging doubt and questions she couldn't answer threatening to rise to the surface. She'd forced it away, the suspicions she'd hid, that her mother wasn't coming back to them. And Jake voiced it aloud. She wiped her eyes and turned her head away.

Snow settled in his black hair. He clapped his hands and shoved past her, bumping her shoulder. "Let's get on with this."

Win staggered but caught up with his long strides. After a long, awkward silence, he threw her a cruel smile, changing tact. More rocks to be thrown.

"Luke won't be able to carry on living with you. You're aware of this, aren't you?"

Win blasted him with a stern look. "What do you mean?"

"I'm not totally *useless*, as you pointed out. I heard what he said loud and clear, as I'm sure your sister did too. Luke's gone and got himself a crush."

Guilt coursed through her like wildfire, recalling his confession. And now he'd convinced himself he needed to break up with Ella. The thought of Ella's heartbreak made Win want to melt into the snow. Jake's remark weighed on her. He was enjoying her dismay, the inevitable. Now there was no turning back. Luke would have to leave her, and it hurt her heart.

"He can't possibly stay there. I know him better than you think, and it'll be eating him up that he can't have you."

"Wow—that's wildly inappropriate."

He chortled, pleased with himself, for finding a chink in her armor. "I'm right, though. It must kill him, seeing you with Grayson. I get him more than you know."

"And you're so alike, right?" she laughed. "He's nothing like you!"

"Wrong again!"

"Would you take him back?" she fired.

His expression soured as he breathed out a long sigh. "I doubt he'd want to."

"But if he had no one else?"

"I'm not a monster, Win."

"That doesn't answer my question!" Angry, she caught his coat lapel between her fingers, so he was forced to stop, yet again.

"And if you cared, why'd you sell the place from under his feet?" Win didn't need an answer. Jake was as petulant as a twelve-year-old. Luke hurt him, and he'd retaliated in the way he understood. Money, worldly needs, it was his wheelhouse. But she appealed to the better nature she hoped lay under all the sarcasm. "Say you won't leave him! If he asks, you won't turn him away?"

He pried her fingers off his coat. "Careful, this is a Tom Ford and cost more than your truck!"

Win burst. "Promise me!"

Now he was looking into her eyes, and she was open, earnest, and begging. His lips twitched into a smile. Win hated the look on his face, lips pressed together, eyes creased, laughing silently at a joke, only he knew the punchline. It made her want to smack him in the mouth.

"You are relentless, Win. A true Hickory if ever I saw one—no wonder you're dad looks old."

Win deflated. It was hopeless trying to talk to him. Imploringly she looked up, not too high and mighty to beg for her friend.

"Please, Jake. Don't be a jerk. He's been through hell, and he won't ever admit it, but he needs you."

His smile dropped, expression thoughtful, and for a moment, Win wondered if she had gotten through.

"Maybe it's not unrequited, after all? Interesting. Does your boyfriend have any idea how you feel?"

"Shut *up*!" Her face flamed. Giving up, she stalked away, only to run right into Grayson.

Oh…crap! Her stomach dropped. He was pale and studying her oddly, partially hidden in the trees. Had he heard? She started toward him, her legs like jelly. As she got closer, he held out his hand, putting his finger to his lips. She nodded, ducking low and following him. She threw Jake a look, motioning for him to do the same. Grayson wound through the snowy track his boots had already made.

She cast a look back at Jake. *You asshole. You knew he was there, listening. And I know you can hear me.*

Jake smiled, his blue eyes boring into hers, thoughtful. *A fox…I think.*

What?

If I could guess what I would have been…I'd be a damn good fox.

Grayson ducked to his knees, motioning with his hands for them to come closer. Ahead, Evan hid in the trees, darting out when she saw them, waving her arms. Above Rowan circled, baring her talons, she swooped, landing in a patch of brambles, hidden from view. Moments later, she hurried out of the trees, half-dressed in the clothes Evan kept for her.

"What is it?" Win called, and Grayson shushed her.

The quiet of the woods exploded. In a frantic frenzy of silver and black, two animals burst out from the bushes and barrelled through the clearing, one toppling the other again and again. Snarls and growls licked the air as Spencer and Luke battled, leaving their bloodied footprints in the snow.

Thirty Three

The question was, at what point did you throw yourself between a wolf and a panther? When they were locked in a bloody, violent brawl and it appeared as though, one way or another, one would be dead by the end of it. Win didn't think. She ran, picking up speed as she sprinted across the snow.

Grayson caught her around the waist, angrily flinging her to the ground. Fur, gnashing teeth, and claws shredding only inches away, as the two large animals struck one another. Luke repeatedly sought dominance, his jaws snapping at Spencer's neck, forcing him to the ground while he lunged at his flank with sharp claws. But what advantages Luke gained, Spencer clawed back in brute strength, tossing him aside as if he were feather-light. Grayson knelt, his knee buried in thick, white snow, as he lifted the crossbow and attempted a shot. Win struggled to her feet, angry with him for pulling her back.

Grayson fired, the arrow fizzed through the air, but it missed, soaring over Spencer's head.

"What are you doing? Don't shoot Luke!" she yelled. Grayson ground his jaw, squeezing one eye and taking aim.

"Who do you think I'm aiming for?" he growled. "Get the hell away from them, Win. You can't get in the middle of this!"

Jake barrelled up beside her, his face contorted in dismay. "They'll kill each other!"

Grayson drew out another arrow and locked it in the groove, his finger on the trigger. "No," he spat. "Luke is going to lose, there's no way he can win this. Spencer is twice as strong."

Win gaped at the spectacle unfolding before them. Luke whimpered as Spencer toppled him, his teeth circling the slim bones of his hock. Luke whipped out of reach at the last second. Snapping, tearing, the two of them didn't let up, one determined to end the other. She started forward, but Grayson grabbed her wrist.

"Please Win!" he begged, a sheen of sweat breaking out across his brow. "Stay away. You'll get hurt. If there were six more of Luke, he'd stand a chance—a pack would decimate a panther. But it's just him…."

Rowan appeared, her cry cracking through the din. Talons bared she dove, claws shredding the thin muscle along the panther's spine. He yelped and staggered in pain. It didn't buy Luke long, seconds long enough to recover, only for a moment, before the panther lunged again.

Win's heart fired up, throwing a glance back at Grayson, who was running out of arrows.

"Save your arrows!" she ordered. To her dismay, Jake ripped off his coat and was getting involved. He grabbed a log from the trees and ran toward Spencer, flailing it in his direction.

"Spencer, stop! For god's sake…you'll kill him!"

Win stripped off her sweater, discarding it on the ground, watching as above, her sister lunged again. But this time, Spencer was ready, jumping and batting her mid-air with his massive paw. Rowan thudded in the snow, and Evan was already running toward her.

Rowan no! Win couldn't hold back any longer.

"He does have a pack," Win yelled at Grayson before sprinting in the direction of the fight. "*Us*. We're the pack!"

You can do this! She closed her eyes, calling to the earth, breathing in air so cold, it scolded her lungs. She leaped and burst from her skin, her clothes fragmenting mid-air, and landed on four paws with a guttural growl. Luke's eyes snapped in her direction.

Win, do not get in the middle of this. He wants to kill you!

He's going to have to try harder!

Spencer drew back, jaw open and panting out hot breath, fogging on the air. His eyes were filmy, hurt, and he was limping. The three of them circled one another, but the way Win felt right now, she could tear him apart, strength coursed through her, every muscle alight. She pounced, snarling, and rolled Spencer through the snow like a ball, but he flipped back, pounding her across her muzzle with a splayed paw.

Win jerked, recoiled in pain but rushed at him again, barrelling him off his feet. Luke was at his neck, his jaws gaining purchase, sinking into flesh, forcing the panther to his belly.

Spencer exploded out from under them in a rage, clawing at Win with his back legs and tossing Luke like a cat toy. Win momentarily flicked her eyes to Rowan, who was back in human form, struggling into a shirt, and breathing hard as she staggered to her feet. Helpless, and hurt she looked on. Grayson crossed round the fight, shrugging out of his jacket to hand to her.

Win, don't die, please! Rowan begged, and Win ignored her, leaping away as Spencer lunged, snapping at her hind legs. Win screeched and rolled, her back arching in the snow, as Spencer bellied her, pinning her with his front paws on her shoulders. She kicked him off with her back legs, making sure she sliced at his underbelly.

The ground quaked. Tremors sent birds rocketing from the

trees, the snow crumbling. Spencer drew back, quivering as the earth shook, the stone appearing from a fine, hazy blue mist. Its light reflected off the snow.

"Win, get away from it!" Evan yelled, balling her fists, violet balls of light appearing in her palms. The stone pulsed and the three of them scattered as shards of light danced around the clearing. Trees bent in its wake, torn from their roots, like an unstoppable tsunami, it careered toward them.

"What is that?" Jake yelled, ducking behind Grayson like he was a human shield. While Spencer was distracted, he aimed, firing off an arrow, but as it plowed through the blue light, it disintegrated into dust.

Spencer was too late to escape the light. It caught him, holding him rigid, while it tore at his body, reverting him to the mutated, half-human he was. Luke was next, his eyes frantic as he tried to bolt but was bound, like being stuck in jello, and Win had no choice but to watch in grim horror as he twisted in pain. The light blazed around him. He yelled as his body cracked and bent into a half-wolf, half-man, dense black fur covering his lower half right up to his chest. She didn't understand what was happening. No one ever told her you could be half an animal. But it seemed this generation of Therian was different. Wildly, he was spat free of the light, landing right by her, and she nudged him with her snout.

What has it done to you?

She could have wept as he lifted his head, long elongated fangs and wild, frightened eyes, hands, and feet clawed. He stared at Spencer, assessing the deplorable, mutated state of his brother.

"Maybe this makes us equal now?" Luke panted, his eyes rolling in pain as he tried to stand.

Win got in front of him. *No, he'll kill you.*

"He's weak and injured." Luke stood straight, towering over six feet. His body mutated and beyond recognition. "All I need is one good hit."

Please don't kill him, Luke. You'll never live with it. He has to pay for the lives he's taken, pay the right way. Luke stared at her, his clawed fingertips stroking her head.

"He won't stop, Win," he said. "If I don't do this, he won't ever stop trying to hurt you."

In those seconds, the world slowed, and her choices slimmed down to one. Spencer wouldn't stop—and neither would Luke. Luke wasn't a brawler, she'd never seen him hit or fight anyone, but he was somehow holding his own in his mutated form. Win couldn't allow him to do this, not alone.

Then we do this together. Running past him, she drove straight into the blue light.

She heard Rowan screaming, Grayson begging her to stop, but she didn't listen. The light held her captive, suspended mid-air. It fizzed and crackled around her body like a lightning storm, her muscles tearing and shredding, pushing her into a human shape. Jaguar rosettes bloomed up her legs, back, torso and chest, along with a covering of soft, golden fur, leaving her hands with ten razor-sharp claws and glistening fangs. Red fire crackled in her hair. Win sensed the rush of power, alighting every fiber in her body, surging with strength, her eyes wide, blazing with light.

This was the dark power Mary spoke of. The power of the last Therian born. Win opened her eyes and walked free of the light as it sparked and rippled around her legs. Any doubts of joining the fight melted away. Win trusted her body, right now pumped full of adrenaline, feeling like she could kick down a wall.

"You are so dead, Spencer!" she snarled.

Luke's mouth dropped open, his heated gaze raking her top to bottom. "Shit, Win! You are so messed up!"

The blue light crackled around her, and she laughed. "It's probably best you don't look in a mirror!"

Rowan jogged to Grayson, ducking to her knees beside him. "Can't you just shoot the guy? I thought you were supposed to be good at this!"

He threw her a glare. "If he stopped moving, he would be dead by now!"

Win and Luke stood back to back as Spencer circled them. He was angry, wild, and wanted this over, but Win buzzed with energy. She'd never felt this kind of strength, sensing the depth of its magic, the darkness from where it had been forged. Power coursed through her muscles. Determined to see him in jail, she didn't care if he got wounded in the fight.

Spencer barrelled toward them, oafish, careless, and Win kicked him, sending him skidding through white clouds of snow, his blood making a grisly trail. But the more she pushed, the stronger and more crazed he became, until he was uncontrollable, a wall of muscle.

Together, they fought him back. Luke grappled Spencer's waist, forcing him to the ground while Win landed on top of him. Spencer was toying with them, and they were both growing weaker and more tired as time ticked by.

"I don't know how much more I can take," Luke said at her back, wiping blood off his chin. "He isn't going to stop."

Even Win's earlier bravado slipped by increments. Hurt, growing in exhaustion and her nerve endings shredded. She found Rowan's eyes across the clearing.

He isn't going to stop Win, Rowan said. *He'll not stop till we are all gone.*

Till he ends the line…

As the sky emptied a snowdrift upon them, it fizzled and crackled off the blue light. Win recalled the day she was pushed into a pit by the man who stalked around them. On that day, he'd tried to end her life with no thought or regret, and all this time, he'd waited to get his chance again. He'd controlled Rowan, working from the inside, yearning for this day. And if he could wait this long, he would never stop trying. No love, no mercy.

I can't kill him, Win admitted. *I won't do it. I'll be no better.*

Rowan stared at the stone. *Didn't you say that thing was a door?*

Win jerked sideways as Spencer lunged. She flipped over Luke's back, he threw her into the air, and she round housed Spencer to the ground with one stroke. Staggering to her feet just in time to see Spencer grab Luke, twisting his neck so hard it looked like he'd break his head clean off. Win barrelled into him, air whooshing through her red mane of hair, her back stinging as he sliced at her spine.

She fell flat in the snow, her chin crashing into the ground. Grayson let an arrow fly; it soared above her head, hitting Spencer between the shoulder blades. He roared, pulling it free, and flung it to the ground. Grayson stared at her helplessly. He was out of arrows.

Evan stood on the edge of the crackling light. She squinted through the dense, white fog. "Blood opens the door, Win!" she yelled. *"Blood opens the door!"*

Painfully, her spine protesting, Win crawled to her knees, then her feet, breathing hard as she ran through the blue light. Her palms were already bleeding, scratched up, and splintered. The blue light seared her skin. She squeezed her eyes shut, holding up both her palms to the stone. It sent her careering back with such a whack she landed on her back, between Luke and Spencer, still growling and warring above her.

She rolled, finding Rowan across the clearing. "It's open!" she screamed.

Time rolled to a slow crawl. Having guessed Rowan's plan, Grayson pulled a long curved blade from his belt, locking eyes with her as she bolted past him. She caught the knife with her outstretched hand as he tossed it to her. Rowan skidded to her knees, her back arching as she landed under Spencer, and with both hands plunged the blade up, between his ribs.

Wild-eyed, sobbing with exhaustion, Rowan managed to dodge his slow, desperate attempt at a killing blow before he dropped to his knees.

"Now!" Evan screamed. "*Do it now!*"

Luke and Win locked eyes, each of them taking one of Spencer's limbs and, with what little left between them, ran with him toward the stone. They threw him, trapped in the crackling fire.

"Close the door! *Close it!*" Rowan yelled before collapsing.

Using the sharp, clawed end of her nail, Win dragged it along her palm, so blood welled in the cut, then held up her palm to the stone, her hair flying behind her, as she shielded her eyes.

The stone pulsed, then exploded, vanishing in a blaze of blue thunder, taking Spencer with it. Flung out of the path of the light, Win and Luke flailed as they landed on their backs. When Win opened her eyes, her limbs throbbed, and she felt the tickle of snow hitting her raw skin.

Spencer was gone.

Groaning, she rolled onto her tummy, stark naked. Next to her, Luke moaned in pain.

Rowan collapsed by her side and struggled out of Grayson's jacket, flinging it over them. "You did it!" She wrapped her in a tight hold, her tears wet on Win's face. "You both did it!"

Win rolled to her side, facing Luke, crawling close enough to throw her arm over his chest. He was dumbfounded, staring skyward, eyes watering. He glanced at her, and they shared a smile, but his smile faded quickly, longing in his gaze.

Instinctively she knew what he was thinking. She didn't have to read his mind. Time had run out, and decisions had to be made. The words were out there, truth floating between them. He loved her, deeply, more than a friend should. It broke her heart she couldn't return it.

Win held his hand, taking the back of it and kissing it. *You don't have to go. We can make it work…somehow.*

His eyes filled up. *You're my best friend, and I want it to stay that way.*

Luke gazed at her, hair like fire in the snow; her eyes still a vibrant yellow. Jake appeared and tossed him a coat. Luke glanced up at him gratefully. "Just protecting your modesty...you looked kind of cold," Jake informed him with a smirk.

"Thanks, Dad," Luke puffed out a laugh. "I don't know how many hot baths will fix this. I'm broken."

"Where is he?" Jake asked, an edge of panic creeping into his voice. "Where the hell did you send him?"

"I don't care, Dad!" Luke moaned. "I just don't care."

Jake whirled in Evan's direction. "Bring him back…you can't leave him to die."

Evan withdrew, huddling at Rowan's side. "I have no idea where he is, Jake. But I know, if we hadn't acted, one of your sons would be dead by now."

Win sat up, clutching the jacket to her chest, drawing up her knees. The explosion singed the ground, a chared black hole where the stone stood only moments ago, leaving her to wonder where on earth they had sent Spencer.

Thirty Four

Bleary-eyed, Win awoke in her bed, blinded by white light. Outside it was still snowing, and she had no idea how she got home.

When she sat up in bed, she hissed. Every part of her body protested, every muscle pulled, and forced her to lie back down. Rolling her head right, she carefully inched up, her head as still as she could muster. She held out her arms and saw she'd been bitten *everywhere*.

"Hold fire!" Ben barked, bouncing from the chair, steadying her as she attempted to stand. "Take it easy."

Win's head was cloudy, like cotton balls. "Where's Luke? Grayson?"

Ben eased her back to the mattress. "Luke is in his room, face down in some kind of coma. Grayson went home. I think the poor guy needed a break, and I told him to go. That's okay right?"

Win half smiled. "Yeah, of course." Though she wished he had stayed. "How long have I been…?"

"Only a couple of hours." He wrinkled his nose. "Excuse the bluntness, but I think you need a shower. Honestly, you smell like a cat peed all over you."

Disgusted, she sniffed her skin. "That's gross."

He gave her a gentle pat on the knee. "A shower, and you'll be as good as new."

Win's lip dropped, allowing her emotions to seep in. She didn't think she would ever be good as new. The remaining traces of the blue light tingled under her skin, forever altered, she was different from them, and the one person who could understand was about to leave her.

It was all so stupid, she hated him for loving her, and he'd ruined everything. She wanted him here, with her, her friend, her companion, and now it was all going away.

"Win." Ben touched her ratty hair. "You did a good thing. You saved Luke, and you sent Spencer god knows where. Though Jake isn't too happy."

Win wrinkled her nose, thinking Jake could jump off a bridge for all she cared. Momentarily, the conversation in the woods with Jake floated back to her. His words... *"I knew her better than you ever did,"*...echoed in her mind. She opened her mouth but quickly closed it. It wasn't the right time, and she wondered if her father would even tell her the truth. Like a true Hickory, he had a knack for bending reality.

The thought churned her stomach; somewhere in time, Spencer was alive, or at least he was when he went through the door. Her eyes snapped up. "How's Rowan?"

Ben smiled fondly. "She's sleeping, and I'm kind of glad the guy has gone from her life. One way or another, he paid for what he did. And he won't hurt anyone else."

"What about the cops?"

Ben scratched his head. "They cleared out a few hours ago. Officer Chase called it off, for now. As far as they are concerned, it has moved on."

As Ben led her to the bathroom, she thought if Rowan even felt for a second the way she felt for Luke, then Spencer would never truly be gone. He'd always be there, a nagging doubt, the last thing she thought of before she slept—a ghost lurking in the shadows. Under the hot spray, she winced against the sting, clean and dry before wrapping herself in a towel.

In the hall, Luke waited for her, and she stopped dead, drawing in her breath. She hadn't properly looked at him, not since the change, and he was…bigger. His hair thicker and longer needed a good brush. With a man's jaw, shadowed with scruff, his eyes sparkled blue. He didn't look anything like the seventeen-year-old who'd died in the woods. Massive arms crossed a broad chest as he folded them, his lip curling in a smile at her reaction. Two pinch marks were still visible on either side of his nose where his glasses once sat. He even smelled different, like pine needles, which stabbed her heart. The Luke she'd known was lost. Win clutched her towel tighter and covered her mouth before she laughed nervously.

He drew his brows together. "What's so funny?"

She snorted. "You're *enormous*. You look like you spent a weekend doing steroids!"

Luke's pouty mouth cracked into a smile. He smirked. "I wonder if anything else got bigger?"

Win punched his shoulder. "Don't be gross!"

He stretched out his arms, giving her a boyish smile. "Sorry, couldn't resist. Are you done?"

Awkwardly, she nodded, grabbing him a dry towel from the rail and pressing it into his hands. She smiled, heat creeping up her neck. "I promise not to turn on any faucets while you're in there."

"I guess that's one thing I won't miss." His eyes glassed, and voice cracked, and Win thought she might dissolve into tears. He flung down the towels and threw his arms around her, squeezing her so hard she could feel her bones creak. She wept into his neck, and he was breathing hard into her hair.

"Please, don't leave," she sobbed. "Don't go. We can go back to what we were. Please, *don't* break up with Ella."

"I can't stay here." Luke held her tight, his skin warm, and she could feel every muscle flex under his shirt. Her heart fired up, in time with his. When he let go, she could hardly breathe. He let her slip back to the balls of her feet.

"I can't stay," he said again. "But I want you in my life. I can't *not* have you in my life. If I stay, it'll be Rowan and Spencer, all over. And I don't ever want that to happen to us."

He went into the bathroom and locked the door. Win scuttled back to her room, falling into bed, pulling on an old sweater, and falling into an exhausted sleep, every inch of her bitten, chewed, and scratched. She opened her eyes when she felt a weight pressing on the bed. Evan sat, her hand out stroking her back, a soft, violet light seeping out of her hands.

Win went limp, her eyes rolling and heavy. Evan smiled. "Sleep, baby." She smiled. "Just try to sleep."

Win woke, pain-free, and rolled into a sitting position. Rowan jumped in fright, and Win could tell she'd surprised her. She sat in the chair by the window, her legs propped on the edge of the bed, scanning through one of Win's tattered books.

"It's okay!" she said, leaning forward in her chair. "You're okay!"

"What happened? How long have I been out?"

Grimly, Rowan smiled. "Two days?"

"No…oh…Grayson…is he?"

Rowan uncurled her legs from under her. "He's been here, don't worry. But he left about an hour ago when you were still dead to the world."

Win struggled to sit, eyeing her sister suspiciously. “I hope you were nice to him.”

Rowan grinned savagely, stretching out her legs and yawning. “I think I can give him a pass…for now. He made himself pretty useful in the woods.”

The woods…the memory floated back to her. Win uncovered her legs, revealing the faded remains of bites, scratches, and bruises. “Holy crap!” She gritted her teeth but then looked at her sister, knowing her wounds ran deeper. “Are you…okay?”

Rowan sucked in her breath, the question she dreaded by her expression. “Slightly frazzled, knowing Spencer is finally gone. It’s a good thing.”

“You ended him, Rowan. You were so brave. And I know… how you must have loved him once.”

“The question is, where did we send him?” Rowan mused. “And will he be able to get back?”

Win looked thoughtful. It was disturbing, knowing Spencer was out there somewhere. But, now, he was someone else’s problem. Win lay back for a moment, trying to recover her thoughts, remembering the way the stone’s light transformed her into something terrifying. The power and the strength, she could still feel it itching under her skin.

“Did you know we could be half-human?”

Rowan laughed shortly. “Uh, no. I would have remembered something important like that, and I don’t want it to happen again. It looked intense…and painful!”

Win nodded, pressing the tender flesh of her thigh. It was healed. Only Spencer’s bite mark was visible. “It was intense,” she agreed. “Look what it did to Spencer.”

Rowan suppressed a shudder, and Win knew she was likely to bolt. She teetered too closely to discussing her real feelings, and Rowan was too guarded. Instead, Win tilted her head. “And is Evan still here? Dare I ask?”

“She’s cleaning the kitchen,” Rowan said. “Trying to pretend I’m not angry with her.”

"She has a lot of explaining to do," Win mused, pulling on the covers. "I'm still not entirely sure I understand this whole immortality thing."

Wordlessly, Rowan stood and tidied around Win's room, folding up clothes and stacking them away. Watching her, she picked at her nails, reaching for her phone, and thumbing through the messages, surprised to see there were none from Ella, no voicemails or texts. Her stomach dropped. *Oh…god, no!*

Her face drained, and she sat up. "Rowan…is Luke awake?" she croaked, and Rowan threw her a confused look.

"Yeah, he's been with Jake this afternoon. Think they have been working stuff through."

"When did he wake up?"

"Um…He was awake yesterday….why?"

Win flung back the covers, wincing as her feet hit the floor. She threw on clothes, her heart hammering as she fled downstairs, scrambling into her shoes and grabbing the keys to the truck. She ignored Rowan calling after her as she started the engine. The snow was beginning to turn a slick, sludgy grey.

Shit!…please, don't let him have spoken to her! Butterflies partied in her stomach, her nerves jangling as she turned the truck onto the main road. The wipers swished away stray flakes of snow as she drove out of town, not stopping till the tires crunched over the gravel in Ella's yard.

Knuckles wrapped softly on wood. Win inched back on the welcome mat, standing outside Ella's front door, a small, white-clad colonial build about three miles outside of town. Stamping her cold feet, she stood back, peering up at the house, the drawn curtains in Ella's front bedroom.

Her mouth grew drier the longer she waited, a knot tightening in her stomach. When there was still no answer, she took a few steps back, wandering around to the family room window, cupping her eyes, and peering inside. There was movement; she saw Ella's mother dart past with a coffee in her hand. Win waved, noticing how the woman's face tightened when she spotted her.

The door rattled as it unlocked, and Ella's mother answered, her icy gaze sweeping Win from head to foot. Win's expression fell, her hopeful smile fading.

"Hey, Mrs. Torres. Is Ella home?"

Ella's mom was short, with deep olive skin and shiny, short black hair, a fuller build, and the same round, open eyes as her friend. But right now, her expression was pensive; she nervously looked over her shoulder. "Ah, Win. I don't think now is the best time."

Win choked. "Oh…I just really need to see her."

"Well, perhaps she doesn't want to see you."

Win could feel any courage she'd built dissolving, her insides turning to mush. Nervously she balled her hands, nails digging into her skin. She forced back tears.

"Okay…maybe tell her I called by?"

"Mom, wait, it's okay!" Ella's voice called from behind the door. But it wasn't her usual cheery tone, her voice was thick, snuffly, and Win fell apart when she pulled back the door. Ella's face was red, swollen, her eyes dull and raw. Folding her arms, she stood in the doorway, pulling her robe tight. Mrs. Torres gave her daughter a warm squeeze of her shoulder before stepping aside and leaving them.

Ella drew in a raspy breath, leaning on the doorframe, and Win didn't know what to say. She could feel her chest tightening, knowing anything she said would sound lame, pathetic.

"Ella…I'm so sorry."

Ella's eyes filled with water, her chin wobbling. "He came by last night, and he broke up with me."

Guilt choked and strangled Win's voice, her heart clenched like a fist. Sorry didn't cut it. It wasn't enough.

Ella tilted her head. "He looks so different. Was it awful? Seeing it happen to someone else?"

Win couldn't form words; it hurt too hard to speak. She merely nodded, and Ella wiped her eyes.

"He's leaving," Win said. She sniffed, wiping her nose. The snow was starting to fall, gently, muffling the sound in the air. But she could hear Ella's slow heartbeat. A heart crushed to pieces, sluggishly beating in her chest.

"He told me he'll stay with his dad at the old house—if they can get along. At least he'll always be in your life," Ella said. "You are connected now—more than ever."

"It's not like that…."

"Win, it is! He's in love with you."

Win groaned, pushed back her hair, scrubbing at her watery eyes. "Ella, I don't know how this happened. I'm so sorry. I never did anything….there was never a chance."

Ella nodded weakly, hanging off the door as though it were keeping her upright. "I know. I know you never did anything to make him think there was a chance. You never betrayed me."

"I would never hurt you!" Win could feel herself bubbling, close to breaking. "This is killing me!"

But Ella didn't seem to be listening.

"In all the time we dated, he never once said he loved me, never. I kind of hoped he would say it one day, and I imagined how he'd drop it in the conversation. You know him, he is awful at emotional stuff, and sometimes, I even *thought* he'd said it, and I'd somehow missed it."

"Ella…"

"I tried to ignore the way he looked at you. I could see how devastated you were after Grayson. And I even told him to look out for you, like a big brother, and I loved how everything was so perfect—just us three. But last night, he came over and ended things, said he didn't want to hurt me anymore. And he said he *loved* you. He just *said* it. As easy as breathing."

Win's face crumpled into hot tears. "Ella…I'm so sorry."

Ella left the safety of the door and stumbled into Win's arms for an awkward hug. Win held her tightly, her fingers gripping her soft robe, not letting her pull away. Finally, Ella stepped back, her smile wobbly as she pushed wet strands of hair out of Win's face.

"Win, I need some time, okay? I can't just pretend this didn't happen."

Win faltered. "What do you mean?"

"It means right now—I don't want you in my life."

"Ella, no, *please*," Win begged. This was falling apart; everything about to dissolve under her feet. "You're my best friend."

"And you're mine," Ella said, frantically dabbing at the corners of her eyes. "But I loved him Win, and the entire time, he felt nothing for me."

"That's not true!"

"It is, Win," she said, stepping back inside the house. "It is true. I know it's not your fault. But right now, I can't even look at you."

Ella stepped inside and shut the door, and the click hit Win with a sense of finality, leaving her standing frozen on the porch.

In a numb state of shock, Win drove home, hardly able to recall the journey. As she approached the entrance to Hickory House, she spotted a black Mercedes pulling out of the drive. Her heart sped up, tears blurring her eyes as she pulled the truck to the side of the road, the engine still running as she chased the car down. Feet slapped over wet asphalt, her lungs tight, relieved when the car stopped and Luke jumped out of the passenger side. He was ashen, apprehensive as he jogged toward her.

She shoved him in the chest; it was like hitting a stone wall. "How could you?" she wailed. "How could you do this to her? You've screwed *everything* up!"

"I'm sorry." His face blotchy and red, hands tore through his messy locks as he paced in front of her.

"You go back there right now and fix this! Tell her you made a mistake!"

"Win, I'm not going to. She's already hurt enough."

Win threw her hands up in despair. "So, you're leaving…going back to him?"

"Where the hell am I supposed to go? Perhaps he needs me, Win, did you think of that? Perhaps it isn't all about you, *all the time?* He's my father, and he lost his son. It's time to start forgiving one another. Maybe, we can be there for each other?"

Win knew her motivations were selfish. She'd do anything to keep him, her playmate, her friend, knowing it was killing him. She wouldn't give him what he truly wanted. As long as she wasn't alone, she would cling to him like a life raft, lost at sea. Where else could he go? She all but put the idea in Jake's head, reunited them. She'd begged him to take Luke back because she was terrified he'd be alone. But she didn't want Luke to go back to his old ways, cold and aloof. She let out a desperate sob. "And were you even going to say goodbye? You were just going to leave?"

He scrubbed at his face. "Win, it's too hard to say goodbye. This is just too hard!"

Someone climbed out of the driver's side, Jake leaned on the open door, watching them, and to her surprise, for once, he didn't look amused or pleased with himself. He just looked sad.

"I hate you!" Win seethed, tears streaking her face. "I *hate* you for what you've done!"

He caught her arms, pinning her, so she was still and bawling into his shoulder. Cradling her, he kissed the top of her head. "I need to go. Please let me go!"

"No, you can't leave me," she sobbed, her fingers fisting his shirt. "You're my best friend, and I can't do this on my own. Please, please don't leave. *Don't go!"*

Gently, he eased her off him, and to her horror, he was crying. She'd never seen him cry. "I'm leaving now. But I'm not leaving you, you understand me? I'm still here—across the woods. If I stay, I'll end up wanting more than I can have. *Please*, Win, let me go."

It was useless, knowing there was nothing she could do to make him stay. She let go of his shirt, falling back on the balls of her feet.

Flinging her arms around his neck, she held him tight, breathing him in one more time. “Don’t change,” she begged. “Don’t go back to what you were, cold…like him.”

He smiled, wiping at his eyes. “I won’t change, Win,” he said. “You’re part of me now.”

He left her standing on the side of the road. As his father drove away, Jake did something uncharacteristic, reaching out and cupping the back of his neck. She could see them through the back window.

Win shook, her hands like rubber on the wheel as she nursed it back into the drive. She didn’t remember slamming the door or stumbling up the porch steps. Luke’s den was open, all of his things gone, the bed stripped and folded back into a couch, like the days where it was just her grandfather’s office. Trembling, she opened the door, her teeth chattering as she looked around the room. Rowan’s shape filled the door behind her.

“I tried to get him to wait,” she said, but Win didn’t hear her. Instead, she walked to the bedside cabinet where his spare glasses rested on top of a book. She picked them up, turning them over in her hands, before shrieking and throwing them against the wall.

Rowan’s lip quivered as she bent to scoop Win from the heap she’d crumpled to on the floor.

“I’m so sorry, honey,” she soothed. “God, I’m so sorry.”

Win didn’t move. She lay still and bawled into her sister’s lap.

Thirty Five

Mist covered the road, the light in the cab flickered. It was past midnight. Win wiped at her eyes with her free hand, the truck bouncing along the road. She stole a glance at the bags packed, thrown on the floor of the cab, her clothes stuffed in the small case, its contents spilling over the top as the vehicle bumped.

After returning home from Ella's, Win sat numbly on the edge of her bed. Closing her eyes, she tried to shut out the sound of Rowan and Evan arguing in the next room. How had things gone so wrong? And what hurt was there was no escape. Luke wasn't downstairs, where she could crawl into his room and hide while he read, and she scrolled through her phone. He was gone, leaving a raw, open wound. Therian wounds didn't heal well.

Ella wasn't going to be there to help pick up the pieces, to call or share endless messages. Win held in a sob, stuffing the heel of her hand into her mouth. She wondered if Ella would ever speak to her again, could even stand to be near her, knowing what she'd unwittingly stolen. Sitting on the edge of her bed, hands shaking and her chest muscles tightening, she knew she had lost two of the most important people in her life. And her mother was nowhere to be seen.

Mom, where are you? I wish you were here…

Win's temper flared, a hot spark of bitterness settling on her tongue. She was angry. No matter what she did, she lost people. And her mother wasn't here. She was alive, out there somewhere, and hadn't come home. Win paced the floor, wiping her eyes on her sleeve, a hot fuel building in her gut. Alice left them, and it was too much to bear.

Transported back to a year ago, where she was an outcast, lonely and unliked, her one and only friend, Aimee, turned against her, leaving her like a stranded cat in the wilderness. Ella accepted her, loved her, and been her confidante, even a few nights ago; she was ready to risk *everything* to help her.

Now she didn't want to see her again. Win closed her eyes, knowing she'd unwittingly broken Ella's heart.

Stifled, the suffocation was too much to bear, and Win did the only thing she could think to do. She ran.

Packing some things, she'd crept out of the house, tiptoeing down the stairs at midnight. She'd nearly been out the door when she heard footsteps behind her. Whirling about, she caught sight of her father standing in the kitchen.

He gave her a sad smile and a nod before she closed the door behind her. He let her go.

She pulled the truck onto the main road out of town, her wipers swishing frantically, knowing there was only one place she could go.

As she drove, her mind pulled her back to a glorious day in the summer, where she, Ella, and Luke laid out a giant blanket in the yard, talking and eating under the dying sun. Win shook up his coke can so hard when he cracked it open, fizz exploded from the can, leaving him dripping in sticky liquid.

Ella fell about laughing while he chased Win across the yard, catching her around the waist and hauling her across his shoulder. He threatened to dump her in a trash can, turning her upside down, so she shrieked with laughter, tears running down her face. They'd all recovered on the blanket, and Rowan bounded across the yard, snapping a photo on her phone of the three of them, still giggling like kids. Luke propped on his elbow, Ella leaning across his stomach and Win with one arm around his neck. She'd printed the photo at the drugstore, and it was on a corkboard in her bedroom at home.

But it was all over now. The snow fell and covered her tracks.

Grayson managed to open a water bottle with his teeth, necking it back, darting a quick look at the girl asleep next to him in the cab. He patted her hand, checking she was warm under the woolen blanket and adjusting the blower. Wipers swished frantically back and forth, batting away the snow before it settled on the windscreen.

Her head lolled, tumbling red curls falling across her face, and in her sleep, she shivered and then changed position, resting her head on the passenger window.

He'd been fast asleep when she appeared at his door at one in the morning, bleary-eyed. He'd let her in and held her while she sobbed on the bed next to him. She'd gazed at him with glistening eyes.

"Please take me away," she begged. "Anywhere. You said you would once."

He stroked her face, tried to calm her down, but she was insistent, utterly heartbroken. She'd told him about Luke and then Ella, hardly able to breathe between sobs, like an inconsolable toddler.

"Win, we can't just take off," he said, but this only made her more upset.

"I need to get away. Luke is gone, and now Ella won't talk to me...."

Grayson had a horrible suspicion this was the problem. Anyone with eyes could see the kid harbored a huge crush, and Win loved him deeply, with her huge heart, and would've never seen it coming.

Grayson agreed to take her away, but reluctantly. He was thinking ahead, trying to plan where they might go, find a quiet spot where Win could shift in safety, where she could vanish. He knew of a couple of motels near West Point, not too far out. Somewhere they could be alone, but not too out of the pull of Cedar Wood.

Pulling Win's truck to the roadside, he stepped out into the cold air and called her house. He gave a rushed sigh of relief when Ben answered, his tired voice at the other end of the line. "Win is with me. I thought you should know."

Ben made a gruff noise at the other end of the line, he didn't sound happy, but he wasn't Rowan. Win's sister probably would have hunted him down like prey, despite the grudging truce they'd formed while Win recovered. "I'll call when we settle somewhere," Grayson promised.

"Thank you, Grayson," Ben replied stiffly. "I know you'll take care of her."

"She just needs space," Grayson said, and Ben laughed.

"I think we could all use that right now."

The truck bumped along in the dark snow, and Grayson lost himself in thought, casting a glance at her, the glow of the freeway lights glinting off her face. It heated his blood, imagining them together, every morning and every night, going to sleep together, and waking. He would never have to share her, and she'd be his, for however long it lasted.

It wouldn't be long if he knew Win, which he did. The pull to go back to her family would eventually draw her home. He guessed a couple of weeks at best.

Snow beat down on the truck. It bumped over a pothole, jostling it left, right, and Win made a noise but settled back to sleep. An object glinted in the breast pocket of her shirt, something glass twinkling in the dimness of the cab, and he carefully plucked it out of her shirt between his fingers.

Her cheeks were shiny, wet lashes spiked, and even in her sleep, she whimpered like a lost child. Grayson studied the thin wire-framed glasses. They were broken, smashed, a crack exploding across one of the lenses like a spider web. He placed them back in her pocket before she woke up and saw he'd found them.

Tightening his grip on the wheel, he pushed away his jealousy, knowing now was not the time. She was distraught, and he'd no right to push her, and it was unbelievable he was even in her life at all.

And she chose you, a voice in his head kept saying. *So suck it up and forget it.*

The glasses jangled in her pocket, right above her heart, and he kept driving.

Flakes of snow fell in pretty patterns, settling on the old, rusty engines. Rowan sat on the back of an abandoned truck, her legs curled up under her, watching the snow glisten as it rested on the trees. The yard was quiet, the ground hard, and inside she was trembling. The sun was coming up.

Evan was packing her things, and Rowan didn't know if she had the strength to stop her. Every nerve ending shredded, trust she built with her destroyed like a fallen tower. And yet, she couldn't let her go.

In her fingers, she held Win's note. *I'm sorry, I need some time. I'm with Grayson, and we'll be okay.*

Footsteps crunched through the ice, and Rowan's gaze flicked up. Ben settled on the truck next to her. "Room for another?" He smiled, hopping up and snaking one arm around her waist. Even after all this time, his affection was restrained, tentative, and a little shy. She smiled weakly, resting beside him.

"Win's gone," she said, holding out the note.

"I know. I heard her leave."

"And you didn't try to stop her?"

He chuckled lightly, the sound floating on the still air. "No, Rowan, I didn't."

"But...she has school, and her friends...she can't just take off?"

He exhaled, breath fogging in the air. "Let her go, Rowan. Let her be a teenager. I know you want the best for her, and you don't want to see her fail. But she has to make some of her own mistakes...what did you say to me once? Wild animals shouldn't be locked in cages?"

Rowan sniffed. "I never meant to hurt her."

"Of course you didn't, and she knows that. She's a good kid, and she'll come home. And she's with Grayson. I trust him. Even if you don't."

She licked her dry lips, salty from all the tears she'd cried. "I was wrong to keep him away. He isn't Spencer."

"You did what any sister would do, but we are allowed to make mistakes. They've found one another again. That's what matters."

Rowan cocked her head, giving him a sideways look. "You are awfully calm about all this? I would've bet you'd have called the cops by now."

He laughed. "I'm dying inside, don't worry. I'm just trying to look like I have things in hand."

"Hmm, sounds like me."

He rubbed her shoulder. "Yeah. You aren't letting Evan leave, are you?"

Rowan groaned inwardly. "I don't know."

"You can't." He turned her shoulders to face him. "Don't you believe in second chances? In redemption?"

"I guess."

"Then don't let her go. She loves you, and she is good for this family, for you! If you can forgive me…."

"That's different," Rowan said as flakes of snow settled on her hair. "It's Mom. Of course, you hid it from us, I understand. But Evan…"

"I know!" Ben insisted. "I know, but we have to start forgiving one another. Luke is gone, and Win has flown the coop—I need Evan around too. She's a good person—and she isn't Spencer."

Rowan's chest heaved as she looked skyward, letting bites of snow tickle her face. Spencer was gone, finally out of her life, paying with his for the awful things he'd done. "I said some terrible things…."

"She'll forgive you."

She fell into his open arms, snuggling under his chin while he rocked her. He made an odd noise in his throat, as though he was choking back tears, and when he finally let her go, she saw his eyes were wet and shiny. He pinched her chin.

"It's freezing out here. I'm going inside and going to catch Evan before she disappears." He hopped off the back of the truck. "But…uh…I think there might be someone here to see you."

Frowning, she watched as he jogged back to the house. He gazed across his shoulder and smiled into the distance. Rowan turned, wondering what he was looking at.

A woman stood partially hidden in the treeline, a flicker of movement, a flash of blonde hair, and Rowan dropped from the truck, her limbs numb.

The woman stepped out timidly, her arms wrapped around herself. Dressed in an old faded hoodie, wearing nothing but a ratty nightshirt underneath, her pale legs bare as she padded across the yard, her short blonde hair spiked with the wetness of snow. They locked eyes, and the woman stopped dead, staring straight at Rowan, her eyes brimming with recognition.

Rowan smiled through tears. “Mom?”

Alice trembled with apprehension and walked toward her, holding out her arms as she picked up speed.

Rowan sobbed and ran to her mother.

Epilogue

His eyes opened, and saw flecks of yellow light, blinking and struggling to adjust. He breathed in, wincing, like the knife was still there, wedged between his bones, every raspy choke splintered his insides.

Oddly though, he was warm, laying on something scratchy but spongey. Wrinkling his nose, he smelled…hay. Was he on a farm?

He recalled hurtling through the blue light, encased in darkness and sucked into its depths, the languid feeling of being pulled through warm water. Now, he woke, confused and in pain, and hot with fever. Perhaps, this was it. Was he finally dying?

"Lay still," a voice spoke softly. Female, young, her outline a blur in his vision. He blinked awake, drinking her image in. Small boned, young, hair the color of dirt. Spencer groaned, eyeing her dress, a long, white nightgown. Behind her, in the barn door, he saw the sun rising. The first glimpses of morning rising over a very different time. He sucked in air, she smelled different. *Strong*.

"Who are you?" he rasped, his head lolling back on the hay. He was weak, frail. A rosy blush streaked the girl's face.

"You shouldn't talk," she warned him shyly. She kept looking at her hands, folded in her lap. "Save your strength. I brought you here."

"You did?"

He could hardly believe it. She looked about twelve, and judging by her bone-white skin and thin arms, she didn't have the stamina to drag a bale of hay, let alone a man his size. Spencer glanced down his body, the mutant he was. Groaning inwardly, he knew he must look ghastly. Thick, soft panther hair covered him foot to chest, not to mention the claws…and the teeth. He narrowed his eyes at her. "Aren't you afraid of me?"

Her face stilled. She was looking deep into his eyes. "I've seen demons before."

He cocked a brow, coughing as he laughed. "Oh, have you now? Bet they didn't look like me."

"I think," she said, swallowing. "You're beautiful."

He smiled, and at first, she drew back in alarm, his teeth glistening, but then she smiled back. He saw colors floating around her head, the way he always saw things. Cursed all his life to see people for what they were, shapes, colors, and sounds. Her aura was bright, despite her empty, black stare—bright, golden light, as hot as the sun.

"What's your name?"

She ducked to her knees, crawling a little closer. Spencer thought she was either brave or foolish. "Mary Hickory."

Recognition sparked within him. "And, how old are you?"

She bit her lip shyly. "I'm thirteen."

He guessed about right, and she was so young. "And, have you got sisters?"

At the mention of siblings, Mary's face fell, reluctant to answer. "I have two. My eldest sister died."

Spencer sat up, brushing strands of hay off his skin. "So, then, you would be the *youngest*?"

Her earnest gaze open, like an eager pup, she nodded. *Jackpot,* Spencer thought. No wonder she glowed. It was the power coursing through her blood that set her on fire, like a beacon he would have recognized anywhere. Like all those years ago, in the woods, the day he'd first set eyes on Win. A girl with golden light surrounding her like a halo. A girl who could end the curse.

"What's your name?" she asked timidly. Spencer gave her a lazy smile.

"Do demons have names?"

"I don't know. Our reverend says some do. You don't look too frightening, though?"

"I'm Spencer," he said, weighing her reaction, how she whispered it back to herself.

"What a funny name."

"Hmm, I guess it probably is. What year is it?"

"1807."

He stretched his massive arms, yawning and noticing the way she blushed and looked away. Spencer guessed she hadn't seen a half-naked man before, let alone one who looked like him. "Do you know what happened?" he asked. "Where I came from?"

"I was in the woods," Mary explained. "And I heard the stone humming. I feel like it calls to me sometimes. It lit up like a wild blue fire, and then, you were there…with a knife stuck in you."

He grimaced, gazing down at his torso, noticing for the first time he'd been bandaged, a bloody stain blanching the fabric. Despite the pain, he gazed up at her and bestowed her with a charming smile. "Did you do this for me?"

Mary nodded, her breathing shallow. She glanced over her shoulder. "I can get you some food if you like? No one is awake yet indoors."

He smelled the pigs, his stomach growling. He chuckled darkly, thinking how incredible it was. He wound up *here,* in the Hickory hay barn. His knife wound itched, he ground his teeth. *Rowan… Rowan and the witch.* They'd sent him here, probably thought they were so clever, rid of him for good. Luke knew, about the curse, knew one way or another he had to be dealt with. He could almost give his little brother props, he'd sworn he wouldn't let him hurt Win, and he'd won. Maybe Luke had some balls, after all?

Mary studied him and noticed she carried a cloth and a bowl of hot water beside her. Timidly, she scooted closer, fanning out her dress, pressing the hot material to his temple. He didn't look away as she washed his face, wiping the blood off his mouth, and he admired her guts. She was trembling, the kind of scared he liked. And right now, with his stomach growling, he knew it wasn't pigs he was interested in. He knew how to make his wound heal faster.

"Mary." He straightened, stretching out his legs, so she was forced to edge her knees. She pushed strands of his dirty, blonde hair out of his face, dabbing him clean. "Have you ever been kissed before?"

She startled, her black eyes widening, alarmed but intrigued. She let out a breathy laugh. "Uh…only by my mother."

Spencer's eyes darkened. "No, I mean, by a man."

She drew back on her knees. Fear leaked out of her, and he drank it in. "No…I haven't."

This kind of scared made his blood run liquid hot. And right now, she was terrified. Spencer lifted a finger and drew a line from her eyebrow down to her bottom lip, earning a deep shudder from her.

Their eyes met. He stared at her lower lip, teasing her, breathing shallow as he leaned closer—and struck. He sank his fangs into her jugular, and the girl thrashed wildly in his arms. With waning strength, she beat and clawed at his back with dull, short nails until she slackened across his lap. Spencer drank her blood like she was lemonade, lapping it up, till he felt her heart slow to a crawl, then fade to nothing. He dropped her, and she rolled to a crumpled heap on the hay, her dark hair spraying across her face. Spencer rose to his feet, stretching, and smiled to himself.

Well, that's better, he thought. The girl's blood mingled with his, renewing his strength, making him whole, healing him. Staggering to the barn door, he stared up at Hickory House, his mission clear, if he ever stood any chance of getting home and ending this once and for all.

Out here somewhere, in this time, was the person he needed. A woman, with knowledge and power in her veins, a healer and an insufferable meddler, capable of annihilating Rowan and bringing her family to their knees—where they belonged.

Spencer needed to find the witch.

Hardback Exclusive Story

Paper birds

1990

"Everyone knows your old man is a freak."

The statement, laced with venom, came from the mouth of a boy with a mop of black hair, so dark it reflected blue as the sun beamed through the church window and bounced off his head. The boy had a cold, steel blue glare, fixed on the girl sitting opposite him. Alice Hickory swallowed down anger, boiling under her skin. She *hated* him. Even the way he dressed bugged her. Who wore a pressed linen grey suit and a neat stripy tie to church club? With a black-framed pair of reading glasses sat perched on his snub nose, his hair gelled so a rouge curl fell in his eyes, the kid resembled a mini Clark Kent. She stared down at her grubby knees, splattered in mud and her frayed dungaree shorts.

They were both eleven years old, but he looked younger, and she'd made the fatal error of assuming he was a second grader on their first session. She'd playfully ruffled his hair, and he hadn't forgiven her yet.

Alice crossed her legs at the ankles, tossing him a sneer with as much acidity as she could muster. She might be only eleven years old, but she knew a jerk when she saw one. And this one had just got her kicked out of church club for the second week running. This time it was because she'd slugged him in the nose. It was swelling up, bruising a greyish purple, and he was carefully holding an icepack to his face.

He got what he deserved, she thought, ignoring a spark of guilt.

He successfully stuck gum in her hair, and now Mrs. Flanders was looming over her in the chair, a pair of scissors in her shaky, seventy-five-year-old grasp and breathing coffee fumes in her face. The scissors snipped in her ear, and Alice watched as a long lock of strawberry blonde hair floated into her lap. She gritted her teeth.

He deserved a good kick in the balls. Alice's hair was an unruly crown, blessed with so much, she doubted it would show. She peered up at him under thick waves of straw-colored locks. Staring at him, dressed in his neat, crisp attire, she thought of the ultimate comeback and licked her lips.

"Well—everyone knows your old man bangs his nurse."

Jake Fraser's eyes darkened, his mouth pinched, but Mrs. Flanders gasped in horror.

"Alice *Mary* Hickory!" The older woman clutched her chest and dropped the scissors onto the table with a clatter. "I ought to wash out your mouth. What a thing to say! I can't imagine what your mother will have to say about this!"

Alice sensed a tingle of regret, her stomach coiling at the inevitable phone call about to be made. She exhaled long and hard as the older woman stalked out of the room. Seconds later, her frail, wobbly voice filtered down the echoey hall, profusely apologizing down the phone. Church club had been Gloria, her mother's bright idea.

There were a handful of kids in the town, and they got bored, and this was an opportunity to craft and create while their parents could relax and have a break under the watchful gaze of the Lord. When Alice finished school, she was excited and looking forward to a long summer vacation of hanging upside down in trees in the woods or going hunting with her father. But her mother had other plans and wasn't about to let Alice jump rivers, climb trees, ruin clothes, and learn more curse words from her father for the whole vacation. Gloria dropped her here every Sunday directly after church, and escaped off for some 'mommy time' while her father spent the afternoon in Hardy's, the local bar. This was her second session and the second time Jake Fraser screwed it up.

Alice cast a wary eye at him across the room, nursing his bruised, swollen nose, his eyes running, and felt a prickle of something…guilt maybe. Even though he was a jerk and stuck blueberry gum in her hair, he was just—so small.

Compared to her, everyone was small, but Jake was tiny, little hands, thin shoulders drowning in that stuffy suit. He didn't look eleven. Alice was well aware she didn't look eleven either, towering a foot proud of most of her classmates, long-limbed and gangly, freckly skinned and pale. Plus, with her height and complete lack of grace came some clumsiness. This had been the issue week one adding serious insult to injury after petting him like he was a six year old. Passing his table, sucking on a juice carton, she'd spun a little too enthusiastically and knocked orange, sticky liquid all over the paper birds he'd made.

He'd spent a great deal of time crafting them, folding the paper neatly, symmetrically, the edges crisp and sharp, his eyes narrowed, and his tongue stuck out. He'd even used a ruler and a pen to mark the folds—she admired his attention to detail. She'd watched him across the hall, her crumpled birds no doubt trash bound, and she'd smiled, thinking how cute and *little* he was. But that changed when she'd spilled the juice and witnessed his vile temper.

"Stupid Hickory trash," he'd spat. Alice kicked him in the shin so hard he burst into tears.

Alice's violent temper and Jake's unkind language earned them both an instant dismissal from the group. Week two rolled around, and Alice 'looked at him the wrong way,' and he'd shoved the greyish, sticky gum right in her untidy mane.

Mrs. Flanders came back to the room, wringing her knobbly hands. She shook her head at the sorry pair. "Your mother says you can walk home," she said to Alice, who shrugged nonchalantly. "And…" Her watery eyes drifted to Jake. "I'm afraid no one is picking up at your house, despite your nanny saying she was there all afternoon."

Alice snickered. "Wonder what *she's* up to," she muttered under her breath but shut her mouth when she saw Jake staring at her, nostrils flaring. He let the ice pack drop into his lap, an expression on his face too mature for a boy his age.

"It's fine. I can walk home."

The older woman didn't look convinced. "I'm not sure you should."

"I'm the same age as *her*!" he spat, flicking his eyes at Alice, who had taken the opportunity to pick a scab off her elbow. "I can walk home fine."

Mrs. Flanders peeked through the door into the main hall, the noise from the other children concerning her, she worked her mouth wordlessly. "Then you both better go." She stood over them, hands-on-hips, her expression sour. "I don't want a repeat next Sunday, do you understand? Or I might have second thoughts on having you back at all."

"Hmm— such a shame," Jake muttered as he slipped to his feet, and Alice snorted. Outside, the trees wilted in the late summer sunshine, the humidity suffocating as they both trudged along the dirt path from the church hall. Alice lagged behind him.

The path wound down a cobbled stone track, eventually branching off into town, another dirt, grassy path snaked off leading straight into the depths of the infamous Cedar forest, which would mingle after about a mile with the two plots of land owned by the feuding families, the Hickory's and the Frasers. Two families at war for over two hundred years.

No one could say for sure when the feud between them started, only it began with Callum Fraser's death, the reverend's son, who was in love and planning to run away with Vivienne Hickory. They were both eighteen, but Callum's father frowned upon the match. Even then, all Hickory's were trash, despite the head of the family being a military captain. Callum vanished, never to be seen or heard from again, and Vivienne got the blame. A plague of witchcraft washed through New England, and Vivienne was locked in the local jail, where she died from pneumonia, but oddly, her body was never found. Only a tiny kestrel remained in her place, frozen to the ground. A ghost story for tourists was born, and the rest dead and buried history.

Alice knew all the stories and lived with the rumors daily. Only…they weren't rumors, and the Hickory family were strange, as was the woodland they were both about to walk through. Alice came alive in the woods, and it ran through her blood. She breathed in the humid air and longed to run as they trekked closer. She cast a glance at him, walking stiffly ahead, the sun beating down on him, clearly ignoring her.

Something about him tugged on her conscience. He didn't have a mother, and that made her sad. Gloria irritated the heck out of her, but imagining her gone, caused a knot to form in her throat. John Hickory, her father, was about as far from dad material as it got. Alice imagined him attempting to braid her hair, and she giggled.

Alice saw Jake's shoulders slump and wondered what he was carrying around in his leather book bag. It reminded her of something her old Uncle Willard would carry, neat and expensive looking. God, Jake was so uptight. He cast a wary look over his shoulder as he walked as if he expected her to boot him in the ass.

Not that the thought hadn't crossed her mind, but the further away he got, the smaller he became, and it tugged on her gut.

I shouldn't have hit him. What did her mother always say…Take a long deep breath before you ball up your fist. It wasn't the first time Alice had been reprimanded for fighting. She was pretty famous for it in her schoolyard, often coming home with a fat lip or black eye. Gloria was mortified while her father cackled into his beer. Alice groaned, looked skyward, clasping her bag as she jogged after him. Jake jerked in surprise when she fell into step with him.

"What?"

"Look—I'm sorry," she said, dry-mouthed. "I shouldn't have hit you."

He sniffed, wiped his nose on his clean, linen cuff. "S'okay. It didn't hurt. You hit like a girl anyways."

Alice pursed her lips and swallowed back her temper. What did her mom always say? Be the bigger person. She decided she would try it, even if he was an irritating little shit.

"You don't go to our school," she said, more of a statement than a question. Jake shrugged.

"I'm home-schooled."

"Bet that's boring!"

"Father doesn't want me mixing…with…." He abruptly cut off his sentence, and Alice rolled her eyes.

Nice family! Jake glanced in her direction. "But I'm going to Furlow's High next semester."

Alice frowned. God, she hoped he would grow a few more inches by then. Furlow's would be hell for a kid his size, plus he'd be all weird and socially awkward. "Don't you have any friends your age?"

They walked into the woods, the shade of the canopy engulfing them. It was cooler, and Alice stripped off her sweater, down to her t-shirt underneath, and tied it around her waist. She noticed him stiffen, glance at her bare arms, and she wondered if he must be sweltering under that suit. He adjusted the button at his neck, and she grinned.

"Father says I'll make plenty when I get to high school, but for now, my studies are important."

"Sure," Alice agreed, half-heartedly, though she wasn't much of a bookworm, and she preferred being outdoors. "Though you must get lonely in that house, all by yourself?"

Alice spotted a gnarled Rowan tree and hurried toward it. She crawled up the trunk, huffing as she hoisted her torso over a low branch. The tree was ripe and full of red berries, some of which fell to the grass as she dislodged them.

Jake watched as she lunged, her knees hooked around the branch as she hung upside down, blood rushing to her cheeks and her stringy hair tumbling in her face. He shrugged, disinterested and unimpressed. "Not really. I can entertain myself."

"You watch cartoons?"

"Sometimes." His mouth twitched into a smile. Alice noticed the change in expression, her interest piquing. *So he can smile!* Perhaps if he weren't so stuck up, he'd be fun to hang around with? She'd love to have a boy to talk to.

"What'd you like? Let me guess— ninja turtles?"

Jake paused, his eyes pulling into a cold frown. "I'm not sure why you're speaking to me like I'm five years old."

Alice realized her blunder, uncurling from the branch, and dropping to the ground. She shook her head. "I'm sorry… it's just that…."

"I know I'm small for my age!" he bit, his voice not as immature as his stature. "I get that I look young. But I'll grow. Father says I will shoot up one day just like he did. And he's six foot four now."

Alice made a face, recalling seeing old Robert Fraser in church, hunched over, frail, a man in his seventies in a wheelchair. Her father was tall, toned, and strong and in his seventies too. But you would never guess. Therians concealed their age well— too well. And they lived forever. Well, not quite forever, but long enough to watch decades drift by.

"You want me to show you how to climb?"

His lip curled at her abrupt subject change, widening his eyes. "Thanks but *no*. I'm good."

"It's fun!"

"Well, yes to *you*, maybe. I'll ruin my clothes."

She sniggered, hooking one hand around the branch and practicing pull-ups. Sweat broke out under her arms, her hair sticking to her forehead. "You can take them off, you know? Maybe lose the jacket?"

"I don't think so."

Huffing, she dropped and bent her knees, straightened, and they carried on walking through the shelter of the pines. Alice lifted her hair off her neck. She thought of something wicked and grinned, slapping his shoulder as they walked side by side. "You know these woods are haunted, right?"

Jake snorted. "I don't believe in that stuff."

"*Really?*" She folded her arms. "What if I told you I'd seen something?"

He paused, his eyes vaguely interested in her hook, but the moment passed, and he snorted indignantly. "You mean my ancestor, Callum Fraser? *Everyone* knows about him."

Alice beamed, enjoying herself immensely. "No—I mean the *other* ghost."

Jake stopped dead, his complexion draining of color. "What are you talking about?"

Jackpot! She had his attention. She crept closer, clawing up her fingers devilishly. "I mean the one who walks."

Jake's lip dropped, he drew in a shallow breath. "Do you mean…the girl?"

Alice froze. She was teasing, playing, and vying for a reaction, but suddenly goosebumps broke out on her arms. She didn't think anyone knew about *her*. These woods were Hickory Fraser property, sometimes the odd hiker came by, but with the strange wolf sightings, it was secluded, shadowy, and private. Alice shuddered and rubbed her arms briskly. She didn't believe poor Callum Fraser haunted these woods—but someone else sure did.

Alice had been six and out for a hunt with her father. The old, shaggy grey wolf trotted alongside, and she'd held his mane of fur as they crossed the rushing brook. Prickles of fear crept over her shoulders, and she'd glanced about to spot a girl in the woods, with long dark hair, wearing a long, old dress. When she'd pointed her out, the wolf did a short turn, nudging her with his snout, and marched her back swiftly in the other direction. Later, when she asked why he was so spooked, he only replied. "We don't talk about her."

Now Alice stared at Jake, her fun game of enticing him over. "You've seen her?"

Why wouldn't he have seen something? This was his woods too. But in all the years Alice played out here, she and Jake never crossed paths. He sneered, shaking his head, his good mood dissolving. He pursed his lips angrily. "You've had your fun—leave me the hell alone!"

He marched off, but she caught up with him quickly. "I'm sorry. I was teasing, but…." Alice faltered, her potential playmate staring at her like she was something unpleasant he'd stepped in.

"Leave me alone!"

She grabbed his shoulder. "Jake, please wait!"

"Get your filthy hand off me…Hickory bitch!" Jake reacted as though she'd stung him, and she snatched her hand back. The look he threw her was enough to root her to the spot. Her eyes welled up with hurt tears, but she sniffed them back, determined not to give him the satisfaction of seeing her cry.

At her side, her fists balled. *Do not hit him! Be bigger, be better!*

His bottom lip trembled, and she could tell he was backtracking, regret crossing his face. Alice shrugged, sweat gathering at her nape under all her sweaty hair.

"Whatever," she sighed. "Guess I'll see you next week." She shoved him hard, right in the collar bone, and he toppled backward and landed on his ass. It didn't make her feel better, but she was glad he got to stare up at her, towering over him, as she got the last word. His paper birds toppled out of his bag, and she stared at them in the grass, wishing she had the patience to have made something as beautiful.

She stalked away, tears hot in her eyes, but she wiped at the corners.

"What a dick," she muttered. His rebuke cut like a knife. Humiliation welled in her throat, and she wondered what she expected. He was a Fraser, and they were weird; everyone knew that. But she was a Hickory, and they weren't exactly normal either. But they weren't bad. And she wasn't a *bitch*.

She only wanted a friend. Alice wiped her nose on her wrist, pushing through low trees, determind to forget him and beg her mother never to send her back to that dumb church club.

Behind her, Jake screamed. She jolted to a stop, ice flying up her bare arms, having gone a few yards into the trees.

It tore right through her, froze her insides. Without pausing, her feet moved like lightning. She trekked back through the vines pushing aside branches, where only moments ago, he'd landed on his backside.

"Jake?"

He was gone. Only his bag remained, sprawled out on the dirt track and the disregarded paper creations from club. Panic mounted in her belly. "Jake—where are you?"

Her eyes darted around the small, wooded area, her neck tingling. Nothing moved, oddly and eerily still, only rustling in the bushes above. Her voice wobbled as she called out again. The finally, she heard a groan.

"Jake?" she cried in relief, whirling around, though she couldn't see him. "Where are you?"

"Down here," he cried. Alice looked around the small area, her eyes scanning the dirt. She stepped forward and cried out, her arms flailing as she managed to save herself from toppling. There was a massive hole in the ground, and she dropped to her knees, peering into the darkness.

"Holy crap, Jake! Are you down there?"

"I fell." *Oh god, he's crying.* Her heart thumped.

"How did you not see a great big hole?"

"Same way you didn't," he shot back. "It just appeared, and I stepped and fell straight in."

"Are you hurt?"

She was greeted by silence, then a muffled snuffling nose, probably him wiping his nose. “I think I broke my wrist.”

Alice breathed out humid air. “Thank god that’s all you’ve broken.” She looked down the hole, noticing some twisted vines buried deep in the impacted dirt. “Look, there are some vines here. Can you climb out?”

“I can’t see anything,” he moaned in reply. “And my arm hurts.”

Alice bit her lip, thinking. “Okay…okay…” she muttered. “Maybe I should run home and find your dad?”

“No!” he wailed, his voice needy and scared. “Don’t go. Don’t leave me.”

Alice sat back on her heels, her head buzzing. “I don’t know what to do.”

“Look in my bag…I’ve got a lighter. Can you toss my bag down?”

Alice grabbed up the expensive looking bag, and without thinking, stuffed the paper birds inside before zipping it up. She held it by the strap and hovered it over the hole. “Okay, I’m throwing it down.”

Her fingers released the strap, and it vanished into the hole. Seconds later, she heard a thud and Jake’s relieved, “Got it!”

A few moments after, a glow emerged from the dark, and she could see his dirt-splattered, sweaty face peering up at her. Alice smiled in relief. He didn’t look too damaged, just afraid.

“I can’t climb out of here,” he said hopelessly. “My arm…I’m not strong enough.”

Alice bit her lower lip, trying to think, while the dying sun was determined to beat on her back. “How big is the hole?”

Jake wafted the lighter around, coughing as dirt fell on his head. “It looks like a tunnel—there’s even some wooden slatting down here.”

Something clicked in her mind. This was a tunnel! One of the infamous tunnels dug in the 1700s. “Jake!” she cried. “You’re standing in one of the old tunnels. This will come out on your land, or even mine." She cast an eye over her shoulder, gazing back at the worn path from the church, and shivered, it must have lain untouched for years, and she wondered what else could be underneath her feet.

Shaking off her creepy sensation, she did the only thing she could think of. She grabbed at an exposed vine, knotting her fingers around it tightly and tugging it so she could ensure it would take her weight. She threw herself down the side of the hole and, with her biceps screaming under strain, walked down the crumbly wall. Jake's eyes widened as she dropped the last few feet and landed next to him.

"Are you some kind of moron?" he asked. "What are you doing?"

She brushed the dirt off her hands and flexed her shoulders. "I got in the hole with you."

He cocked a brow. "I can see that. Now we're both stuck down here."

"Ah yes, but you have a lighter, and this is a tunnel. And perhaps we can get out of this together?" She slapped his shoulder, forgetting his injury, and he winced in pain. "Maybe it's a good idea to have some friends, and not worry about studying so much. You know, in case you fall on your ass?"

She winked, and he ducked his eyes, and she swore he'd blushed, which made him look cuter than he already was. Filthy, he stripped off his suit jacket and undid the buttons on his cuffs.

"Whoa, Clark Kent is taking the jacket off!" Alice teased, giggling. "You better not roll up those sleeves, or I might faint!"

"Shut up," he muttered but grinned when she wasn't looking. Jake held up the lighter, and it flickered about, the draft in the tunnel catching it.

"Why do you have a lighter? Do you smoke?"

Jake stared at her, incredulous. "It was a gift—from my father."

"Weird ass gift!" Alice remarked, wondering what kind of Christmas this kid endured every year. "I bet you have a real fancy set of pens, too."

Jake smirked, despite the acidity of her joke. "I have a bureau. And a drawing board."

Alice burst out laughing, her attention drawn to the shadows around them.

"There!" Alice pointed in the direction of the waft of flame. "We go this way."

"But…" Jake sputtered as she stepped blindly into the darkness, her arms waving in front of her face. He grabbed the back of her shirt and flung himself in front of her.

"I should go first."

Alice snorted. *"Really?"*

Jake's expression soured. "I have the lighter, and I kind of feel like it should be me who goes first."

Alice was about to open her mouth and chastise him for his sexism, because he was a *boy*, he should be the one to go ahead, but when she met his gaze, she knew he was only trying to be gallant, in his way.

"Okay, well after you." She gave him a mock bow, managing to swipe a sweaty streak of dirt across her face as she pulled her hair back. Even though she'd been teasing, once they made the first steps into the dark cavern, her bravado slipped, and she found herself grappling for the walls either side.

Her chest heaved as the walls pressed closer. Alice's throat thickened, tasting dirt, and her limbs grew prickly and heavy. This was new, and she tried to shake herself free of the odd, numbing sensation traveling up her arms, panic quickly setting in. Alice was used to being outdoors, free to wander and climb, jump rocks over the brook or lay in the grass. Right now, the dark was creeping in, and she couldn't breathe. "Jake…"

"I know. It's a tight fit," he replied, sensing her fear.

"I can't." Her arms pinned to the wall, she could barely lift them. "I can't do this." In the dark, his clammy fingers grasped hers.

"Keep going. Maybe you are claustrophobic? Don't lose it on me, okay?"

She swallowed, tears escaping her eyes. "Okay."

Jake started well, taking long, careful strides through the dark. The tunnel crowded them on both sides and got progressively narrower the further they got. The moment Alice was forced sideways, feeling dirt crumbling into her hair, she struggled to fight down a wave of panic. It was damp, the soil clammy and cold. The facing wall close enough to graze her forehead, she felt her own breath on her cheeks. Something tickled her hair, then ran down her bare arm, and she shrieked.

"What?" Jake yelled.

"A spider—or something crawled down my arm!"

"Is it gone?"

Alice steadied her breathing, taking in great gasps of air. "I hope so."

He squeezed her hand in the dark. "Can you see much?"

"Not much," he said through gritted teeth. "It's cold down here."

"You're very brave."

She heard him snort. "I'm not a six-year-old, Alice."

She rolled her eyes. "Sorry."

They carried on in silence, and for a section of the tunnel, the facing wall became so narrow it compressed against her chest, making her draw in her ribcage, her breathing shallow. Alice sweated under her hair, panic lacing its way into her thoughts. "Maybe we should go back? I can hardly move."

"No, keep going," he said, the light flickering ahead of him. "I can feel air moving."

"I can't do this," she choked, and he squeezed her hand.

"Yes, you can."

"It's too tight."

"Keep going, Alice. You jumped in here with me, and I'll make sure we get out."

His tone was older than his years as he forced her to carry on, despite her knees trembling. The dark crowded in around her, vines poking her skin and dirt slipping underfoot. She never guessed being stuck, trapped would be something that would cripple her with fear, strike her almost unmovable. Alice made a note to remember this if she ever got in a closet or elevator in the future.

"Here!" Jake yelled, triumphant. "I see steps!"

Alice breathed out claggy air, swallowing saliva into her dry throat. "Really?"

Jake kicked his foot and Alice heard the dull thud of wood. Miraculously the tunnel widened so they could move about freely. Ahead the tunnel carried on, and Jake shone the lighter, his expression strange.

"Wonder what's down there?" Alice wondered aloud. "If we kept going—not that I want to!"

"I don't want to find out." Jake shuddered. "Alice…"

They locked eyes. "What?"

"Nothing."

"What?"

He bit his lip, his skin glistening with a sheen of sweat. "Did you really see *her*?"

Alice knew who he meant, and her neck tingled, her spine shivering. Solemnly, she nodded. "Have you?"

Jake audibly gulped. "Yeah."

Next to him, Alice shuddered in the dark. "Let's get out of here. How sturdy do you think that ladder is?"

Jake glanced up at their ramshackle chance for escape. "I mean, it looks ancient. But I'm willing to risk it." He let go of her hand and shone the light toward an old, rickety-looking ladder nailed to the wooden slats against the wall. Alice rejoiced, raking her eyes up the ladder to a gnarled trap door. "That's incredible. I wonder where we are."

"I don't care," Jake said, putting one foot on the bottom rung. "I want to get out of here." He climbed up the ladder, nursing his limp, swollen arm, and attempted pushing on the door wedged tight above their heads. "It's stuck."

"Let me have a go," she insisted as he slipped back down the ladder. He looked pale in the low, flickering light, and she thought he must be in a lot of pain. She pushed up the ladder and shoved the door hard with her shoulder. Gritting her teeth, she tried again with everything she had. Dirt crumbled inward.

"It's grassed over," she said. "That's why it's so tough." She dug her nails into the soil impacted around the door. Like a raccoon, she scrubbed it away till her fingertips stung and bled. Jake peered up at her anxiously.

"Don't hurt yourself!"

"It's coming away," she said, ignoring him. "I have to loosen it. God knows how long this has been here."

Jake made a face, holding the lighter as steady as his arm would allow. Alice coughed and revealed a patch of light after a few more clumpfuls of dry, compacted earth fell in her face. She whooped in joy and wedged her hand through. "I can feel air!"

A great gust of air swept through the tunnel, and Jake's lighter blew out. He gasped, his fingers clicking it in the dark, sucking in a breath when it wouldn't light. Alice forced down a surge of panic, knowing she would have to get them out blind.

"Keep pushing!" Jake encouraged her. Using her shoulder as a lever, Alice pushed her shoulder tight against the old wood door, pain splintering along her neck as muscles strained. With watering eyes, she forced her legs to hold fast, gripping the ladder with her free hand, and with a groan, the grass split and pulled away from the earth. Light flooded the tunnel as she flung it open with an animalistic grunt.

"We did it!" she yelled, pushing up into the light, the sun streaming through the hole. She crawled out and met the daylight, rolling onto her side and panting hard. She remembered Jake and leaned back into the hole. He was already halfway up the ladder, balancing on the rickety rungs using his good arm to hoist himself to freedom.

Alice met his eyes, grabbed his forearm, and with a cry, tugged him the rest of the way out, her bicep biting. He rolled next to her, staring skyward at the trees and breathing hard. "Thanks," he said, at last. She let her head roll in his direction.

"Where are your glasses?"

He rubbed at his eyes. "Lost 'em somewhere down there."

Alice's brows flew skyward. "How bad is your eyesight?"

He half smiled, squinting at her. "Well, put it this way, all I can see is your hair. You're a blurry mess right now."

He'd dragged her through that tunnel, unable to see a thing. She gaped at him, kind of glad he couldn't see her smiling.

Jake sighed. "Maybe I should get contacts."

"You look cute without them," she said, nudging his shoulder, again forgetting his injury, and he hissed in pain, cradling his arm to his chest. She was on her feet and held out her hand. "Come on. We should get you home."

He sat up. "I'm not a kid!"

Alice huffed. "I know that, Jake. I mean, we should get you back. Your wrist is swelling up."

They shuffled a few steps, eyeing the massive trap door. "What should we do with it?"

"It's dangerous," Alice said. She kicked the door closed and spent the next few minutes gathering twigs and branches to cover it. They were still in the middle of the forest, but she recognized this part. They were on the borders of the Mercy/Hickory land. She pointed to the large oak shooting skyward. "We'll know it's here. The oak marks the spot. I don't know how many times I've walked past this place and never seen it."

Jake leaned heavily on the tree. He was staring at the trunk of the oak and the hollowed-out knot etched into the bark. "It's like a hiding place," he said, thoughtfully. She didn't listen, too busy flattening earth over the now wobbly old door. A sense of dread crept over her, knowing they'd been lucky to get out of that tunnel. Something felt off down there, old and forgotten, like whispers, and she wondered about the old ghost stories. Did the ghost of Callum Fraser still walk this wood?

Alice closed her eyes. *The girl with dark hair…the one who walks…*

Her father's grim expression as he'd marched her home. "We don't talk about her…."

"Why are you covering it up?" Jake asked, bringing her back to the present, wincing as he attempted to flex his wrist. Alice stared at the mass and rolled her shoulders, a shiver creeping over them.

"Feels like…I don't know. It feels wrong. Like an open grave or something."

"Well, that's creepy."

"I know," she agreed. "We can't go back down there, and it was covered up for a reason."

Alice walked him back to the gates of Mercy, gazing up at the oppressive, looming old place she'd passed many times on her travels, somehow knowing Jake had been inside the whole time made it a little less intimidating. Alice felt a tug in her chest, imagining him rattling around in there by himself, an only child, like her. She boyishly shoved her hands in her dungaree pockets, blowing a stray hair off her face with a puff of breath. "So, I guess I'll see you around sometime."

"Next week." He gave her a charming, boyish smile, which she found herself returning. "Unless, we manage to get ourselves kicked out again."

"How about you keep the gum away from my hair?"

"How about you try not to slug me?"

They both laughed. Nodding, her words dried up, and she grinned, turning to walk away.

"Do you play Chess?" Jake called. She turned on her heels in a pile of leaves.

"No."

He stepped up timidly, blushing and scratching the back of his neck with his good hand. "I got a set for Christmas, but my father…." He looked at the ground. "He doesn't have time. I could teach you…and maybe you could show me how to do that tree swinging thing— it looked kind of cool."

Alice beamed. "Sure!" She headed off. "See ya, Clark Kent."

He snorted and muttered something as she wandered off, her grin splitting her face.

Alice wandered back to the house, bracing herself for the almighty telling off she was about to receive. Luckily, John was still at the bar, and once she explained her disheveled appearance to her mother, Gloria only sighed and wrung her hands in despair. After a good soak in the bath and detangling her locks, Alice found herself wandering in the woods, heading back to the spot where they'd come up through the door.

Twilight touched the woods, the sun setting low, casting a pink glow through the canopy. The chilly atmosphere from earlier vanished, and it only seemed peaceful and quiet. She reached the oak and smiled at what she found in the hollow—a paper bird.

She took it out carefully and examined it in her hand, wishing again she possessed the patience to make something as pretty. It felt wrong not to leave anything for him, so she dug around in her dungaree pocket and found a stick of gum, grinning as she poked it in the hole.

She stalked back to Hickory House, jumping over the shallow brook, splashing her ankles in a puddle, when her neck tingled and her eyes tore to the trees, spotting the familiar, dark outline hidden among them. A girl in a long, ragged nightdress watched from the shadows. Teasing Jake earlier was a game, but when she learned he'd also seen *her*, the look on his face was enough to chill Alice's blood. She didn't want to tell him, she knew exactly who walked these cursed woods— and where she came from.

Alice lifted her chin. "Get lost, Mary," she sneered, balling her fists to cover how utterly terrified she was. "You don't belong here."

Other Books in the series

The Curse of Win Adler
Huntress
The Short Story Collection

Also by Victoria Wren

A Season of Darkness (Knock, Knock and Iron Heart)

If you love this series please consider sighing up to my newsletter for regular updates, free short stories and art reveals! Join at www.victoriawrenauthor.com

ACKNOWLEDGMENTS

Once again, I'm floored that I'm writing an acknowledgement section for this book. But this time I will keep it short and sweet, if I can.

Writing a book is rewarding, thrilling and exciting and I love nothing more than spending time with these characters. But it is also a lonely business at times, and I want to thank my amazing writer friends for being a pillar of support during this process. So thank you Bethany, Alex, Alicia, Orla, Kent, Hannah, Richard, Dan, Day and Chris! You are all so talented and I love being in your gang.

Thanks Ian for listening (at least I think you do) and being such an amazing, gorgeous husband, and my two girls Eva and Grace, my two little stars, I love you so much.

Thank you to Greg and Natalia at Enchanted Ink and to Thea who blows my mind with her art.

I would also like to make a special note of a lovely man, a member of the Choctaw Nation, who took the time to sensitivity read this book for me, thank you so much for your love and support!

Thank you all my wonderful readers!

Until we meet again,

Victoria x

VICTORIA lives in Essex in the United Kingdom, with her husband, two girls and three cats. Since the age of thirteen she has written short stories and novels for young adults, creating worlds she wished were real and characters who are dear to her soul. She is a huge fan of paranormal fiction, loves scaring the life out of her kids and anyone who wants to read her work. Victoria is the proud author of the young adult series 'Wild Spirit' and looks forward to publishing more books in the series this year.

Lightning Source UK Ltd.
Milton Keynes UK
UKHW012038151121
394023UK00004B/38/J